George S. Mann

Mann Memorial - A Record of the Mann Family in America

Genealogy of the descendants of Richard Mann, of Scituate, Mass. Preceded by

English family records

George S. Mann

Mann Memorial - A Record of the Mann Family in America
Genealogy of the descendants of Richard Mann, of Scituate, Mass. Preceded by English family records

ISBN/EAN: 9783337223076

Printed in Europe, USA, Canada, Australia, Japan

Cover: Foto ©Andreas Hilbeck / pixelio.de

More available books at **www.hansebooks.com**

MANN MEMORIAL.

A Record of the Mann Family in America.

GENEALOGY

OF THE DESCENDANTS OF

RICHARD MAN

OF SCITUATE, MASS.

Preceded by English Family Records,

AND AN ACCOUNT OF THE

WRENTHAM, REHOBOTH, BOSTON, LEXINGTON, VIRGINIA, AND
OTHER BRANCHES OF THE MANNS WHO SETTLED
IN THIS COUNTRY.

By GEORGE S. MANN.

BOSTON:
PRESS OF DAVID CLAPP & SON,
1884.

CONTENTS.

LIST OF PORTRAITS, ETC.

(Eighteen wood-cut fac-similes of Autographs in the volume.)

Man. **Mann.**

The above armorial bearings represent, with slight differences, eleven
out of fifteen families of this name, as given in Burke's General Armory.
[See pp. 15 and 16 of this work.] Both families were of Co. Kent at
various periods. It has not yet been possible to connect the New-England
families with their English ancestry.

───────

NOTE.—Some of the elder New-England families have in their possession a coat
of arms, similar to the above on the left. They were evidently painted by John Coles,
and their genuineness is considered doubtful by heraldic authorities.

PREFACE.

AT the solicitation of friends I submit the following genealogical records to those of the family who are immediately or remotely interested. In view of the hundreds of personal subjects treated, together with the impossibility of producing a publication of this nature without errors and imperfections, it is with diffidence that it is sent forth from the press, especially so, since the author considers who will be his readers. Primarily, it was not my purpose to publish a genealogy to be exposed to the animadversion of any possible censorious critic. This is not intended to be a work of literary merit, otherwise it would have been submitted to an expert, and revised before publication. Therefore, if any thing is found of error or is peculiar in orthography, the compiler would ask the indulgence of a discriminating posterity.

I have spared no pains to give a perfect record of the families represented, though not as full as I have desired. A few accounts sent me by correspondents are at variance with the records or other data. These I have harmonized as best I could. The biographical sketches of most persons mentioned are necessarily brief, while others are more full. Undoubtedly, not a few whose history is very briefly sketched are as much deserving of an extended notice as any who have received it; but their merits failed to reach the author. The MANNS in England were honored in successive periods with royal favor, and their offspring were, no doubt, among the early fathers of our country. There is a growing interest at the present day manifested by the descendants of the early settlers to know the names and history of their ancestors. This interest is laudable, and the gratification generally gives genuine satisfaction to the living, and will be the means of insuring an invaluable legacy to the coming generation. Moreover, pedigrees are invaluable aids to the student of history.

The plan adopted in this work is the comprehensive one in use by our New England Historic Genealogical Society, and is easily understood. The children of each head of a family are to be found

(V

directly under his or her name. When the information concerning the children is limited, and their posterity not numerous, the whole record is generally given at once. When otherwise, the name is designated by a number at the left, carried forward, on a subsequent page, in brackets, and makes the starting point of a new family. The names in Italics which are in parenthesis at the beginning of each new family, by the aid of the exponent number at the right, carry the line directly back to the original ancestor. These small exponent figures at the right of christian names should be carefully noted, to determine at sight to what generation the subject belongs, and to assist in tracing out each family. The abbreviations common to all works of this kind are used to facilitate the labor and lessen the cost of the book. To trace a line of descent in the American families, seek the Index.*

In the prosecution of the work the author is indebted to the valuable library of the New England Historic Genealogical Society, and to the obliging custodians of both Plymouth and Massachusetts colonial and probate records. I am under great obligations to those who have procured and sent me dates and facts, and herewith express to them all my sincere thanks. For special information I am indebted to Alrick H. Man, Esq., and Rev. Brady E. Backus, D.D., of New York city; Henry Dutch Lord, Esq., of Boston; Herbert A. Backus, Esq., of Detroit, Mich.; Addison C. Miller and Frederick G. Fincke, Esqrs., of Utica, N. Y; Matthew D. Mann, M.D., of Buffalo, N. Y. Albert Holbrook, Esq., of Providence, R. I.; Horace Mann, Esq., of Natick, Mass.; Stafford Mann, Esq., of Lincoln, R. I.; Mrs. Charlotte M. Phelps, of Hebron, Conn., and many others. For a portion of the records of the Randolph (Mass.) family line, I am indebted to the efforts of Miss Luthera H. Mann, of that town; and for many Ohio records thanks are due Mrs. Ellen S. Lockwood, of East Plymouth, Ohio. The printers of this Memorial are also deserving of thanks for the creditable manner in which they have performed their part of the work.

If the perusal of these pages, by this and future generations, should serve to animate any latent desires for a nobler life and higher culture, and if its readers are stimulated to guard with jealous care the fair fame they inherit, and emulate the heroic examples of virtue, excellence, and pious endeavor of their ancestors, in their love for civil and religious liberty, then the labor and money expended on this compilation may not have been in vain.

G. S. M.

Boston, November, 1884.

---

* The English Records etc., or the first sixteen pages of this work, not Indexed.

INTRODUCTION.

THE name Man or Mann* appears very early in English history, and, no doubt, earlier in Germany as a patronymic; but as the author has not made any extended effort to trace the genealogical order of the family beyond the confines of the United States, the sphere of this volume is necessarily confined to this country, and to the period since the beginning of the first settlements made here by our honored forefathers. A few general facts which are gleaned from various English records, and inserted on the first few pages of this work, are sufficient to show that the family have lived in England from a remote period. There were a number of the name who early left the Old Country, came to America, settled, and had families. Of the foregoing, those whom I have found recorded in history are mentioned in this volume, in order, if possible, to stimulate and facilitate more extended research in the future. These families may be found on the pages immediately following the English records. Whether any of these first settlers were brothers, or otherwise related, the author has not been able to determine. The branch that is mainly and more fully treated in this volume, is the line of which RICHARD MAN, of Scituate, Mass., was the head. The descendants of this early New England settler have been pretty thoroughly traced, and their lives briefly sketched. The records of this family occupy the main body of this work.

In briefly treating the various other Manns in this country as pre-
liminary to the main (Richard Man) branch, I have made considerable effort to trace the descendants of William Man, the early settler
of Cambridge, Mass., through his only son, Rev. Samuel, of
Wrentham, Mass., and down a few generations (some lines to the
present), in order to separate* and distinguish these families from
the Richard Man branch, above alluded to; for I have found persons
bearing the name who had supposed that these two lines were of one
and the same branch, though without apparent reason.

---

* The late R. R. Hinman, of Hartford, in his "Early Puritan Settlers of Connecticut," claimed [erroneously] that the Hebron branch of the name in Conn. descended
from William of Cambridge. An extract of a "correspondence" may show wherein,
no doubt, he was led unadvisedly to this belief.

"HARTFORD, Dec. 9, 1847.

To Gov. J. S. PETERS, of Hebron, Conn.
        SIR:—To-day, R. R. Hinman, Esq., and Dr. Hitchcock called upon
me, with an old pamphlet containing some historical facts of the family. The Dr.'s
mother was a Mann before marriage. I want to inquire at what time did Grandfather
John Mann come to Hebron, from what place did he come, who was his father, or
what was the name of my great-grandfather, and where did he reside? * * * *
I give some of the names and dates taken from the pamphlet, etc.
                                                BENNING MANN."

In this pamphlet, William Mann the early Cambridge settler is mentioned, also his
descendants. Nathaniel (grandson of William) is underscored as being the Hebron
ancestor.—ED.

The following is a brief extract of Gov. J. S. Peters's reply.

"MY DEAR SIR:
        Your grandfather, John Mann, stated to me many years ago that
his ancestors came from England to Massachusetts, that his father emigrated to Mans-
field in this State (Conn.), and gave the town his name, Mans-field, from thence to
Hebron, and located on the farm that Cyrus lives on, and that his name was Nathaniel.
Nathaniel, John, Andrew, and Cyrus have succeeded each other in the possession of
the farm.   J. S. PETERS."

The reader will readily see in the personal sketches of the family, in the body of
this book, that John Mann above must have been in error. Mansfield, Conn., was
probably named in honor of Col. Moses Mansfield, of New Haven. Nathaniel, alluded
to in the above pamphlet, was grandson of William, and died in Wrentham, Mass.,
leaving a will. Nathaniel of Hebron was grandson of Richard of Scituate.—ED.

Derivation of the name Man or Mann.

R. FERGUSON, London, 1864, has the following derivation in the "Teutonic Name System," p. 57: "There are several names of which the etymological meaning is simply Man * * * * And the words seem to be used, *par excellence*, as we apply the terms manly and beautiful. * * * * At the head of the list is MANN, which is in a more direct manner connected with hero worship than the rest, if, as is probably the case, its use as a name is to be traced up to the Mannus of Tacitus, the fabled son of the hero or god Tuisco, and the founder of the German nation. We do not, however, meet with the name in after times, at least in its simple form, before the seventh century, though in a compound form it is found as early as the fourth century. Two other forms are Men and Mon, the latter of which was Anglo-Saxon, and is still used in the Lowland Scotch."

Man   { Old German—Manno, Manni, Meni (7th century). }   Simple
(homo)   { Anglo-Saxon—Mann, Manni, Mon.   }   forms.

(Fr. S. H. NEEDLES, Philadelphia.)

ENGLISH RECORDS.

ONE of the earliest notices of the family name of MAN, in England, is to be found in the Domesday Book in 1086, where "Willelmus filius Manne" (William the son of Man) is mentioned as a landholder in the County of Hants. In "Our English Surnames," by C. W. Bardsley, M.A., the names Henry le Man and Richard le Man are cited to show the most ancient form of the name of the Man family, but no other particulars are given. A book entitled "Patronymica Britannica" states that the name Man signifies in old French, "Norman." Also, that in Dutch, de Man means "the man," a hero.—(Ib.)

CORNELIUS DE MAN, a celebrated (Scotch?) painter, was born at Delft, Holland, 1621, and died there in 1706.

In 1322, REGINALD LE MAN, of Diss., was Lord, who, in 1337, left it (Watton's Manor) to Alice, his wife, etc.—(Blom. Hist. Norfolk Co.)

2

In the 31st of Edward III. [1358], JOHN LE MAN held a third part of the manor of John de Denham, etc.—(Ib.)

In the 13th of Richard II. [1390], William Ode, who married Matild., dau. and heir of John Man, held their part of this manor till about the end of the reign of King Henry VI., when it was conveyed to Richard Sparwe, Gent., of Oxburgh, who, in 1482, settled on a chantry which he then founded in the Church of Oxburgh.—(Ib.)

ALEXANDER MAN was the 15th R. C. Bishop of Caithness, Scotland, A.D. 1389.

A very ancient family of Mans is referred to in the History of Northamptonshire (by Bridges, in Astor Library, N. Y.), as having lived in that County about 1326, and, from that time on, William, Robert and Thomas Man are mentioned.

JOHN MAN, A.M. [son of John Man, of London, Gentleman], was warden of Merton College, Oxford, 1562. In 1565 he was made Dean of "Gloster," and in August, 1567, was sent by Queen Elizabeth on an embassy to Spain, where he was accused of speaking irreverently of the Pope, and was excluded from the Court. He was recalled, and died in 1568.—(For Arms and Tabular Ped. see Vis. Essex.)

DANIEL MAN was professor of Astronomy in Gresham College, Oxford, in 1601.

HENRY MAN, R. C. Dean of Chester, was the 41st Bishop of the Isle of Man, in 1546.—(Beatson's Political Index.)

THOMAS MAN, condemned for heresy by the Roman Catholic Bishop of London, March 29, 1518, was delivered to the sheriff, who was on horseback in Paternoster row, and the same afternoon the said Thomas Man was burned at Smithfield.—(Fox's Book of Martyrs, p. 417.)

RICHARD MAN was in London in 1586, where he had a servant by the name of Phillippe Colston.

THOMAS MAN, Esq., sword bearer to the city of London, about 1675, m. Rebecca, dau. of Sir William Peake.—(Le Neve's Ped. of Knights.)

JOHN MAN(a), of Poole [Dorset co., Eng.], b. 1495; m. (1) Aug. 17, 1525, Eleanor Whytt, and had seven chil., viz.: Sukey, 1528; William, Feb. 5, 1530; John, Feb. 4, 1531; Margaret, 1532; Thomas, Sept. 1, 1534; Edith, 1535; Agnes, 1537. He m. (2) Amy Ryve, a widow, dau. Thomas Harvye, Sept. 30, 1547, by whom had chil., viz.: Bartholomew, Au 24, 1548; George, ——; Edward, May 11, 1551; Amy, 1552.

EDWARD MAN(b), b. May 11, 1551; m. (1) Feb. 7, 1575, Temperanc Hassarde; m. (2) 1579, Margaret Faunt le Roye, widow, dau. of John Aly gentleman; m. (3) 1585, Eleanor Darre (she being only 15 years of age

He had the following chil.: 1 by first wife; 3 by second, 5 by third, viz.: John, June 27, 1578; Amy, 1580; Temperance, 1582; Edward, Jan. 4, 1583; Temperance, 1586; Edward, Sept. 17, 1588; Amy, 1590; Jane, 1592; Theophilus, Dec. 15, 1600.

THEOPHILUS MAN, b. Dec. 15, 1600; m. May 8, 1629, Ann Warham, by whom had seven chil., viz.: Edward, Feb. 16, 1629; Eleanor, 1631; Theophilus, Feb. 24, 1633; Anne, 1635; John, Feb. 1637; Elizabeth, 1640; James, Dec. 16, ——.

EDWARD MAN, b. Feb. 16, 1629; m. (1) 1656, Anne Clavering; m. (2) Sept. 19, 1673, Mrs. Lucy (Warren), by whom the two youngest chil. were b. in Third Haven, Talbot County, Maryland; 8 chil. by both wives, viz.: A son, dead born, 1657; Anne, ——; John, July 23, 1661; Elizabeth, Feb. 15, 1663; Robert, Spring, 1667; A son, 1669, died in infancy; Lucy, March 8, 1679; Mary, Aug. 24, 1687. [This family, probably, ultimately settled in Virginia.—ED.]

ELIZABETH MAN, b. Feb. 15, 1663, dau. of Edward and Anne (Clavering) Man; m. in Virginia, Oct. 24, 1682, John Needles, the son of Lieut. John Needles and Frances his wife, of Pianketank River; 6 chil.

(a) JOHN MAN,
B. 1495,—D. 1578.

Mo. that I John Man was married ye vj day of awguste an° 25 (1525) yn ye xvij yere of ye Reyn of Kyng harry ye viij unto Elenor whytt ye Dawther of thomas whytt she bey'g [being] of ye adge [age] of xxij yeres ye xxj day of may lest [last] pass'd & I John man bey'g [being] of ye adge of xxx yere ye xvij day of october nexs [next] comy'g.

(b) EDWARD MAN,
Son of JOHN MAN.

my father John man was maryed the vj daye of auguste in an° D'm 1525 to one Elenor Whytt the Dawghter of thomas whytt of poole by whom he hade vij chyldren suckye [Susie] wyllyam John margaratt thomas edith & agnes.

John man wentt awaye from my fathers and wee never herde of certayne what became of hyme butt thomas whytt of poole said that hee dyed in Holande [Holland.]

NOTE.—The record of the foregoing Mans of Poole, Eng., is from a work entitled, "Man, Needles, and Hambleton Families." It says: The MS. record of the Man family was originally commenced in Poole, England, by John Man, b. Oct. 17, A.D. 1495, d. 1578. It appears that the account of births of this branch was preserved up to the year 1600. From this time up to 1629 there was a lapse in the records (a very unfortunate circumstance for the American genealogist). John Man was mayor, A.D. 1539, and other years. Edward Man, mayor in 1589. Another Edward Man, mayor, 1663.

Among the oldest records in the church at Poole are two brass plates, about 50 x 10 inches each, saved from the old church, and now screwed on the inside of a closet door of the vestry. One reads: "Here lyeth the body of Edward Man of this Town and County of Poole, Marchat, whoe died Deceb. XXII., An Domi, M.D.C.XXII. His wife Eleanor made this Memoriall of Him."

> "This marchant Man purchast a Jewell rare
> When to gain Christ (God and man) he took care."

1492, Jan. 21. Ego Cecilia Walpole de Burnham Westgate in mea pura
viduetate [To Cecily Man, 6s. 8d:—To Richard Man, 5 marks.] Item lego
Cecitie Man antedict uná magnam patellam [Residee to John Robertson,
clerk and vicar of Geystroyk, and Richard Man of Burnham Westgate,
to each for their labour xx s.]

                    (From Visitation of Norfolk, 1563, Vol. 1.)
[Burnham Westgate is on the sea coast, Norfolk, England.—Ed.]

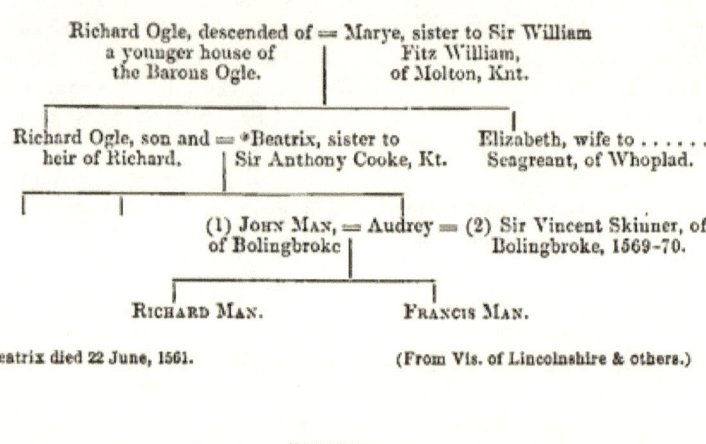

* Beatrix died 22 June, 1561.   (From Vis. of Lincolnshire & others.)

MAN, OF DRAX ABBEY.

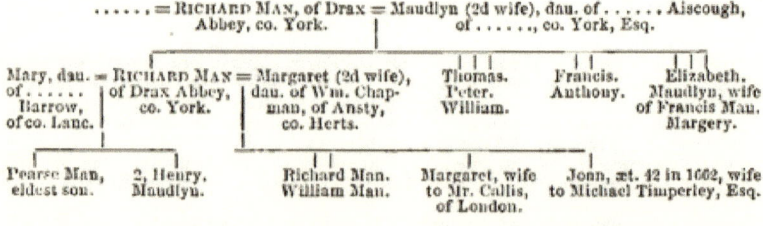

                    (From Visitation of Yorkshire, p. 627.)

Edward[1] Man, of Bramley, co. York.
William[2] Man.
William[2] Man.

                    [Ib.—p. 562.]

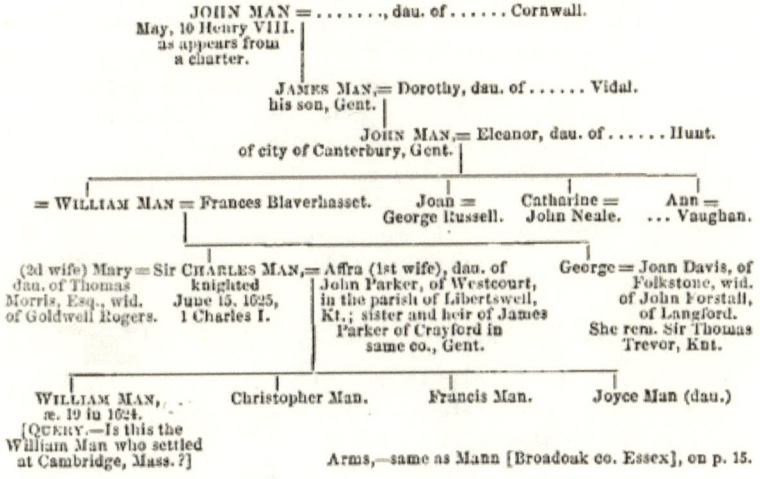

JOHN MAN = ..., dau. of ...... Cornwall.
May, 10 Henry VIII.
as appears from
a charter.

JAMES MAN, = Dorothy, dau. of ...... Vidal.
his son, Gent.

JOHN MAN, = Eleanor, dau. of ...... Hunt.
of city of Canterbury, Gent.

= WILLIAM MAN = Frances Blaverhasset.   Joan =   Catharine =   Ann =
                                        George Russell.   John Neale.   ... Vaughan.

(2d wife) Mary = Sir CHARLES MAN, = Affra (1st wife), dau. of   George = Joan Davis, of
dau. of Thomas   knighted   John Parker, of Westcourt,   Folkstone, wid.
Morris, Esq., wid. June 15, 1625,   in the parish of Libertswell,   of John Forstall,
of Goldwell Rogers. 1 Charles I.   Kt.; sister and heir of James   of Langford.
                                     Parker of Crayford in   She rem. Sir Thomas
                                     same co., Gent.   Trevor, Knt.

WILLIAM MAN,   Christopher Man.   Francis Man.   Joyce Man (dau.)
æ. 19 in 1624.
[QUERY.—Is this the
William Man who settled
at Cambridge, Mass.?]   Arms,—same as Mann [Broadoak co. Essex], on p. 15.

(Compiled from "Berry's Ped. of Families," by Alrick H. Man, Esq., N. Y.)

GREGORY MAN, of Much Ayston = ...
(Easton), in Com. Essex.

ROBERT MAN, = Phillip, dau. of Thomas Moore,
of London, grocer.   a proctor of the Arches.

WILLIAM MAN, = Cathcrin, dau. of ..... Arkenstall.
of Hornchurch, 1634.   relict Daniell Moore.

(Vis. Essex.)

RICHARD MAN, buried in Woodeforide, June, 1561. —(Reg. Lanc. and
Cheshire.)

SIR WILLIAM MANN, Knt., of Kent, m. Frances, dau. of Sir Edward
Master; the latter was Gov. of Dover Castle.

SIR CHRISTOPHER MANN, Knt., b. about 1580.

JOHN MANN, Esq., Dorsetshire, in Queen Elizabeth's time.

RICHARD MANN, city of York; b. near 1660.

WILLIAM MAN, of Hempton, about the time of Queen Elizabeth.

FRANCIS MAN, of Lincoln, Norfolk, merchant, about 1600.

ROBERT MANN, Esq., of Bolingbroke, Lincoln (16th century).

WILLIAM MAN, m. Sarah Moseley, 1654; Parish Ch. of Calverley.

JAMES MANN, church warden, 1764-5 and 6, of Calverley.

JOHN MAN, lord of Egington, Buzzard, co. Bed., deceased [1657].—"Par. burial."

EDWARD MAN or MANN [he signed both ways], comptroller of His Majesty's port of Ipswich, in the reign of Charles I. (See Arms, p. 16.)

The following were early pupils in the "Merchant Taylor's School," London.

JOHN MAN, b. May 6, 1602; entered 1617.

JAMES MAN, b. June 6, 1615; entered 1623-4.

SAMUEL MAN, b. Dec. 20, 1616; entered 1626.

FRANCIS MAN, b. Aug. —, 1617; entered 1626.

GEORGE MAN, b. Aug. 15, 1619; entered 1626.

THOMAS MANN, b. ———; entered 1698.

ROBERT MANN, Esq. (possibly a son or grandson of Edward of Ipswich), who settled at Linton, in Kent, Eng., was father of Sir Horace, Galfridus, James and Edward [the three last were army clothiers]. Sir Robert Walpole, in 1737, appointed Mr. Horace Mann to the English Legation at Florence, Italy, and two years later to be Minister, which office he retained through life. He died at Florence, unmarried, Nov. 16, 1786, æ. 85. "On the 15th of Feb. 1755, Mann was raised to the dignity of a Baronet, with reversion to his brother Galfridus." Mr. Chute, at Sir Horace Mann's request, furnished him with a motto for Mann's shield of arms, and in part allusion to the goats in Mann's arms, happily suggested "*Per ardua stabiles*,—steady in difficult places. "All your friends approve it," wrote Walpole. "It alludes so well to the goats," wrote Mann, "that I am justified in taking it." Sir Horace in life never returned to his native land; but by a pre-arrangement with his distant cousin Sir Horace Walpole, son of Sir Robert, the Prime Minister, he maintained a continuous correspondence with him, covering a period of more than forty years. "Sir Horace Mann's body was deposited at Linton (Kent), where Walpole had erected a monument to his twin brother, Galfridus." The Baronetcy reverted to Horace, the eldest son of Galfridus,—thus, the second Sir Horace Mann; but the latter "did not again marry." Dr. Doran, in his work entitled "Mann and Manners at the Court of Florence," adds: "Linton, however, has continued in the family 'by the distaff.' Catharine, daughter of Galfridus

Mann, in 1771 became the wife of James Cornwallis, fourth Earl Cornwallis [Arms below], and subsequently Bishop of Litchfield and Coventry. Their son James, the fifth and last Earl inheriting Linton, dropped his family name, and took that of Mann only. This last Earl's only surviving daughter, Lady Julia Mann, married in August, 1862, William Archer Amherst, Viscount Homesdale, eldest son of Earl Amherst." "The House is fine," said Walpole, in 1757, "and stands like the Citadel of Kent. The whole country is its garden. So rich a prospect scarce wants my Thames." "The house is occupied by Lord and Lady Holmesdale, and Mann's old home could hardly be in better keeping." (See Sir Horace Mann's letters in Walpole's works; also, Dr. Doran's "Mann and Manners," the latter rich in illustrations of Court life in Italy, from 1740 to 1786.)

English Coats of Arms.

(From Burke's General Armory, London, 1842.)

MANN [Broadoak, co. Essex]. Or. a chev. ermines betw. three lions ramp. sa. *Crest*—A tower or, issuant from the top five tilting spears ppr. *Motto*—"Virtus Vincet invidiam."

MANN [Ireland; Reg. Ulster's Office]. Same *Arms*, *Crest* and *Motto*.

MANN [Dunmyle and Corvey, co. Tyrone: confirmed to Deane Mann, Esq., of Dunmoyle, and the descendants of his grandfather Henry Mann]. Or, on a chev. engr. ermines between three lions ramp. sa. a trefoil of the first. *Crest*—A tower or, charged with a trefoil vert issuant from the battlements five spears ppr. *Motto*—"Virtus Vincit invidiam."

MANN [Earl of Cornwallis. See Cornwallis, Marquis and Earl of Cornwallis, extinct 1852. James Cornwallis assumed, 1814, by royal license, the surname of his mother's family, Katharine, sister of Sir Horatio Mann, last bart. of Linton. when the following coat was exemplified to him; he s. as fifth Earl of Cornwallis, 1824]. Quarterly, 1st and 4th sa. on a fesse counter-embattled betw. three goats pass. ar. as many pellets, for Mann; 2nd and 3rd sa. guttée d'eau on a fesse ar, three Cornish choughs ppr. for Cornwallis. *Crest*— 1st, A demi dragon sa. guttée d'eau, for Mann; 2nd, on a mount vert a stag lodged reguard. ar. attired and unguled or, gorged with a chaplet of laurel vert, vulned in the shoulder ppr., for Cornwallis.

MANN.* Ar. three antique boots sa. spurs or. *Crest*—A demi man ppr. wreathed about the temples and loins vert, holding over the dexter shoulder an arrow ppr.

MAN [co. Lancaster]. Per fesse embattled ar. and az. three goats pass., counterchanged, attired or.

MAN [Long Sutton, co. Lincoln]. Or, three chevronels sa. in chief as many pellets.

MAN [Bullinbrooke, co. Lincoln]. Per fesse embattled ar. and gu. three goats pass., counterchanged.

MAN [Newcastle]. Sa. on a fesse betw. three goats pass. ar. as many pellets.

MAN, or MANN [Ipswich. co. Suffolk: granted 2 March, 1692]. Sa. on a fesse counter-embattled betw. three goats pass. ar. as many pellets. *Crest*—A demi dragon with wings endorsed ar. guttée de poix.

MAN [London]. Az. on a fesse counter-batelly betw. three goats pass. ar. as many pellets. *Crest*—A dragon's head betw. two dragons' wings expanded gu. guttée d'or.

MAN. Or, a fesse cotised az.

MAN, Isle of. Gu. three legs conjoined in the fesse point in armour ppr. garnished and spurred or.

MAN [Linton, co. Kent, bart., extinct, 1814: descended from Edward Man, Esq., of Ipswich, co. Suffolk. temp. Charles I.]. Sa. on a fesse embattled counter-embattled betw. three goats pass. ar. as many pellets. *Crest.*—A demi dragon, wings endorsed sa. guttée d'eau, inside of wings and talons ppr. *Motto*—"Per ardua stabillis." (See p. 14.)

MANN [Norwich, co. Norfolk]. Same *Arms*.

---

* Another Coat of Arms is found which resembles the one above, viz.:
MAN [Scotland], gules, three boots argent, spurred sa.

CAMBRIDGE OR WRENTHAM BRANCH.

1. WILLIAM MAN,* who early settled at Cambridge, Mass., it is said, was born in England (Kent County ?) about the year 1607, and was the youngest of eleven children. He married first, in 1643, Mary Jarred (who also came from England). He married for a second wife Alice Tiel, June 11, 1657. He died in 1662, leaving a will and schedule of his property without his signature (see Mid. Prob. Rec.). His only child and son was:

2. i. Rev. Samuel² Man,† B.A., of Wrentham, Mass., b. in Cambridge, July 6, 1647. The record says "his parents were esteemed truly religious," and that they early designed their son for the ministry. He was graduated at Harvard College in 1665. May 13, 1667, commenced to teach in Dedham, and taught five years there. He preached to the small society in the part of Dedham, now Wrentham, till March 30, 1676, when the inhabitants were drawn off by reason of "an Indian war," after which the Indians burnt all the dwellings but two. He appears again in Dedham as a teacher, in the years 1676, 1677 and 1678. Nov. 13, 1677, the town of Rehoboth "voted, that an invitation might be given to Mr. Man for to be helpful in the work of the ministry for this winter." Early in the spring of 1678 he was engaged to preach at Milton; but returned to Wrentham, with "divers of the inhabitants," Aug. 21, 1680. There he continued his ministerial labors till a church of ten persons was gathered; April 13, 1692; was ordained and preached his own ordination sermon. Oct. 26, 1699, "in dead of night," his dwelling house with the church records were burnt. It is said that he was much afflicted with bodily weakness and infirmities, and that for twenty-five years before his death did not go out of his own town. One of the first men of the Province said that "he was not only a very good, but

---

* From one who has made research in England:

"I am inclined to believe that William was eldest son of Sir Charles Man, of Hatton Bradock, in Kent, knighted in 1625 by Charles I."
(Ext. Alrick H. Man's letter).   (See Tab. Ped., p. 13.)

† What is supposed to be the private record of Rev. Samuel Man, reads: "Oct. 25, 1699. My house was burned and all records," and as his "memory doeth serve my father William came from the other England and was the youngest of eleven children, born about the year 1607."—(Ext. letter of William R. Mann, Esq., of Sharon, Mass.)

a very great and learned man." See his work containing advice to his children who were soon to enter the married state (New Eng. Hist. and Gen. Reg., vol. x. p. 19). "His ordinary sermons were fit for the press," and yet such was his humility that he thought nothing of his worth publishing. He died at Wrentham, May 22, 1719. He m. May 19, 1673, Esther, b. Sept. 28, 1655, dau. of Robert and Margaret (Hunting) Ware, of Dedham. She d. Sept. 3, 1734. —Ext. "Sibley's Harvard Graduates," vol. ii. p. 190. He was beloved by his people. His last sermon, March 1, 1719, was from the text in Ecclesiastes i. 14: "I have seen all the works that are done under the sun, and behold all is vanity and vexation of spirit." Will in Suffolk Probate—Rec. No. 4195.

(2.)   REV. SAMUEL[2] MAN (*William[1]*), by wife Esther had children born in Wrentham and Milton, Mass., viz.:

     i.   MARY,[3] b. April 7, 1674; m. Samuel Dearing, May 4, 1708, and had *Mary,[4] Esther,[4] Margaret,[4]* and *Samuel.[4]*
3.   ii.   SAMUEL,[3] b. Aug. 8, 1675; d. 1732.
4.   iii.   NATHANIEL,[3] b. in Milton; d. in Wrentham, May 11, 1756.
5.   iv.   WILLIAM,[3] b. in Milton, May 1, 1679.
6.   v.   THEODORE,[3] b. Feb. 8, 1680; d. July 29, 1761.
7.   vi.   THOMAS,[3] b. Oct. 24, 1682; d. Sept. 10, 1756.
     vii.   HANNAH,[3] b. Jan. 12, 1685; m. Samuel Davis, April 30, 1707.
     viii.   BERIAH,[3] b. March 30, 1687; m. Daniel Hawes (b. March 30, 1684), Dec. 20, 1710, and had *Daniel,[4] Samuel,[4] Pelatiah,[4] Moses,[4] Aaron,[4] Ichabod,[4] Timothy,[4] Beriah,[4] Josiah,[4] Joseph,[4]* and *Mary.[4]*
8.   ix.   PELATIAH,[3] b. April 2, 1689; m. Jemima Farrington.
     x.   MARGARET,[3] b. Dec. 21, 1691; m. Nathaniel Whiting, April 18, 1711, and had *Margaret,[4] Esther,[4] Nathan,[4]* and *Nathaniel.[4]*
     xi.   ESTHER,[3] b. June 26, 1696; m. Isaac Fisher, Dec. 30, 1719, and had *Jonathan,[4] Esther,[4] Isaac,[4] Anna,[4] Margaret,[4] Timothy,[4] Experience,[4] Beriah,[4]* and *Hannah.[4]*

(3.)   SAMUEL[3] MAN (*Samuel,[2] William[1]*), born Aug. 8, 1675; died 1732; married Zipporah Billings, Oct. 13, 1704, and had:

     i.   *SAMUEL,[4] b. 1705; d. 1740; m. Mehitable Nicholson, December, 1736, and had *Samuel,[5]* Dec. 2, 1737 (the latter had a son *Samuel[6]*).
     ii.   *MARY,[4] b. 1705; m. ——— Bacon.
     iii.   *EBENEZER,[4] b. 1707; prob. m. Mary Gould, July 23, 1739. He d. leaving a will in Worcester County, in 1782. His "wid. Mary Mann" was admitted to the church in Shrewsbury,

---

   * Births thus (*) designated in Samuel's[3] family are recorded in Dorchester Records.

from that in Wrentham, in 1783. He had the following children born in Wrentham: *Chloe*,[5] May 15, 1741. *Lucy*,[5] June 8, 1743. *Molly*,[5] Nov. 16. 1745. *Anne*,[5] May 15, 1747. *Lucretia*,[4] Oct. 29, 1750. *Ebenezer*,[5] July 14. 1753, who lived in Shrewsbury. and died there May 18, 1840; he m. in 1828, widow Mary Foster, of Boylston; she d. Aug. 14, 1843, æ. 64. Dr. *Oliver*,[5] June 5, 1756, d. July 4, 1832; settled at Castine, Me., and had *Lucy*,[6] *Polly*,[6] *Ebenezer*,[6] *Reuben*,[6] *Oliver*,[6] *Lucretia*,[6] *Harriet*,[6] and *Nancy*.[6] Dr. *Peres*[5] (mentioned in will), b. Nov. 30, 1758; settled at Burlington. Conn. His first wife was Mrs. Miletee White. Their daughter, *Miletee*,[6] b. 1787, who m. Dr. Aaron Hitchcock, of Burlington, in 1808, and had eight children. In 1792, Dr. Peres[5] m. second, Frances Treat, and they had *Frances*,[6] b. Jan. 4, 1793, who m. Correl Pettibone in 1815, and had four children.

iv. *BERIAH,[4] b. 1708; m. Kezia Ware, Jan. 1, 1733, who had *Bathsheba*,[5] March 9, 1736; *Hannah*,[5] July 16, 1737; *Jonathan*,[5] Sept. 8, 1739; *Keziah*,[5] Aug. 13, 1741; *Mary*,[5] Oct. 20, 1743; *Beriah*,[5] Nov. 17, 1746; *Betty*,[5] Dec. 24, 1748.

v. *ZIPPORAH,[4] b. 1709; m. Thomas Throop, April 28, 1742.

vi. *RICHARD,[4] b. 1711; m. ——, and had *Sabin*.[5]

vii. *JOSIAH,[4] b. 1712.

viii. *HANNAH,[4] b. April 24, 1714; m. Thomas Brastow, Dec. 7, 1738. Eleven children.

ix. *JONATHAN,[4] b. 1715.

x. ELIZABETH.[4]

xi. BENJAMIN.[4]

xii. ESTHER.[4]

xiii. BEZALEEL,[4] b. June 15, 1724; m. Bede Carpenter. He was a noted physician in the town of Attleboro', Mass., for nearly fifty years. He had the unlimited confidence of the people, and the record says, that his wife was a "bright genius; of few words, and much reserved in mind." He d. Oct. 3, 1796. She d. 1793, aged 61. Among his children were the late Dr. *Preston*[5] *Mann*, of Newport, R. I. Dr. *J. Milton*[5] *Mann*. *Mary*,[5] m. Josiah Draper. Dr. *Herbert*[5] *Mann*, who was frozen and died in Plymouth Harbor, in the 21st year of his age, December, 1778. *Newton*[5] *Mann*, who removed to Whitesboro', N. Y., and had *Bezaleel*,[6] *Mehitable*,[6] *Abbie*[6]; he was a cotton manufacturer, and the village of Manville was named for him.—(Attleboro' Chron. of Nov. 15, 1873.) Dr. *John Preston*[7] *Mann*, of New York city, is a son of Bezaleel.[6] *Eunice*,[5] who married Dr. Seth Capron.

(4.) NATHANIEL[3] MAN (*Samuel*,[2] *William*[1]), born at Milton, Mass., about 1677. He married Elizabeth George, Dec. 19, 1704, and died May 11, 1756. He made a will Oct. 19, 1754, calling him-

self of Wrentham, and mentioned his wife and all the children, except
Timothy.   His son Richard executor.—(See Suffolk Prob. Rec.)
The following children were probably born at Wrentham:

   i. GEORGE,[4] b. Sept. 29, 1705; m. Zipporah Hall, March 10,
      1734, and had *Mercy*,[5] March 21, 1734-5; *George*,[5] Sept. 27,
      1741; *Rhoda*,[5] m. Moses Guild; *Mary*,[5] m. Edward Gay.
   ii. JOHN,[4*] b. Aug. 12, 1707; m. Mahitabel Man, Oct. 10, 1744,
      and had *John*,[5] 1745-6; *Esther*,[5] *Beriah*,[5] *Jason*,[5] and *Row-
      land*.[5]
   iii. NATHANIEL,[4] b. Aug. 6, 1709: m. ———, and probably had
      Nathaniel,[5] *Ebenezer*,[5] and *Abijah*.[5]
   iv. MARY,[4] b. July 24, 1711.
   v. ROBERT,[4] b. April 11, 1713; m. ——— Pratt, and had *Rob-
      ert*,[5] and *Nathan*[6]; probably by second wife, Esther, had
      Eldad,[5] Jan. 1, 1749.
   vi. JEREMIAH,[4] b. May 26, 1715; m. Abigail Monk, July 3, 1740.
   vii. JOSEPH,[4] b. Aug. 13, 1717.
9. viii. EZRA,[4] b. Oct. 13, 1719; m. Esther Newland, July 16, 1752.
   ix. TIMOTHY,[4] b. May 3, 1722.
   x. RICHARD,[4] b. Aug. 17, 1723; d. July 14, 1796.

    (5.)   WILLIAM[3] MAN (*Samuel*,[2] *William*[1]), cordwainer, born in
Milton, Mass., May 1, 1679; married Bethia Rocket, Dec. 1, 1701;
was a selectman in 1706, and a representative in 1733. He had the
following children, who were probably born in Wrentham:

   i. WILLIAM,[4] b. Oct. 15, 1702.
   ii. BETHIA,[4] b. March 3, 1704; m. Daniel Farrington, April 21,
      1731.
   iii. DOROTHY,[4] b. Oct. 20, 1705.
   iv. HEZEKIAH,[4] b. Oct. 27, 1707; graduated at Harvard College
      in 1731; d. 1739.
   v. ELIJAH,[4] b. April 11, 1709; d. April 7, 1750; m. 1733, Jemi-
      ma Skinner, of Norton, Mass., and had *Elijah*,[5] May 25, 1736;
      Obadiah,[5] March 4, 1738; *Jemima*,[5] Nov. 21, 1739; *Amos*,[5]
      Oct. 16, 1741; *Nathan*,[5] July 20, 1743, d. at Reading, Vt.,
      in 1826 (who m. Esther Baker, who d. at Alstead, N. H., in
      1816; settled first at Marlboro', Mass., and had *Betsey*,[6] 1774;
      William,[6] 1775; *Cynthia*,[6] 1778; *Sally*,[6] Oct. 17, 1782, who
      m. Wm. P. Shed; and two others); *Jacob*,[5] Oct. 23, 1745;
      Sarah,[5] July 27, 1748; *Ebenezer*,[5] Oct. 25, 1750.
   vi. MARY,[4] b. March 19, 1711.

---

   * Hinman claimed, erroneously, that this Nathaniel and son John settled in Mans-
field and Hebron, Conn. (See Richard Man Branch; also on p. 8.)

vii. MICHAL,[4] b. March 12, 1712; m. first, Ephraim Pond, 1736; second, Ephraim Whitney, 1749.

viii. MEHITABEL,[4] b. Sept. 1, 1713; m. Daniel Boyden, of Needham, Sept. 24, 1734.

ix. JOSEPH,[4] b. April 22, 1715.

x. ICHABOD,[4] b. June 9, 1719; m. Sarah ———, and had Sarah,[5] March 17, 1746; Abigail,[5] Sept. 26, 1747; Mary,[5] March 30, 1750; Hezekiah,[5] Feb. 21, 1752; Samuel,[5] April 5, 1753; Leonard,[5] April 15, 1755; Hannah,[5] Sept. 13, 1756; Lois,[5] Oct. 4, 1759; d. Nov. 27, 1801; she m. Pallu Pond in 1780, who resided in the north part of Wrentham. He was in the Revolutionary war, and died in 1843.

xi. ELISHA,[4] b. July 13, 1721; m. Susanna ———, and had Elisha,[5] Feb. 21, 1752; Susanna,[5] Jan. 2, 1754; Asa,[5] baptized April 5, 1755; William.[5]

(6.) THEODORE[3] MAN (Samuel,[2] William[1]), born Feb. 8, 1680; married Abigail Hawes, Feb. 28, 1702. He was a deacon in the church at Wrentham, selectman and representative in 1722. He died July 29, 1761. Children:

i. THEODORES[4] (dau.), b. Aug. 9, 1703; d. Sept. 1, 1703.

ii. MARY,[4] b. July 16, 1704.

iii. PHEBE,[4] b. Feb. 16, 1706; m. John Gould, March 22, 1732.

iv. THEODORE,[4] b. March 6, 1708; m. Abigail Day, Feb. 22, 1738, and had Joseph,[5] Benjamin,[5] Elias,[5] Jabez,[5] Timothy,[5] Daniel,[5] Seth,[5] Ralph,[5] and Theodore.[5]

v. ABIGAIL,[4] b. Sept. 16, 1710; m. Eliphlet Whiting, Mar. 7, 1733.

vi. MARGARET,[4] b. Oct. 15, 1712.

vii. SARAH,[4] b. May 6, 1714.

viii. DANIEL,[4] b. Sept. 8, 1716.

ix. BERIAH,[4] b. April 27, 1719; m. Daniel Kingsbury, Jr., Nov. 3, 1737.

10. x. THOMAS[4] (Dea.), b. Oct. 11, 1721; m. Mary Blake, Oct. 11, 1744.

xi. JERUSHA,[4] b. Nov. 12, 1724; m. Gamaliel Gerauld, Oct. 11, 1751.

(7.) THOMAS[3] MAN (Samuel,[2] William[1]), born Oct. 24, 1682; married Hannah Aldis, Dec. 27, 1709. He died Sept 10, 1756, and she Oct. 27, 1756, aged 70. He settled in that part of Wrentham, now Franklin, Mass., in 1719. He cut down the forest trees, built his house and reared his family. This place was in the family name one hundred and eighteen years, and until a recent date called "Mann's Plain." Children:

i. HANNAH,[4] b. March 3, 1711; m. Eleazer Ware, May 20, 1736.

ii.   ESTHER,[4] b. Aug. 19, 1712; m. Robert Ware, May 1, 1735.
iii. RACHEL,[4] b. July 8, 1714.
11. iv.   NATHAN,[4] b. Oct. 15, 1716; m. Esther ———.
v.   RUTH,[4] b. Jan. 15, 1720; m. Benjamin Rockwood, Jan. 9, 1745.
vi.   HEPZIBAH,[4] b. May 7, 1722; m. Pelatiah Metcalf, Jan. 14, 1742.
vii. MARY,[4] b. July 15, 1725; m. Jabez Ware, Dec. 16, 1746.

(8.)   PELATIAH[3] MAN (*Samuel,[2] William[1]*), born April 2, 1689; married Jemima Farrington, Feb. 18, 1719.   Children:

i.   DANIEL,[4] b. March 29, 1721.
ii.   JEMIMA,[4] b. Dec. 21, 1722; m. Jonathan Everett, Sept. 5, 1744.
iii. DAVID,[4] b. Aug. 30, 1724; m. Anna ———.   He was the *David[4] Man*, probably, who was many years an "inn-holder," and father of the celebrated *James[5] Mann*, M.D. (B. U. 1815), A.A.S., Surgeon, etc., b. at Wrentham, Mass., July 22, 1758 or '59; d. (N. Y.) Nov. 7, 1832; H. U. 1776, Surgeon U.S.A., etc.   Dr. Mann published two monographs, which gained prizes in 1804, and "Medical Sketches of the Campaigns of 1812-14,"—8vo., in 1816.   He m. Mary Tyler, and had five children.   (2) *Amherst,[5]* b. July 7, 1760.   (3) *Nancy,[5]* who m. first, Dr. Tyler, of Uxbridge, and second, Col. Whitney.
12. iv.   JAMES[4] (Capt.), b. Nov. 3, 1726; m. (1) Abigail Willard.
v.   EUNICE,[4] b. March 9, 1729; m. Seth Brewster, June 9, 1752.
vi.   SUSANNA,[4] b. Feb. 17, 1731; m. Royal Kollock, Aug. 11, 1748.
vii. MELATIAH,[4] b. Feb. 12, 1733.
viii. LOIS,[4] b. Dec. 25, 1734.

(9.)   EZRA[4] MAN (*Nathaniel,[3] Samuel,[2] William[1]*) born Oct. 13, 1719; died March 26, 1760; married Esther Newland, July 16, 1752.   Children:

i.   OTIS,[5] b. Dec. 26, 1753; d. Oct. 13, 1756.
ii.   RUFUS,[5] b. Aug. 26, 1755; m. Jan. 25, 1781, Sybil Allen, and had children:
    (1) *Sarah,[6]* b. Jan. 2, 1782; m. Daniel Everett, Jan. 1, 1807; no children.
    (2) *Rodney,[6]* b. March 15, 1784; died a bachelor at Buenos Ayres. South America, April 16, 1826.
    (3) *Susanna,[6]* b. Sept. 5, 1785; m. July 26, 1812, Maj. Timothy Palmer Whitney; had four children.
13. (4) *George Henry,[6]* b. Sept. 16, 1793; m. Rhoda Fisher.
iii. ESTHER,[5] b. Sept. 14, 1757; m. John Hewes.
iv.   JEREMIAH,[5] b. Oct. 7, 1759; d. May 8, 1814; m. July 1, 1790, Olive Ware; no children.

(10.) DEA. THOMAS⁴ MAN (*Theodore,³ Samuel,² William¹*), born Oct. 11, 1721; married Mary, daughter of James Blake, Oct. 11, 1744. See Dr. James Mann's letter about Dea. Thomas Man, living at Wrentham in 1809, aged 87.—(Mass. Hist. Coll., vol. x. p. 141).

  i. HANNAH,⁵ b. Oct. 16, 1746.
14. ii. ARIEL.⁵ b. June 20, 1748.
15. iii. MOSES,⁵ b. Feb. 18, 1749.
16. iv. AARON,⁵ b. Jan. 31, 1752.
  v. JACOB⁵ (Maj.), b. March 12, 1754; m. first, Mary, dau. of Joseph Brownell, of Portsmouth, R. I. He was chief of a brigade staff.—(See Peirce's Contributions.) See a pamphlet entitled: "A Sermon delivered at the House of Major Jacob Man, July 7, 1813, by John Cleaveland, A.M. etc." He was the author of the unique "Man Family Chart," executed in 1814. He was of large size. He had *Brownel,*⁶ who d. in 1810.
  vi. DAVID,⁵ b. Feb. 6, 1756.

(11.) NATHAN⁴ MAN (*Thomas,³ Samuel,² William¹*), born Oct. 15, 1716; farmer, in what is now Franklin, Mass.; by wife Esther had children:

  i. NATHAN.⁵
  ii. ESTHER,⁵ b. Dec. 7, 1743.
  iii. LOIS,⁵ b. March 30, 1746.
  iv. ABIAL,⁵ b. June 30, 1750.
  v. MARY,⁵ b. Dec. 4, 1752.
  vi. ELIAS,⁵ b. July 27, 1754.
17. vii. THOMAS,⁵ b. Dec. 24, 1756; m. Rebecca Stanley.

(12.) CAPT. JAMES⁴ MAN (*Pelatiah,³ Samuel,² William¹*), born Nov. 3, 1726; married first, Abigail Willard. He was a butcher, and lived until 1747 in Holliston and Sherborn. He purchased a farm of sixty acres in Natick, where he died in 1785. "Capt. Mann was a very conspicuous person in Natick," filling the various town offices, etc. He served in the campaign near Lake George in 1752, was commander of the "Natick Minute Men" in 1775, and at the Bunker Hill alarm, June 17th, marched with his company. In 1778 he went with his company to Rhode Island, and for forty days again in 1780. He married second, Anne Parker. Children by first wife:

  i. MARY,⁵ b. at Holliston, 1744; d. at Natick, 1755.
  ii. ABIGAIL,⁵ b. at Sherborn, 1747; m. Thomas Broad, of Natick.

iii.　JAMES[6] (Col.), b. at Natick, 1747; settled at Dover.
iv.　ELIZABETH,[6]) b. 1748; killed by falling from a cart in 1751.
v.　JOSEPH,[6] 　 { b. 1748; twins; d. of scarlet fever in 1755.
vi.　SARAH,[6] b. 1749; d. of scarlet fever in 1755.
vii.　MOSES[6] (Capt.), b. 1752; m. Rebecca Bullard, of Needham,
　　　　and settled there.
viii.　EBENEZER,[6] b. 1753; studied medicine; m. Zepporah Goulding,
　　　　of Natick. Entered the army, and d. at Rhode Island in
　　　　1776.　　　　　　　　　　　　　　[Needham and Dedham.
ix.　ELIZABETH,[6]) b. 1755; school teacher; m. E. Farrington, of
x.　JOSEPH,[6] 　 { b. 1755; twins; d. at Natick in 1758.
xi.　MARY,[6] b. 1758; m. first, Oliver Curtis; no children. She
　　　　married second, Jacob Foster, of Boston, the builder and
　　　　owner of "Foster's Wharf."
xii.　JOHN,[6] b. 1760; m. Hannah Bacon, of Needham, in 1788. He
　　　　d. (insane) in 1810.

Capt. Man married, second, Anne Parker, and by her had:

xiii.　PHEBE,[6] b. 1761; m. Dea. William Goodnow, of Natick; he
　　　　was one of the last Revolutionary pensioners in that town.
　　　　She d. in 1843.

(13.) GEORGE HENRY[6] MANN (*Rufus,*[5] *Ezra,*[4] *Nathaniel,*[3]
Samuel,[2] *William*[1]), born Sept. 16, 1793; married, May 10, 1820,
Rhoda Fisher. Children:

i.　GEORGE RODNEY,[7] b. June 30, 1821; m. June 6, 1843, Laura
　　　Crehore Johnson; residence Sharon, Mass. No children.
ii.　WILLIAM RUFUS,[7] b. Oct. 30, 1823; m. first, June 7, 1849, Mary
　　　Hewins; she d. March 6, 1878. He m. second, July 13, 1881,
　　　Esther Eliza (Barney) Ladd. He is a manufacturer at
　　　Sharon, Mass., and resides there. Children by first wife are:
　　　(1) *Mary Elia,*[8] b. July 9, 1850; m. May 14, 1884, James E.
　　　Greensmith, of Taunton, Mass. (2) *George Hewins,*[8] b.
　　　Feb. 28, 1856; m. Dec. 5, 1883, Lizzie Cass Stoyle.
iii.　CAROLINE FRANCES,[7] b. June 18, 1829; d. Oct. 21, 1846.
iv.　SARAH ELIZABETH,[7] b. Feb. 5, 1834; d. Oct. 6, 1855; m.
　　　William C. Mills, Nov. 2, 1853, and had *Helen Curtis' Mills,*
　　　b. Oct. 15, 1854.

(14.) ARIEL[5] MANN (Dea. *Thomas,*[4] *Theodore,*[3] *Samuel,*[2] *William*[1]), born June 20, 1748; m. ——. He died early, and his
widow married second, a Boyden of Sandwich, Mass. Children:

i.　BERIAH,[6] b. ——; m. widow Carpenter, of Augusta, Me.
　　　He was a Justice of the Peace in Hallowell, Me., 1848. No
　　　children.

Geo H Mann

ii.   ARIEL.[6] (Dr.), b. at Wrentham, May 14, 1777; d. March 16,
1828, at Hallowell, Me., where he had an extensive practice.
He m. Phebe Morse, and had the following children: (1)
Elizabeth,[7] b. 1811; m. first, Samuel P. Benson, of Winthrop,
Me.   (2) *William Theodore,*[7] b. 1814; d. ——; no children.   (3) *Ariel Warren,*[7] b. 1816, m. Harriet Sanford, and
had *Mary,*[8] b. 1845, m. E. L. Sturtevant; *Anna,*[8] b. 1853, m.
Theodore T. Whitney; *Hattie,*[8] b. 1858, m. E. L. Sturtevant
(second wife).   The three last mentioned families reside in
Boston.   (4) *Henry Edward,*[7] b. 1819, m. Anna Sanford;
they reside in Boston, and have the following children: *Henry
Sanford,*[8] b. 1853; *Elizabeth Benson,*[8] b. 1854, who m. Benjamin C. Hawes; *Louisa Sewall,*[8] b. 1858; *William Theodore,*[8]
b. 1861; *Hattie,*[8] b. 1855; *Ariel,*[8] b. 1859; *Horace,*[8] b. 1862;
the three last died in youth.   (5) *Charles Thomas,*[7] b. 1822;
m. dau. of William Leake, of Mississippi, and have *William
Leake,*[8] and two daughters; residence, Yazoo City, Miss.

(15.)   MOSES[5] MANN (Dea. *Thomas,*[4] *Theodore,*[3] *Samuel,*[2] *William*[1]), born Feb. 18, 1749; married ——.   Child:

i.   SALMON,[6] who m. Phœbe Howe, of Marlboro', Mass., and was
a farmer in that part of Wrentham called "North Wrentham,"
now Norfolk.   Salmon,[6] by wife Phœbe Howe, had: (1)
Charles G.,[7] b. about 1811, living in New York city, who had
E. H.[8] (late of Clayton, Ill., who m. a dau. of N. P. Mann,
of Boston), and *Kate Maria.*[8]   (2) *Caroline,*[7] m. Arsy
Blanding, of Attleboro'.   (3) Dea. *Levi,*[7] b. about 1816, living on the old homestead at Norfolk, Mass., and has children,
viz.: *Thomas H.,*[8] a physician in Woonsocket, R. I. (who m.
Julia Backus, of Ashford, Conn., and have children: *Bertha
V.,*[9] b. about 1870; *Mary I.,*[9] b. about 1873; *Josephine,*[9] b.
about 1875; *Henry L.,*[9] b. about 1877; *Philip,*[9] b. about
1880).   *William E.,*[8] on homestead at Norfolk, m. Jennie
Rice, of Nova Scotia; *James W.,*[8] d. at Port Hudson, 1879;
Edward W.,[8] has canning factory and grist-mill at Norfolk,
Mass.; *Franklin W.,*[8] physician at Woonsocket, R. I.   (4)
Lowell,[7] b. about 1818, m. ——, and has *Rhoda,*[8] *Maria,*[8]
and *Herbert,*[8] all living with their father on a farm at South
Walpole, Mass.   (5) *Mary Ann,*[7] b. about 1825; m. William
Ward, farmer and millwright, Norfolk, Mass.   (6) *Charlotte,*[7]
b. about 1827; m. Dr. H. M. Paine, of Albany, N. Y.   (7)
Ariel,[7] b. about 1829.

(16.)   AARON[5] MAN (Dea. *Thomas,*[4] *Theodore,*[3] *Samuel,*[2] *William*[1]), born Jan. 31, 1752; settled in Providence, R. I., and was for
many years engaged in the hardware business. He married June

4

4, 1789, Grace Speare Willis Flagg, daughter of Col. Josiah Flagg, of Boston. She was born in Boston, Aug. 11, 1773(?) and died in Providence, Oct. 29, 1843. He died April 4, 1834. He was a captain in Gen. Sullivan's expedition to Rhode Island, and received honorable mention for gallantry shown in the service at that time. *Children :

    i.   SAMUEL,⁶ b. July 21, 1791; d. Sept. 28, 1792.
   ii.   SAMUEL F.,⁶ b. June 18, 1793; d. Sept. 17, 1847. He was a prominent cotton manufacturer, for whom was named the village of Manville, now in Lincoln, formerly Smithfield, R. I.
  iii.   THOMAS,⁶ b. ——, 1795; d. ——, 1880; author.
  iv.   ARLON,⁶ b. Dec. 29, 1797; d. Dec. 16, 1845.
   v.   ORVILLE,⁶ b. Aug. 30, 1800; d. Aug. 8, 1839.
  vi.   ELIZA.⁶
  vii.   ANN.⁶
  viii.   GEORGE F.⁶

(17.)   THOMAS⁵ MANN (*Nathan,⁴ Thomas,³ Samuel,² William¹*), born Dec. 21, 1756; died June 20, 1809. He married June 29, 1786, Rebecca Stanley, of Attleboro', Mass., who was born Feb. 23, 1761, and died March 19, 1837. He was a substantial farmer in Franklin (formerly a part of Wrentham), Mass. Children:

     i.   REBECCA,⁶ b. May 14, 1787; m. (1815) Calvin Pennell; he d. 1824. She d. 1850. Children: (1) *Calvin S.,⁷* 1816; (2) *Rebecca M.,⁷* 1821; (3) *Eliza M.,⁷* 1822; (4) *Marcia E.,⁷* 1824.
18.   ii.   THOMAS STANLEY,⁶ b. Dec. 6, 1788; d. 1835; m. Eliza Scott.
   iii.   STEPHEN,⁶ b. Dec. 23, 1792; d. July 22, 1810.
19.   iv.   HORACE⁶ (LL.D.), b. May 4, 1796; d. Aug. 2, 1859.
   v.   LYDIA B.,⁶ b. July 30, 1798 (teacher half a century); residence, Westerly, R. I.; unmarried.

(18.)   THOMAS STANLEY⁶ MANN (*Thomas,⁵ Nathaniel,⁴ Thomas,³ Samuel,² William¹*), born in Franklin, Mass., Dec. 6, 1788, and died in 1835. He married in 1816, Eliza Scott, who died in 1862. Children:

    i.   MARIA R.,⁷ b. Sept. 4, 1817; teacher for half a century.
   ii.   MARY ANN D.,⁷ b. July 29, 1819; d. Nov. 30, 1825.

---

    * This family have held to the present time to the orthography of the single "n" in their name.

iii. THOMAS S.,[7] b. Sept. 26, 1821; d. Nov. 23, 1825.
iv. JENCKS S.,[7] b. July 6, 1823; d. Nov. 30, 1825.
v. ELIZA S.,[7] b. Sept. 6, 1824; m., 1849, William H. Wilbur,
M. D., who d. Oct. 12, 1879. They had (1) *John*,[8] M.D.,
1850; (2) *Sarah*,[8] M.D., 1853; (3) *Caroline Eliza*,[8] 1859.
Eliza S. resides at Westerly, R. I.
vi. SARAH ANN,[7] b. April 16, 1826; d. March 4, 1878.
vii. ELLEN S.,[7] b. Nov. 21, 1828; d. May 15, 1836.
viii. THOMAS S.,[7] b. May 17, 1830; d. Nov. 21, 1882; m. first,
Minerva Freeman; second, Mrs. Ellen Burdick, in 1880.
Children by first marriage: (1) *Ella M.*,[8] b. March 12, 1853;
m. Rev. George Tilton, and have three children. (2) *Mary
P.*,[8] b. Aug. 25, 1861; teacher.
ix. CHARLOTTE M.,[7] b. Aug. 23, 1832; m., 1872, Isaac Cooper.

(19.) HORACE[6] MANN, LL.D. (*Thomas*,[5] *Nathan*,[4] *Thomas*,[3]
Samuel,[2] *William*[1]), statesman and educational philosopher, was born
in Franklin, Mass., May 4, 1796. He was graduated at Brown
University, and commenced the study of law. Elected to the Massachusetts Legislature in 1827. His first speech was in favor of religious liberty; his second a plea for railways. He was the founder
of the State Lunatic Asylum, and an advocate of temperance. He
removed to Boston, and about 1836 was President of the State
Senate. He edited the Revised Statutes of the State, and was for
eleven years Secretary of the Board of Education. For many years
he devoted his whole time to the cause of education, introduced
normal schools, paid committees, etc. In 1843 he visited the educational establishments in Europe, and his report was reprinted both
in England and America. He was an incessant worker, and conducted a large correspondence. He was elected to Congress in
1848, as successor to John Quincy Adams, and opposed the extension
of slavery. At the close of his congressional term he accepted the
presidency of Antioch College, at Yellow Springs, Ohio, where he
labored successfully until his death, Aug. 2, 1859. For a more particular account, see "Life of Horace Mann," by his widow, Mrs.
Mary Mann.* He married first, Sept. 29, 1830, Charlotte, daughter

---

* Mrs. Mann has kindly furnished the following "sketch" for publication:

"Horace Mann was born in Franklin, Mass., on the 4th of May, 1796. His father,
Mr. Thomas Mann, was a farmer; his mother, Miss Stanley, was a woman of good
intellect and fine moral sense. Horace Mann's parents had not the means to give him

of President Messer of Brown University. She died without children, Aug. 1, 1832. He married second, Miss Mary T. Peabody
(who still survives), May 1, 1843, by whom he had children:

    i. HORACE,[7] b. Feb. 25, 1844; grad. Lawrence Scientific School;
        naturalist; d. Nov. 11, 1869.

    ii. GEORGE COOMBE,[7] LL.B., b. Dec. 27, 1845; grad. Har. Univ.
        1867; teacher in Jamaica Plain district, Boston. He m.
        Aug. 22, 1877, Esther Lombard. Child: (1) *Horace*,[8] b.
        Oct. 20, 1881.

    iii. BENJAMIN PICKMAN,[7] b. April 30, 1848; grad. Har. Univ.
        1870; m. July 12, 1878, Louisa Van de Sande. He is in
        the Agricultural Department, Washington, D. C.; entomo-
        logist.

---

early advantages; but they inspired in him an adoration of learning; and late in life
he enjoyed some small opportunities of acquisition, of which he made the most. His
naturally logical mind served him in his self-education, and the mere dry bones were
but a trifling element in his development. He said of himself in a letter to a friend,
'My teachers were very good people, but they were very poor teachers. Looking
back to the school days of my mates and myself, I cannot adopt the line of Virgil,

               ' O fortunatos nimium sua si bona norint!'

I deny the *bona*. With the infinite universe all around us, all ready to be daguerreo-
typed upon our souls, we were never placed at the right focus to receive its glorious
images. With all our senses and our faculties glowing and receptive, how little were
we taught! or rather how much obstruction was thrust in between us and nature's teach-
ings. Of all our faculties, the memory for words was the only one specially appealed to.
All ideas outside of the book were contraband articles, which the teacher confiscated or
rather flung overboard.' These few words are a key to his character and life-work.
That others should be put 'at the right focus' was the aim of his life. He studied
law at the Litchfield School, and entered upon a great career, but he turned aside
from it to devote himself to education; and after remodelling the original common
school laws of Massachusetts, he accepted the presidency of Antioch College, where
unsectarianism and co-education were the basal principles. His training in the Legislature of his native State, where he held the highest position, gave him a great advantage in training young men for life. A sketch of his uneventful life—uneventful
except to himself—may be found in Livingstone's Magazine of eminent Americans,
which carries him to the period when he left his native State for Ohio. His congressional life is embodied in a volume of his speeches, and his educational essays have
been published in two volumes since his death.

                                  MARY MANN."

REHOBOTH BRANCH.

JAMES MAN's wife, of Rehoboth, Mass., was "presented to court for continuing a meeting from house to house on the Lord's Day, Oct. 2, 1650."—(Plymouth Court Rec.)

JAMES MAN (probably the foregoing), is found among the "enrolled freemen" at Newport, R. I., May 17, 1653. An account of a portion of his will, made Nov. 13, 1689, is in the Providence, R. I. records. He made liberal bequests to "cousins John Parker and Hester his wife," and to several of their children of "West New Jersey."

(1.) THOMAS¹ MAN (was he son of the foregoing James?) was a landholder in Rehoboth, Mass., in 1676, and later. Rachel, daughter of Jonathan Bliss, of Rehoboth, was his first wife. She was buried there with her child in June, 1676. He married second, "9th of April, 1678," Mary Wheaton, who survived her husband, and married a Darling. He (Thomas) was probably one of Capt. Michael Pierce's guides in the famous Indian fight in that town. Bliss, in his "History of Rehoboth," says: "Thomas Man on the 27th month, 1676, has just returned with a sore wound."[*] He removed to Providence, R. I., in 1692-3, and died there July 18, 1694, leaving a will. The following children, except the youngest, were born at Rehoboth, Mass.:

    i.   RACHEL² (Richard?), b. April 15, 1679.
    ii. MARY,² b. Jan. 11, 1680-1; m. 1708, Ebenezer Sprague.
    iii. BETHIA,² b. March 2, 1682-3; d. 1712; m. Jonathan Sprague.
2. iv. THOMAS,² b. Jan. 24, 1684; d. in Smithfield, R. I.

---

[*] Deane gives the credit of this "sore wound" to Thomas Man, of Scituate; but the Ed. thinks Deane was in error.

v.   MEHETABLE,* b. April 17, 1687; probably m. July 6, 1733,
        D. Aldrich.
vi.   JOANNA,[2] b. Sept. 24, 1689; d. Sept. 28, 1731; unmarried.
vii. DANIEL,[2] b. Feb. 16, 1691-2; d. 1744; m. first, ———; sec-
        ond, 1733, Jerusha Mowry, who d. 1758. He lived in
        Glocester and Smithfield, R. I. Six children by first wife;
        four by second, viz.: (1) *Bethiah*,[3] who m. 1736, Moses
        Arnold; (2) *Andrew*[3]; (3) *Daniel*[3]; (4) *Richard*[3]; (5)
        Hutchins[3](?); (6) *Sarah*[3]; (7) *Susanna*[3]; (8) *Abraham*[3];
        (9) *Rhoda*[3]; (10) *Thomas*[3].
3. viii. JOHN,[2] b. about 1694; m. Abigail Arnold.

(2.)   THOMAS[2] MAN (*Thomas*[1]), born in Rehoboth, Mass., Jan.
24, 1684; died in Smithfield, R. I., Oct. 24, 1754; married Mary
Whiting, and had the following children born in Providence, R. I., or
Wrentham, Mass.—(See Wrentham Records):

i.   THOMAS,[3] b. June 21, 1713; probably m. Rebecca ———, and
        had (1) *Robert*,[4] 1735; (2) *Sarah*,[4] 1737; (3) *Amos*,[4] 1739;
        (4) *Kezia*,[4] 1741; (5) *Mary*,[4] 1743.
ii.   MARY,[3] b. Aug. 2, 1715.
iii. OLIVER,[3] b. Nov. 30, 1718; m. Mercy Arnold; settled in Smith-
        field, R. I., and had (1) *Anna*,[4] 1748; m. Israel Aldrich.
        (2) *Lucy*,[4] 1749; m. Ezra Allen. (3) *Joseph*,[4] b. 1754; m.
        Jerusha Comstock; children were: *Lucy*,[5] m. Marcus Arnold;
        Sophia,[5] m. George Aldrich; *William*,[5] m. Betsey Kimball,
        and had *Mary*,[6] *Lucy*,[6] *Nancy*,[6] *Arnold*,[6] and *William H.*[6]
        (4) *Alfred*,[4] b. 1762; m. Lydia Metcalf; children were:
        Oliver,[5] 1793; *William Metcalf*,[5] 1794; *Anna*,[5] 1797; *Mercy*,[5]
        1799; *Catherine*,[5] 1802; *Stephen*,[5] 1804; *Lydia*,[5] b. Feb. 5,
        1807. (5) *Sophia*,[4] 1764.
4. iv. MOSES,[3] b. Feb. 23, 1719-20; m. Alice ———.
v.   JOHN,[3] b. May 28, 1722; m. ———; had son, *Joab*,[4] who had
        Ariel,[5] 1781; *Elisha*,[5] 1787; *Mary*,[5] 1792; *Phila*,[5] 1795;
        Bonaparte,[5] 1798.
vi.   PATIENCE,[3] b. Feb. 18, 1726; m. Robert Aldrich.
vii. ROYAL,[3] b. March 28, 1731.
viii. PHILIP,[3] b. May 13, 1733; and probably, ix. DAVID.[3]

(3.)   JOHN[2] MAN (*Thomas*[1]), born about 1694 (probably in
Providence, R. I.). He purchased part of the farm, of his brother
Daniel, where Stafford Mann now resides, in Lincoln, R. I., and lived
on it until Dec. 17, 1782, the time of his death, in the 88th year of
his age, and was buried in the family burial ground on the farm. He

married, June 29, 1720, Abigail, daughter of Eleazer Arnold.
Children:

    i. ABIGAIL,[3] m. Benjamin Bollard.
    ii. SARAH,[3] d. March 23, 1801, aged 77; unmarried.
    iii. MARY,[3] m. Benjamin Lapham.
    iv. DORCAS,[3] m. ——— Harrenden.
5. v. JOHN,[3] d. Oct. 9, 1807, aged 72; married first, Marcy Stafford.

(4.) MOSES[3] MAN (*Thomas,[2] Thomas[1]*), b. Feb. 23, 1719-20;
married Alice ———. He was a seafaring man for twenty years
(he shot a snake in the West Indies some twenty-five or thirty feet
in length, and brought home the skin); then owned a farm, probably
in Smithfield, R. I. Children:

    i. RACHEL,[4] m. Ahas Mowry.
    ii. SAPHRONIA,[4] b. June 14, 1785; m. George Pierce, and had
        twelve children, who all lived to grow up. She resides in
        Chesterfield, N. H.; still living.
    iii. ALPHA,[4] m. Newell Mowry.
    iv. DIANNA[4]; unmarried.
    v. CURTIS[4]; unmarried.
    vi. THOMAS WHIPPLE,[4] b. May 21, 1795; m. ———, and died at
        Chesterfield, N. H., June 30, 1864. He was a scythe manu-
        facturer in that town. Children: (1) *Emily M.[5]*; (2) *Ruth E.[5]*;
        (3) *Dianna[5]*; (4) *Susan C.[5]*; (5) *William,[5]* who was b. in
        1820, was a farmer and coal merchant in Franklin, Mass.
        The latter has children: (1) *Emily,[6]* b. 1851; (2) *Harriet,[6]*
        b. 1854; (3) *William A.,[6]* b. 1857, d. 1865; (4) *Alden T.,[6]*
        b. 1861.

(5.) JOHN[3] MAN (*John,[2] Thomas[1]*), was a farmer, blacksmith,
member of the Town Council and Court of Probate of Smithfield,
R. I. He married first, Mary, daughter of Thomas Stafford of War-
wick, R. I.; she died in 1781, aged 47. He married second, widow
Anna Aldrich; she died in 1825, and he Oct. 9, 1807, aged 72.
Children by first wife:

    i. SAMUEL,[4] b. ———; m. Amey Brayton. He resided in Smith-
        field, R. I.; was justice of the peace, coroner, farmer, black-
        smith, and town clerk. Children: (1) *John,[5]* m. Nancy
        Kelly. (2) *Marcy,[5]* m. Marcus Arnold. (3) *Amey,[5]* m.
        Abraham Winsor. (4) *Daniel,[5]* m. Phebe Harris. (5)
        Sarah,[5] m. Nathan Mowry. (6) *Joanna,[5]* m. Dr. Tyler
        Briggs. (7) *Ann Eliza,[5]* unmarried. (8) *William Brayton,[5]*

d. 1874; m. first, Margery Chase; second, Rosa West.   (9)
Stephen Stafford.[3]   (10) *Thomas Arnold,*[5] and others.

    ii.   HANNAH,[4] b. Jan. 30, 1768; m. Jonathan Lapham, who died
            1845, in Greenfield, N. Y.
6. iii.   THOMAS[4] (Judge), b. Sept. 2, 1769; m. Lydia Lapham.

(6.)   JUDGE THOMAS[4] MANN (*John,*[3] *John,*[2] *Thomas*[1]), born in
Smithfield, R. I., Sept. 2, 1769, and died there April 17, 1852.   He
married, May 2, 1802, Lydia, daughter of Augustus Lapham, who
died Oct. 11, 1858.   Mr. Mann, who was a farmer, inn-keeper, and
manufacturer, occupied many positions of trust.   He was a member
of the Town Council and Court of Probate, a member of both
branches of the Rhode Island Legislature, an Associate and afterwards Chief Justice of the Court of Common Pleas for Providence
County, and for twenty-three consecutive years Town Clerk of
Smithfield, R. I.   Children :

  7.   i.   JOB SCOTT,[5] b. March 21, 1803; m. Olive L. Hill.
  8.   ii.   ARNOLD,[5] b. June 1, 1804; m. first, Adelia Ann Chase.
      iii.   RUTH,[5] b. Dec. 8, 1805; unmarried.
      iv.   MARY,[5] b. Dec. 13, 1807; unmarried.
      v.   STAFFORD,[5] b. Feb. 21, 1814; unmarried; a prominent citizen
           of Lincoln, R. I.   He resides on a part of the original farm
           (formerly his great-grandfather's).
      vi.   ABIGAIL LAPHAM,[6] b. June 8, 1816; died unmarried, Nov. 7,
           1869.

(7.)   JOB SCOTT[5] MANN (*Thomas,*[4] *John,*[3] *John,*[2] *Thomas*[1]), born
in Smithfield, R. I., March 21, 1803; m. Olive Lapham, daughter of
Samuel Hill, Jr., of Smithfield; she died May 8, 1880.   Mr. Mann
resides in Lincoln, R. I.; is a farmer; was a machinist, and member
of the Town Council and Court of Probate of the old town of Smithfield.   Children :

     i.   PHEBE EMMA,[6] b. Oct. 12, 1832; m. Pliny Fiske Johnson (his
        second wife), of East Providence.
    ii.   THOMAS STAFFORD,[6] b. Oct. 3, 1834; m. June 8, 1865, Eliza
        Ann Martin, b. April 13, 1839.   He is a clerk; resides in
        Providence.   Children: (1) *Flora Emily,*[7] b. May 9, 1866;
        (2) *Annie Idelle,*[7] b. Jan. 27, 1868; (3) *Lizzie Ellen,*[7] b. Jan.
        4, 1871; (4) *Hattie Eliza,*[7] b. Nov. 7, 1873; (5) *Olive
        Louise,*[7] b. Oct. 20, 1876.
    iii.   ARNOLD AUGUSTUS,[6] b. April 12, 1836; resides in Lincoln,
        R. I.; a farmer.   He m. March 28, 1866, Philena Augusta,

dau. of Stillman Estes, of St. Albans, Me. Children: (1) *George Eugene,*[7] b. March 9, 1867; (2) *Bertha Irene,*[7] b. Nov. 8, 1868, d. 1869; (3) *Frederic Arnold,*[7] b. Dec. 7, 1869; (4) *Mabel Augusta,*[7] b. Sept. 1, 1871; (5) *Elgie Anna,*[7] b. Dec. 27, 1873; (6) *Grace Isabel,*[7] b. Nov. 10, 1875; (7) *John Stafford,*[7] b. April 4, 1878, d. July 22, 1880; (8) *Ervin Hillsgrove,*[7] b. Jan. 21, 1881.

 iv. ADELIA CHACE,[6] b. April 12, 1842; unmarried.

(8.) ARNOLD[5] MANN (*Thomas,*[4] *John,*[3] *John,*[2] *Thomas*[1]), born in Smithfield, R. I., June 1, 1804; resides in Florence, town of Northampton, Mass.; was a machinist. He married first, Adelia Ann Chase, of Smithfield; she died in 1834. He married second, in 1846, Mary Smith, daughter of Samuel L. Hill, of Northampton, who was born Sept. 22, 1828. Three children by first wife; four by second, viz.:

 i. and ii. Two infant sons, b. April 6, 1830; died the same day.
  iii. ADELIA ALVIRA,[6] b. Oct. 18, 1833; d. Sept. 30, 1834.
  iv. GEORGE,[6] b. Sept. 10, 1847; d. Aug. 31, 1848.
  v. SAMUEL HILL[6] (Dr.), b. Aug. 11, 1848. He is a physician; resides in Providence, R. I.; m. Nov. 23, 1881, Eleanor Augusta, b. June 27, 1853, dau. of George L. Mason, of Providence. They have (1) *Mary Louise,*[7] b. Aug. 18, 1882.
  vi. CHARLES ARNOLD,[6] b. Aug. 30, 1849; is a machinist in Providence, R. I. He m. Sept. 18, 1872, Emma Elmira, dau. of Pliny Fisk Johnson by his first wife. She was b. Dec. 1, 1848. Children: (1) *Hattie Julia,*[7] b. July 7, 1873; (2) *Helen Sophia,*[7] b. March 24, 1878; (3) *Henrietta Clara,*[7] b. March 20, 1880.
  viii. HERBERT,[6] b. Jan. 17, 1852; died unmarried, Nov. 17, 1879.

EARLY BOSTON MANS.

1. JOHN[1] MAN, an early resident in Boston, and by trade a baker. He had real estate transactions with the trustees of Harvard University, as seen in Suffolk Register Deeds. His first wife was Mary —————— (a widow Willis), who died May 27, 1678, aged 42. He married second, about 1679, Hannah A. ——————. He was deceased in 1693, and his widow, Hannah A., in 1705. The latter left a document, recorded in Suffolk County, concerning her eldest daughter; it says : "Rebecca to have her portion if she does not marry Richard Coe, of London." All of the children by first wife, except Joseph, were baptized at the Old South Church, Feb. 26, 1669-70. Children :

 i. MARY,[2] b. ——————; d. Nov. 16, 1678, aged 21.
 ii. HENRY.[2]
 iii. JOHN.[2]
 iv. BENJAMIN,[2] b. May 26, 1666 (perhaps the Benjamin of Sudbury).
 v. HANNAH.[2]
 vi. JOSEPH,[2] b. June 30, 1672.

Children by second wife :

 vii. REBECCA,[2] bap. April 25, 1680-1.
 viii. ANNA,[2] bap. Oct. 2, 1681-2; m. Nov. 19, 1705, John Brewer (mariner).
 ix. MARY,[2] bap. Sept. 23, 1683-4; m. Thomas Thurber (mariner).

1. NATHANIEL[1] MAN (mariner), and Deborah, his wife, were early residents of Boston. He died in 1704. The widow who survived died in Boston, Dec. 22, 1718, aged 69. She left a will, remembering many of her grandchildren.

Judge Samuel Sewall in his Diary thus alludes to this family :

"1689, Mch 20. Fear [I] shall never hear of Nath. Man or the Fidelity* any more."

---

* Fidelity, a vessel, probably commanded by Nathaniel Man, on which, no doubt, Judge Sewall had property.—ED.

"1691, Sept. 14. Nine Companys Train etc. Dined at Mrs. Man's: had the Governour, Mr. Willard, Bayley, Capt. Dumer."

"1718, Dec. 25. In the evening Mrs. Deborah Man, a very good woman, a Dorcas aged 69 years, was burried. Bearers, Sewall, Townsend, Bromfield, Stoddard, Williams, Marion."

Children of Nathaniel[1] and Deborah Man, of Boston :

2. i. WILLIAM,[2] b. Feb. 19, 1671; m. Rebecca Burnham.

    ii. PRISCILLA,[2] b.————; m. Daniel Loring, Feb. 2, 1698, and had children: *Daniel,*[3] *Isaac,*[3] *Nathaniel,*[3] and *Priscilla.*[3]

    iii. NATHANIEL,[2] b. March 17, 1674; probably died young.

    iv. NATHANIEL,[2] b. Jan. 27, 1679; probably m. Abigail Shore, Oct. 5, 1714. He was a glazier in Boston. He d. Sept. 6, 1718. Children: (1) *Deborah,*[3] b. May 29, 1715; (2) *Abigail,*[3] b.————.

    v. DEBORAH,[2] b.————; m. David Craigie, and had *David,*[3] *John,*[3] *Nathaniel,*[3] and *William.*[3]

    vi. ELIZABETH,[2] b. July 18, 1684; m. Jonathan Bull, Jan. 1, 1707.

    vii. SARAH,[2] b. July 18, 1684.

    viii. JOHN,[2] b. June 26, 1688; m. Abigail, dau. of Joseph Belknap, of Boston, June 14, 1711; she was b. Feb. 29, 1691. Their children were born in Boston, where he was called a "taylor." He and wife, of "Cohenrey, Penn., merchant," deeded lands in Boston, March 5, 1725. Children: (1) *Deborah,*[3] b. Sept. 8, 1712. (2) *Elishaway,*[3] b. March 8, 1714-5; she made Barratt Dyre, of Boston, her guardian in 1732, mentioning her late father of Penn. (3) *Yelverton,*[3] b. Oct. 20, 1718; d. September, 1734. (4) *John,*[3] b. Feb. 19, 1720; d. Sept. 6, 1721.

(2.) WILLIAM[2] MAN (*Nathaniel*[1]), born in Boston, Feb. 19, 1671; married Rebecca, daughter of Thomas Burnham, Esq.,* of Wethersfield, Conn. He resided in Boston up to about 1702. A constable in 1699 and 1700. Subsequently settled in Wethersfield, Conn. He died there about 1735-6, leaving a will. The following children born in Boston, except the two eldest:

    i. WILLIAM,[3] b. about 1691; d. 1735; m. Hannah Hill in Boston, Feb. 5, 1712. He settled at Marblehead, Mass., about 1718, where he was an "inn-holder." Children; born in Boston and Marblehead: (1) *Thomas,*[4] b. March 11, 1713-4; (2) *Han-*

* Thomas Burnham, Esq., a shrewd criminal lawyer, was born in 1617, and died June 24, 1688. He sailed from Gravesend, Eng., to Barbadoes early, and thence to Connecticut.—ED.

            nah,[4] b. Nov. 17, 1715; (3) *Rebecca,*[4] b. Aug. 21, 1717; (4) *William*[4]; (5) *Sarah*[4]; (6) *Mary.*[4]

  ii.   CHARLES,[3] b. probably about 1692; a distiller in Boston in 1718.—(See Suffolk Deeds.)

  iii.   THOMAS,[3] b. Feb. 25, 1694; died at Barbadoes, 1715; "merchant."

  iv.   JONATHAN,[3] b. Jan. 25, 1696; probably died early.

  v.   REBECCA,[3] b. Jan. 11, 1699; m. first, Josiah Lupton, June 16, 1720 (died before 1825); second, John Rennals, Jr., of Wethersfield, Conn,, to whom the father of Rebecca gave his brazier's tools, pewter, brassware, and 10 £. They had *John,*[4] *Hannah,*[4] and *William.*[4]

"Sar⁴ JOSIAS MAN" resided in Boston, Aug. 15, 1674.—(See "Book of Possessions.")

JOSIAH MAN, of Boston (probably the above Josias Man), was in Capt. William Turner's company, that went out in pursuit of the Indians in 1675-6. This company was in Medfield, Mass., Feb. 22, 1675-6.—(Drake's History of Boston.)

ALMON MANN, among the "burnt out" in the great fire in Boston, 1760. (Ib.)

LEXINGTON BRANCH.

1. JAMES[1] MAN, married Nov. 8, 1711, Priscilla Grice (daughter of Samuel and Priscilla Grice, of Boston), who was born in Boston, April 12, 1692. They were married in Boston by Cotton Mather, D.D. Their children, born in Boston, were:

    i. ANNE,[2] b. Sept. 2, 1712.
2. ii. JAMES,[2] b. Nov. 19, 1714.

(2.) JAMES[2] MANN (probably the above James,[2] born Nov. 19, 1714), married Mary Simonds, Sept. 29, 1736; she was born March 10, 1717. He deeded real estate in Methuen, Mass., early, and was next settled at Lexington, Mass., where he was a real estate owner, and by trade called a cooper. He was a soldier in the "French war, 1759-60." He died at Mason, N. H., Dec. 23, 1780. His wife died there Oct. 9, 1781. Their children were:

    i. MARY,[3] b. March 29, 1737; d. Nov. 4, 1738.
3. ii. BENJAMIN[3] (Capt.), b. Oct. 23, 1739; m. Martha Deane.
   iii. SARAH,[3] b. Aug. 17, 1743.
   iv. JOANNA,[3] b. April 12, 1747.
    v. MARY,[3] b. 1749; d. Dec. 23, 1764.

(3.) CAPT. BENJAMIN[3] MANN (*James,[2] James[1]*), was born at Lexington, Mass., Oct. 23, 1739, and married Martha Deane (probably in Waltham), who was born Feb. 18, 1743, and died May 17, 1808. The last few years of his life he resided with his daughter at Troy, N. Y., where he died Dec. 7, 1831. The following is from Hill's History of Mason, N. H.:—Benjamin Mann, Esq., removed with his family from Woburn (Mass.), to Mason, about 1771. His father and mother, James Mann and wife, and his brother-in-law, Simon Ames, removed to Mason about the same time. Mr. Ames's wife was Mr. Mann's sister. About 1780, Abraham Merriam, whose wife was an aunt of Benjamin Mann, came also from Woburn, and settled on the Wilton road on the lot east of Mr. Mann's. Soon after he came he was employed in public offices in town; was moderator of the annual town meetings twelve years; town clerk four years; several times a delegate to conventions; in the New Hampshire Legislature many years; a member of the committee of safety, etc. He commanded a company in the battle of Bunker Hill, also in the army in Rhode Island. He built the house in the Centre Village now owned (1858) by Asher Peabody, and kept a tavern there, also a small store of goods. That village is also indebted to him for the noble elm trees which adorn the common. He was the first person appointed a justice of the peace in town. About the year 1800 he sold his estate in Mason, and removed to Keene, and from that place to Troy, N. Y. Children:

    i. BENJAMIN,[4] b. April 10, 1763; d. at Mason, N. H., July 24, 1776.
    ii. JOSEPH,[4] b. Jan. 21, 1765; d. July 1, 1766.
4. iii. JAMES,[4] b. Feb. 15, 1767; m. Lydia Cooke.
    iv. POLLY,[4] b. Jan. 26, 1769; d. May 9, 1851; m. 1790, Elisha Buss, who was born at Leominster, Mass., January, 1768, d. March 17, 1829. Children: (1) *Polly*,[5] b. July 30, 1791; (2) *Lucy*,[5] b. March 23, 1794; (3) *John*,[5] b. Nov. 14, 1796; (4) *Elisha C.*,[5] b. May 7, 1799; (5) *Betsey Mann*,[5] b. Sept. 20, 1801; (6) *Francis*,[5] b. Dec. 27, 1803; (7) *Alfred*,[5] b. May 28, 1808; (8) *Emeline*,[5] b. Dec. 29, 1810; (9) *Elisha C.*,[5] b. April 28, 1813.
    v. JONAS[4] (Gen.), b. April 17, 1771. He was a merchant at Brattleboro,' Vt., thirty or forty years, and a General of the State militia. About 1824 he removed to Syracuse, N. Y., where he continued his mercantile pursuits until his death, Sept. 6, 1831. He married for second wife in 1813, Mary, dau. of the late Joel Negus, Esq., of Petersham, Mass.
    vi. BETSY,[4] b. April 23, 1773; m. Samuel Wilson.
    vii. LUCY,[4] b. June 12, 1775; d. Sept. 10, 1777.
    viii. PATTY,[4] b. Oct. 31, 1777; d. Nov. 2, 1777.
    ix. LUCY,[4] b. Nov. 17, 1778; d. Oct. 8, 1779.
    x. PATTY,[4] b. Aug. 5, 1780; d. Jan. 11, 1875; m. July 25, 1805, Ebenezer Daniels, born at Surry, N. H., Nov. 8, 1775. Children: (1) *Mary Baldwin*[5] (daughter of Daniels by previous marriage), b. Jan. 19, 1802; d. 1861. (2) *Esther Mann*,[5] b. April 29, 1806; d. 1882. (3) *Ebenezer Deane*,[5] b. June 26, 1809; d. 1842. (4) *Martha Elizabeth*,[5] b. Oct. 1, 1812. (5) *Charles Wilson*,[5] b. April 18, 1815. (6) *Sarah*,[5] b. April 28, 1818.
    xi. LUCY,[4] b. Nov. 12, 1782; d. May 10, 1785.

xii. SALLY,[4] b. June 21, 1785; m. ——— Allen.
xiii. BENJAMIN,[4] b. May 15, 1788; d. July 27, 1860; m.———;
had one or two children.

(4.) JAMES[4] MANN (Capt. *Benjamin,*[3] *James,*[2] *James*[1]), born
Feb. 15, 1767, in Waltham, Mass.; died Sept. 22, 1835. He married Lydia (born Dec. 17, 1770), daughter of Benjamin Cooke, of
Cambridge, Mass. Mr. Mann was a merchant at Keene, N. H., in
1806. During the years 1807, '8 and '9 was at the head of the house
of Mann, Adams, Nazro & Co., importing merchants of Boston. The
difficulties with England coming on, they closed up, and he went to
Troy, N. Y., where he was a merchant seven or eight years. In
1817 he removed to Onondaga County, N. Y. His wife died Aug.
27, 1822. Children:

i. HARRIET,[5] b. March 16, 1794; d. Aug. 18, 1796.
ii. ELIZA,[5] b. May 24, 1796; d. Dec. 1, 1877; m. Joel Dickeson.
iii. HARRIET,[5] b. June 22, 1799; d. May 6, 1878; m. John C.
Ellis.
iv. JAMES CHAUNCY,[5] b. Dec. 16, 1801; d. March 14, 1821.
v. CAROLINE,[5] b. March 12, 1804; m. first, William P. Morse;
second, James Benson.
5. vi. SETH HUNT,[5] b. April 8, 1806; m. first, Mary Holbrook.
vii. MARTHA ANN LYDIA,[5] b. Oct. 7, 1810; m. Samuel K. Haring.

(5.) SETH HUNT[5] MANN (*James,*[4] Capt. *Benjamin,*[3] *James,*[2]
James[1]), born April 8, 1806, at Keene, N. H.; married first, at
Whitesboro', N. Y., Sept. 6, 1830, Mary, daughter of Deacon Luther
Holbrook, who was born at Keene, N. H., May 5, 1807; she died
Oct. 6, 1877. He married second, Dec. 16, 1880, Charlotte A. Joy,
of Nantucket. His sixty years of business life have been spent almost wholly in merchandizing and banking; largely the latter. He
has also written considerable for the press on banking and currency,
slavery, intemperance, and other subjects. Thus he has entertained
opinions, which he dared to express freely. Residence, Washington,
D. C. Children:

i. HARRIET,[6] b. June 25, 1831; m. Watts T. Miller (then of
Chicago), Aug. 16, 1854. Children: (1) *Harriet Mabel,*[7] b.
July 8, 1856; m. Charles H. Smith, of Brooklyn, N. Y., Jan.
17, 1881. (2) *Charles Watts,*[7] b. Jan. 11, 1858. (3) *Mary
Mann,*[7] b. July 13, 1859. (4) *Robert E.,*[7] b. Nov. 17, 1868.

ii. JAMES COOKE[6] (Maj.), b. Aug. 20, 1834; residence, Denver, Col.; m. first, Oct. 23, 1856, Mary E. Stem, of Rock Island, Ill.; second, March 9, 1864, Minnie M. Scott, of Ripon, Wis.; third, Dec. 24, 1882, Frances Nettie Bean, at Denver, Col. Children: (1) *Mary Grace*,[7] b. April 16, 1859; m. Joseph L. Brown, at Denver, Col., Oct. 20, 1878. (2) *Benjamin Abbott*,[7] b. Aug. 20, 1866. (3) *Archie Scott*,[7] b. Aug. 16, 1868.

iii. CHARLES HOLBROOK[6] (Rev.), b. Sept. 11, 1839, at Syracuse, N. Y.: m. at Chicago, Ill., March 14, 1867, Clausine Kristine Riborg Borchsenius, who was b. Aug. 23, 1840. He is a prominent Swedenborgian clergyman; settled at Orange, N. J.; editor of the "New Jerusalem Messenger." Children, all born at Orange: (1) *Horace Borchsenius*,[7] b. April 4, 1868; (2) *Charles Riborg*,[7] b. July 12, 1869; (3) *Clausine*[7] (daughter), b. Nov. 10, 1871; (4) *Kristine*[7] (daughter), b. Aug. 29, 1873; (5) *Anna Root*,[7] b. April 6, 1877; (6) *Holbrook*,[7] b. Feb. 18, 1883.

iv. WILLIAM CHAUNCY,[6] b. at Syracuse, N. Y., Aug. 17, 1841; m. Nov. 10, 1864, Mary E. Seeley, at Ripon, Wis.; residence, Denver, Col. Children: (1) *Philip Seeley*,[7] b. Dec. 24, 1866. (2) *Mary Maud*,[7] b. Jan. 20, 1873; d. June 25, 1873. (3) *Royal Holbrook*,[7] b. Aug. 17, 1875; dead. (4) *Ralph Byington*,[7] b. May 25, 1879.

EARLY MANNS NOT IDENTIFIED.

THE following list of persons bearing the family name, has been taken from town records and other sources. The reader may recognize some of them as belonging to branches mentioned elsewhere, and thus be aided in further research.

WILLIAM MAN[1] was one of the early settlers and original "Proprietors" of Providence, R. I. The lands transferred by Roger Williams to his associates, were subsequently divided into what were called "home lots" and "six-acre lots," and in a list of fifty-four persons in 1638, appears William Man.—(R. I. Col. Rec., vol. i. p. 24.) He, among others, signed the first compact in 1640. (Ib. p. 30.) He married Frances, daughter of William and Joanna (Arnold) Hopkins, who was born May 28, 1614 [sister of Thomas Hopkins, born in England, April 7, 1616]. William's widow (Frances) complained to the Council that the overseers of her late husband's will were "negligent in their attention to it." This complaint was presented the "27th of the 11th mo. 1650," showing that his death occurred at an earlier date. They had two children, viz.:

     i. ABRAHAM,[2] b. ———, never married. He was admitted a freeman in 1672, and was one of the few Providence men who "staid and went not away," during the scare in King Philip's war. He was wounded in an encounter with the "Red men."—(R. I. Col. Rec., vol. iii. p. 165.)

    ii. MARY,[2] b. ———; m. ——— Lapham, and had (1) *John*,[3] b. ———. (2) *Mary*,[3] b. ———. This Lapham family probably removed to Dartmouth, Mass.

JOHN MAN and Alcie (Alice) Bourne were married in Braintree, Mass., Dec. 4, 1672. She was a daughter of John Bourne of Marshfield, Mass., and was born in 1649. They had:

6

ALCE,² b. (in Quincy, Mass.) June 23, 1675.
The following children of JOHN MAN were b. in Milton, Mass.
MARY,² b. Jan. 21, 1680; TIMOTHY,² b. ———, 1682; SARAH,²
b. Feb. 4, 1684; ANNA,² b. March 18, 1687. (Town Rec.)

TIMOTHY¹ MANN,(?) born about 1720; lived in New Jersey; subsequently at Montgomery, Mass., from thence to Dummerston, Vt., where he died. His children were *Stephen,² Nathaniel,² Darius,² Richard,² Rachel²* and Rev. *James² Mann* (Baptist minister). The latter was born at Montgomery, Mass., Feb. 6, 1768. He moved to Dover, Vt., in 1813, and died there Feb. 11, 1854. He had the following children, all born at Dummerston, Vt.:

i. JAMES,³ Jr., b. July 13, 1790; d. Oct. 6, 1876; has *Gilbert Hosea,⁴* b. Sept. 28, 1838, who resides at Zoar, Mass.
ii. ABIJAH,³ b. May 3, 1792; d. in Ohio.
iii. GEORGE,³ b. Dec. 11, 1793; d. in Sullivan, Ohio, Nov. 22, 1862. Children: (1) *James Dennison,⁴* b. Feb. 9, 1820. (2) *Elliot,⁴* b. April 6, 1824; lives Sullivan, O. (3) *Merrill Newton,⁴* b. July 4, 1828; lives Sullivan, O. (4) *George Adin,⁴* b. June 27, 1840.
iv. BETSEY,³ b. Aug. 28, 1796; d. in Ohio.
v. SALLY,³ b. Sept. 4, 1798; d. in Dover, Feb. 14, 1862; m. Daniel Leonard.
vi. HOSEA,³ b. Oct. 18, 1801; now living in Dover, Vt. He has children: (1) *Hosea,⁴ Jr.,* b. July 13, 1858, who is a lawyer in Wilmington, Vt.
vii. WM. RILEY,³ b. Dec. 16, 1806; d. in Dover, May 30, 1869. Children: (1) *Nathan Dean.⁴* b. Nov. 11, 1832; living in Wilmington, Vt.; who has *Frank B.,⁵* b. May 3, 1865. (2) *Wm. Hosea,⁴* b. Oct. 10, 1834; living in Dover, Vt.; who has *Henry L.⁵* b. March 5, 1863, and *Clifford E.,⁵* b. Sept. 30, 1873. (3) *Frank R.,⁴* b. July 18, 1839; living at Dover, Vt.; who has *Willie F.,⁵* b. Aug. 24, 1863, and *John Earle,⁵* b. June 6, 1877.—[Ext. letter of Hosea Mann, Jr., Esq., Wilmington, Vt.]

HENRY¹ MANN (a German), resided in Schoharie Co., N. Y., prior and subsequent to 1746. He had:

i. WILLIAM,² b. about 1746; d. Oct. 19, 1816. He had (1) *Peter W.,³* who had *John H.,⁴* now living at Fulton, Schoharie Co., N. Y. (2) *Jacob W.,³* who had *P. I.,⁴* now living at Girard, Mich. (3) *William,³* who died childless.
ii. JACOB.² He had: (1) *Peter.³* (2) *George,³* who had Judge *John E.,⁴* now of Milwaukee, Wis.

iii. And possibly Capt. GEORGE[2] MANN, a gentleman of great wealth and influence, who during the Revolution attached himself to the Royal cause, and figured conspicuously in Schoharie Co., N. Y.—(See Sabine's Am. Loyalists, also Simms's His. of Scho. Co. and Border Wars.)

EBENEZER[1] MAN, M.D., married January 4, 1759, Anne, daughter of Nathaniel Berry, at Kent, Conn., and lived there until 1789–90, when he removed to Addison, Vt. He served as brigade surgeon under General Washington, at White Plains, and was at the surrender of Lord Cornwallis at Yorktown. Among his children were:

Dr. ALBON[2] MAN, a surgeon in Gen. Wilkinson's army, in 1813–14. ALRICK.[2] ELIZABETH,[2] who m. Matthew Hubbell, of Utica, N. Y. LODEMA,[2] who m. Dr. Buel Hitchcock, of Ft. Covington, N. Y. ANNIE,[2] m. Barzilla Hitchcock. And others.

Among the descendants are:

Albon P. Man,[3] lawyer, of New York city. *Alrick H. Man,*[4] Esq., in same city, the latter's son. The wife of Hon. Hugh McCulloch, of Washington, D. C. *Buel Man,*[5] of Addison, Vt. And others.

PETER MANN, of Portsmouth, N. H.; m. first in 1750, Sarah Card, and had *Elizabeth, Thomas, Peter, Sarah, Benjamin.* He m. second, about 1765, Elizabeth ——, and by her had *Elizabeth ; William* [b. Jan. 22, 1768, m. Susanna Hanson, of Dover, N. H., and had *Rebecca ; Geo. Gaines,* 1795, m. Hannah Alcott; *Statia; William,* 1805, m. Sophia Nickerson; *Joseph,* 1807, m. Mrs. J. Knowles; *Miranda,* and others who d. in infancy]; *Joseph,* 1769; *John,* 1771; *Mehitable, Patience, Hannah, Thomas,* 1777; *Mark,* 1779, d. 1783; and *Geo. Gaines,* 1782, d. 1783. ("Chron. Rec. of Eng. Manns," by J. B. Mann.)

AMOS MANN had a son *Thomas,* who m. Alice Arnold (prob. in R. I.). The latter had children *Jesse, Mary,* m. —— Hammond; a daughter who m. —— Arnold, whose sons *Welcome* and *Christopher* were merchants in Providence, R. I., and *Asa,* b. in R. I., who m. first Hepzibah Conant. The latter had Col. *Josiah,* b. 1792, in Dudley, Mass., and *Lavinia* who m. Charles Hull, a younger brother of Commodore Isaac Hull. Rev. *Joseph R. Mann,* D.D., of New York city, is a son of Col. *Josiah* above. *Asa* (above) m. second —— Clark, and had *Walter Mann,* Esq., now of St. Paul, Minn., and *Eliza.*—(Ex. letter of Joseph R. Mann, D.D.)

There was a family of MANNS in Blandford, Mass., about the time of the Revolution. Among the names were *Joseph, Nathan, William,* b. 1764, *James,* and *David. Loomis Mann,* a descendant, lives at Ionia, Mich. *Franklin J. Mann,* and others, reside at No. Blandford.

BENJ. MAN, was chairman of a committee at Monson. Mass., who under date of April 5, 1775, addressed a letter to the "Inhabitants of Boston." The following is added in postscript: "We have eighty stout fellows in this district, a great part of which are not only disciplined, but excellent marksmen. I dare be bold to say that at about thirty rod distance, they would pick up tories as fast as so many hawks would pick frogs from a frog-pond."—(His. Coll.)

DANIEL MAN, killed by Indians May 31, 1748, was with Capt. Melvin, near Crown Point. (Ib.)

SAMUEL MAN and Mary his wife of N. Stratford, Conn., who had *Samuel*, Jr., b. March, 1756.—(Hinman papers.)

DANIEL MANN, b. 1763, in Richmond, N. H.; m. Annie Jillson.—(Jillson Gen.)

JOHN MAN and DANIEL MAN, freemen, in Providence, R. I., in 1720. (Sons of Thomas Man, of Rehoboth, Mass.)

BENJAMIN MAN, was one of the deputies of Providence, R. I., 1770-'1 and '3.

CHARLES MANN (prob. from Chester, Vt.), distinguished himself at the battles of White Plains and Monmouth, N. J.—(Olcott Gen.)

JAMES MAN, on muster roll of Daniel Moore's regiment at Goffstown, N. H., July 22, 1776.

GIDEON MANN (prob. Rehoboth stock), b. April 19, 1764, Smithfield, R. I.; settled in Delaware County, Ohio. Many descendants; John G. Mann, Esq., of Jackson, Tenn., one.—(Letter.)

WILLIAM MANN. Strasburg, Penn.; descendants; some went to Bedford Co., Penn.—(Letter.)

JAMES MANN and JOHN MANN (and prob. Daniel Mann), settled in Pembroke, N. H., between 1730 and 1740. They probably came in the Londonderry colony. Descendants now in that town and vicinity.—(Ext. letters.)

THOMAS MANN, of Bedford, N. H., had Col. James Mann, b. March 29, 1773, who m. Lucena Davis, 1779; had large family and settled West.—(See Davis Gen.)

JOHN MANN, b. in Elgin, Moray Co., Scotland, June 4, 1756; d. Hampstead, N. H., 1831; had James and William, who settled in N. H.—(Ext. letter.)

MANNS near Brunswick, Maine, in 1815, from the North of Ireland.—(Nason's His. Freeport, Me.)

NATHANIEL MAN, by wife Hannah ———, of Needham, Mass., had *Nathaniel*,[2] b. 1719, who with wife Mary (daughter of Rev. Jonathan Townsend), was in Natick in 1753. The latter had children: *Samuel*,[3] settled in Dover, Mass.; *Nathaniel,*[3] removed to Conn.; *Abijah,*[3] d. in French War, 1757; *Mary,*[3] m. Dr. Isaac Morrill, of Natick; and *Ebenezer,*[3] who removed to Westminster, and was a pensioner in 1840.—(Ext. letter of Horace Mann, of Natick.)

ADRIAN MAN, b. about 1661 (wife Hester); shopkeeper, city of New York. He deposed as witness, concerning the "negro riot," June 11, 1690. His will 15 Jan., 1736, wherein is mentioned children of his son John, deceased.

EDWARD MANN, had son Abraham (wife Ruthe), who left a will bearing date March 2, 1748. Island of Nassau, Kings Co., N. Y.

EDWARD MAN (wife Mary). City of New York. Will March 18, 1767; had Edward, Jr. (who had Edward), and John; the latter had Edward and Abraham.

EDWARD MAN, baker, New York city, probably son of Edward, Jr., above; leaves in will to wife Mary, and to children Mary, Edward, William, Elizabeth, Archibald and Margaret.

JAMES MAN, of New York city, mariner; will April 4, 1756, leaves to mother, Margaret, living in Barbadoes, also son John Strange.

John MAN, Sr., of New York, cordwainer; had Philip, blacksmith, of New York city, who left a will dated July 1, 1760.

August 17, 1674, mortgage by JOHN MAN to John Shakerly, merchant, of New York, a plantation house, barn, etc., at Jamaica, L. I.—(Col. of N. Y. Hist. MSS., p. 25.)

January 22, 1679. Petition for an order that RICHARD MAN, JOHN MAN, et al., appear to answer on a bond at Southampton Court.—(Ib. p. 76.)

ISAAC MAN, et al., Dec. 5, 1763, petitioned for an appointment of a justice of the peace, at Stillwater, they being owners of the Saratoga land patent.—(Ib. p. 745.)

GEORGE MAN, Orange Co., N. Y., April 24, 1767; certificate of minister Weygand of the Lutheran church, etc.—(Ib. p. 768.)

PETER MAN, Goshen Precinct, signed against rebellion, etc., May 24, 1775.—(N. Y. Rev. MSS.)

JAMES MAN, Jamaica, L. I., Nov. 7, 1775, voted "no deputies to the Provincial Congress."—(Ib.)

Capt. RICHARD MANN (called a British officer), m. Jerusha, daughter of Dr. Micah Moore, of Hempstead (?). She was b. 1757; d. 20 April, 1777.—(v. Charles B. Moore's compilation.)

"Att A court Helde att New haven the 7th of The 2[d] Monday 1640, SUSANNA MAN, servant to Mr Goodyeare, haveing accused John Thomas for stealing a piece of stuff, valued att 3' 6'. She now confessed thatt she had slaundered him. and said thatt God had given her oner to the Devill to make her lye. wherevpon it was ordered that she should pay to her ma' double the price of the stuff as the said Joh: Thomas should have done if he had beene guilty, according to the law of God in thatt case."—(N. Haven Col. Rec.)

"Benj. Mann was in the Pequot war, in 1637."—(Hinman papers, N. E. Hist. Gen. Soc., Boston.)

"Benj. Mann had a house-lot in N. W. part of the village of Hartford, in 1640."—(Ib.)

"Richard Mann was a witness to a deed given by Gie Sachem, at Setauket, L. I., to Richard Woodhul, dated Nov. 19, 1675."—(Ib.)

"Brookhaven (probably Windham Co., Conn.), (Hist. by Town Clerk, p. 44), Richard Mann (elsewhere called Mr. Richard Man), witness to deed and counter-deed. from and to Indians at Brookhaven" (Ib. p. 46). Also a few pages further on he is mentioned, also John Man, perhaps his son.—(Comp. of A. H. Man.)

Robert Man, of Sudbury, Mass., m. Deborah Draper, April 1, 1664; she d. May 11, 1665.—(Mid. County Rec.) It appears he took for a second wife, the widow of John Bush, Dec. 20, 1671. At this date his age was 35.—(Mid. Court Files.)

Dorothy Man m. Edmund Goodenow, in Sudbury, Mass., June 6, 1686.

Benjamin Man, of Sudbury, 5 July, 1709. "Went to sea on a voyage for Jamaica. Dyed intestate."—(Mid. Pro. Rec.)

Benjamin Man, by wife Dorothy, of Sudbury, had Abigail, b. Dec. 2. 1688.—(Mid. Rec.)

Died in Sudbury. Mass. Dorothy Mann, d. Feb. 2. 1690-1; Elizabeth, wife of Robert Mann, d. May 4, 1705; Sarah, wife of Robert Mann, d. July 19, 1710; Robert Mann, d. Sept. 10, 1719.—(Town Rec.)

Thomas Man, m. in Billerica, Mass., Jan. 23, 1731-2, Ann Haseltine.

"vj Jvnij 1635." The following persons imbarked in the "Thomas and John, Richard Lambard, Mr." at Gravesend, England, for Virginia: Tho. Mann, aged 23; Wm. Mann, aged 25.

Leave was granted in England to the following persons to pass the sea. May 2, 1635, Ann Mann, æt. 17, to Barbadoes; ship "Alexander." Nov. 20, 1635, John Mann, æt. 21, to Barbadoes: ship "Expedition."

Among the inhabitants in and about St. Michaells, Barbadoes, in the year 1680, were: Jno. Man and wife, five children and six slaves; Barnard Man and wife, one servant and two slaves.

Annanias Man, senior, buried June 4, 1678, at Barbadoes.

PERCIVAL MAN was dead in Virginia (Martin's Hundred), 1622-3.

Feb. 1, ——— (early), the King by patent appointed JOHN MANNE, Gent. (prob. Mann), to be chief surveyor of the island of Jamaica, during pleasure.—(See Hotten's Emigrant List.)

EDUARD MAN, Chairman of the Hon. Board of Directors of the West India Company, chambers at Amsterdam (Holland), signed documents from about 1650 to 1660.—(Col. Hist. N. Y., vol. i.)

EDWARD MAN was a justice of the peace in Talbot, Maryland, in 1693. —(Mann-Needles Gen.)

Among the Delaware Patents sealed the 24th July, 1676, was EDWARD MAN, five hundred acres.—(Col. Hist. N. Y., vol. xii. p. 544.)

Mr. ABRAHAM MAN was one of the magistrates of Delaware, on the "West Side at Newcastle," in 1678.—(Ib. p. 634.)

VIRGINIA MANNS.

"HERE* Lyeth ye Body of JOHN MANN, of Gloucester County, in Virginia, Gent. Aged 63 years. Who Departed this life ye 7th Day of January, Anno Domini 1694," and of his wife.

"Here Lyeth Intered the Body of Mrs. MARY MANN, of the County of Gloucester, in the Colony of Virginia, Gentlewom, who Departed this life the 18th day of March, 1703-4. Aged 56 years." The only child of the above JOHN MANN and Mary, was MARY MANN, b. 1672, d. 24th March, 1707, aged 35 years, and buried at Rosewell, Gloucester County, Va. She m. in 1689, Hon. Mathew Page, of Rosewell. Hon. Mathew Page had only surviving child, viz.: Mann Page [Hon. Mann Page]†, from whom all the Virginia Pages are descended. Mann Page m. first, 1712, Judith Wormley. By her he had an only surviving child and daugh-

----

* Timberneck Bay, Gloucester Co., Va., the ancient seat of the Manns.

† Hon. Mann Page, grandson of Sir. John Page, "was probably the wealthiest land-holder of his time in Virginia, with the single exception of the Fairfaxes." It it said "he united in his person the rich inheritances of the Manns and the Pages." He built the historic and costly mansion called "Rosewell House," in Gloucester County, one of the most venerable relics of antiquity in Virginia. His landed estates were eleven thousand acres called "Pageland," in Prince William County; eight thousand acres in Frederick; forty-five thousand in Spottsylvania; one thousand acres in King William, called "Pampike"; two thousand acres in Hanover; fifteen hundred in James City; besides others elsewhere, and the magnificent plantation on the York River, to which Rosewell gave its name.—(See Henning's Statutes, vol. v. p. 227. Also "Old Churches and Families of Virginia," by Bishop Meade.)

ter, Maria Judith Page, who m. about 1735, William Randolph, of Tucka-
hoe, Goochland County, Va. William Randolph and Maria Judith Page,
his wife, had issue: Thomas Mann Randolph, being third child and only
son, b. 1741, m. 18th Nov. 1761, Anne, eldest child of Col. Archibald
Cary. Their eldest son and fourth child was Thomas Mann Randolph,
Jr., of Edge Hill, who m. Martha Jefferson, daughter of Thomas Jefferson.
—(Ext. letter of R. C. M. Page, M.D., New York city.)

JOHN MAN was one of the Commissioners for the County of Gloucester,
Va., 1676.—(Hist. Coll.)

BENJAMIN MANN, b. in Wales, came to Virginia and fought through the
Revolution. He m. Millie Timberlake, and had twenty-three children.
After the Revolution he removed to Lexington, Ky., thence to Campbell
County, Ky., near Alexandria, where he d. æt. 77. Among his children
were Richard, b. in Va.; Thomas, Elijah, Tannie, Arch, Susan, Sarah,
Lucy, Peggie, Nancy, William, James, Francis, Benjamin, and others.
The descendants are numerous in Kentucky and adjoining states. RICH-
ARD MANN, an extensive farmer and one of the first men of Pendleton
County, Ky., is a descendant. He has about seven hundred acres of fine
land under a high state of cultivation. ELIJAH G. MANN, Esq., Associate
Principal of Harrodsburg Classical and Commercial College, Kentucky, and
his brother ELI B. MANN, M.D., of Oldenburg, Indiana (sons of James),
are descendants.—(Ext. E. G. Mann's letter.)

Hon. A. DUDLEY MANN, b. in Virginia, 1805, was a Commissioner of
the United States to the German States, 1845 and 1847. Special Com-
misssioner to Hungary, 1849. Minister to Switzerland, 1850. Private
secretary to President Pierce in 1853. In 1861 he was sent on a special
mission to induce the European governments to recognize the Southern
Confederacy; subsequently associated with Messrs. Mason and Slidell.

RICHARD MAN

(OF SCITUATE, MASS.)

AND HIS DESCENDANTS,

WITH AN INDEX.

(PRECEDED BY A BRIEF SKETCH OF THE TOWN
IN ITS EARLY HISTORY.)

COVERING A PERIOD OF TWO HUNDRED AND FORTY YEARS.

1644—1884.

7

EARLY SCITUATE AND ITS INHABITANTS.

THIS historic old town, one of the first settled in Plymouth County, is situated on the coast about mid-way between Boston and Plymouth. The earliest notice of settlement on record bears date 1628; it is certain, however, that the Pilgrims of Plymouth explored the shores somewhat earlier, and took notice of this favorable place for a settlement. History affirms that many of the first settlers of this town were "men of education and easy fortune, who left homes altogether enviable, save in the single circumstance of abridgment of religious liberty." The "Men of Kent," as they were called (from Kent County, England), settled at and near what is now called the Harbor, and on the cliffs bordering on the sea shore. It is said, "early as the year 1639, Scituate contained more men of distinction and fair fortune than at any period since." Some of them were "celebrated in English history for gallantry, loyalty and courtly manners." Of these, were: Vassall, Hatherly, Gilson, Cudworth, Hinckley, Foster, Tilden, Stedman, Saffin, Annable, Chittenden, Clapp, Cobb, Josselyn, Adams, Robinson, Stetson, Hatch, King, Preble, Turner, Williams, Sutton, Hoar, Ensign and others. A few years later came in the families of Otis, Barstow, Ticknor, Brooks, Briggs, Barker, Church, Chandler, Clarke, Collamore, Bryant, Bird, Bourne, Allen, Cushing, Curtis, Delano, Man, Ewell, Hewett, Holmes, Jacobs, Jones, Litchfield, Lincoln, Cowen, Lewis, Little, Lowell, Lombard, Fuller, Parker, House, Merritt, Nash, Pierce, Pierpont, Randall, Rogers, Stockbridge, Sylvester, Torrey, Jenkins, Hobart, Wade, Wanton, Willard, Winslow, Wilson, Woodworth, Young and others. Descendants of the above are now found located in nearly every State in the Union. The early clergymen who were born in England were: Giles Saxton, John Lathrop, Charles Chauncy, Henry Dunster, William Witherell and Nicholas Baker. Dunster and Chauncy were the first and second presidents of Harvard University. William Vassall was the shining literary light, who bitterly opposed Rev. Dr. Chauncy, and disrupted the church. Foster, Hoar, Saffin and Barker were the first lawyers of the town. John Hoar, the lawyer and farmer, removed to Concord, Mass., in 1659 or '60, and his descendants are well known in the State and Nation.

The Cushing and Otis families have been very prominent. William Cushing, LL.D., one of the first justices of the United States Supreme Court, who administered the oath of office to President George Washington, lies buried here in his own selected enclosure, and near his once famous mansion. Of the long list of persons mentioned in this article, Mr. Timothy Hatherly deserves a brief notice. With his abundant fortune, he preëminently enhanced the early prosperity of Scituate. He first arrived at Plymouth in the ship Ann, 1623, and erected a house there, which was destroyed by fire. He went to England in 1625, but returned hither in 1632, and settled in Scituate, where he came into possession of a grant of land nine miles square, called " Conihassett Grant." A portion of this land had already been taken by "squatters"—the early settlers—but adjustments were made, whereby a deed of copartnership was signed in 1646. These Conihassett partners (twenty-six in number, see p. 57) appointed their clerks, surveyors, committees, agents, etc., and conducted their affairs with all the efficiency of a corporate town. They laid out and maintained roads until 1715, and records which fill a large volume were kept of all their transactions in perfect order. Their last meeting on record was 1767. Of the two ancient burial grounds, where lie buried the venerable fathers, one is barely visible by its ancient and weather-beaten head-stones; the other, where lie the ashes of Rev. William Witherell* and others, was long since desecrated by ruthless hands, who removed the slabs and ploughed the soil.

---

* Rev. William Witherell, who antagonized Dr. Chauncy's mode of infant baptism, and who baptized Gov. Josiah Winslow, was born in England in 1600 ; ordained pastor at Scituate in 1645, and died in 1684. He administered at Scituate six hundred and eight baptisms. Many anecdotes are related of him ; one as follows : Mr. Bryant entered the church after services commenced. Mr. Witherell at close of prayer thus addressed him : " Neighbor Bryant, it is to your reproach that you have disturbed the worship by coming in late, living as you do within a mile of church. Especially so, since here is goody Barstow, who has milked seven cows, made a cheese, and

This town suffered early by the Narraganset Indians. March 26, 1676, Capt. Michael Pierce, of Scituate, with less than eighty whites and friendly Indians from the neighboring towns, had a desperate encounter with the foe near what is now the town of Rehoboth, Mass. He was killed with fifty-two Englishmen of his company. The Indians being in great force, then marched towards Scituate, burning houses and murdering the inhabitants. Deane informs us, that in their progress over "Walnut Tree Hill" they entered Ewell's house, which stood at the "turn of the road." Ewell's wife was alone, save an infant grandchild, John Northey, sleeping in the cradle. The house being situated beneath a high hill, they had no notice of the approach of the savages until they were rushing down the hill towards the house. In the moment of alarm she fled towards the garrison, which was not more than sixty rods distant, and either through a momentary forgetfulness or despair forgot the child. She reached the garrison in safety. The savages entered her house, and stopping only to take the bread from the oven (which she was in the act of putting in when she was first alarmed), they rushed forward to assault the garrison. After they had become closely engaged, Ewell's wife returned by a circuitous path to learn the fate of the babe, and, to her happy surprise, found it quietly sleeping in the cradle as she had left it, and carried it safely to the garrison. Shortly after the house was burnt.

The court records abound with curious items. A. D. 1660, "William Holmes' wife was accused of beinge a witch. Dinah Sylvester,

---

walked five miles to the house of God in good season." Mr. Witherell wrote verse superior to the poetry of Dunster. In an elegy on the death of his friend, Gov. Josiah Winslow, after extolling highly his many virtues, he suddenly breaks forth thus:

> "But why do I burn Tapers in the sun,
> Or midst great cannons, let fly my pot-gun;
> His worth transcends the weakness of my quill,
> As lofty mounts o'ertop the pismire hill.
> *   *   *   *   *   *   *
> Had I an hundred eyes like Argus, I
> Would weep them all purblind, or pump them dry.
> I'd rather drink the tears of my old eyen
> For sweet JOSIAH, than quaff muskadine.
> *   *   *   *   *   *   *
> I wish that He, who thee succeedeth next,
> May, like to thee, keep close unto the Text.
> Sacred and civil; He shall have my Vote,
> While I am worth a Tester or Gray Groat."

accuser. Witness sworn said she saw a beare about a stones throw
from the path, but being examined, and asked what manner of tayle
the beare had, she said she could not tell, for the head was towards
her." Probably the bear alleged was William Holmes's wife in that
shape.

The physical changes are marked since the first settlement of this
ancient town. By the constant attrition of the tides and storms the
cliffs are gradually wasting away. The early records mention the
" Live Oak Forests." The first ship building of the colony was
done on the banks of North River, a sluggish stream affected by the
tide. A noticeable feature of the town at this late day is the little
colony of colored people—descendants of the slaves, who in early
times were numerous at this place. This town (which included
Hanover prior to 1727, and South Scituate up to 1849) has many
very ancient and historic mansions; old buildings still standing,
erected 1636 and later. In another way Scituate has been made
famous. Here lived the author of the poem, " The Old Oaken
Bucket." The maternal cottage of Woodworth, the " dairy-house,"
and the " moss-covered bucket " are gone, but still to be seen as of
yore is

> " The wide-spreading pond, and the mill that stood by it;
> The bridge, and the rock where the cataract fell."

The well also remains unchanged, but a flat cover is substituted for
the curb, and the water is taken into the kitchen by a pump. The
historic old mill has been in constant service for two hundred and
forty years, and is now busily at work as in Woodworth's childhood.

RICHARD MAN

AND HIS DESCENDANTS:

RICHARD MAN, of Scituate, Mass., was one of the first bearing the name who, probably, with his wife Rebecca ————, during the reign of King Charles I. of England, emigrated from that country. There is no data sufficiently authentic by which to fix the year of his arrival here; but it was, no doubt, a few years previous to 1644. The first appearance of his name on record is found with thirty-one other persons in the town of Scituate, Mass., as having taken the "Oath of fidelity." This act bears date "January 15, 1644."

Rev. Samuel Deane, in his history of Scituate, published in 1831, says:

"Richard Man [planter] was a youth in Elder Brewster's family, and came to Plymouth in the Mayflower, 1620. He was one of the Conihassett partners in Scituate, 1646. His farm was at Man Hill* [a well known place to this day], south of great Musquashcut pond, and north of John Hoar's farm. There is no record of his marriage here. His children: Nathaniel, born 1646; Thomas, 1650; Richard, 1652; Josiah, 1654. Nathaniel lived in Scituate, but left no family. In 1680 he made over his estate to his brothers, Richard and Thomas, and took a bond for support. This was on account of infirm health. Josiah deceased early, or removed. Thomas had children: Josiah, born 1676; Thomas, 1681; Sarah, 1684; Mary, 1688; Elizabeth, 1692; Joseph, 1694; Benjamin, 1697. Thomas had lands at Rehoboth, and probably deceased there. He was in the Rehoboth battle with Capt. Pierce, 1676, and was severely wounded. Richard

---

* "Man Hill." A beautiful, but gentle rise of land bordering on the sea shore, located at the N. E. part of Scituate. Known by this name since 1648. Now covered by a few elegant summer residences. The old Man cellar-hole is still visible on the west slope of this hill.—ED.

had children: John, born 1684; Rebecca, 1686; Hannah, 1689; Nathan.., 1693; Richard, 1694; Elizabeth, 1696; Abigail, 1698. Rebecca, widow of Richard, Sen., married John Cowen, 1656."

A historian, and more especially the compiler of a genealogical work like the History of Scituate, is not expected to be infallible. Deane, though in error in his statement that Richard Man "was a youth in Elder Brewster's family," and "came in the Mayflower, 1620," was, nevertheless, a good annalist. There was a "youth" in the family of Elder Brewster by the name of Richard More, who married Christian Hunt, Oct. 20, 1636. Deane probably confounded the two names. And his assertion that Thomas Man, of Scituate, "was in the Rehoboth battle; had lands at Rehoboth, and probably deceased there," is another error equally obvious. There was a Thomas Man of another branch (see p. 29), a resident of Rehoboth, who, undoubtedly, was the one who came out of that noted Indian fight in 1676 "with a sore wound."—(See Bliss's History of Rehoboth.) James Savage, LL.D., in his Genealogical Dictionary, claims that Deane must have been also mistaken in his assertion that Richard Man came in the Mayflower, 1620, and adds: "The person who had share with Brewster's lot in the division of cattle, 1627, was not Mann but More (v. Davis's Morton, 382), and Bradford gives the Mayflower Richard More to be counted with the other heads to Brewster, six in number," etc.

Richard Man* (planter) appears next in 1646 with twenty-five other persons in the well known "Conihassett grant†" deed from the venerable Timothy Hatherly.—(See Old Col. Rec.)

---

* Richard Man was one of the twelve men "impannelled and sworne" the 15th of November, 1655, "to looke on the body of the daughter of Willam Pakes.
By the appointment of mee, Timothy Hatherly."

"Wee find Willam Pakes his well to bee very dangerous, as both in that it lyes at the foot of a hill, as alsoe haueing noe fence aboute itt to preserve a child from shooting or tumbling in: soe the child falling or tumbling in the water was the cause of the death of Thankful Pakes."—(Plymouth Col. Rec., Vol. iii. p. 92.)

† Within this territory was included a large tract of land which the Colony Court had granted to four gentlemen, called "merchant adventurers of London." The following court order, A.D. 1633, relates to this subject: "That the whole tract of land between the brook at Scituate, on the N. W. side, and Conihassett, be left undisposed of till we know the resolution of Mr. James Shirley, Mr. John Beauchamp, Mr. Richard Andrews and Mr. Timothy Hatherly." In October, 1637, the above tract was granted to the above named gentlemen, "extending three miles up into the woods from the high water mark in the brook," etc. This grant was purchased by Timothy

1655,
4 October
[Bradford.
Governor.]

"The 16th of February, 1655, they whose names are vnder-written were panneled on a quest of enquiry about the death of Richard Man.

By mee, Timothy Hatherley.

Sworne {
Matthyas Briggs.
Ensigne John Williams.
Serjeant Gilbert Brookes.
Jeremy Hatch.
Rodulphus Elmes.
Gowin White.
}

Sworne {
Willam Pakes.
Jonathan Whetcom.
Thomas Ensigne.
Steuen Viner.
Robert Whetcom.
John Hoar.
}

The verdict of the jury concerning the death of Richard Man:

. Wee find, that by coming oner the pond from his owne house towards the farmes, that hee brake through the iyce, and was in soe deep that hee could not git out, and by reason of the cold of the weather and water made him vnable to healp himselfe, neither could any other psent aford him any healp that could healp him out, though they vsed their best endeauors for the space of about an houre, as is reported to vs by the wittnesses that saw him, in which time hee died. This wee find to bee the cause of his death, as wee all judge."—(P. C. R., Vol. iii. p. 92, 93.)

1655,
5 March
[Bradford,
Governor.]

The Court haue ordered and requested of Mr. Hatherley in respect vnto the estate of Richard Man, late deceased, att Scittuate.

Presentment by the Grand Enquest. Wee p'sent to this honered Courts consideration the death of two men vnattested, vizs. John Granger of Marshfield, and Richard Man, of Scittuate.—(Plymouth Col. Rec.)

Hatherly of the other merchant adventurers before 1646; and in that year he divided it into thirty shares (reserving one fourth part of the whole), and sold it for £180 to a company since called the "Conihassett partners" [Conihassett means a fishing promontory.—Flint's Century Sermon]. Many of this company had already located upon these lands; thus an amicable adjustment was made with those persons. The partners were: Mr. Charles Chauncy, pastor of the church; Thomas Chambers, planter; John Williams, Sen., farmer; James Cudworth, salter; Joseph Tilden, yeoman; Henry Merrett, planter; Thomas Rawlins, Sen., planter; Thomas Tarte, planter; John Hoar, farmer; Richard Sealis, planter; Thomas Ensign, planter; Thomas Chittenden, weaver; John Stockbridge, wheelwright; John Allin, planter; Thomas Hiland, planter; John Whetcomb, planter; John Woodfield, planter; Edward Jenkins, planter; John Hallett, planter; Ann Vinall, spinster; William Holmes, planter; John Whiston, planter; Gowin White, planter; John Daman, planter; Rhodolphus Eallms, planter; Richard Man, planter.

On the fifth of March, 1655, the widow made application to administer on his estate, and letters were granted on the sixth of May following.

The apprisal of Richard Man's real and personal estate on record at Plymouth bears date "14th April, 1655." Some of the items are:

1 dwelling house & barn with 43 acres of upland; 13 acres marsh land & share of Connihassett land undersold,	40	00	00
2 oxen,	10	00	00
one heifer,	3	00	00
2 two year old steers,	5	10	00
3 yearlings,	4	10	00
2 more valued,	09	00	00
3 bushels of barley and 3 bushels of good wheat,	01	05	00
a pair of shoes,	00	06	00
a bushel of Indian corn,	00	02	00
a bushel of mault,	00	04	00
one bed, two old blankets, and a Rugg,	02	00	00
one warming pan,	00	06	00
2 spinning wheels,	00	06	00
one Iron Kettle, one Iron pot, and Iron skillett,	01	02	00
2 frying pans, a little kittle, 1 skillett, 1 pr. of tongues,	00	06	00
1 cradle, 2 old pitch forks, and old pair of cards,	00	06	00
a bible with other books,	00	05	00
1 plow, plow points, 2 axes, 2 hammers and hoe,	00	14	00
2 pieces of bacon,	01	06	00
small shot gun, old box, with 4 old chairs, and pr. of ballances,	00	06	00
2 old hogsheads, one barrell, etc.,	00	08	00
one Sabbath short coat,	00	16	00

(And a few other articles so obliterated by age that I could not decipher them.—ED.)

Sum total,   92 02 00

apprisers { James Cudworth. / Walter Briggs.

[signed] { Timothy Hatberly, Esq. / 2d May, 1656

1656, 6 May [Bradford, Governor.]   The wife* of Richard Man, deceased, doth give vnto her three youngest children, to each of them five pounds: and Captaine Cudworth standeth bound to see the same pformed out of the estate of the said Richard Man.—(Plymouth Col. Rec.)

---

* Rebecca Man (widow of Richard Man) married John Cowen "the last of March, 1656." John Cowen and wife Rebecca lived in Richard Man's house until 1670.— (See controversy Plymouth Col. Rec., also on p. 60.) Their children were: Joseph, b. 1657; Mary, 1659; John, 1662; Israel, 1664; Rebecca, 1666. Joseph Cowen, b. 1657, was killed with fourteen others of Scituate in the Indian fight at Rehoboth, 1676. John Cowen, Sen., was from Scotland. He purchased lands in Conihassett (Scituate), north of Sweet Swamp. His house stood where Stephen Litchfield's did in 1830. As an evidence of his Scottish spirit I insert the following "Court Record":

Nathaniel Man, the Sun of Richard Man, was Borne the 23 of September, 1646.

Thomas Man, the Sun of Richard Man, was Borne the 15 of August, 1650.

Richard Man, the Sun of Richard Man, was Borne the 5 of ffebuary, 1652.

Josiah Man, the Sun of Richard Man, was Borne the 10 of December, 1654.—(Scituate Rec.)

The compiler has not traced the family line in England. By examining what is printed of English Records on pp. 9 to 17 of this work, the reader can judge as well as the author, independent of a more extended research, regarding the ancestry of Richard, anterior to his settlement in Scituate. Undoubtedly, he married (Rebecca ———) in the mother country, and, probably, had no children there. William[5] Mann (*Ensign*,[4] *Ensign*,[3] *Thomas*,[2] *Richard*[1]), a person of intelligence and remarkable memory, on his death-bed in 1861 related to the writer, that his father told him that Richard Man, Sen., came from the County of Cornwall,[*] England, "with" or "had" seven sons. One theory in connection with this statement is, that Rebecca, the widow of Richard, married John Cowen, 1656, and by him had three sons, making "seven sons" in both families, who were probably brought up together and cared for under one roof (see p. 58). But traditional accounts are so unsatisfactory, the writer will refrain from mentioning others.

1671,   Att this Court, John Cowin was indited for speaking contemptable words
5 June,   against the royal dignity of England, in that hee said hee scorned to be in
Prence,   subjection to any English man, and that there was neuer any Kinge in
Gov[r].   England that was an English man but one crooked backed Richard, a
crooked rogue, just like such an one as hee named, vizs. a crooked man
well known in the town of Scittuate. The case being put vpon tryall the
jury brought in not guilty, and soe hee was by open proclamation cleared,"
and

1672-3,   Anthony Dodson, of Scittuate, sued John Cowen and Rebecka, his wife,
4 March.   claiming £100 damage, "for vngroundedly saying and reporting this yeare,
'72, that the said Dodson sayed that John Williams sayed William Rogers
broke vp his house, by which saying and reporting of John Cowin and his
wife, the said Dodson is wronged, reproached, and defamed, and soe comes
to be damnifyed. The jury find for the defendant."

* In reply to a letter of the author, Rev. Charles Noel Mann, of St. Issey Vicarage, Cornwall, Eng., wrote under date "12 March, 1880," regarding Richard Man, thus: "From the Register Books of the Parish—no trace of him exists in any branch of our family."

Richard was a farmer, and one of the original land proprietors. His foresight, no doubt, led him to select one of the most beautiful locations for a residence on the coast. His neighbor on the south was John Hoar, who early removed to Concord, Mass. On the east of him was the sea; north, "Musquascut Pond"; still further north, and bordering the "Pond," were the "Farmes," so-called. In an attempt to cross this pond in February, 1655, on the "iyce," he was drowned (see p. 57). Like most of the earliest settlers, he has no monument to mark his grave. It appears that he was a man of some note, and much respected in the Colony. Among his descendants may be found many in the various professions, trades, etc. A great proportion, however, have been and are farmers. As will be seen, the descendants are now scattered from Maine to California.

RICHARD[1] MAN and wife Rebecca ———, had the following children, born in Scituate, Mass.:

    i. *NATHANIEL,[2] b. Sept. 23, 1646; d. July 20, 1688. No children.

---

* 1670,
  5 July.   Wheras Nathaniel Man, of Scittuate, formerly sued his father in law, John Cowin, att the Court of the celectmen of Scittuate, for vseing and improveing his house and lands without his order, and that Court tearmed it a vexatious suite, and find not themselves in a capasitie to issue the difference, althoe the said Man sued not vpon title, but for trespass, to the damage of thirty niue shillings, and being noe way releived by the judgement of the above said Court, the said Man was necessitated to appeale from the judgment of that Court to his Maties Court held heer this day. This appeale was not pleaded to. Soe as refered to the jury, but was otherwise determined. See Booke of Orders, July Court, Anno 1670.—(Plymouth Col. Rec., Vol. vii. p. 160.)

In 1680 Nathaniel made over his estate to his brothers, Thomas and Richard; and Thomas signed a bond for his support. This was on account of infirm health.—(Plymouth Prob. Rec.)

DEATH OF NATHANIEL MAN, THE VERDICT.

Scituate, July 21, 1688.
    Doe find that said Nathaniel Man hath formerly been troubled with fitts, his falling sickness, and sometimes hereterfore hath been distracted or out of his witts. And that on the 19th of this instant, July, at evening, at the house of his brother Thomas Man, at Conihassett in Scituate aforesaid, greviously distracted or Lunatized & in a raging manner so continued till towards break of the day & then ran out of the said house & tore off his clothes &. ran away in the said distracted frame, & on the 20th Instant was founed in the scarf of the Sea between high water & low water mark amongst a body of Rocks lying against little Pond and was dead, that he Running amongst the said Rocks they being very slippery, did fall upon some of them & wounded his head whereof he died.—(Plymouth Prob. Rec.)

His estate consisted of about 30 acres of upland and meadow, besides cows, swine, books, etc., to the am't of £13 3s. 0d.

2. ii.   THOMAS,[2] b. Aug. 15, 1650; m. Sarah ———; d. 1732.
3. iii. RICHARD,[2] b. Feb. 5, 1652; m. Elizabeth Sutton.
    iv.   JOSIAH,[2] b. Dec. 10, 1654; probably deceased early, though
          possibly he may have been the Josiah who was in Boston,
          1674-5-6 (See p. 36).

The following receipt appears on the " Court Record ":

" Received this 30th of October" [prob. 1671], " of my father in law Cowin
five pounds for the vse of Josiah Man, which hee was to have by the Court
order, of his father Cowine; wee owne it received by vs, Thomas Man and
Richard Man, as witnes wherof wee have hearvnto sett our hands.

THOMAS MAN.
RICHARD MAN."

(2) THOMAS[2] MAN

(*Richard*[1]) was born in Scituate, Mass., Aug. 15, 1650.   He
married Sarah ———, had
five sons and three daughters,
all of whom (except Ensign,
who is mentioned in the will) are recorded in the town of Scituate
record of births.   His name appears in the Old Colony Records,
deeds, etc., and he was one of a coroner's jury " 26th March, 1677."
In 1680 he was " propounded as a freeman for the next year if approved." He probably came into possession of that portion of his
father's estate whereon the buildings stood, prior to 1679.   From
time to time, he added to his lands and estates.   There appears
more than twenty transfers to and from him, in marsh and uplands,
in the town of Scituate.—(See Plym. Co. Registry.)   In one or two
deeds, he is called a wheelwright. The following receipt may be
found in Old Col. Rec., vol. v. p. 174.

1675 1 June, Winslow Gov[r]	Received this 4th of July, 1671, of my father in law John Cowin, of Scittuate, the sume of five pounds, and is full satisfaction for my portion allowed mee out of my father, Richard Mans estate, by the honored Court of New Plymouth; I say received by mee

(Signed) THOMAS MAN.

Witnessed by James Cudworth.

In 1703, Thomas purchased of his brother Richard, lands situated on south side of "Man Hill," and April 9, 1713, deeded the same to his second son, Thomas Man, Jr. Feb. 24, 1719, Thomas Man, Sen., deeded a considerable lot of land to his sons Joseph and Benjamin Man. Thomas, Sen., March 6, 1722, con. £75, "for the love and affection to my beloved son Ensign Man, housewright," deeded him "one half moiety part" of his estate. And in 1723, sells "one half part" of an estate to son Joseph Man.

Thomas, Sr., died in 1732, leaving a will, the following a copy:

THOMAS MAN, Sen., WILL.

In the name of God Amen. this thirteenth day of February Anno Domini. One thousand seven Hundred & twenty three: I Thomas Man of Scituate in ye County of Plymouth in New England, Husbandman. being aged & Infirm of Body, but of sound mind & memory [Praised be God] do make & ordain this my last Will and Testament in manner & form following viz. Principally and first of all I commend my Soul to God that gave it. and my Body to a decent Burrial at the Discretion of my Executor hereafter named. And touching my Worldly Estate where with God hath blessed me in this life. my just Debts & funeral charges being first paid & Discharged. I give, Devise & Dispose of ye same in manner following. That is to say, I having already Disposed of all my Housing & Lands & Settled them upon my Sons Thomas Man, Joseph Man, Ensign Man & Benjamin Man by Deeds under my hand & seal to each of them respectively made & passed. And having also provided considerably for my Daughters, I Give & Dispose of ye Remainder of my movable Estate as followeth viz: I give to my son Thomas Man, Jr. the sum of five pounds. I give to my son Benjamin Man the sum of five shillings. I give to my son Ensign Man, the sum of five shillings. I give to my Daughter Sarah Gibbs the sum of five shillings. I give to my Daughter Mary Man, the sum of five shillings. all the above Legacies to be paid out of my movable Estate by my Executor within one year after my Decease. Item, I give to my Daughter Elizabeth Man ye Bed where she usnally lyeth With all the Bedding & furniture belonging to it and all ye Rest of my movable Estate of what kind or nature soever & wheresoever lying & being I give ye same to my sd son Joseph Man forever, whom I hereby nominate & appoint to be Sole Executor of this my last Will & Testament. In Witness Whereof I have hereunto Set my hand & Seal ye Day & Year first above Written

Signed sealed Published & Declared by ye sd Thomas Man first mentioned to be his last Will & Testament In the presence of Ebenezer Stetson, Jacob Vinall, Nicholas Vinall.

(Signed)   THOMAS MAN   [SEAL.]

Will approved & allowed ⎫ Administrators Inventory filed July 12, 1732.
by Court July 12, 1732. ⎭   (Signed)   JOSEPH MAN, Executor.

(Plymouth Pro. Rec., vol. vi.)

THOMAS MAN, Sen., by wife Sarah ———, had the following children born in Scituate, Mass. :

      i.   JOSIAH,[3] b. March 11, 1679; d. 1708. Letter of administration granted to his father, Thomas Man. Unmarried.

4. ii. THOMAS,[3] b. April 5, 1681; m. Deborah Joy.

    iii. SARAH,[3] b. Nov. 15, 1684; m. ——— Gibbs.

    iv. MARY,[3] b. March 15, 1688; unm. 1723.

    v. ELIZABETH,[3] b. March 10, 1692; unm. 1723.

5. vi. JOSEPH,[3] b. Dec. 27, 1694; m. Mary ———.

6. vii. BENJAMIN,[3] b. Feb. 19, 1697; m. Martha Curtis.

7. viii. ENSIGN,[3] b. about 1699; m. Widow Tabitha Vinal, 1738.

(3) RICHARD[2] MAN

(*Richard[1]*), born in Scituate, Mass., Feb. 5, 1652; married Elizabeth Sutton, born 1662; eldest daughter of John Sutton, of Scituate, and granddaughter of Elder Nathaniel Tilden.* [The latter a wealthy citizen who emigrated from Tenterden, in Kent, England, before 1628, and settled in Scituate.] Richard was three years old at the time of his father's death, and only four when his mother married John Cowen.† At eleven years of age he was apprenticed‡ to Mr. Thomas Hinckley [Governor of Plymouth Colony from 1681 to 1692], of Barnstable, for the term of ten years. He received a grant of land in Connecticut, for his services in the "Indian War."§

---

* Sarah [dau. of Nath¹ Tilden], b. in England; m. George Sutton, of Scituate, 1641, and had John, b. 1642, who m. Elizabeth, daughter of Samuel House, 1661. John Sutton, by wife Elizabeth, had Elizabeth, b. 1662, who m. Richard Man.

† Received, the seauenth of June, 1673, of my father in law John Cowin, one red horse, and is in full satisfaction for fiue pounds, which the Court ordered him the said Cowin to pay mee as a portion determined by the Court for mee out of my father Richard Man's estate; I say I have receiued the said horse, in full satisfaction for the portion of five pounds. In witnes wherof, I have haerunto sett my hand

                            The marke of R. RICHARD MAN

Witnessed by James Cudworth

                          (Old Col. Rec., vol. v. p. 174.)

‡ For an episode in the history of the boyhood of Richard Man, see Plym. Col. Rec., vol. iv. p. 34.

§ Richard Man deeds to "my well beloved son Nath¹ Man a tract of land granted by yᵉ General Assembly of yᵉ Mass. Bay. I being one of the shoulders (soldiers) in yᵉ former Indian War and especially in yᵉ Narragansette Sortie Fight commonly so called." The foregoing "tract of land" lies in Hebron, Ct., where the deed is recorded. It bears date Nov. 21, 1728.—(Letter of Mrs. C. M. Phelps.)

In 1703 he sold his farm in Scituate, to his brother Thomas, and about the same time calling himself a "planter," deeded six and two thirds acres of "Connihasset lands" to Gershom Ewell. At Plymouth Registry Deeds, vol. v. p. 125-6, is a copy of a deed dated 13th of April, 1703, where John Allyn sells his homestead and other lands in Middleboro', Mass., to Richard Man and Benjamin Booth, of Scituate. These lands, "by estimation," were more than three hundred acres, and described as being "near the Comons as ordered by Gov. Prince to Maj. Church." The author has not observed any subsequent transfer of this estate. Soon after, we find Richard Man* and family, residents at Lebanon, Conn., where he probably ever after lived, and died. The first conveyance of land to him at Lebanon, Conn., was July 6, 1705, by which one hundred acres were purchased for £25.—(Lebanon Rec., vol. i. p. 150.) He conveyed land to his son Nathaniel Man, of Hebron, Conn., Feb. 9, 1725-6, also to his son Richard, Jr., Dec. 7, 1724. Either he or son Richard conveyed a farm (situated at the north-east part of Lebanon) in 1743 to Eldad Kingsley. The place is now owned by John D. Kingsley. "There is upon the old homestead, a building now standing, which tradition says was erected about 1695, for a Quaker meeting-house. The building is two stories, and is now used for a wagon-house and granary."—(Ext. of a letter of W. G. Kingsley, Esq., of Lebanon.)

The following were the children of Richard Man and wife Elizabeth; all except Elisha were born at Scituate, Mass.:

  i. JOHN,[3] b. April 7, 1684. He was in Lebanon, Conn., 1719. (No doubt but that he removed to New Hampshire or Western Massachusetts and had a family.) Nathaniel Man, of Hebron, Conn., March 16, 1719, conveys "to my brother John, of Lebanon."—(Leb. Rec., vol. iii. p. 179.)

 ii. REBECCA,[3] b. March 22, 1686; m. Isaac Tilden (second wife), of Lebanon, June 4, 1716, and had *Rebecca*,[4] b. March 7, 1717; *Jonathan*,[4] April 21, 1719; *Judith*,[4] April 2, 1721; *Martha*,[4] Oct. 12, 1723; *Mercy*,[4] Aug. 15, 1725; *John*,[4] Jan. 28, 1729.—(Mudge Gen.)

---

* Richard Man and Elizabeth his wife, of Lebanon, Conn., Oct. 17, 1715, sold all right, title, interest, claim, and demand, of their interest in a salt marsh in Scituate, Mass., "which was sometime Marsh land of Nathan Sutton, deceased, and now in possession of Abigail Sutton, one s⁴ part being one third part thereon as set off to s⁴ Elizabeth Man, as her part of said portion of Nathan Sutton deceased."—(Plym. Reg. Deeds, vol. xiv. p. 53.) Nathan Sutton was a brother of Elizabeth Man.—Ed.

    iii. HANNAH, b. April 13, 1689.

8.   iv. NATHANIEL, b. Oct. 27, 1693; m. first, Mary Root.

    v. RICHARD, b. March 10, 1694; prob. m. Mary Culver,* July 23, 1719. Settled at Lebanon, Conn., and had *Esther*,[4] b. Dec. 18, 1721. He probably removed to Western Massachusetts or New Hampshire, where he no doubt left descendants.

    vi. ELIZABETH, b. Aug. 27, 1696.

    vii. ABIGAIL, b. Feb. 23, 1698-9; prob. m. (at Lebanon) April 6, 1721, Simon Baxter.

    viii. ELISHA,* b. [not on Scituate record.] He sold property Jan. 22, 1729, to his brother Nathaniel Man, of Hebron.—(Leb. Rec.) [Probably removed.]

(4) THOMAS[3] MAN

(*Thomas,*[2] *Richard*[1]), born in Scituate, Mass., April 5, 1681; m. Deborah Joy, Dec. 8, 1714. He probably resided at "Man Hill"— on the southern slope of the hill. This farm was granted him by his father April 9, 1713, it being the premises formerly owned by his uncle, Richard Man, Jr. In the deeds of record he is called a "cordwainer." His brother, Ensign Man, owned the adjoining farm on the north. The following were his children, all born in Scituate:

9.   i. JOSIAH,[4] b. Dec. 9, 1715; m. Mary Chubbuck.

10.   ii. THOMAS[4] (Capt.), b. Nov. 26, 1717; m. first, Ruth Lamon.

    iii. DAVID,[4] b. Nov. 9, 1719; lived at "Man Hill"; m. Alice Healey, May 31, 1746. "David Man died Oct. 16, 1801, aged 84; a Inhabitant of Scituate."—(Hanover Town Rec.)

    iv. DEBORAH,[4] b. Feb. 20, 1721; m. Abner Curtis, of Hanover, Mass., 1749, and had: *Abner,*[5] *Deborah,*[5] *Seth,*[5] *Huldah,*[5] and *Rebecca.*[5]—(Barry's Hist. of Hanover.)

    v. SARAH,[4] b. Feb. 20, 1721; m. Jesse Curtis, of Hanover, Mass., 1739, and had: *Elijah,*[5] *Abel,*[5] *Jesse,*[5] *Deborah,*[5] *Gershom,*[5] *Sarah,*[5] *Charles,*[5] *Amos,*[5] and *Orpha.*[5] Jesse Curtis, Sen., died in Hanover, 1759, and his widow, Nov. 17, 1802, aged 80.—(Ib.)

11.   vi. EBENEZER,[4] b. Dec. 28, 1725; m. first, Rebecca Magoun.

---

* In August 1725, a party of "Rogerenes" [a religious sect, so-called, and fully described in Mrs. Caulkins's His. of Norwich, Conn., p. 290], consisting of John Rogers, John Bolles, and Joseph Bolles, of New London; John Culver, Andrew Davis, James Smith, John Waterhouse, and Sarah Culver, from Groton, were going to Lebanon at the request of Mary Mann, of that place, "who sent us word," said John Rogers, "that she desired to be baptized by our Society." She was baptized after they arrived in Lebanon, and a few days later they baptized Elisha Mann.—(Caulkins's Lebanon, p. 292.)

9

(5) JOSEPH³ MAN

(*Thomas,² Richard¹*), born at Scituate, Mass., Dec. 27, 1694; m. Mary ———. His father deeded him a portion of his estate on "Man Hill" Feb. 24, 1719. He probably lived there until June 17, 1732, at which time he sold this estate to Jeremiah Pierce, and removed to Boston, Mass. Nov. 15, 1734, con. £300, Joseph Man [of Boston], is deeded by Gideon Thayer, of Braintree, Mass., a farm of "about eighty acres, more or less," situated at the "South Precinct" in Braintree. This part of Braintree was incorporated March 9, 1793, and called Randolph. In 1742, he calling himself of Hanover, Mass., transfers a portion of the above estate to his brother, Benjamin Man, of Hanover. He died in Braintree (now Randolph) about 1747. This farm is still in the family of the sixth and seventh generation from Richard.¹ A very old house is still standing on this estate. It is situated about two miles north of the village of Randolph, Mass. Joseph³ Man was executor of his father's will in 1732. His children were all born in Scituate:

12.   i.   JOSEPH,⁴ b. Oct. 10, 1722; m. Elizabeth Niles.
13.   ii.   SETH⁴ (Lieut.), b. 1724; d. Jan. 28, 1815, aged 91.
14.   iii.   EPHRAIM,⁴ b. 1728; m. Sarah Glover.
     iv.   MARY,⁴ b. 1730; m. Moses Littlefield, Aug. 27, 1751.
     v.   DELIGHT,⁴ b. 1732; m. Ephraim Hunt, Jr., Oct. 11, 1750. They had: Dea. *Elisha,⁵* b. Nov. 30, 1771, of Boston; a carpenter. He d. June 21, 1845. His wife d. 1876.

(6) BENJAMIN³ MAN

(*Thomas,² Richard¹*), born in Scituate, Mass., Feb. 19, 1697; married Martha Curtis (born Feb. 14, 1701), of Scituate, Feb. 4, 1724, who died Jan. 26, 1769, and he March 2, 1770. His father sold him lands on "Man Hill," Scituate, Feb. 24, 1719. He settled in that part of Scituate incorporated and called Hanover, 1727. "He lived, it is said, on Main St., in the ancient mansion now (1853) occupied by Mr. Hanson, not far from the Bap. M. Hs."—(Barry's Hist. of Hanover.) He was selectman in 1745. In his will, which was made Dec. 3, 1762, he mentions all of his children but Sarah. He gave his daughter Mary (who married her cousin, Elijah⁴ Man) her "full portion, £66 13s. 4d." Children, who survived infancy:

i. MARTHA,[4] b. Jan. 6, 1725; m. William Curtis, Nov. 13, 1747, and had: *William*,[5] *Martha*,[5] *Abel*,[5] *Joel*,[5] *Samuel*,[5] and *Margaret*.[5]

15. ii. BENJAMIN,[4] b. Aug. 4, 1727; d. 1816.

iii. REBECCA,[4] b. Aug. 13, 1729; m. Abner Curtis.

iv. SARAH,[4] b. Feb. 8, 1730; m. Robert Gardner, June 5, 1760.

v. RUTH,[4] b. May 12, 1735; d. July 29, 1808; m. Lemuel Curtis, Jan. 16, 1752, who d. Jan. 11, 1807. Mr. Curtis was a man of influence in Hanover. Their children were: *Lemuel*,[5] *Ruth*,[5] *Olive*,[5] *Lillie*,[5] *Reuben*,[5] Esq., *Consider*,[5] *Sarah*,[5] *Lydia*,[5] *Lemuel*,[5] and *Nathaniel*.[5]

vi. MARY,[4] b. Aug. 13, 1737; m. Elijah[4] Man (cousin), born at Scituate, Sept. 2, 1742. They had one son, *Joseph*,[5] who died (unmarried) in Hanover, June 26, 1851, aged 80. Elijah[4] Man died at Petersham, Mass., April 27, 1823, and his widow died at same town, April 7, 1825. He was a great reader, but became nearly blind before he died. She was a kind hearted woman. They lie buried in the small burying lot at the north part of Petersham (see p. 68).

(7) ENSIGN[2] MAN

(*Thomas*,[2] *Richard*[1]) was born in Scituate, Mass., about the year 1699. He seems to have been the youngest of the family. This christian name (Ensign) now singularly appears for the first time in any branch bearing the name. [Was his mother of the Scituate Ensign family?] His birth is not on the Scituate town records with the other children; but he is mentioned in his father's will (see p. 62). His name appears in real estate transfers in Scituate, from 1722 to 1759, and he is called "housewright" in the deeds. "6th of March, 1722," his father (Thomas Man) deeded him "one half moiety part" of his farm on "Man Hill"; and on the 29th of March, 1750, he sold this farm and a salt marsh for £1350, in "Bills of creddit of the province of the old Tennor" to Benjamin House. Soon after he removed to Boston, and owned a house near the corner of Cambridge and Chambers Streets. He was married by Rev. Nathaniel Eells, of Scituate, July 19, 1738, to "widow Tabitha Vinal, late of Scituate." He and his wife died within seven weeks of each other, with fever, about 1762. They had the following children, born, probably, on "Man Hill," in Scituate:

16. i. ENSIGN,[4] b. July 15, 1740; Harvard Coll. 1764.

ii. ELIJAH,[4] b. Sept. 2, 1742; m. Mary[4] Man (his cousin), of Hanover, Mass.; she was the daughter of Benjamin[3] Man,

and was born Aug. 13, 1737. His brother, Ensign, deeded
him about sixty-eight acres of land with buildings, at north
part of Petersham, Mass., March 2, 1771, bounded by estates of Elisha Ward, Daniel Duncan, John and James Stock-
well. The father of the author remembers both him and his
wife. He was a great reader, and became nearly blind and
dependent before his decease, which occurred April 27, 1823.
His widow died April 7, 1825, being very aged. They were
buried at Petersham, in the "North Burial Ground." She
was a kind hearted woman. They had one son only, viz.:
Joseph,[5] who, at one time, owned a small farm in the town of
Hanover. He was unmarried, and died there June 26, 1851,
aged 80 (see page 67).

iii.   PRISCILLA,[4] b. Dec. 9, 1746; died (unmarried) in Scituate,
July 29, 1831, aged 84.

Priscilla Mann* was one of the most strongly marked characters of the
vicinity in which she lived. For strength of mind, moral worth and intellectual ability, probably she was not surpassed by any of her sex bearing
the family name; indeed, as much could be said of her brother Ensign, whom
she revered and loved. Whether these mental traits were inherited from
the father or mother, or from both, is hard to determine. From all accounts
at hand, we judge their parents were of quiet mien, intelligent and of high
moral character. Priscilla was a paragon of excellence in her penmanship;
some of her letters now in existence abound with good advice to those she
addressed. In a letter to her niece bearing her name, dated at Hanover,
Mass., Nov. 26, 1813, she thus briefly gives a little sketch of herself:
"Tenderly watched under the eye of a kind mother for sixteen years, I was
in seven weeks & one day bereft of both my parents, & ushered into the
world a perfect stranger to every thing but what I had gain'd from books,
for I was always at home; having no sister I had but little inclination to
roam abroad, and being in town" (probably Boston) "my acquaintance
was small. When I came into the country I had everything to learn & no
instructor, but Nature, theory, & your father" (Ensign Man). "A constant
correspondence with him was of use to me. He was my monitor. He bid me
beware of the intrigues of the world, and cautiously to retain my own
secrets, which I found of infinite use to me, being well assured, from what
I have since seen, that by communication we put wings to our words which
we can never recall." On the subject of matrimony in the same letter, she
adds: "It is cruel to damp the ardour of youth; I have been young & hope
I am not so very an old maid, as to think a girl of twenty three can be in-
fluenced by the same feelings of a woman almost seventy. I ever had a
niceness in my choice, and could as soon have ceased to live, as to have
married a man in whose character or conduct I discovered material defects.
I early resolved upon a single life. My occupation gave me an unwish'd
for fore-knowledge of the married world. But I love married folks as well

---

* Priscilla Mann wrote her name with a double "n." Her brother, Ensign, with
a single "n" up to 1795; after that with a double "n."—ED.

as single ones, and I never had any reason to think they shun'd my company. Thus much for my own excuse for being single. But I recommend it to no one further than their own choice. But I would advise all girls who marry, to look for partners of steady habits, good tempers, prudence, & a sense of the moral obligations of religion."

In a letter to her brother, Ensign Mann, of Petersham, dated June 25, 1814, is extracted the following:

" Your British friends have landed at Scituate Harbour, burnt & carried off the Vessels. We have frequent alarm. But your Good Governor * can't spare any Cannon for fortifying, so the artillery & soldiery turn out when call'd for. If the Pious old gentleman dont act a little more like a man his Tory friends will get mad at him. One of the red hot Tories at the Harbour was the greatest sufferer. His loss was estimated at 5000 Dollars, & we find they flinch when property is touched just like other folks. We are in a queer state enough, a Generalissimo at Northampton: so good, so wise & so prudent, so *Merciful*. What a happy People, to be so blest with such a Head! I have seen America in one war when Our Laws were abolish'd by British tyranny. But we had men who knew how to govern themselves; and then indignantly look'd down on the obsequious addresser of Britons Governor Gage!" etc. " I know how little you will relish this letter. But in brotherly kindness you will pass it over since my scolding will do neither good nor hurt to your favourites," etc.

And in another letter to her brother Ensign, dated Feb. 25, 1820, after commenting upon the imaginary ill conduct of his long lost son William, she closes the letter as follows:

" Necessity only will keep a vicious man from pursuing forbidden paths, until he is convinced that sin is misery, and virtue alone makes happiness. All rational, innocent indulgences are allowed us by the Author of our being, nothing forbidden but what is hurtful in the moral world. How strange that our reason is so obscured by our passions! that experience can't convince us before we have run into irretrievable ruin. Sin, ten thousand times repeated, leaves its sting behind, when virtue always affords peace and pleasure, such as no misfortune can rob us of. I am fully convinced for myself that nothing can produce a sincere change in us but Supreme Love to God, viewing Him according to our highest conception of perfection as our father and friend, and the bestower of every blessing which our natures require; And that all sin is opposite to His character and nature, and the source of all temporal inquietude and misery, while we travel the journey of life. Thus convinced we shall hate vice for its deformity, and opposition to the Divine Character, and from love to Him shun and abhor it, which in my mind is the only true repentance. Not merely fearing to sin because we think we shall be personally punished for our misdeeds and would gladly sin if we were sure we could escape punish-

---

* Caleb Strong, LL.D., Governor of Massachusetts, from 1800 to 1801, and from 1812 to 1816. He and Ensign Man were classmates at Harvard University, 1760-4.

ment.   Such goodness to me, wont afford lasting peace of mind, or lay any
foundation to build it upon; but keeps the poor marr'd vessel all its lifetime subject to bondage through fear of Death.   *   *   *   *   I board at
Peres Jacobs, son of David Jacobs, whom you once knew, and have made
it my residence for three years past in the Old mansion house that used to
be a tavern.   I am handy to the meeting which I chuse to attend.   I have
heretofore mentioned when absent from here, of being with a child of this
family who was taken sick at her sisters on Cushing's neck, and been confined there for more than two years, was living a few days since, but not
expected to recover.   A woman of superior understanding, and very dear
to me, her mind unreproachable, and stored with useful knowledge, an
ornament to her sex, and a blessing while in the world.   Willing to cease
from suffering, but patiently waiting her Creator's time.   That such may
be our happy frame at the approach of death, is the constant prayer of
                Your affectionate sister,

Priscilla Mann

The late president of Brown University, Alexis Caswell, D.D., in
his memorial address on the life of Hon. John Barstow, in 1864,
thus refers to his old school teacher at Hanover:

"His first preceptress was Miss Priscilla Mann, who taught the town
school at 'Broad Oak,' and who, as another pupil of hers remarks, 'for
more than half a century had been distinguished in that capacity.'   He had
been heard to refer to her with great respect, except that she once punished
him without just cause."

A correspondent writes: "I have often heard my dear mother speak of
Aunt Priscilla Mann.   She commenced teaching at sixteen, and continued
fifty years in Boston, Scituate, Hanover, and vicinity.   She used sportively
to remark, that 'all she knew about cooking was to spread her own bread
and butter.'   I once possessed an original poem on 'Suicide,' from her
able pen, but unfortunately lost it."

From a daughter of Peres Jacobs, born 1798: "She, Miss Mann,
boarded in my father's family when I was married, sixty-two years ago.
She was a very fine writer, was capable of writing deeds and all kinds of
contracts and conveyances, a woman beloved and respected by all.   She
was rather tall, very fleshy, well-proportioned and good looking; could con-
verse on any subject, religious, political, or the topics of the day.   She was
a remarkable woman of her time, likewise she was a moderate snuff-taker."
—(Ext. letter of Mrs. D. R. Wade.)

The following extract of a letter, is from a daughter of the late
able divine, Father Hosea Ballou, and dated Norwich, Conn., April
17, 1881:

"It is a pleasure for me to speak of the life of the distinguished individual who was the subject of your inquiry, my beloved and honored friend,

Ma'am Mann. Her personal appearance was unusually attractive; she was tall and proportionally large, dignified in her demeanor, and moderate in all her movements; her speech was slow, her enunciation perfect. She commanding great attention, no one would think of interrupting her while she was speaking. She was doubtless a great reader, but too courteous to confine herself to books during the few hours that we enjoyed her society in the family circle; at such times she was knitting continually, in which employment she took great satisfaction. It seems very singular that you should have been informed that Miss Priscilla Mann ever wrote a poem. It may be possible, but I distinctly recollect hearing her make a remark like this, ' I never possessed a talent for rhyming, but one day being with a friend with whom I was familiar, I enquired:

> If you and I should chance to die
> Would any mortals think to cry?

My friend immediately replied

> I do suppose for the sake of our clothes
> They would cry enough to wet their nose.

There was so much more wit in my friend's impromptu expression than in my question, that I never made another attempt of the kind.'

Ma'am Mann possessed a spirit of remarkable serenity, her smile was rich and rare. I never knew her to descend into a broad laugh, although in everything that was comical she saw the point at once. She said in my presence that she taught forty-nine years, seven months, and three days. Being fond of argument could carry her part well in a controversy and yield with grace when her opponent got the better of her. I never doubted her being a thorough Universalist; she attended the church of that denomination regularly in Scituate, where Dr. Benjamin Whittemore was pastor. I was a mere child when I left Boston and went to board in the family of Ichabod R. Jacobs. I well remember what I thought of the old lady boarder, how noble, how stately she appeared; her black eyes were so penetrating I almost feared to encounter them; when she addressed me I felt sure of making a silly answer, I was under so much restraint; she seemed so wise and so far beyond my reach. After the lapse of more than half a century, I still consider Miss Priscilla Mann one of the noblest women I ever met. She had few equals, no superiors."—(Mrs.) M. B. Whittemore.

The last few years of her life, she boarded in the family of Ichabod R. Jacobs, in Scituate (now South Scituate), the old family mansion being only a few rods east of the town of Hanover line, and near the Universalist church, in the little village of Assinippi, called "Snappet for fun" in one of Miss Mann's letters. She died there July 29, 1831, and was buried in the Jacobs burial ground in that village. The elderly persons in that vicinity remembering their old school teacher, speak highly of her many virtues and strength of character. No doubt her goodly influence still prevails in that community. She left a will written by herself, which bears date, December 26, 1820.

The author accidentally found the following lines written by Priscilla Mann, at the age of twenty-two. They are not inserted for their elegance or correctness of versification, but to show the general thought and manner of moralizing in verse at that time.

"*Compos'd to the Memory of Mr. JOHN STOCKBRIDGE, unhappily Slain by Falling a Tree, Feb'y the 10th, 1768. Communicated to his only Sister for private use: By a Female Friend.*

Assist Melpomone* my feeble verse
While I a Sad and Tragick Scene reherse
A Hopefull Youth cut down in Natures Bloom
In Height of Action hastening to the Tomb
Whose Rising Sun so flattering clear & Bright
Sits in a Cloud ere the return of Night

With cheerfull Mirth to Labour does repair
Not thinking Death in Ambush waited there
His Nerves with Youth and Vigour Strung does ply
The Cedar Tall by which he is to Die
When Lo the dread Commission Issues forth
Like Trembling Thunders from the distant North
Levels his —— shafts on his defenceless Head
When Instantly he's numbered with the dead
In Natures Boasted pride of airy Forms
He yields to death and mingles with the Worms

Ye Friends to Virtue Touch'd with Grief draw near
Over this Urn let fall a Mournful Tear
With me Lament—Read thus the Dismal page
A Bright Example Left the future Age
Whose Character unstain'd by Envy's Breath
Beloved in Life Lamented much in Death
Draw near Incautious Youth & tell me why
You dare to Live when unprepared to Die
Behold this Scene, nor dont delude your Sence
Youth Strength or Fortune can be no defence
O Youth so fond of Life and Airy prime

Take heed and well improve uncertain Time
Your Boasted Titles cant Secure a Day
When Death shall Summon you must haste away
Fit or unfit to Shades You must repair
Nor no devise or knowledge purchase There
To God your Maker pay your first regard
In Youth and Health Secure the great reward

And now to the bereaved Sister dear
What hardened Heart can blame the Silent Tear
Who Trembling Saw the stately fabrick fall
And stood so nigh it crush'd her down withall
Still may your Griefs with Moderation rise
That ought of Mercy you may not despise
Review your Hope with care & awe profound
And see what Consolation may be found

Train'd up in virtues School his steady mind
To Carnal vain delights was ne'er Inclind
The Graces Early did his Soul adorn
Shone in his Life and Beautified his Form
His Tongue from Oaths or vain expressions clear
Such as in Youths we but too often hear
His Heaven born Soul from vicious passions free
Nor yet unthoughtfull of Mortality

Ye weeping Friends abate your Mournful Strain
Behold him walking on the Ethereal Plains
In Robes of Glory perfect Pleasures where
No change or Sorrow ever enters There

---

* Melpomone: the Muse of Melancholy.

Heaven saw him Meet for more exalted Bliss
In worlds above than could be found in this
Cease your complaints and blame your erring Sight
Shall not the Judge of all the Earth do Right
What though he's pleased to blast our fondest hope
Shall not his Promis bair our Spirits up
Himself still Lives & always is the Same
He gives and takes and Blessed be his Name

With confidence we'll to his Altar go
And Still adore the hand that gave the blow
We'll dying Live to Live when ere we die
To Join in praise to all Eternity.

*   *   *   *   *   *   *

Unstrung my Nerves my Heart does ake
That such a plant must fall
While Hundreds in the Vineyard Stands
Of no account at all

For Miss HANNAH COPLAND of Scituate 1768"

(8) NATHANIEL³ MAN

(*Richard,*² *Richard*¹), born in Scituate, Mass., Oct. 27, 1693. His father, Richard Man, Jr., sold his farm on "Man Hill" in Scituate, in 1703, to his brother Thomas, and about 1704 he removed with his family to Lebanon, Conn., where he purchased a farm of one hundred acres July 6, 1705. A considerable lot of land was deeded to Nathaniel Man, of Lebanon, "4 10 acre lots on Ten Mile River called plow plain fields." Date of this deed was May 29, 1713.— (Lebanon Rec., Vol. ii. p. 387.) A deed dated March 16, 1719, from Nathaniel Man, of Hebron, Conn., to "my brother John, of Lebanon." —(Ib., Vol. iii. p. 179.) Richard Man conveyed to his son, Nathaniel Man, of Hebron, a tract of land; deed dated Feb. 9, 1725-6. Jan. 22, 1729, Elisha Man sold property to his brother, Nathaniel Man, of Hebron (Town clerk of Lebanon). In 1723 Nathaniel Man purchased nine acres of Obadiah Hosford, and seven and a half acres of it given to the town of Hebron for a burial ground. He (Nathaniel) married first, Mary Root,* of Hebron, Feb. 1, 1713; she died May 19, 1728. He married second, Mary Sprague, March 4, 1729, who died Oct. 15, 1735. He married third, Patience Role, Sept. 5, 1736. He had six children by first wife, and two by second, according to Hebron Records. The following were the names of the children,

---

* Mary Root was daughter of Jacob² Roote (the latter was son of John¹ Roote, one of the first settlers of Hartford, Ct.), one of the early settlers of Northampton, Mass. Jacob Roote removed to Hebron, Ct., 1705, and was one of those chosen to run the bounds between Colchester and Hebron in 1710. He died Aug. 9, 1731, aged about seventy. Mary, who married Nathaniel Man, was born at Northampton, Mass., Nov. 24, 1689.—(See Root Gen.)

born in the towns of Lebanon and Hebron, Conn., as furnished the author by the town clerk, and one of his descendants:

17. i. Joseph,[4] b. April 5, 1713 (probably 1714.—Ed.).
     ii. Nathaniel,[4] b. June 16, 1715-16; baptized at Lebanon, Sept. 30, 1716; m. Deborah Tillotson, June 5, 1739. He probably died at Bolton, Conn., leaving no children.
     iii. Benjamin,[4] b. March 3, 1717 (died or removed).
18. iv. John,[4] b. Nov. 20, 1720; married first, Margaret Peters.
     v. Mary,[4] b. June 5, 1723.
     vi. Nathan,[4] b. June 20, 1727; m. Elizabeth Skinner, Feb. 12, 1752, and had: *Elizabeth*,[5] b. May 20, 1753; *Lydia*,[5] Dec. 16, 1760; *David*,[5] April 27, 1762; *Zadock*,[5] Feb. 9, 1764; *Jerusha*,[5] June 20, 1766.
     vii. Abigail,[4] b. Feb. 14, 1730-31.
19. viii. Abijah,[4] b. Aug. 7, 1734; m. Sarah Porter.

(9) JOSIAH[4] MAN

(*Thomas*,[3] *Thomas*,[2] *Richard*[1]) was born in Scituate, Mass., Dec. 9, 1715. He was a resident of that town, and died there in August, 1802. He married Mary Chubbuck, of Wareham, Mass., Jan. 2, 1741; she died in 1800. Children and grandchildren, born at Scituate:

     i. Jonathan,[5] b. March 28, 1745; died at Scituate, Dec. 22, 1822. He married Mary Gilbert, of Hingham, Mass. Children: (1) *George*,[6] b. Dec. 23, 1766, who probably married Mary ———, and had *Sophronia*,[7] ———; residence, Cohasset. (2) *Polly*,[6] b. Dec. 30, 1775. (3) *Betsey*,[6] b. Nov. 25, 1777, who married Gideon Young, 1795. (4) *Leah*,[6] b. June 15, 1779. (5) *Desire*,[6] b. July 18, 1781, who married Jeremiah Grant, of Freeport, 1805. (6) *Jonathan*,[6] b. April 15, 1783. (7) *Noah*,[6] b. Feb. 22, 1787.
     ii. Josiah,[5] b. May 12, 1746; died at " Man Hill," Scituate, Oct. 25, 1820. He married Sage Clark, of Hanover, Mass., 1769; she died 1802. Children, born in Scituate: (1) *Margaret*,[6] b. June 19, 1771. (2) *Sarah*,[6] b. Sept. 5, 1776; m. Jonathan Brown, 1797. (3) *Charlotte*,[6] b. Jan. 12, 1779; m. Asa Cushing Tower, of Cohasset, 1806. (4) *Josiah*,[6] b. June 19, 1783; m. Zilpha Stetson. (The latter had children born in Scituate: *Moses W.*,[7] b. Feb. 19, 1820; *Lucy*,[7] July 16, 1821; *Rebecca H.*,[7] 1822, d. 1823; *Edmund Cooper*,[7] July 13, 1828; *Josiah*,[7] Feb. 11, 1831; *Charles*,[7] July 14, 1833; *Benjamin*,[7] May 17, 1836; Infant, d. Oct. 7, 1840.)
     iii. Deborah,[5] baptized May 13, 1748; died.
     iv. Mary,[5] b. Dec. 28, 1748.

v. Susanna,[5] b. Dec. 16, 1752.
vi. Deborah,[5] b. Oct. 2, 1754; probably never married; d. Sept. 4, 1838. She boarded her brother Josiah on "Man Hill" 1820, and previous.
20. vii. Nathaniel,[5] b. Oct. 9, 1759; m. Abigail Billings.

(10) THOMAS[4] MAN

(*Thomas,*[3] *Thomas,*[2] *Richard*[1]), born at "Man Hill," Scituate, Nov. 26, 1717. He was a man of influence in the town, was called "Captain," and was one of the "Committee of Inspection" of Scituate in 1774. He probably married first, Ruth Damon, Dec. 30, 1742, and by her had no children. He married second, Deborah Briggs, Jan. 10, 1746, who died Feb. 16, 1817, aged 92. He died in Scituate, June 29, 1795, leaving a will (on record) which was made Nov. 26, 1794. Children, by wife Deborah, born ... :

i. Deborah,[5] b. Oct. 6, 1749; pr...
ii. Lucy,[5] b. Dec. 23, 1752; m. W... less." ...Aug. 10, 1...
    and had: *Charles,*[6] *Abel,*[6] G...rch 9, 1793. Lucy. Seth
    Mary[6]; residence, Scituate.   extensive land proprietor,
21. iii. Isaiah[5] (Rev.), b. Feb. 7, 1756 (...onged to his father, situ-
iv. Sarah,[5] b. May 14, 1758.   inhabitants of the town,
22. v. John,[5] b. May 10, 1761; d. 1841.
vi. Deborah,[5] b. June 29, 1766; she di...dwelling-house is still
    Dec. 23, 1846, leaving a will execut...
    gave her niece, Polly Mann, "the u...west suc-
    and use in kitchen to wash and bake." n; two... first,

(11) EBENEZER[4] MAN

(*Thomas,*[3] *Thomas,*[2] *Richard*[1]) was born at "Man Hill," in Scituate, Mass., Dec. 28, 1725. He settled at Pembroke, Mass., and was a shipwright. He early purchased land at the "Brick Kilns," a noted shipbuilding stand in the early history of the town. He also bought lands near North River Bridge, and, later, purchased an estate where Thomas[6] Mann resided in 1881. His first residence was probably at North Pembroke. He and wife Rebecca, of Pembroke, deeded lands to Thomas Man in Scituate, 1763. He married first, Rebecca Magoun, of Pembroke, Aug. 22, 1751, by whom all of his children were born. He married second, Ursula Randall, Oct. 1, 1772. He died in Pembroke about 1805, leaving a will. Children, born in Pembroke:

23.　i.　DAVID,[5] b. Oct. 19, 1752 (O. S.); d. Nov. 22, 1838.
　　ii.　REBECCA,[5] b. Jan. 12, 1755 (N. S.); m. Joshua Turner, June 19, 1783, who was born and resided at North Pembroke.
24.　iii.　EBENEZER,[5] b. Aug. 6, 1757; d. 1836, at Salem, Mass.
　　iv.　BETSEY,[5] b. Oct. 14, 1759; d. Aug. 27, 1851; m. Thomas Nash, Dec. 7, 1780. They had: *Thomas*,[6] *Ebenezer*,[6] *Zebulon*,[6] *Betsey*,[6] and *Charlotte*.[6] The widow resided with her son Zebulon[6] some time.

(12)　JOSEPH[4] MAN

(*Joseph*,[3] *Thomas*,[2] *Richard*[1]), born in Scituate, Mass., Oct. 10, 1722; removed with his parents to "South Precinct" in Braintree, Mass., about 1734, where his father (Joseph, of Boston) bought a farm of Gideon Thayer. This "Precinct" in 1793 was incorporated and called Randolph. He was a taxpayer here in 1780 and 1793; but early deeded all interest in the above estate to his brothers Seth and ... He "was a lame man," yet served for ... in ... war. There is a tradition that when a ... to him that he was guilty of great indis... soldier, as he would be unable to save him... he answered: "I enlisted to fight and not ... account, Randolph Transcript, 1858.) He ... orn in Woburn, Mass., Dec. 8, 1723), daughter ... anton, whose first husband was Peter Niles. He ... s deceased in 1804, and the widow living.* Children:

　i.　RUTH,[5] b. March 9, 1756; d. Dec. 29, 1837; m. about 1779, Nathaniel Holbrook[6] (*Ichabod*,[5] *David*,[4] *Ichabod*,[3] *John*,[2] *Thomas*[1]), b. Oct. 7, 1758; d. July 6, 1845. Children: (1) *Nathaniel*,[7] b. July 8, 1780; d. July 23, 1865; m. Hannah Stetson. (2) *Benjamin*,[7] Oct. 19, 1781; d. May 28, 1842; m. Esther Thayer. (3) *Ruth*,[7] April 20, 1783; m. Ebenezer Hollis. (4) *Mary*,[7] Dec. 30, 1784; d. Nov. 29, 1862; m. James Stetson. (5) *Esther*,[7] Sept. 4, 1786; m. Zenia Thayer. (6) *Abel*,[7] April 5, 1788; d. May 30, 1819; m. Sarah Smith Hopkins, and had: *Albert*,[8] Esq., of Providence, R. I., author of the "Hopkins Family." (7) *Elizabeth*,[7] July 7, 1790; d. ———. (8) *Lydia*,[7] April 5, 1792; d. July 19, 1820; m. Royal Stetson. (9) *Joel*,[7] Nov. 14, 1793; d.

---

* Joseph Man, of Randolph, Mass., petitioned the Probate Court in 1804, for guardianship for his mother, Elizabeth Man, who was deaf. He says: "I desire that the sharpers may not Deprive her of her Interest and living."—(Prob. Rec. at Dedham.)

unmarried, Oct. 14, 1825. Of the above, three married cousins.—(Letter of Albert Holbrook, Esq., of Providence, R. I.)

25. ii. JOSEPH,[5] b. 1760; married first, Mary Dyer.
iii. HANNAH,[5] m. Moses Littlefield, Jr.
iv. PHEBE,[5] m. Noah Whitcomb.

(13) SETH[4] MAN

(*Joseph,[3] Thomas,[2] Richard[1]*) was born in Scituate, Mass., in 1724. He, with his parents, removed to "South Precinct," in Braintree, Mass., about 1734, where his father,  Joseph (called of Boston) purchased a farm of Gideon Thayer, consisting of "about Eighty acres more or less." This "Precinct" was incorporated and named Randolph, March 9, 1793. Lieut. Seth Man (as he was called), was a farmer and extensive land proprietor, and resided on the farm that formerly belonged to his father, situated at the "West Corner," so called by the inhabitants of the town, where his descendants still live. The ancient dwelling-house is still standing on the place, and is in very good repair. He had in succession three wives, who bore him eighteen children; two by the first, ten by the second, and six by the third. He married first, Rachel Spear, Oct. 14, 1745; second, Elizabeth Dyer, Oct. 18, 1750; and his third wife was widow Deborah Dyer, daughter of Nathaniel Littlefield. He died Jan. 28, 1815, leaving a will executed in 1806, in which he gave $333.33 to each of his children, except Elisha and John who had the home farm. His grandson Alvan Mann, who lives on the original farm, remembers him. He had, by his three wives, the following children:

i. DEBORAH,[5] b. April 1, 1746; d. Oct. 4, 1822; m. ab. 1770 Zacheus Thayer, and had four daughters.
26. ii. SETH,[5] b. Dec. 3, 1747; m. Mary Hayward.
27. iii. BENJAMIN,[5] b. ———, 1751; m. Hannah Hayward.
28. iv. EPHRAIM,[5] b. April 3, 1752; m. Comfort Jewett.
v. BETSEY,[5] b. Oct. 20, 1753; d. June 3, 1833; m. ab. 1782 William Blanchard, of E. Stoughton, Mass., who died Jan. 21, 1814, æt. 66. His second wife's children: Samuel, Betsey, Seth, Elisha, and Lemuel.
vi. ENOS,[5] b. March 20, 1755 (deranged); d. æt. 30.
vii. RACHEL,[5] b. Feb. 11, 1757; d. Dec. 29, 1833; m. Joseph Riford, b. June 6, 1758; residence, Braintree, Vt., and had

Joseph,⁶ Samuel,⁶ Rachel,⁶ Polly,⁶ Asa,⁶ Lazarus,⁶ Seth,⁶ Betsey,⁶ Stephen,⁶ and *Ephraim⁶*; all dead except Stephen, who resides at Randolph, Vt.; was hale and hearty (1882), æt. 84.

     viii.   MARY,⁵ b. Dec. 19, 1758; m. Adam Howard, Pomfret, Conn.

29.   ix.   SAMUEL,⁵ b. Sept. 13, 1760; m. first, Nancy Pettee.

     x.   SARAH,⁵ b. July 11, 1762; d. June 2, 1852; m. Micah White, Esq., Dec. 15, 1783, who was b. March 10, 1744; d. Nov. 14, 1841. He was in business at one time at Claremont, N. H. Had nine children.

     xi.   ANNA,⁵ b. May 18, 1764; m. Deacon Eames, went to Maine.

30.   xii.   STEPHEN,⁵ b. March 11, 1766; m. Lucy Pettee.

31.   xiii.   JOB,⁵ b. March 26, 1769; m. Matilda Fuller.

32.   xiv.   ELISHA,⁵ b. Feb. 4, 1771; m. Abigail Whitcomb.

     xv.   PHEBE,⁵ b. Sept. 19, 1772; d. Dec. 20, 1849; m. Samuel Temple, who d. Sept. 19, 1816, æt. 46. They had six children.

     xvi.   OLIVE,⁵ b. Aug. 4, 1774; d. April 9, 1855; m. Deacon Asa Thayer, May 27, 1798, who d. June 13, 1852. They had three children.

     xvii.   ESTHER,⁵ b. Feb. 9, 1776; d. April 19, 1847; m. Rufus Thayer, June 7, 1807. He d. April 23, 1833, æt. 77 years, 4 months, 21 days. They had *Rufus,⁶* and a daughter.

33.   xviii.   JOHN,⁵ b. Nov. 18, 1777; m. Jane Tucker.

(14) EPHRAIM⁴ MAN

(*Joseph,³ Thomas,² Richard¹*) was born in Scituate, Mass., 1728. He probably resided with his parents at "South Precinct," in Braintree, Mass., until he became of age. He early sold his interest in the homestead, to his brother Seth Man, and lived for a time at Castle Island, in Boston harbor. He served in the French and Indian war. His name appears on a list dated May 20, 1756, Capt. Edward Blake. He had considerable real estate, and was a resident in that part of Dorchester now called South Boston; died at "Dorchester Neck," Sept. 23, 1803. He married in 1760, Sarah, born March 4, 1737, daughter of Alexander and Sarah (White) Glover, of Dorchester; she died Oct. 16, 1796. Children:

     i.   SARAH,⁵ b. June 4, 1761; m. Aaron Spear; d. before 1831.

     ii.   MARY,⁵ b. Jan. 6, 1763; m. Moses Marshall, Feb. 3, 1791; res. Dorchester. She was living a widow in Boston in 1835.

34.   iii.   EPHRAIM,⁵ b. Dec. —, 1764; m. Rebecca Lindsey.

     iv.   WILLIAM,⁵ b. Jan. 11, 1766; m. Sarah Foster, Nov. 13, 1794. He with his wife of Milton, Mass., April 15, 1801, for the consideration of $3,793.93 sold eleven acres of land in Boston, to William Tudor, Jr., and Frederic Tudor, "being a moiety of the parcel set off" to said William Mann and his sister Mary Marshall, etc., by their father Ephraim Man.— (Suffolk Reg. Deeds, vol. ccviii. p. 225.)

(15) BENJAMIN⁴ MAN

(*Benjamin,³ Thomas,² Richard¹*), an only surviving son, was born in Hanover, Mass., Aug. 4, 1727. Barry, in his History of Hanover, says of him: "He was selectman in 1763 and '64, and erected the old grist-mill which formerly stood near the bridge, on North street. Married first, Abigail Gill, Nov. 23, 1749; second, the widow of Charles Bailey, who died in 1800; and third, the widow of Abner Curtis, and died Jan. 27, 1816, aged 89." He resided at the north part of the town, on Curtis street, where now (1883) Mr. David Mann lives. His widow died 1820. He had fourteen children, born at Hanover, viz. :

	i.	ABIGAIL,⁵ b. Sept. 9, 1751; m. Asa Turner, June 30, 1771, and moved to Maine, where he d. Aug. 25, 1821, æt. 78, and his widow, April 16, 1853, æt. 72 (prob. second wife); many descendants in and about Orland, and Norridgewock, Me.
35.	ii.	BENJAMIN,⁵ b. March 3, 1753; m. Hannah Sears.
	iii.	OLIVE,⁵ b. April 18, 1754; d. July 20, 1819; m. Thomas Stetson, June 18, 1772, who d. Dec. 24, 1821. They had: (1) *Thomas,⁶* b. 1773, lived in Hanover. (2) *Olive,⁶* b. 1775; m. Samuel Beals, 1796, and moved to Me. (3) *Ruth,⁶* b. 1777; m. David S. Whitman, Bridgewater, 1798. (4) *Elizabeth,⁶* b. 1780; m. Calvin Bates, 1801. (5) *Lucinda,⁶* b. 1783; m. Noah Mason, Ill. (6) *Benjamin,⁶* b. 1786; d. young. (7) *Benjamin,⁶* b. 1790. (8) *Eli,⁶* b. 1794, a millwright, res. Hanover.
	iv.	EZRA,⁵ b. Dec. 11, 1755; was in the Revolution; d. Nov. 26, 1775, at Weymouth, on his way home.
36.	v.	LEVI,⁵ b. Sept. 9, 1757; m. first, widow Anne Cooley.
37.	vi.	JOSHUA⁵ (Capt.), b. July 14, 1759; m. Mary Cushing.
	vii.	BELA,⁵ b. July 18, 1761; m. Ann Bryant, of Scituate, and removed to Lunenburg, Mass., about 1795. He owned real estate at Ashburnham, Mass., 1806, and may have resided there a few years. He was by trade a blacksmith. He d. at Lunenburg, July 29, 1826, and his wife Aug. 3, 1813. In the inventory of his estate at Worcester, filed Sept. 2, 1826, he had "11 acres of land with buildings," at L. Children, prob. b. at Lunenburg: (1) *Anna,⁶* who was living in Boston April 10, 1824, as her father deeded her a "pasture" in L. at that date; *Lydia,⁶ Clarissa,⁶ Emma,⁶ Albert,⁶ Bela,⁶* Jr., *Abigail.⁶* The family left Lunenburg many years ago.
	viii.	SARAH,⁵ b. Jan. 17, 1763; m. Jos. Neal, of Cohasset, Mass., Dec. 6, 1791.

ix. SUSA GILL,[5] b. Oct. 24, 1764; d. Nov. 25, 1842; m. Caleb Whit-
     ing, April 23, 1785, who d. May 20, 1848, æt. 87. He lived
     on Whiting st., Hanover, and had the following children:
     (1) *Caleb,*[6] b. 1788; d. 1792. (2) *Lucy,*[6] b. 1791; d. 1840.
     (3) *Susa G.,*[6] b. 1793; d. 1794. (4) *Caleb,*[6] b. 1795; res.
     Whiting st. (5) *Sage,*[6] b. 1797; m. David Nichols, of Co-
     hasset. (6) *Ezra,*[6] b. 1800; m. Sally Curtis, and lived on
     Main st., H. (7) *Jared,*[6] b. 1804; m. Desire Loring, and
     lived on Whiting st., H. (8) *Lydia P.,*[6] b. 1806; m. Briggs
     Freeman, Ab'n.

x.   CHARLES,[5] b. Nov. 27, 1766; d. 1825; m. Abigail Gill, who d.
     April, 1845, æt. 74. They had children: (1) *Abigail,*[6] who
     m. first, Ithamer Whiting, of Abington; he d. July 31, 1820,
     æt. 34. m. second, Harry Burrill, of Rockland, children:
     Lydia,[7] m. Gideon B. Phillips, of Rockland; *Abigail,*[7] m.
     John H. Marsh, of Worcester; *Stephen*[7] *Whiting,* of Rock-
     land. (2) *Merrill,*[6] who m. Loring Curtis, of Hanover, June
     23, 1828, and had *Nancy H.,*[7] who m. John Poole, of Rock-
     land; *Mary H.,*[7] who m. Hubbard Wardrobe, and lives in
     Hockton, Cal.; *Sarah J.,*[7] who m. Walter W. Wardrobe.

38. xi. PEREZ,[5] b. Nov. 7, 1768; m. Abigail Johnson.

xii. CHLOE,[5] b. Jan. 26, 1771; d. Feb. 2, 1844; m. Charles Bai-
     ley, Oct. 28, 1792. He lived on Main st., Hanover, where
     he d. June 11, 1820. Their children were: (1) *Charles,*[6] b.
     1793, moved to Indiana. (2) *Chloe,*[6] 1795; m. Paul Perry.
     (3) *Benjamin,*[6] 1797. (4) *Betsey,*[6] 1799; m. Josh Dwelley.
     (5) *Barker,*[6] 1801. (6) *Luther,*[6] 1803; d. 1804. (7)
     Martin,[6] 1807; d. 1844. (8) *Mary,*[6] 1809; m. Ensign
     Crocker. (9) *Morcia,*[6] m. Albert Holbrook, 1830.

xiii. SAGE,[5] b. 1773; d. 1791.

xiv. CALEB,[5] b. Sept. 13, 1775; d. Feb. 23, 1840. He m. Betsey
     Pratt, who d. at Hanover, April 26, 1867, æt. 91 years, 8
     mos., 20 days. He ran a market cart. They had a daugh-
     ter *Betsey,*[6] b. 1799, who m. David Mann (her cousin), of
     Hanover; she d. Jan. 29, 1873. Mr. David Mann was
     living in 1883, hale and hearty, at the age of 85.

(16) ENSIGN[4] MAN

(*Ensign,*[3] *Thomas,*[2] *Richard*[1]) was born at "Man Hill," in Scituate, Mass., July 15, 1740. He was the eldest child of Ensign Man,
Sr., by wife (widow) Tabitha
Vinal. His father sold his
real estate and homestead on
"Man Hill," in 1750, and
soon after removed to Boston.

It is said the subject of this sketch was prepared for college by the clergyman of the town. Be that as it may, he was graduated from Harvard University in 1764, the year the college hall and library were destroyed by fire.* At this time Man had a chamber in the Hall, where he had accumulated many books for the purpose of preparing himself to be a tutor. The fire taking all, he resolved to teach, and we next find him the same year (1764), at Lancaster, Mass., a school teacher.† He taught three years in that town, and about 1767 went to Petersham, ‡ Mass., to pursue the same employment.

It is said he had " warmly espoused the cause of liberty," and no doubt the many friends of the government party § in Petersham were ready to throw every obstacle in his path. Rev. Aaron Whitney, one of the committee, not liking his political sentiments, refused to take any part in his qualification as a teacher. " But in spite of all antipathies and objections," says Rev. Mr. Willson, " Mr. Man at length commenced his labors." He was the leader of the party in town who styled themselves " Sons of Liberty," ‖ and met on the 20th of Sept. 1768, and dedicated a " thrifty young elm " to the goddess of liberty. Willson says, " the training which Mr. Man had had in letters, made him a valuable acquisition to the Whigs, who had frequent occasion, no doubt, to avail themselves of his services in drawing up their papers, and putting their resolutions in form." At this time party spirit " ran high " at Petersham.

In August, 1770, Capt. Thomas Beaman (who acted as a guide to the British troops at Lexington and Concord, and afterwards fled,

---

* For an account of this disastrous fire of Jan. 24, 1764, see Pierce's History of Harvard University.

† See Worcester Magazine, vol. ii. p. 238. (Among the teachers were Gen. Warren of Revolutionary fame, President Willard, and others.)

‡ For a historical sketch of Petersham, and more about Ensign Man, see the ably written pamphlet of Rev. Edmund B. Willson, entitled " An Address in Commemoration of the One Hundredth Anniversary" of the incorporation of that town; printed 1855.

§ Petersham at this time was one of the most prominent towns in the state, and many of its first citizens were of the government party, or "Tories." (See Willson's Address.) This romantic hill town of late years, through the influence of James W. Brooks, Esq., Prof. John Fiske, and others, has become a quiet but noted summer resort.

‖ For a fierce letter regarding the "Sons of Liberty " at Petersham, see Boston Evening Post, of March 13, 1769, Mass. Hist. Soc. The "thrifty young elm" is said to be one of the three large trees now standing on the east line of the main road, and just north of the highly cultivated estate of James W. Brooks, Esq.

11

his estate confiscated, etc.) "padlocked" the "obnoxious school-master" out of the schoolhouse. Mr. Sylvanus How and Man "without ceremony broke it open." This action led to a lengthy and bitter law suit, in which the defendants, How and Man, employed as counsel Josiah Quincy, Jr. Soon after "Mr. Man," says Mr. Willson, "had been wounded and taken captive by a subtler warrior, and a hero of more conquests than ever went clad in armor of metal. The minister could not convert him from his idol-worship at the shrine of liberty, nor all the armies of the royal George subdue or bind his spirit; but the minister had a gentle daughter, the glance of whose eye smote his shield through and through, cleft his helmet in twain, and left him defenceless. At the feet of Miss Alice Whitney he had by this time surrendered at discretion."

He married, August 19, 1773, Alice (born in Petersham, September 23, 1748), eldest daughter of Rev. Aaron Whitney,* the first minister at Petersham. Mr. Man purchased a farm at the north part of the town and resided there until about the year 1810; after

---

* Rev. Aaron[5] Whitney (Moses,[4] b. ab. 1690, Moses,[3] b. 1655, Richard,[2] b. 1626, John,[1] b. in Eng. 1600), b. in Littleton, Mass., 1714. Har. Univ. 1737. Ordained minister at Nichewaug (Petersham), 1738; m. Alice Baker, of Phillipston, Mass., July 12, 1739; she d. Aug. 26, 1767, æt. 49; he m. second, the widow of Rev. David Stearns, of Lunenburg. He continued to be the minister of the town up to about 1775, at which time he was barred from the pulpit (being a "tory,"), but continued to preach, holding services in his own house up to the time of his death in 1779. He was also a large land proprietor and extensive farmer. He carried on a large correspondence with his English friends. Children:

    i.   Abel,[6] b. 1740; d. in college, Cambridge, March 15, 1756.
    ii.   Rev. Peter,[6] b. Sept. 6, 1744; grad. Harv. Univ. 1762; m. 1768, Julia Lambert, of Reading. Ordained pastor of the 1st church at Northborough, Mass., Nov. 4, 1767, where he died Feb. 29, 1816. He was the first historian of Worcester County, and the author of several occasional sermons. Many of his valuable MSS. were destroyed by fire at Northborough. They had eleven children. The second child was Rev. Peter[7] Whitney (b. Jan. 19, 1770), of Quincy, Mass. (who was father of Rev. George[8] Whitney, late of Roxbury, Mass., and Rev. Frederic A.[8] Whitney, late of Brighton, Mass., and others).
   iii. Charles,[6] settled at Phillipston, Mass.; d. in Vt.
   iv. Aaron,[6] merchant at Northfield, Mass.
   v.   Alice,[6] b. Sept. 23, 1748; m. Ensign Man. (H. U. 1764).
   vi. Lucy,[6] m. Samuel Kendall, D.D., of New Salem, Mass.; settled at Weston.
  vii. Paul,[6] b. March 23, 1753 (H. U. 1772); d. March, 1795; a physician at Westfield, Mass.
 viii. Abel,[6] b. March 15, 1756 (b. same day the eldest son died); d. March 2, 1807; merchant at Westfield. Eleven children.
  ix. Richard,[6] b. Feb. 23, 1767 (H. U. 1787); d. 1806.
   x. and xi. Names not given. (See Whitney genealogy.)

that lived with his son Thomas, where he died December 21, 1829, in his ninetieth year. His wife died September 20, 1806. Besides teaching, he prepared young men for college, and was called "Master Man," a *sobriquet* that he is still known by. He was of vigorous frame, a great reader, and possessed remarkable memory. He had the Bible, English poets, and many other works almost at his "tongue's end," though he had a slight impediment in his speech. His religious views are best expressed in a letter of his to his sister Priscilla, dated at Petersham, June 4, 1825, then in his eighty-fifth year. An extract of which is:

"My dear sister, I received yours of May 2d, which to my great joy informed me you was alive and well, which dissipated my fears, and gave me great happiness. * * * I feel old age very sensibly creeping upon me. I am very lame, but not so but that I crawl about like an old tortoise. I strive to bear old age well as I can. * * * With you, I have no doubt our vices are punished in this Life. It looks most reasonable, and most suitable to the character of an all-wise and all-merciful God to punish our sins here; than ten thousand years hereafter. * * * There is a book lately published, entitled an 'Inquiry,' by Walter Balfour. I was extremely pleased with reading of it. I read forty years ago Dr. Chauncey's 'Salvation of all Men,' and expected it would have been answered by some pious Divine; but I never heard it was. But this, I expect, will have the Thunders of the Vatican levelled against it, and the author of it doom'd to everlasting punishment in hell fire! * * * I have often wondered why different sentiments in religion and even in politics should create ill feelings in the hearts of men towards each other, but so it is, as Mr. Pope has well expressed it:

> 'What shocks one part, will edify the rest,
> Nor with one system can [we] all be bless'd,
> The very best will variously incline,
> And what rewards your virtue punish mine.'

But how any man can be edified or pleased with the doctrine: 'It is the greatest happiness of the saints in Heaven to look down into hell, and see their friends and relations tormented in flames,' I am unable to conceive. I will say with Mr. Balfour, 'The good Lord deliver me from such a Heaven.'"

Children:

    i. ALICE,[5] b. April 10, 1775; d. July 20, 1805; m. Thomas Lincoln, b. 1780; d. at Greenwich, Mass., 1869. He was a farmer, and had (1) *Ebenezer*,[6] b. Dec. 13, 1803; m. Miss Goddard; is a farmer living in Grafton, Mass. (2) *Thomas*,[6] b. May 6, 1805; d. 1854; m., lived in Dana, Mass.

    ii. LUCY,[5] b. May 9, 1777; d. unmarried at Petersham, Feb. 14, 1859.

39.   iii.   ENSIGN,⁵ Jr., b. July 14, 1778; d. 1810; m. Lydia Filmore.
40.   iv.   THOMAS,⁵ b. May 6, 1780; d. 1853; m. Esther Stone.
       v.   JULIANA,⁵ b. March 2, 1783; d. unmarried at P., March 22,
             1813.
      vi.   WILLIAM,⁵ b. Sept. 2, 1784; d. about 1861, at Petersham.
             He never married. At the age of about 24, he left home
             and was not heard from for twelve years; during this time he
             travelled every state in the Union, peddling combs, etc. On
             his return he lived with his brother Samuel, and never after
             went a mile from the house up to the day of his death. He
             was a man of large size, of good understanding, well read,
             and of remarkable memory. He directed the family to bury
             him in a plain wooden box (without a funeral) in the pas-
             ture, which plan was carried out. The characteristic oddi-
             ties of the family were more apparent in the life of this Wil-
             liam; yet he was a man of honor and strictest integrity.
             (See pp. 59 and 69.)
41. vii.   SAMUEL,⁵ b. Nov. 21, 1787; d. 1856; m. Sarah Luce.
     viii.   PRISCILLA,⁵ b. June 4, 1790; d. July 29, 1836; m. Holland
             Goodnow, of New Salem, Mass., a farmer. He was b. Feb.
             13, 1792; d. Sept. 21, 1861. He was a man favorably known
             in the community where he resided. Children:
                  i.   *Julia,*⁶ b. March 2, 1816; d. Aug. 2, 1840; m.
                        Nov. 1837, Daniel Andrews. They had:
                             (1) *Horace W.*⁷

                 ii.   *Alice Whitney,*⁶ b. April 25, 1818; d. June 8, 1867;
                        m. 1845, David Andrews. Children:
                             (1) *Samuel Holland,*⁷ b. April 28, 1846; m.
                                 Dec. 25, 1873, Gracie Smith.
                             (2) *Charles Sumner,*⁷ b. July 6, 1856.

                iii.   *Priscilla Elvira,*⁶ b. April 5, 1820; m. Leonard
                        Merchant, Nov. 25, 1841. He d. Dec. 12,
                        1866. Children:
                             (1) *Julia Eliza,*⁷ b. Oct. 10, 1843; m. Sept.
                                 29, 1864, Rev. Almond Barrett.
                             (2) *Joseph Adelbert,*⁷ b. Aug. 15, 1846; d.
                                 May 9, 1855.
                             (3) *Augustus Leonard,*⁷ b. Aug. 17, 1851; m.
                                 May 20, 1880, Ellen M. Dickenson.
                             (4) *Alice Whitney,*⁷ b. June 4, 1856.

                 iv.   *Samuel Holland,*⁶ b. Oct. 10, 1821; d. Sept. 17,
                        1843.

                  v.   *Augustus Warren*⁶ (Rev.), b. March 25, 1824; m.
                        first, Aug. 26, 1851, Susan Amelia White, d.
                        March 19, 1873. He m. second, Sarah Glazier
                        Rice, Nov. 3, 1874. He graduated from Am-
                        herst Coll., 1849. Ordained at Royalston, Mass.,

1852; pr. at Stamford, Vt., Wilmington, Vt., No. Sunderland, Mass., Bernardston. Mass., Shutesbury, Mass., and is now at Wilmington, Vt. Children:

 (1) *Milton Augustus,*[7] b. July 31, 1852; m. June 18, 1879, Mary Gorham.
 (2) *Melvin Warren,*[7] b. April 23, 1858; d. Dec. 12, 1863.
 (3) *Anna Marion,*[7] b. April 20, 1861.
  By second wife:
 (4) *Florence Alcesta,*[7] b. Nov. 23, 1876.
 (5) *Grace Warren,*[7] b. Nov. 4, 1881.

vi. *Amos Sawyer,*[6] d. æt. eighteen months.

vii. *Sarah E.,*[6] b. Dec. 16, 1827; m. Nov. 1, 1849, Hollis Wilber, and have:

 (1) *George H.,*[7] b. March 30, 1851.
 (2) *Ellen A.,*[7] b. Nov. 13, 1852.
 (3) *Frederic W.,*[7] b. Feb. 12, 1859; d. Sept. 1865.
 (4) *Henry A.,*[7] b. March 24, 1864.
 (5) *Frankie E.,*[7] b. Feb. 8, 1867.

viii. *Nancy Alcesta,*[6] b. June 25, 1829; d. Dec. 23, 1871; m. April 9, 1848, Rev. Samuel P. Everett, who was b. in Milford, N. H., Jan. 26, 1826; res. South Hampton, N. H. Children: the two eldest b. in Worcester, the others in Rowe, Mass.

 (1) *Jennie M.,*[7] b. March 17, 1850; m. Albert J. Pierce, res. Brightland, Mass.
 (2) *Edward S.,*[7] b. Nov. 13, 1853.
 (3) *Ella A.,*[7] b. May 31, 1858.
 (4) *Walter G.,*[7] b. Aug. 21, 1860.
 (5) *Samuel A.,*[7] b. Feb. 15, 1866.

ix. *Amos W.,*[6] b. Nov. 14, 1832; m. April 12, 1857, Sophia N. Avery. Children:

 (1) *Ida N.,*[7] b. April 14, 1860.
 (2) *Etta J.,*[7] b. April 21, 1862.
 (3) *Louis,*[7] b. Sept. 5, 1864.

x. *Mary Jane,*[6] b. (in Montague) Feb. 8, 1836; m. first, Sept. 27, 1858, Waldo H. Andrews, a dentist, who d. Sept. 27, 1864; she m. second, Oct. 10, 1865, Riley Boyd, of Wilmington, Vt. Children. By first husband:

 (1) *Erwin Wilson,*[7] b. Jan. 13, 1861.
  By second husband:
 (2) *William Riley,*[7] b. July 10, 1867.
 (3) *Robert Whitney,*[6] b. April 14, 1870.

ix. HANNAH,[5] b. July 30, 1792; d. Oct. 3, 1865; m. June 15, 1823, John Briggs, who was b. at Athol, Mass., 1797. This family lived at the extreme north part of Petersham, Mass., up to about 1852-3; from thence the parents and all of the daughters removed to Calhoun county, Mich. Children, b. at Petersham:

    i. John S.,[6] b. May 25, 1824; m. Dec. 10, 1850, Mary Ann Doyle. Number of children.

    ii. Mary,[6] b. Oct. 23, 1825; unmarried; d. in Mich. 1874.

    iii. Julia H.,[6] b. April 16, 1827; m. April 28, 1856, Wm. S. Woodruff, of Mich.; he d. Oct. 19, 1868. She was in early life a school teacher of much talent, and a devoted Christian. She d. June 15, 1882, leaving an only son, viz.:

        (1) *Willis B.,[7]* b. Feb. 3, 1862; res. Battle Creek, Mich.

    iv. Phebe,[6] b. Feb. 7, 1829; m. first, Sept. 1, 1856, Milton M. Woodruff. He d. Aug. 1862. She m. second, a Mr. Spear, a carpenter; res. Dunningville, Mich. Her father lives with them. Children, by first marriage:

        (1) *Alice R.,[7]* b. June 9, 1857.
        (2) *George M.,[7]* b. Dec. 25, 1858.

    v. David,[6] b. Dec. 10, 1831.

    vi. Priscilla Gracia,[6] b. Aug. 6, 1833; m. 1856, M. W. Southworth. He is a farmer; res. Marengo, Mich.

(17) JOSEPH[4] MAN

(*Nathaniel,[3] Richard,[2] Richard,[1]*) was the eldest child of Nathaniel Man, by wife Mary (Root), of Hebron, Conn. He was born, according to the town of Hebron records, April 5, 1713; whether he first saw the light at Hebron, or Lebanon, Conn., is uncertain. His father (Nathaniel) deeded lands, May 29, 1713, calling himself of Lebanon, but soon after resided and owned land at Hebron. Joseph Man married first, Mercy ———, who died April 5, 1738. He married second, Hannah Gilbert, Nov. 27, 1740, who died Aug. 15, 1777. He probably died in Hebron, 1798 or '9. A granddaughter says, "he was a farmer and miller in Hebron." He had fourteen children, two by the first wife, and twelve by the second, all of whom were born at Hebron, viz.:

      i.   ARODA[5] (dau.), b. Jan. 27, 1734-5.
      ii. MERCY,[5] b. Sept. 7, 1736; m. Zebedee Howard.
     iii. JOEL,[5] b. Sept. 4, 1741; prob. d. young.
42. iv. JOEL,[5] b. Oct. 1, 1743; m. Mercy Man [cousin No. 18, v.].
  ~ v. HANNAH,[5] b. Nov. 17, 1745; m. John Weed, of Malta, N. Y.;
          farmer.
     vi. FRANCES,[5] b. Aug. 21, 1749; m. Solomon Bailey.
    vii. JOSEPH,[5] b. Nov. 12, 1751; d. Oct. 21, 1758.
   viii. ABALINE,[5] b. May 31, 1754; m. Levi Bissell, of Hebron, Conn.
     ix. DEBORAH,[5] b. Sept. 30, 1756; m. Eleazer Phelps, and lived
          in Lenox, Mass.
43. x. ZADOCK,[5] b. Feb. 7, 1759; m. first, Esther Warner.
     xi. JOSEPH,[5] b. Oct. 25, 1761; d. July 29, 1843; m. Patience
          Barber. [In will, real estate to two of his wife's nieces and
          a yearly stipend to the church.]
    xii. CANDIS,[5] b. Jan. 9, 1764; m. Ezekiel Brown, of Hebron. He
          d. 1843.
44. xiii. JAMES,[5] b. Feb. 24, 1768; m. Tryphena Tarbox.
    xiv. JOHN,[5] d. young.

(18) JOHN[4] MAN

(*Nathaniel,[3] Richard,[2] Richard[1]*), fourth son of Nathaniel, of Hebron, Conn., by wife Mary (Root), was born in that town, Nov. 20, 1720, and died June 4, 1806. A representative of the family, Mrs. C. M. Phelps, writes: "The Mann farm in Hebron contains about 250 acres; the present house was built in 1782 by Andrew Mann (b. 1755). It is a large house, in good repair. The place was never sold after Nathaniel Man bought it, until my father died." From a letter of his written in 1791, directed to his brother-in-law, Rev. Samuel Peters, D.D., LL.D.,[*] then

---

[*] Samuel Andrews Peters, D.D., LL.D., born at Hebron, Conn., 1735; died 1826; grad. Yale Coll. 1757. In 1758 he visited Europe, returned to Conn. in 1759, and became a clergyman of the Episcopal church and had charge of the churches at Hartford and Hebron. His toryism was so pronounced that he was obliged to take flight to England, where in 1781 he published a "History of Connecticut," setting forth a code of "blue laws" which was somewhat untruthful. He published in New York, in 1807, a History of Rev. Hugh Peters, his great-uncle; and a History of Hebron. He visited the Falls of St. Anthony in 1817, and took up a claim there of large extent of land. Trumbull called him "Parson Peter," in "M'Fingal." He was remunerated by the Government for losses during the Revolutionary war.

   The author was kindly loaned a very interesting letter of his, dated "London, Oct. 24, 1786," and addressed to John and Dr. Nath[l] Man, of Hebron. An extract of which is: "I have appointed you (John[4] Man) & your Son Nathaniel jointly & severally to be my Attorney & Attorneys not believing that the State of Connecticut is now graced with two other men of equal virtue & honor," etc.

in London, one would judge him to have been of good business talent and education. He married first, Jan. 1, 1740-1, Margaret Peters (b. Aug. 1724), of Hebron, "aunt of Gov. Peters, of Hebron." She died June 2, 1789. He married second, about 1790, Hannah, widow of Samuel Kellogg, of Marlborough. He had the following children, born at Hebron, by his first wife. (Hebron records.)

     i. MARY[5] (prob. Margaret), b. April 14, 1742; m. Mr. Cross, settled at Montreal, Canada, and had *John*[6] and *Aaron*.[6]

45. ii. JOHN,[5] b. Dec. 25, 1743; d. 1828; m. first, Lydia Porter.

    iii. MARY,[5] b. Feb. 25, 1745-6; d. May 18, 1817; m. Oct. 16, 1768, Jacob Loomis, b. at Andover, Conn., May 20, 1745; d. May 9, 1813. They had *Mary*,[6] *Jacob*[6] and *Abigail*.[6]

    iv. HANNAH,[5] b. 1747.

    v. MERCY,[5] b. March 5 or 16, 1749; m. Joel Man (cousin). See No. 42.

    vi. ELIJAH,[5] b. Aug. 9, 1751; m. first, Aug. 20, 1771, Mary Perkins, who d. 1781. He m. second, Nov. 14, 1782, widow Baxter, of Lebanon. Children: (1) *Mary*,[6] b. May 17, 1772; d. July 19, 1866; m. 1790, Asa Strong, who d. April 3, 1859, æt. 93 (prob. Colchester, Conn.). (2) *Enoch*,[6] who prob. had *Enoch P.*,[7] *Levi*,[7] *Harriet*,[7] *Fanny*,[7] and others. (3) *Elijah*.[6] (4) *Bernsley*.[6]

46. vii. ANDREW[5] (Capt.), b. March 18, 1755; m. Harriet Phelps.

    viii. Dr. NATHANIEL,[5] b. Aug. 11, 1757. He was educated at Dartmouth College, soon after went to England and perfected his education as physician and surgeon, and was for a time in a hospital in London. On his return to this country, m. Miss Owen, of Hebron, May 6, 1787. For a short time he imported drugs, medicines, etc., from England. He had *Harriet*[6] and *Sophia*,[6] no sons. He removed to Georgia, where he practised medicine, and finally died there.

    ix. PHEBE,[5] b. Aug. 6, 1763 (or '68); prob. m. Mr. Buel.

    x. HANNAH,[5] b. June 5, 1772; m. Theophilus Baldwin, b. Aug. 25, 1769; lived for a time in Bradford, Conn.; removed to Holland, Erie Co., N. Y., where they died. They had four or more children.

(19) ABIJAH[4] MAN

(*Nathaniel*,[3] *Richard*,[2] *Richard*[1]) was born at Hebron, Conn., Aug. 7, 1734. He was the youngest child and sixth son of Nathaniel Man, by his second wife, Mary Sprague. It is said he lived in the western part of the town of Hebron. "The house in which he lived is now (1874) standing, but unoccupied." He died (probably with a cancer) in 1809, at Hebron. He married Sarah Porter, of that town, in November, 1757, and the following ten children were born there, according to the town records, viz.:

47.   i.   ABIJAH,[5] b. Dec. 21, 1761; d. 1856; m. Levina Ford.
48. ii.   AARON,[5] b. Oct. 16, 1764; m. Chloe Clark.
     iii.   SARAH,[5] b. Sept. 13, 1766.
49. iv.   OLIVER,[5] b. Nov. 14, 1768; m. Content Hills.
50.   v.   DANIEL,[5] b. Jan. 18, 1771; m. first, Molly Case.
     vi.   ELISHA,[5] b. Aug. 4, 1773; m. first, Mary Perkins; second, Ruby Baxter. Had *Sarah.*[6]
    vii.   AMASA,[5] b. Nov. 4, 1775; probably settled in Franklin, N. Y.
   viii.   ALEXANDER,[5] b. Sept. 10, 1777; unmarried; a silversmith.
     ix.   ABIGAIL,[5] b. July 21, 1780.
      x.   MOLLY,[5] b. Oct. 9, 1782.

(20) NATHANIEL[5] MANN

(*Josiah,*[4] *Thomas,*[3] *Thomas,*[2] *Richard*[1]) was born at Scituate, Mass., Oct. 9, 1759, and died there Oct. 2, 1839. He was a farmer, and lived in Jesse Dunbar's house. He married Abigail Billings. Children, born in Scituate:

      i.   EDMON BILLINGS,[6] b. May 12, 1786; m. ———, and had: (1) *Barnabas N.,*[7] b. about 1824, who was 1st Lieut. in Col. T. C. Amory's Regiment; it is said he fired "Chain Bridge"; he died in "Libby Prison" Oct. 8, 1864. (2) *Mary,*[7] m. ——— Thayer or Hager, of Chelsea, Mass.
51. ii.   CHARLES,[6] b. Nov. 16, 1790; m. Mary D. Lothrop.
     iii.   BARNABAS,[6] b. Feb. 14, 1793.
     iv.   THEODORA BILLINGS,[6] b. Aug. 12, 1795; m. Oren Faxon, of Boston.
      v.   NATHANIEL,[6] b. March 30, 1798; m. Maria Fenner, of Quincy. He died of cholera, in Milton, Mass., 1849, leaving a will. No children mentioned in the will.
     vi.   REBECCA,[6] b. March 28, 1800.
    vii.   ABIGAIL,[6] b. May 30, 1802.
   viii.   MARY,[6] b. Nov. 21, 1804.
     ix.   MALINDA,[6] b. April 18, 1807.
      x.   SARAH F.,[6] b. Nov. 16, 1809.

(21) REV. ISAIAH[4] MANN

(*Thomas,*[4] *Thomas,*[3] *Thomas,*[2] *Richard*[1]), the eldest son of Capt. Thomas Man, of Scituate, Mass., was born there Feb. 7, 1756. He was graduated from Harvard University, 1775. He had a call from the church in Falmouth, Mass., Oct. 25, 1779; but on account of the

12

severity of the winter of 1779-80, and not duly receiving his certificate of church membership from Scituate, the ordination did not take place until Jan. 19, 1780. He continued in the ministry at Falmouth up to April 2, 1789, at which time he died. He married Zipporah, daughter of Isaiah Nickerson, of Falmouth. They had one son:

    i. ISAIAH THOMAS,[6] b. 1788; m. ———. He resided at Ashburnham, Mass., and died there March 18, 1847.

(22) JOHN[5] MANN

(*Thomas,*[4] *Thomas,*[3] *Thomas,*[2] *Richard*[1]), the youngest son of Capt. Thomas Man, was born at "Scituate Harbor" in Scituate, Mass., May 10, 1761. He married first, Patience Rogers, who died Dec. 14, 1799, aged 39. He married second, June 18, 1803, Rebecca Briggs, who died Oct. 3, 1857, aged 88. He died suddenly June 6, 1841. He had twelve children—eight by first wife, four by second; all of them born in Scituate, viz.:

    i. PATIENCE,[6] b. April 5, 1782; m. John Broaders, of Boston, and had *Edward R.*[7] and others.
52. ii. PELEG,[6] b. Feb. 3, 1784; m. Margaret Tufts.
53. iii. JOHN,[6] b. Nov. 1, 1785; m. Kate Harrington.
    iv. SARAH,[6] b. Dec. 16, 1787; d. Dec. 18, 1846; m. John W. Clark, of Haverhill, Mass., and had: (1) *Elizabeth,*[7] who m. Wm. Buswell, of Haverhill. (2) *John W.*[7] Jr., who m. Sarah W. Hutchinson, of Haverhill; he was killed in "Civil War." (3) *Sarah Ann,*[7] who m. Wm. Buswell. (4) *Abigail,*[7] who m. James Stuart, of Haverhill, and had: *George,*[8] *Charles,*[8] *John,*[8] *James,*[8] *Frank,*[8] *Richard*[8] and *Emma.*[8]
    v. ISAIAH,[6] b. Dec. 23, 1789; d. in Boston, March 20, 1823; m. Hannah Elliot, and had: (1) *Thomas Elliot*[7]; unmarried. (2) *George,*[7] who is married, and has a son *Charles.*[8]
    vi. POLLY,[6] b. Aug. 12, 1792; d. unmarried, Jan. 8, 1880.
    vii. THOMAS,[6] b. June 17, 1795; d. Feb. 6, 1882; farmer at Scituate. He m. Emma Trim, 1871. Had three children, one died July 25, 1882, aged 8 years.
    viii. NANCY,[6] b. Nov. 21, 1797; d. May 12, 1852; m. Hilliard Smith, of Maine; lived in Roxbury, Mass.: had only one child, *Charles,*[7] who d. unmarried.
    ix. LOUISA,[6] b. Oct. 1, 1804; unmarried; lived at Scituate; d. Feb. 9, 1881.
    x. BRIGGS,[6] b. Jan. 7, 1807; mason by trade; retired; residence, Poplar Street, Boston; m. Sophia Ann Gould. No children.

   xi. LYDIA CURTIS,[6] b. Dec. 24, 1808; m. Noah Bodge, of Boston. He is dead. Has a son who is a physician, and daughters who are school teachers in Boston.

   xii. REUBEN,[6] b. Nov. 21, 1811; is a well-to-do farmer in Scituate.

(23) DAVID[5] MANN

(*Ebenezer,*[4] *Thomas,*[3] *Thomas,*[2] *Richard*[1]), the eldest child of Ebenezer Man, Sr., was born in Pembroke, Mass., Oct. 19, 1752 (O. S.). He was called a shipwright in deeds. It is said, also, that he was a farmer, and a deacon in the " First Church " in Pembroke. He died there Nov. 22, 1838, leaving a will. He married Betsey Bates, of Duxbury, Mass., Dec. 24, 1778; she died at Pembroke, 1828, aged 68. Children, all born in Pembroke :

     i. HULDAH,[6] b. Aug. 7, 1780; d. June 19, 1851; m. at 18, Jabez Josselyn, and had two girls and seven boys, among whom were : *Isaiah,*[7] of South Boston; *Daniel,*[7] of Hanson, Mass.; *Rebecca,*[7] who m. Otis Perry, and resided at Hanson.

54. ii. DAVID,[6] b. Nov. 29, 1782; m. Rebecca Oldham.

   iii. COMFORT,[6] b. July 11, 1785; non compos.

55. iv. EBENEZER,[6] b. Oct. 12, 1788; m. Alma Josselyn.

    v. ISAIAH,[6] b. May 22, 1791; d. Oct. 9, 1814.

   vi. DANIEL,[6] b. Nov. 8, 1793. He was at Fort Independence during the war of 1812; went away and never returned.

   vii. THOMAS,[6] b. June 10, 1796; d. about 1882; farmer in Pembroke. He m. first, Miss —— Butler; second, Betsey Brown; both dead. No children.

  viii. BETSEY,[6] b. April 18, 1799; m. John Turner, of Pembroke; had two boys and two girls.

56. ix. JOSIAH,[6] b. Oct. 16, 1801; m. first, Hannah Smith.

    x. MELINDA,[6] b. June 4, 1807; m. Moses Carr, of Hanson. Had two children.

(24) EBENEZER[5] MANN

(*Ebenezer,*[4] *Thomas,*[3] *Thomas,*[2] *Richard*[1]) was born in Pembroke, Mass., Aug. 6, 1757. He located at Salem, Mass., in 1783. He commenced ship-building there on the North River, and continued in the business until about 1800, at which time he engaged in the grocery trade on Boston street, in a store that he erected. For names of vessels built by him in Salem, see His. Collections of Essex Institute, vol. vi. pp. 186-9. They were six ships, fifteen brigs, two barques and eighteen schooners, ranging from fifty to two hundred and fourteen tons. He was a pew-holder in the "North Church," and probably a member. He married Dec. 30, 1791, Sarah Buffington, daughter of James and Prudence (Proctor) Buffington (b. Sept. 27, 1772; d. May 17, 1851). He died in Salem, March 19, 1836. Children, born in Salem:

    i.   EBENEZER,[6] b. Nov. 30, 1792; d. Nov. 19, 1808.

    ii.   JOHN,[6] b. Sept. 15, 1794; d. in Andover, Mass., July 21, 1846, childless. Was a farmer. He m. Zoe Clark, of A., July 6, 1837; b. 1797; d. Nov. 28, 1882, at Andover.

    iii.   DAVID,[6] b. Oct. 30, 1796; d. unm. in Brunswick, Me., March 4, 1844.

    iv.   SARAH,[6] b. Oct. 18, 1798; d. in Salem, March 20, 1879; m. James Lord, b. in Ipswich, Mass., Jan. 9, 1799. He settled at Salem; in early life was a tanner. They had *Daniel A.,[7] James A.,[7] Frank,[7] Sarah,[7] William.[7]*

    v.   ELIZABETH N.,[6] b. Jan. 7, 1801; d. in Salem, Aug. 19, 1876. She kept a private school for over fifty years. She was an active member of the "South Church" (orthodox), and did much for the poor and sick.

    vi.   LUCY FROST,[6] b. Feb. 9, 1803; d. in Andover, Mass., Feb. 14, 1880; m. David Baker, of Andover (farmer), 1827, b. March 12, 1803. The children are: *Elizabeth,[7]* who m. Edward Abbott, of Andover; *George,[7]* who m. Charlotte Blanchard, of A.; and *Caroline,[7]* who m. A. Berry, of A.

    vii.   IRA PRESTON,[6] b. Feb. 4, 1805; d. April 27, 1831, unm.

57. viii.   JAMES BUFFINGTON,[6] b. June 14, 1809; m. Susan F. Ruee.

(25) JOSEPH[5] MANN

(*Joseph,[4] Joseph,[3] Thomas,[2] Richard[1]*), born probably in what is now Randolph, Mass., in 1760. He married first, in 1781, Mary, daughter of Peter Dyer. He married second, widow of Elijah Bradley, about 1798. He had fourteen children, seven by each wife, probably all born in Randolph:

58. i.   JOSEPH,[6] b. Nov. 17, 1781; m. first, Mary Dyer.

    ii.   Infant, b. Nov. 17, 1781; died.

    iii.   ISAAC,[6] m. Hepsibah Vose, July 31, 1806; removed to Maine.

59. iv.   JONATHAN,[6] b. Sept. 4, 1786; m. Polly Bradley.

    v.   MARY,[6] m. John Hartshorn, Nov. 1, 1808.

    vi.   LUCINDA,[6] m. Mr. Knapp.

    vii.   JACOB,[6] m. Harriet Belcher, Jan. 29, 1815; removed to Providence, R. I.

    viii.   SARAH,[6] m. Benj. Henry, Buffalo Co., Ohio.

ix. MAHALAH,[6] m. Gilbert Blaisdell, Quincy, Mass.
  x. BETSEY,[6] res. Randolph.
 xi. RUTH,[6] m. John Sloan, Canton, Mass.
 xii. HANNAH,[6] m. John Sylvester, 1820, Canton, Mass.
xiii. PHEBE,[6] m. Ephraim Spear, Canton, Mass.
xiv. NANCY,[6] b. March 15, 1812; m. Lott Madan, Dec. 28, 1828;
     res. Canton, Mass.

(26) SETH[5] MANN

(*Seth,*[4] *Joseph,*[3] *Thomas,*[2] *Richard*[1]), the eldest son of Lieut. Seth
Man, was born in what is now Randolph, Mass., Dec. 3, 1747. He
was in Capt. Abijah Bangs's company, 1776, and settled near the
" Blue Hills River " about that time. He married first, 1769, Mary,
daughter of Aaron Hayward, who died Dec. 17, 1776, aged twenty-
eight; married second, Deborah Dyer, born Oct. 6, 1746, who was a
daughter of his father's wife by her first husband.

He purchased a farm at Braintree, Vt., Oct. 30, 1792, for £32
16s.; removed there, was one of the first settlers, and helped
build a log school-house. At the time his children went to school,
there was only one arithmetic and that owned by the teacher. He
was a generous and upright man, and was one of the overseers of
Braintree, 1806,–7,–11,–12, and 14. He died July 20, 1822; had
fourteen children, two by first wife, twelve by second, viz.:

    i. MARY,[6] b. March 5, 1770; d. July 26, 1851; m. Dea. Abiel
       Howard, a farmer of Braintree, Vt., who was b. 1771 and d.
       Dec. 25, 1859. They had 11 children.
   ii. RELIEF,[6] b. May 3, 1772; m. Jacob Niles, of Randolph, Mass.;
       had 4 children.
  iii. SALLY,[6] b. Jan. 23, 1778; d. May 11, 1855; m. Solomon Hol-
       man, of Braintree, Vt., in 1793, and had thirteen children.
       He b. in Sutton, Mass., 1766, and d. in B., Nov. 26, 1862.
  iv. RUTH,[6] b. July 27, 1779; m. John Kidder; lived in Alexan-
       dria, N. Y.; had *Hosea,*[7] *Earl,*[7] *Sidney,*[7] and two girls.
60. v. SETH[6] (Esq.), b. April 4, 1781; m. first, Betsey Mann (cousin).
61. vi. SAMUEL,[6] b. July 16, 1783; m. Rachel Mann (cousin).
62. vii. MICAH,[6] b. June 21, 1785; m. Sarah Bass.
  viii. TRIPHENA,[6] b. Sept. 13, 1787; d. Sept. 26, 1870; m. first,
       Jacob Bailey, in 1805, a farmer, and had five children; m.
       second, Squire Claflin, of Brookfield, Vt., April 9, 1829; one
       son, *Trueman,*[7] m. Sally Loomis, and lived in Gilmantown,
       Wisconsin.
63. ix. LEVI,[6] b. May 21, 1789; m. Mary Mann (cousin).

64.   x. JOEL,[6] b. May 28, 1791; m. Louisa Mann (cousin).
65. xi. STEPHEN,[6] b. June 30, 1793; m. first, Eliphal Bracket.
66. xii. ELISHA,[6] b. Oct. 4, 1795; m. Ruth Smith.
    xiii. OLIVE,[6] b. Jan. 10, 1799; d. aged about three months.
    xiv. BETSEY,[6] b. Jan. 10, 1799; m. Henry Smith, 1819; he b. 1792, and d. at Roxbury, Vt., 1838. They had nine children, five living in 1882.

(27) BENJAMIN[5] MANN*

(*Seth,[4] Joseph,[3] Thomas,[2] Richard[1]*), the eldest son of Lieut. Seth Man, of Randolph, Mass., by his second wife Elizabeth Dyer; was born there in 1751. He was a farmer at what is called "West Corner," in Randolph; was a deacon in the Baptist church under the pastoral care of Rev. Joel Briggs, in the south part of the town. He served fifteen days in Capt. Sawin's company, 1776, and was employed by the town on the school committee. He died in Randolph, Dec. 14, 1827, aged seventy-seven.

He married Hannah, daughter of Aaron Hayward, who died July 10, 1844, aged ninety. Children, all born in Randolph:

67.   i. BENJAMIN,[6] b. Dec. 3, 1776; m. first, Polly Hunt.
    ii. HANNAH,[6] b. Dec. 18, 1778; m. Nathaniel Tucker.
68. iii. JOSHUA,[6] b. Dec. 7, 1780; m. Sally White (cousin).
    iv. BETSEY,[6] b. Feb. 17, 1783; m. Seth Mann, Esq. (cousin).
    v. RACHEL,[6] b. March 17, 1785; m. Samuel Mann (cousin).
    vi. NATHAN,[6] d. young.
    vii. JOSIAH,[6] d. young.
    viii. POLLY,[6] b. March 25, 1795; m. Seth Mann, Esq. (second wife).
    ix. LOUISA,[6] b. May 25, 1798; m. Joel Mann (cousin).

(28) EPHRAIM[5] MANN

(*Seth,[4] Joseph,[3] Thomas,[2] Richard[1]*) was born in what is now Randolph, Mass., April 3, 1752. The following is from Dr. Ebenezer Alden, of Randolph, 1858: "Ephraim Man, son of Lieut. Seth, married Comfort Jewett, first settled in this town near the present residence of Joseph Jones, then removed to Canton on the York road,

---

* Benjamin and Ephraim Mann, and thirty-one other persons of Braintree, Mass., were among the original proprietors of Braintree, Vt.; only six out of the thirty-three settled there. Ephraim Mann sold his Right, Nov. 6, 1783, to Deacon Samuel Bass. (Bass's Hist. Braintree, Vt.)

and afterwards to Pownal or Bennington, Vt. In 1775, after the battle of Lexington, he enlisted into the army and was a member of the company commanded by Capt. Silas Wild." His wife Comfort was daughter of Thomas and Eunice (Slafter) Jewett, born Sept. 13, 1763; died at Pownal, Vt., Sept. 12, 1831. Children:

    i. ERNICE,[6] b. July 25, 1782; d. Sept. 20, 1860; m. Joseph Parker, April 13, 1802; b. Nov. 27, 1779; d. March 10, 1855. They had eleven children.

    ii. POLLY,[6] b. Feb. 28, 1784; m. Solomon Bennett, March 4, 1810. They had eight children.

    iii. TRIPHENA.[6] b. Aug. 23, 1789.

    iv. TRIPHOSA,[6] b. Aug. 23, 1789; d. June 1, 1863. [Her son Homer Ephraim Mann was b. Dec. 14, 1809. See Slafter Memorial.] She m. Dr. Cranmer Bannister, about Jan. 1, 1814, and had six children.

69.   v. THOMAS[6] JEWETT, b. 1791; m. Betsey Wideman.

(29) SAMUEL[5] MANN

(*Seth*,[4] *Joseph*,[3] *Thomas*,[2] *Richard*[1]), son of Lieut. Seth, of Randolph, Mass., was born there Sept. 13, 1760. He went to Claremont, N. H., and was for a time engaged in business with his brothers Benjamin and Stephen, and his half-brother Micah White. From thence he went to Middlesex, Vt., and afterwards to the "Holland Purchase," Ohio. From 1812 until his death in 1837, he owned a farm within two miles of Mechanicsburgh, Ohio, where he manufactured saleratus. He married first, Nancy, daughter of Capt. Reuben Pettee; she died June 3, 1791, aged twenty-six. He married second, ———, who died before him.

The following account of the children is from Samuel M. Mann, of Mechanicsburgh, Ohio:

    i. SAMUEL,[6] d. unmarried about 1832, at Mechanicsburgh, Ohio.

    ii. OREN,[6] d. 1845, near Mechanicsburgh; m. first, Miss Gill; second, Mrs. Frankenberger. They had (1) *Strange Young*.[7] (2) *Fletcher*.[7] (3) *Nancy*.[7] (4) *Martha*,[7] m. Bland, and lives near Milford Centre, O. All were married, and all are dead but Martha; farmers.

    iii. REUBEN[6] (Dr.), d. 1863, at Milford Center, O.; m. Betsey Alden, and had *John*,[7] studying to be a physician.

    iv. BENJAMIN,[6] d. 1860; m. Jane Gray [who lives within six miles of Mechanicsburgh, O., with her daughter Hester, who is unmarried]. They had (1) *Warren*.[7] (2) *June*,[7] m. ———

Hobbs. (3) *William.*[7] (4) *Harriet.*[7] (5) *Silva,*[7] m. Burnham. (6) *Hester.*[7] (7) *Melissa.*[7] (8) *Edward.*[7] (9) *Abby.*[7] (10) *Clinton.*[7]

v. JOHN,[6] d. at New Orleans, 1849; m. Jane Clement, and had: (1) *Hester,*[7] m. Dr. Carpenter, at Amity, O. (2) *Elvira,*[7] m. Robert Baker. (3) *Azro,*[7] d. in the army. (4) *Adaline,*[7] who resides at Indianapolis, Ind.

vi. LOREN,[6] d. 1867; m. Samantha Timons, who d. 1880; had *Reuben,*[7] who d. aged three.

vii. LEONARD[6] (Dr.), d. 1833.

viii. AZRO,[6] b. 1812; d. 1873, at Mechanicsburgh, Ohio, where he was engaged in the mercantile business. He m. Mary Morgan, 1835, who d. 1867. They had one son *Samuel M.*[7] who is married, resides at Mechanicsburgh, Ohio, and have had the following children: *Charles,*[8] *George,*[8] *Arthur,*[8] *Edith,*[8] *Minnie,*[8] and *Lulu Bell.*[8]

ix. NANCY,[6] d. in Milton, 1850; m. Neman Mitchell, who d. 1835, at Mechanicsburgh, O. They had *Erastus,*[7] *Leonard.*[7] *Seth,*[7] *Reuben,*[7] *Emeline*[7]; all dead but Erastus, who lives at Roundhead, Ohio.

(30) STEPHEN[4] MANN

(*Seth,*[4] *Joseph,*[3] *Thomas,*[2] *Richard*[1]), the youngest son of Lieut. Seth Man, of Randolph, Mass., by his second wife Elizabeth Dyer, was born there March 11, 1766. He located at Claremont, N. H., and for a time was engaged in the mercantile business in company with his brother Samuel; after a while they were burned out. It is said that Stephen acquired a good estate. He married Lucy Pettee for first wife, who died March 11, 1805, aged thirty-five; he married second, Alice Ainsworth, who died June 13, 1845. He died April 6, 1833. He had seven children—four by first wife, three by second, viz.:

i. STEPHEN,[6] b. 1794; d. April 6, 1834; m. Esther Jones, 1818, and had *Susan D.,*[7] May 18, 1819; m. George Merrill, a currier by trade, of Salisbury, Mass., in 1851; now resides at Peabody, Mass.

70. ii. JOSEPH P.,[6] b. 1796; d. April 14, 1864; m. Susan Jones.

iii. HARRIET,[6] b. 1799; d. May 6, 1864; m. George Woodwell, and had: *Mary E.,*[7] and *Jane Mann.*[7]

iv. LUCY ELVIRA,[6] b. 1800; d. July 17, 1875.

71. v. CHARLES HENRY,[6] b. April 28, 1806; m. Vespersia Howard.

vi. ELIZABETH MARY,[6] b. March 29, 1810; d. July 26, 1881, at Claremont, N. H.; m. William Jones, May 19, 1830, and had: (1) *Harriet,*[7] who m. the well-known English title

lawyer, Columbus Smith, Esq. (son of Joseph Smith), of
Salisbury, Vt., who grad. Middlebury Coll. 1842. (2)
Helen,[7] m. Geo. F. Davis, of Windsor, Vt., a farmer. (3)
Lucien E.,[7] resides at the homestead. (4) *Alice A.,*[7] who
died very suddenly Dec. 16, 1882; she was much interested
in genealogy and antique things.

vii. ALICE JANE,[6] b. 1819(?); d. Feb. 22, 1847(?); m. Timothy
D. Kimball, of Claremont, N. H., had two daughters, *Eliza-
beth Alice,*[7] and *Catharine Jane,*[7] now Mrs. Bullen and Mrs.
Tupper, in California.

(31) JOB[5] MANN

(*Seth,*[4] *Joseph,*[3] *Thomas,*[2] *Richard*[1]), eldest son of Seth Man, Sr.,
of Randolph, Mass., by third wife Deborah (Littlefield) Dyer, was
born there March 26, 1769. About 1792 he located at Braintree,
Vt., and purchased a farm, lot No. 14, second Div., Nov. 2, 1793.
Was selectman in 1803 and '4. He died there in 1813. He mar-
ried April 16, 1794, Matilda Fuller. She survived him and married
Isaac Lathrop, about 1815. She was born Dec. 28, 1781, and died
Nov. 14, 1867. The children of Job Mann, of Braintree, Vt.:

i. RELEPHA,[6] b. Aug. 31, 1795; d. Feb. 26, 1815.
ii. MATILDA,[6] b. April 3, 1797; d. in Penn. Dec. 1855; m. first,
Benj. H. Warriner, Sept. 29, 1814. He was formerly of
Conn., lived in Braintree a few years, then moved to Steuben
County, Penn.; m. second, Ebenezer Littlefield, of Easton,
Mass. She has six children living in Penn.
iii. ASENETH,[6] b. Feb. 14, 1800; d. April 17, 1848; m. Ebenezer
Littlefield, Dec. 4, 1821, and have one daughter living in
Braintree, Vt.
iv. JOB,[6] b. Dec. 17, 1801; d. May or Aug. 9, 1806.
v. JEHIEL,[6] b. Sept. 12, 1803; d. May 14, 1806.
vi. BETSEY,[6] b. Feb. 1, 1805; m. first, Wm. Lyons, 1825; second,
David Wellington. She d. April 28, 1878. She has five
children now living at Brookfield, Vt.
vii. PHILINDA,[6] b. April 5, 1807; d. Aug. 21, 1821.
viii. JOB,[6] b. Jan. 7, 1809; d. Feb. 27, 1832.
72. ix. IRA,[6] b. July 23, 1811; m. first, Polly Morse.

(32) ELISHA[5] MANN

(*Seth,*[4] *Joseph,*[3] *Thomas,*[2] *Richard*[1]), the fourteenth child of Seth
Man, Sr., of Randolph, Mass., was born Feb. 4, 1771. He was a
farmer at "West Corner," having come into possession of one half

13

of his father's farm by will. He was admitted a member of the First Congregational Church in Randolph in 1800; elected deacon in 1819, and resigned in 1841. He married Abigail, daughter of Lieut. Jacob Whitcomb, who was born in 1775 and died in 1843. Dea. Elisha Mann lived to a ripe old age. He was living in 1858. The following were the children, born in Randolph:

     i.   MARY,[6] b. May 4, 1798; d. March 13, 1848; m. first, her cousin, Levi Mann, Jan. 16, 1817; second, Dea. Ziba Spear, July 15, 1834; third, a Rollins.

     ii.   LORENA,[6] b. Oct. 7, 1800; m. Warren White, of Randolph, Mass., March 13, 1828; had children: (1) *Charles Warren*,[7] b. Dec. 17, 1828, who m. Emeline Stanton, 1857; she d. 1857; and he m. Eliza Lambert, 1858, and has *Charles Warren*,[8] Jr., b. Aug. 20, 1859; residence, Boston Highlands. (2) *Ephraim Mann*,[7] b. March 7, 1830; m. Mary Frances Niles, 1855; she d. 1859; and he m. Carrie Richards, 1861. Was a member of the 47th Regiment Mass. Vols., and d. at Randolph, July 4, 1869. Had by first wife, *Herbert Warren*,[8] b. Nov. 12, 1859, a graduate of Harvard College, and a physician at Boston Highlands. (3) *Rufus Thayer*,[7] b. Dec. 30, 1833; m. Carrie H. Clancy, 1859. He d. Dec. 13, 1861. He had *Everett*,[8] b. Jan. 20, 1861; d. Dec. 16, 1861. (4) *Lucy Ann*,[7] b. July 9, 1836; d. unmarried, May 1, 1862. (5) *Elisha Mann*,[7] b. June 20, 1841; m. Amelia Hopkins, Jan. 17, 1865. He was graduated at the Jefferson Medical College of Philadelphia, and was surgeon of the 37th Regiment Mass. Vols. Now in business in Boston, Mass. Has one son, *Franklin Warren*,[8] b. Oct. 23, 1869.

73. iii.   ELISHA,[6] b. March 31, 1803; m. first, Catharine Tucker.

74. iv.   ADONIRAM JUDSON,[6] b. March 28, 1805; m. Rosetta Howard.

     v.   RACHEL,[6] b. May 17, 1807; d. Dec. 23, 1857; m. Dea. Wales Thayer, June 21, 1827, who d. Feb. 16, 1856; residence, Randolph, Mass. Children: (1) *Wales*,[7] b. May 2, 1829; m. Sarah A. Packard, 1850. The widow of *Wales*[7] resides at Malden, and has a son, *Alvah Wales*,[8] b. Feb. 5, 1857, who resides there, married, and has children: *Frank A.*,[9] and *Wales G.*[9] (2) *Mary Ann*,[7] b. Nov. 4, 1833; m. June 8, 1854, Abner L. Cushing, a lawyer, of New York city. No children. (3) *Edward*,[7] b. Jan. 17, 1836; d. Jan. 12, 1862; an industrious and amiable young man.

     vi.   ESTHER,[6] b. Aug. 6, 1809; d. March 11, 1881; m. Thomas Lamson, of Randolph, Vt., and had: (1) *Irvin*.[7] (2) *Jasper*.[7] (3) *Mary Helen*.[7] (4) *Edwin*.[7] (5) *Joseph*.[7] (6) *Elisha W.*[7]

     vii.   ABIGAIL WHITCOMB,[6] b. Nov. 1, 1811; d. suddenly Dec. 1, 1829.

     viii.   LUCINDA,[6] b. April 12, 1814; d. Sept. 4, 1879; m. Zachariah Tucker, of Canton, Mass., and had: (1) *Dexter*.[7] (2) *Fred-*

eric.[7] (3) *Albert.*[7] (4) *Mary Abby.*[7] (5) *Annie,*[7] m. Willie
F. Brett, of Brockton, Mass., and have *Arthur*[8] and *Mary
Lucinda.*[8]

75. ix. ASA[6] (Rev.), b. April 9, 1816; m. Mary W. Bruce.
      x. ANNA,[6] b. April 9, 1816; m. Ira Odell, of Randolph, Mass.,
          about 1834, and had: (1) *Laura Ann,*[7] b. December, 1834;
          m. Sept. 23, 1863, Charles Conner, of Exeter, N. H. (2)
          Janette F.,[7] m. Samuel A. Capen, of Randolph, 1861, and
          had *Carroll,*[8] b. April 17, 1875. (3) *Herbert,*[7] b. Nov. 29,
          1841; m. May 3, 1871, Emma Bellows. He is a member
          of the firm of Thompson & Odell, Boston, where he resides.
          They have *Herbert F.,*[8] b. August, 1872. (4) *Alice,*[7] b. Aug.
          29, 1843; m. March 28, 1871, Elmer W. Holmes, of Brock-
          ton, Mass., and removed to California. They have *Annie
          L.,*[8] b. May 21, 1872.
76. xi. EPHRAIM,[6] b. April 18, 1820; m. first, Mary Jane Leeds.

(33) JOHN[5] MANN

(*Seth,*[4] *Joseph,*[3] *Thomas,*[2] *Richard*[1]), the youngest of eighteen children, was born at the old homestead in Randolph, Mass., Nov. 18,
1777. He always lived on the farm that was purchased by his
grandfather, Joseph Man, in 1734. He was a substantial farmer,
and a respected citizen of the town. He died Aug. 28, 1865, aged
nearly 88. He married first, Jane, daughter of Dea. Benjamin
Tucker, in 1804, who was born July 23, 1783, died May 4, 1846.
He married second, in 1847, Lydia, daughter of William Reed, whose
first husband was James Holbrook, of Braintree, Mass. "During the
1812 war, John Mann and Noah Thayer (the latter went in place
of Dea. Elisha Mann, who took charge of his brother's farm during
their absence) went to Richmond, Va., for their nephew, Seth Mann,
Esq., a Boston merchant, carrying 6,000 pounds weight each of West
India goods, flour, tea, etc., bringing home tobacco and cigars.
They went with two yoke of oxen and a horse each, and were gone
from home about six months. The horses stood the journey well;
but only two of the oxen returned."—(Letter of Miss L. H. Mann,
of Randolph, Mass.) John Mann by wife Jane had the following
children, born in Randolph:

77. i. JOHN,[6] b. Jan. 11, 1805; m. Emily Howard.
78. ii. ALVAN,[6] b. Dec. 6, 1806; m. Emeline Mitchell.
     iii. JANE TUCKER,[6] b. March 23, 1808; m. Artemas Aldrich, May
          30, 1830. Mr. Aldrich removed from Randolph to Wrentham,

Mass., in 1837, and was chosen one of the trustees of the Congregational Church of that town in 1853, and served as such ever since. He was one of the selectmen in Wrentham for the years 1863–'64, and from 1870 to 1875; chosen a deacon in 1868. Children: (1) *Sarah Jane*,[7] b. July 17, 1832; d. 1860. (2) *Harrison Artemus*,[7] b. Jan. 29, 1841; m. Cora Bearse, 1873, and have two children; residence, Dorchester District. (3) *Harriet Eliza*,[7] b. Dec. 24, 1844; d. June, 1883; m. George A. Stanton, Jr., 1882; residence, Wrentham. Has two sons: *John Mann*,[8] in college, and *Frank*.[8] (4) *Charles Mann*,[7] b. July 22, 1846; m. first, Harriet A. Fisher (one son); m. second, Eva Harris (one daughter).

79. iv.　SETH,[6] b. April 1, 1810; m. Eliza Hunt.

v.　DEBORAH,[6] b. April 16, 1812; m. George Jones, May 23, 1833. Had two children: (1) *Soreans M.*,[7] b. Feb. 20, 1836; m. Mary Orcutt, and have one child; residence, Randolph. (2) *Elizabeth A.*,[7] b. Dec. 31, 1833; m. John Bigelow; residence, Randolph, Vt.

80. vi.　BENJAMIN[6] (Dr.), b. March 31, 1814; m. Emily C. Morse.

81. vii.　JONATHAN[6] (Dr.), b. March 16, 1816; m. Marietta Rollins.

viii.　SUSAN,[6] b. March 27, 1820; d. Sept. 9, 1859; m. Otis Ryder, April 5, 1838, and went to Wisconsin. Had eleven children, four now living, viz.: (1) *Waldo*,[7] m. and resides in Burlington, Iowa. (2) *Ella Frances*,[7] b. 1843; m. J. M. Foster; resides in Crystal, Iowa. (3) *Abby Ann*,[7] m. S. Wilcox, a farmer in Baraboo, Wis. (4) *Ebenezer*,[7] resides in Bushnell, Ill.; employed by Chicago & Great Eastern Railroad.

(34) EPHRAIM[5] MANN

(*Ephraim*,[4] *Joseph*,[3] *Thomas*,[2] *Richard*[1]), the third child and eldest son of Ephraim Man, Sr., of Dorchester, Mass., by wife Sarah Glover was born there in December, 1764. He (?) was in Lemuel Clap's company in 1780, and probably resided in South Boston, Mass., as he had considerable real estate there. He probably died in 1803, as his will, or his father's (same name), is recorded at Dedham, Mass. He married Rebecca Lindsey, of Charlestown, Mass., Oct. 30, 1797, who died there (a widow) March 15, 1832, aged 72, leaving a will. They left a son William, and perhaps Sarah and Mary. Child:

i.　WILLIAM,[6] b. probably about 1798; m. probably twice. He owned real estate in Weston, Mass., in 1833; a resident and real estate owner in Holliston, Mass., in 1835, and later. He had the following children, living in the town of Holliston and vicinity in 1857: (2) *Caroline*.[7] (3) *James*.[7] (4) *Benjamin J.*[7] (5) *Sarah J.*,[7] m. Sewall Partridge, of Medway, Mass.

(6) *Ann Maria[7]*; (7) *Emeline,[7]* who was dead in 1837.—See Middlesex Deeds, Vol. 367, p. 145; also Rebecca Mann's will,—Suffolk Prob. Rec., No. 29,838. Probably the eldest son by first wife was *William,[7]* who m. Sophronia ———. He died in Billerica, Mass., 1852, leaving a will. No children mentioned.

(35)   BENJAMIN[5] MANN

(*Benjamin,[4] Benjamin,[3] Thomas,[2] Richard[1]*) was born in Hanover, Mass., March 3, 1753, and died there Dec. 12, 1820. He was the eldest son of Benjamin Man, Jr., probably by first wife, Abigail Gill. His name is on the pay roll of Capt. Joseph Soper's company, "to Bristol," 1776. His residence was on Curtis Street, in Hanover, south of where the Baptist meeting-house now stands. He married Hannah Sears, of Halifax, Mass., Aug. 20, 1774, who died at Hanover, May 21, 1827, aged seventy-five. Children, born in Hanover:

i.   HANNAH,[6] b. Jan. 3, 1776; d. Nov. 2, 1859; m. first, Thomas Whiting, June 8, 1797; he was born Aug. 16, 1776, lived on Whiting Street, Hanover, Mass., and d. 1806. Children: (1) *Marcia,[7]* b. May, 1798. (2) *Jairus,[7]* moved to N. Y. state. (3) *Oren,[7]* (m. first, Sarah C. Faxon, who d. Feb. 20, 1827; m. second, Mary Jones, 1831, lived on Whiting St., and had *Lewis,[8]* 1832; *Oren T.,[8]* 1834; *Lucius,[8]* 1837; *Abel H.,[8]* 1841, d. 1842; *Abel H.,[8]* 1843; *Albert,[8]* 1846; *Jno. B.,[8]* 1849. (4) *Lewis.[7]* (5) *Hannah,[7]* m. Elisha Faxon, of Abington, Mass. *Hannah[6]* (widow) m. second, Elisha Faxon (b. in Braintree, Mass., Dec. 7, 1771), Oct. 1818. No children.

ii. SARAH,[6] b. 1778; m. John Curtis, of Hanover, 1798 (selectman, 1822). He d. 1851, aged eighty. Had (1) *Sally,[7]* b. 1799; m. Ezra Whiting. (2) *John,[7]* 1801; d. 1817. (3) *William,[7]* 1803. (4) *Benjamin,[7]* 1807. (5) *Martin,[7]* 1810. (6) *Alathea,[7]* 1812. (7) *John,[7]* 1816, who m. Marian A. Fuller, of Boston, 1845, and was a merchant in Boston. (8) *Lucinda,[7]* 1819; m. Joseph H. Studley, 1839.

iii. RUTH,[6] b. Oct. 14, 1779; m. Isaac Wilder, and lived on Main Street, in Hanover, where he died, March 30, 1818, aged forty-one. The widow survived many years. They had: (1) *Ruth,[7]* b. 1803; m. Vaniah Prouty, Sept. 11, 1822. (2) *Isaac M.,[7]* June 19, 1805, trader at Hanover; m. Lucinda Eells, Feb. 5, 1834, and had: *Isaac,[8]* Nov. 15, 1834; *Joseph E.,[8]* 1839; *Lucinda,[8]* 1841. (3) *Hannah,[7]* 1807; d. 1829. (4) *Jno.[7]* 1809; m. Mary Tolman, and lived at Bridgewater, Mass. (5) *David,[7]* 1812. (6) *Caleb,* died young.

(36) LEVI³ MANN

(*Benjamin,*⁴ *Benjamin,*³ *Thomas,*² *Richard*¹), of Hanover, Mass., was
born there Sept. 9, 1757, and died January 12, 1818. He was one
of an independent company stationed at Hull, March 1, 1777.* Soon
after, he went to New York, married Anne Cooley (a widow),
and had two children. She died, and he returned to his native town
and erected a house on Main Street, about 1790. He married second,
Patience Donnell, who died March 8, 1845, aged eighty-five, leaving a
will. All the children except the two oldest were born in Hanover.

    i. EZRA,⁶ b. in N. Y., April, 21, 1780, located at Beverly, Mass.,
      m. there, Nabby Glover, of Beverly, and had: (1) *Abigail,*⁷
      b. June 20, 1802; d. in Quincy, Mass., Oct. 18, 1822. (2)
      *Ezra,*⁷ b. Oct. 1806; went to sea, and never heard from.

82. ii. LEVI,⁶ b. in N. Y., Jan. 6, 1782; m. Margaret Ames.
    iii. ALEXANDER,⁶ b. Feb. 9, 1785; d. in South Carolina, Nov. 17,
      1812.

83. iv. JAIRUS,⁶ b. Oct. 7, 1787; m. Desire Whiting.
    v. PATIENCE,⁶ b. May 1, 1791; m. first, Ebenezer Arnold; second,
      Joseph Cole; third, Job Pratt.
    vi. ANNE K.,⁶ b. Dec. 2, 1792; m. Henry Stoddard, who lived in
      Hanover, Mass., had: (1) *Ann C.,*⁷ b. 1815. (2) *Mary C.,*⁷
      1817. (3) *William B.,*⁷ 1820. (4) Capt. *Duncan T.,*⁷
      1823. (5) *Abby S.,*⁷ 1825. (6) *Isabella R.,*⁷ m. Henry
      Mann, June 13, 1850. (7) *Joseph A.,*⁷ 1830. (8) *Henry
      A.,*⁷ 1833. (9) *Patience E.,*⁷ 1835. (10) *Levi M.,*⁷ 1838.

84. vii. JOHN,⁶ b. Jan. 25, 1795; m. Harriet Turner.
85. viii. JOSEPH,⁶ b. Oct. 12, 1797; m. Eunice Jacobs.
    ix. SARAH,⁶ b. June 12, 1799; d. Dec. 21, 1832.
    x. MARY,⁶ b. June 27, 1801; d. Jan. 6, 1884; m. Wm. Henderson,
      1821; d. in California about 1848. His widow lived in
      Hanover after 1853. They had: (1) *William L.,*⁷ b. May 18,
      1823 (who now owns a farm at North Marshfield, Mass.).
      (2) *Mary M.,*⁷ 1830. (3) *Samuel A.,*⁷ 1833. (4) *Lloyd
      G.,*⁷ 1836. (5) *Joseph M.,*⁷ 1840.
    xi. AMY or EMMA,⁶ b. April 30, 1803; m. Dea. John Brooks, of
      Hanover, Dec. 4, 1823. Mr. Brooks was a "respected and
      intelligent farmer," and lived in the house built by Levi
      Mann, about 1790. Children: (1) *John S.,*⁷ b. 1824. (2)
      *Levi C.,*⁷ 1827. (3) *Joseph W.,*⁷ 1829. (4) *Emma,*⁷ 1831.
      (5) *Sarah M.,*⁷ 1832. (6) *Ara,*⁷ 1835. (7) *Mary E.,*⁷
      1837. (8) *Hannah E.,*⁷ 1840. (9) *Thomas D.,*⁷ 1843.
      (10) *Elizabeth,*⁷ 1845. (11) *George M.,*⁷ d. 1850.

* See Marshall's Washington, vol. i. p. 106.

(37) Capt. JOSHUA[4] MANN

(*Benjamin,*[4] *Benjamin,*[3] *Thomas,*[2] *Richard*[1]) was born in Hanover,
Mass., July 14, 1759, and was third son of Benjamin Mann, Jr., of
the same town. His name appears on three different pay-rolls from
1776 to 1778, as having served in the Revolutionary war. He was
afterwards a captain of one of the military companies of the town of
Hanover, and lived on Whiting Street. Was selectman from 1799
to 1802, and in 1812 was one of the " Committee of Safety." He
died in Hanover, Oct. 20, 1827 (Grave-stone Rec., Dec. 20, 1827).
He married Mary Cushing, of Hingham, Jan. 30, 1783, who died
July 2, 1849, aged ninety-three. Children, born in Hanover :

	i.	Joshua,[6] b. 1784; d. Oct. 3, 1792.
	ii.	Molly,[6] b. 1785; d. Sept. 23, 1792.
86.	iii.	Benjamin[6] (Esq.), b. 1788; d. 1861; m. first, Lydia Josselyn.
	iv.	Mary,[6] b. 1794; m. Oren Josselyn, Feb. 14, 1816, and had: (1) *Oren,*[7] b. 1817; d. 1819. (2) *Mary C.,*[7] 1820. (3) *Eli C.,*[7] 1822. (4) *Charles,*[7] 1826. (5) *Jane R.,*[7] 1829; d. 1830. (6) *George R.,*[7] 1834. Mr. Josselyn lived on King Street, Hanover, and was connected with the foundry. He was Representative from 1842-'44, town clerk 1839 and '41 and from '43-'45, also selectman a number of years.
87.	v.	Joshua[6] (Maj.), b. July 4, 1796; d. 1875; m. Bethia Curtis.
88.	vi.	David,[6] b. Sept. 7, 1798; m. Betsey Mann (cousin).*

(38) PEREZ[5] MANN

(*Benjamin,*[4] *Benjamin,*[3] *Thomas,*[2] *Richard*[1]), son of Benjamin Man,
Jr., by wife Abigail (Gill), of Hanover, Mass., and was born there,
according to the Hanover records, Nov. 7, 1768. The family records say, "Nov. 4-17-1769." Before arriving at his majority,
we find him located at Beverly, Mass., where he lived, and died
Aug. 20, 1848. He was a real-estate owner in the centre of the
village, and it is said he was one of the builders of the "Beverly
Bridge," in 1788. He married Abigail, daughter of Capt. Israel
Johnson, of Beverly, at the age of seventeen, who was born Aug.
31, 1774, and who died there June 25, 1851. Children :

| | i. | Israel J.,[6] b. June 2, 1791; d. Sept. 12, 1792. |
| | ii. | Perez,[6] b. Jan. 15, 1794; lost at sea 1814. |

---

* The information concerning Hanover families is taken in part from Barry's Hist.
of Hanover.

iii. ABIGAIL,[6] b. April 6, 1796; m. Col. Henry Batchelder, and had fourteen children. Dr. Batchelder, of Salem, a son.

iv. ANNA,[6] b. Feb. 3, 1798; d. Aug. 23, 1876; m. Capt. Jeremiah Porter, who died 1878, aged eighty-seven.

v. OLIVE,[6] b. Dec. 18, 1799; d. Aug. 18, 1800.

vi. ELIZA,[6] b. Sept. 26, 1801; d. 1872 or '3; m. Oct. 6, 1826, Col. David Upton, b. Dec. 6, 1799; d. 1882 or '3.

vii. OLIVE,[6] b. July 20, 1803; d. May 6, 1837; m. —— Elliott.

viii. ISRAEL,[6] Jr., b. July 5, 1805; lost at sea Aug. 22, 1829.

ix. HARRIET E.,[6] b. June 21, 1807; d. Nov. 1881; m. —— Needham.

x. CHARLES,[6] b. May 28, 1810; d. in Cuba, May 23, 1826.

xi. GEORGE and EDWARD,[6] b. May 26, 1811; d. May 29, 1811.

xii. LUCY JOHNSON,[6] b. Nov. 1, 1812; d. Jan. 4, 1876; m. —— Larrabee.

xiii. EMELINE,[6] b. April 22, 1815; d. April 21, 1835.

(39) ENSIGN[5] MANN, JR.

(*Ensign,*[4] *Ensign,*[3] *Thomas,*[2] *Richard*[1]), third child and oldest son of Ensign Man, of Petersham, Mass., by wife Alice (oldest daughter of Rev. Aaron Whitney), was born there on the farm at the north part of the town, July 14, 1778.

It is said he was a young man of great promise, energetic in purpose, kind-hearted, and of vigorous frame, but afflicted from youth with what was called "bilious colic," and died in a severe attack of that disease May 11, 1810, with the injunction on his lips, "take good care of my son William," then an infant of nine and a half months. He was buried near his mother, in the yard at the centre of the town, in the north part of the Rev. Aaron Whitney's burial lot. He owned the homestead farm, in company with his brother Thomas, it having been deeded them by their father April 16, 1806. In addition to this, he and Thomas had purchased an estate and mill privilege adjacent, the old growth pine timber of which (since sold) proved to be one of the most valuable lots in the county. In the division of this property after Ensign's decease, the widow made choice of the homestead estate (she not realizing, at the time, the prospective value of the timber), while Thomas reluctantly accepted the timber lot and mill property as his share. The original farm is owned by the descendants, having been in the family more than a hundred years. Ensign, Jr., married about 1808, Lydia (born about 1782), daughter of George and Sarah (Norcross) Filmore,* of Shrewsbury, Mass., and by her had two children, born on the Thomas Mann farm (prospectively Ensign, Jr's.), in Petersham. The widow married second, James J. Sanderson, 1815, and died April 23, 1865.

89.   i.   WILLIAM,[6] b. July 25, 1809, m. Abigail Cook, Nov. 20, 1833.
      ii.   SALLY NORCROSS,[6] b. Oct. 16, 1810; m. May 23, 1833, Peter Harwood Marsh, a carpenter, of Petersham; he d. March 21, 1873. Children: (1) *Charlotte*,[7] b. May 29, 1834; m. Wm. E. Lehman; four children. (2) *Sarah*,[7] b. Sept. 27, 1835; m. Henry S. Hager; four children. (3) *James S.*,[7] b. 1837; d. 1839. (4) *Ensign A.*,[7] b. Aug. 11, 1839; m. Lydia Rice; three children; a farmer; residence, Petersham. (5) *Julia J.*,[7] b. 1842; d. 1846. (6) *Amos A.*,[7] b. 1844; d. 1846. (7) Infant, d. 1845. (8) *Julia A.*,[7] b. 1847; d. 1852. (9) *Henry A.*,[7] b. 1850; d. 1851. (10) *Ella*,[7] b. July 10, 1852; m. Edgar L. Barrows; three children.

(40) THOMAS[3] MANN

(*Ensign*,[4] *Ensign*,[3] *Thomas*,[2] *Richard*[1]), the second son of Ensign Man, of Petersham, Mass., by wife Alice (Whitney) Man, was born there on the homestead farm May 6, 1780. After he became of age we find the two brothers, Ensign, Jr., and Thomas, in joint ownership of the farm, formerly their father's, and a large tract of timber land, with mill privilege adjacent. After the decease of Ensign, Jr., in 1810, by adjustment, Thomas came in possession of the last mentioned estate, settled upon these lands, took his father (whose wife had deceased in 1806) to support, and by the rapid growth of the pine forests accumulated a handsome property. He was of slender frame, good height, a man of strict integrity, moderate in movement, and had a well balanced mind. (The editor of this work lived in this family during the summer of 1848.) He died suddenly at Fitchburg, Mass., Dec. 24, 1853, of heart disease, while on a busi-

* George Filmore, born about 1742, it is said, in Martin, Surrey Co., England, served in the Continental Army, and enjoyed a pension. He died at Shrewsbury, Mass., Sept. 29, 1832, aged about 90. His widow survived, and died in Petersham, Mass., in 1840, aged about 95.—(See Ward's Hist. of Shrewsbury.)

14

ness trip. He married Miss Esther Stone, of Petersham, who survived him, and died May 7, 1858. Children, all born in Petersham:

    i. CLARK,[6] b. June 11, 1808; d. unmarried in Petersham, Dec. 12, 1845. He was a carpenter, built the house, and owned the estate next south of the Dr. William Parkhurst place in Petersham.

    ii. JOSIAH,[6] b. Sept. 24, 1810; d. unmarried, Nov. 11, 1875.

    iii. ALICE W.,[6] b. Sept. 8, 1812; d. at Athol, Mass., February, 1878; m. Joseph Stratton, of Athol, July 14, 1842. Children: (1) *Horace M.,*[7] b. May 12, 1843. (2) *Clark M.,*[7] b. Nov. 3, 1845; d. April 3, 1846. (3) *Frederic E.,*[7] b. July 5, 1847; grad. Williams College; m. ——— Goldsbury.

    iv. ELIZABETH S.,[6] b. Aug. 12, 1814; unmarried; d. Sept. 10, 1834.

    v. DWIGHT,[6] b. July 20, 1816; d. Aug. 31, 1849, in Grafton, Mass., where he owned a farm. He m. Ann Carpenter, who d. Sept. 23, 1848, aged 28. One son, *Charles C.,*[7] d. Aug. 2, 1849, aged 11 months 4 days.

90. vi. LOTT,[6] b. Oct. 24, 1818; m. Mrs. Emily Dennis.

91. vii. THOMAS MARSHALL,[6] b. June 30, 1821; m. M. E. Ferguson.

    viii. ESTHER ELVIRA,[6] b. May 28, 1823; d. unmarried, Dec. 20, 1855.

    ix. PRISCILLA A.,[6] b. Dec. 4, 1825; d. April 3, 1853; m. Austin Ellenwood, of Athol. Had one daughter, *Eliza Maria*[7] (M. D.), b. June 16, 1849; she is a practising physician in New York State; unmarried.

    x. ANGELINE F.,[6] b. March 14, 1828; d. unmarried, June 18, 1859.

(41) SAMUEL[5] MANN

(*Ensign,*[4] *Ensign,*[3] *Thomas,*[2] *Richard*[1]), the youngest son of Ensign Man, of Petersham, Mass., by wife Alice (Whitney) Man, was born Nov. 21, 1787, in that town, within a few rods of where he afterwards lived. Early in life he purchased the estate adjoining the homestead of his father; was a substantial and "well-to-do" farmer. He was a man of large frame, intelligent, honest, and of a religious cast of mind. He had a slight impediment in his speech, as was the case with his learned father. He died June 21, 1856. He married Sarah Luce, May 16, 1824, who survived her husband, and died Nov. 14, 1883. Children:

    i. RICHARD BAXTER,[6] b. Feb. 25, 1825; d. Feb. 7, 1835.

    ii. HARRIET MARIA,[6] b. Sept. 18, 1826; m. Frank Wheeler, Sept. 8, 1851, who owns the homestead farm. Children:

       (1) *Arthur Henry,*[7] b. March 8, 1858. (2) *Frank Mann,*[7] June 28, 1865. (3) *Sarah Marian,*[7] May 29, 1869.

    iii. CAROLINE LUANA,[6] b. Sept. 27, 1828; d. unmarried Oct. 6, 1850.

    iv. ASAPH,[6] b. Oct. 12, 1830; d. Jan. 25, 1832.

92.   v. SAMUEL,[6] b. Oct. 21, 1832; m. Maria Antoinette Luce (cousin).

    vi. WILLIAM HENRY,[6] b. Sept. 8, 1835; d. at New Iberia, La., April 23, 1865. He enlisted in Capt. John G. Mudge's Petersham company, Oct. 17, 1862, and lost his life in the service. He was a school-mate of the author, a brave and talented fellow. He married Susan Bancroft, March 6, 1856. No issue.

(42) JOEL[5] MANN

(*Joseph,*[4] *Nathaniel,*[3] *Richard,*[2] *Richard*[1]), the eldest son (who survived infancy) of Joseph Man, Sr., by second wife, Hannah (Gilbert) Man of Hebron, Conn., was born there Oct. 1, 1743. He married his cousin, Mercy Mann, daughter of John and Margaret (Peters) Man, of Hebron, Oct. 16, 1768. He was a farmer and a highly respected citizen of the town. About the year 1793 or '4 he removed to Milton, Saratoga County, N. Y., where he purchased a farm, and died there Nov. 24, 1824, and his wife May 17, 1820. Children, all born in Hebron except Joseph:

93.   i. RODOLPHUS,[6] b. June 8, 1769; m. first, Lydia Horton.

94.   ii. JEREMIAH,[6] b. Nov. 14, 1771; m. first, Lydia Norton.

95.   iii. SAMUEL,[6] b. June 18, 1776; d. March 23, 1831.

    iv. MERCY,[6] b. April 7, 1779; d. Sept. 8, 1848; m. Dr. Elijah Hanchett, and had: *Mary Ann,*[7] b. at Salisbury, N. Y., Oct. 26, 1804, who m. Russell Mann, 1829.

96.   v. JOEL[6] (Dr.), b. Sept. 16, 1784; m. Sallie Merrick.

    vi. HIRAM[6] (Dr.), b. Aug. 21, 1787; d. Oct. 2, 1855, at Lyons, N. Y. "He m. 1819, Sophia Bigelow, a cultivated lady of Poultney, Vt., settled at Lyons, N. Y., in 1833, was sheriff of Wayne County, of high standing in society and in the Episcopal church. Mrs. Mann died at Lyons, March 19, 1871, aged eighty-one. She had a memorial window placed in the church for the doctor and her son. There is a very handsome monument and well kept lot with stone and iron fence around it, etc. Their only son, *Bigelow,*[7] was drowned June 28, 1839, aged seventeen." [Letter of Mrs. G. Van Marter.]

    vii. JOSEPH,[6] b. Oct. 26, 1794 (non compos.); d. Oct. 13, 1883.

(43) ZADOCK⁵ MANN

(*Joseph,*⁴ *Nathaniel,*³ *Richard,*² *Richard*¹), of Ashtabula, Ohio, was
born at Hebron, Conn., Feb. 7, 1759, and was the eighth child and
fourth son of Joseph Man, Sr., of that town, by second wife Hannah
Gilbert. He married first, Esther Warner, of Waterbury, Conn.,
Sept. 18, 1780, who was thrown from a wagon and killed, in Ashtabula, July 9, 1825, aged sixty-six. He early removed to Ashtabula,
where he was called a farmer, by trade a cooper. He and a
few other persons established the Episcopal church in that town.
He married second, Hannah Williams, who died Jan. 24, 1846, aged
seventy-six. He died from the result of a fall from the scaffold in
his barn, at East Plymouth, Ohio, Sept. 29, 1846. Children by first
wife :

96a.　i.　Eliel,⁶ b. Sept. 3, 1781; d. in Conn.
　　　ii.　Esther,⁶ m. Dr. David Warner, and had ten children.
97.　iii.　Warner,⁶ b. Feb. 16, 1784; m. first, Amanda Blakeslee.
98.　iv.　Joseph,⁶ b. April 12, 1792; d. 1867.
　　　v.　Maria,⁶ b. 1796; d. Dec. 15, 1880; m. Collins Wetmore,
　　　　　Dec. 31, 1813 (farmer), of Plymouth, Ohio, who was a
　　　　　soldier in 1812, b. Sept. 16, 1786, d. Aug. 15, 1859.
　　　　　They had: (1) *Nancy Maria,*⁷ b. Dec. 6, 1816; m. H. J.
　　　　　B. Seymour, of Ashtabula. (2) *Gilbert M.,*⁷ Nov. 5, 1818.
　　　　　(3) *Juliaette,*⁷ Nov. 20, 1820; m. Burton Seymour, of
　　　　　Cal. (4) *Joseph Warner,*⁷ Feb. 7, 1823; m. Sarah Hall.
　　　　　(5) *Collins,*⁷ d. (infant) 1825. (6) *Eleanor,*⁷ Aug. 12,
　　　　　1826; m. Milton Payne, of Kansas. (7) *Collins,*⁷ Feb. 4,
　　　　　1830; m. (8) *Horace Mann,*⁷ May 7, 1832, (farmer in
　　　　　Kansas, and m.) (9) *Theresa,*⁷ 1836. (10) *Jesse Cor-
　　　　　win,*⁷ June 4, 1840; m. Florence Buell; d. 1881 (soldier
　　　　　in civil war). Three died young.
　　　vi.　Fanny Mira,⁶ b. July 16, 1799; d. April 14, 1880; m. Jo-
　　　　　siah White, March 15, 1815, b. Feb. 19, 1789, d. Oct. 1,
　　　　　1863. They had: (1) *Sarah Jane,*⁷ b. July 9, 1816; m.
　　　　　Arthur Howard. (2) *Emory,*⁷ Oct. 3, 1818; m. Lucy
　　　　　Wood. (3) *David B.,*⁷ May 30, 1821; d. ——. (4)
　　　　　*Eliza,*⁷ Dec. 27, 1823; m. J. B. Robinson; d. ——. (5)
　　　　　*Perry,*⁷ Oct. 26, 1826; m. Phebe Clark, 1859. (6) *Wil-
　　　　　liam,*⁷ May 3, 1829; m. Adelia Cady, and resides at
　　　　　Monterey, Mich., and has *Orris,*⁸ *George,*⁸ *Perry,*⁸ *Lee.*⁸
　　　　　(7) *James,*⁷ Nov. 11, 1832; m. Anna Groff, 1855. (8)
　　　　　*Amanda M.,*⁷ May 25, 1837; m. A. Mallory, in 1858, res.
　　　　　Mich.

(44) JAMES⁵ MANN

(*Joseph,⁴ Nathaniel,³ Richard,² Richard¹*), the thirteenth child and
last surviving son of Joseph Man, Sr., of Hebron, Conn., was born
in that town, Feb. 24, 1768. He married Triphena Tarbox (born
Dec. 27, 1765) of Hebron, about 1790, in the Episcopal church, by
Rev. Dr. Bronson. In 1791 they removed to Ballston, N. Y., and
settled on a farm about one mile west of Ballston Springs, where
they resided until their decease. She died Nov. 1, 1850, and he
March 21, 1856, having been, at his death, forty years senior warden
of the Episcopal church. Children, born at Ballston, N. Y.:

	i.	HARVEY,⁶ b. and d. Sept. 26, 1791.
99.	ii.	JAMES,⁶ b. Aug. 10, 1792; d. 1873; m. Abigail Hedges.
	iii.	PATIENCE,⁶ b. Sept. 27, 1795; d. April 12, 1816.
	iv.	SOLOMON,⁶ b. Oct. 22, 1797; d. Sept. 5, 1805.
	v.	FANNY,⁶ b. Oct. 22, 1799; d. April 29, 1816.
	vi.	ELECTA,⁶ b. Oct. 16, 1801; d. Dec. 16, 1883, unmarried, at the homestead in Ballston. She was an intelligent correspondent and furnished the author with considerable genealogical information regarding this family.
100.	vii.	JOSEPH,⁶ b. March 21, 1804; m. first, Eveline Barrow.

(45) JOHN⁵ MANN*

(*John,⁴ Nathaniel,³ Richard,² Richard¹*), the eldest son of John
Man, Sr., of Hebron, Conn., by wife Margaret (Peters) Man, was
born there Dec. 25, 1743. He mar-
ried in 1765, Lydia, born March
17, 1746, daughter of John Porter,
of Hebron, "moved with her on horse-back" to Orford, N. H., in
Oct. 1765, and took possession of a lot of land (then a wilderness)
given him by his father. They arrived the 24th of Oct. 1765,
and passed the winter with a family who had previously arrived,
reared a hut and covered it with bark. "That family moved away,
so that Mr. Mann and wife were the first abiding settlers of the

---

* For a more minute account of this family and some of the descendants, see Rev.
Joel Mann's pamphlet, printed about 1873. In dealing with the earlier families, Rev.
Mr. Mann (adopting the views of the late R. R. Hinman, of Hartford) is in error
in claiming both William Man, the early settler of Cambridge, and Richard Man, the
early settler of Scituate, as ancestors of this Hebron, Conn., branch. See on p. 8.—ED.

town." After the arrival of other settlers and much clearing had been done, Mr. Mann purchased other lots, making a large farm, and fixed his residence in what has become the centre of a thriving village. He died there May 9, 1828, where a beautiful monument has been erected to his memory. His wife Lydia died March 5, 1805. It is said he married second, in advanced life, a widow Barber. He had fifteen children by wife Lydia, born at Orford, N. H., all of whom lived to marry and have children, except the two youngest.

101.   i.   JOHN,⁶ b. May 21, 1766; m. first, Lydia Dutton.
102.   ii.   SOLOMON,⁶ b. Aug. 19, 1768; m. Miss Parkhurst.
103.   iii. JARED,⁶ b. Nov. 6, 1770; m. Mindwell Hale.
104.   iv.   IRA,⁶ b. Sept. 8, 1772; m. first, —— Bailey.
105.   v.   AARON,⁶ b. July 21, 1774; m. first, Sally Melvin.
        vi.   LYDIA,⁶ b. Sept. 17, 1776; d. at Littleton, N. H., Dec. 29, 1851; m. Joseph Pratt, and had: *Joseph*,⁷ *John*,⁷ *Lydia*,⁷ and *Henry*,⁷ a landscape and portrait painter.
        vii. SARAH,⁶ b. June 4, 1778; d. at Orford, N. H., Nov. 5, 1864; m. Dr. Rogers, and had *Sarah Relief*.⁷
106.   viii. NATHANIEL,⁶ b. Dec. 29, 1779; m. Mary Mason.
107.   ix.   BENNING⁶ (Judge), b. Nov. 25, 1781; m. Phebe Mann.
108.   x.   ASAPH,⁶ b. Sept. 30, 1783; m. Mary Barker. *Barber*
109.   xi.   CYRUS⁶ (Rev.), b. April 3, 1785; m. Nancy Sweetser.
        xii. PHEBE,⁶ b. March 7, 1787; d. Nov. 25, 1871; m. Samuel Sargent, and had: *Asenith*,⁷ *Mary Jane*,⁷ *Mercy S.*,⁷ *William*,⁷ *George*,⁷ *John M.*,⁷ *Simon Bolivar*.⁷
110.   xiii. JOEL⁶ (Rev.), b. Feb. 7, 1789; m. Catherine Vernon.
        xiv. ABIJAH,⁶ b. April 3, 1791; d. March 8, 1809.
        xv.   Son, died in infancy.

(46) CAPT. ANDREW⁵ MANN

(*John*,⁴ *Nathaniel*,³ *Richard*,² *Richard*¹), the third son of John Man, Sr., by wife Margaret (Peters) Man, of Hebron, Conn., was born there March 18, 1755, and died in same town Oct. 5, 1846. He married April 29, 1779, Hannah (born Feb. 3, 1759), daughter of Sylvanus and Hannah Phelps, and settled on the old family farm, "which has been handed down without deed from father to son until the present generation." Mr. Mann served in the Revolution, and had a pension from the government. He was made captain at the time the British burnt New London, and marched there with his company. He was short in stature. "On his last birthday he went into his cooper shop, made a packing barrel, and afterwards walked

John Mann

BORN, DEC. 25th, 1743.

Picture taken shortly before decease, at 85 years.

a mile to visit one of his sons, and returned." His widow died
March 9, 1819. Children, born in Hebron :

     i. ANNE,[6] b. Jan. 18 or Feb. 14, 1780; m. Judah Porter.
        Children: *Charles*,[7] d. unmarried; *Randolph*;[7] *Flavel*,[7] m.
        Eliza Cook; *Samuel*,[7] m. ―――― Fitch; *Nathaniel*,[7] d. un-
        married; *Frank*,[7] m. Julia Hendee; *George M.*;[7] *Epaphro-*
        ditus[7]; *Abby*,[7] unmarried; *Mary Ann*,[7] m. ―――― Bliss.

111. ii. REUBEN,[6] b. April 18, 1782; m. Anna M. Phelps.
112. iii. ANDREW[6] (Col.), b. Sept. 14, 1784; m. Nancy Phelps.
     iv. PHEBE,[6] b. 1787; m. Judge Benning Mann (cousin).
     v. MANLIUS,[6] b. Jan. 2, 1789; d. July 12, 1809.
     vi. CYRUS,[6] b. June 20, 1794; d. Aug. 20, 1796.
     vii. MARTHA,[6] b. Feb. 9, 179–; d. Feb. 8, 1822; m. Elisha
        Wakeman.
113. viii. CYRUS[6] (Judge), b. July 27, 1797; m. Elizabeth Worthington.
     ix. HANNAH,[6] b. Feb. 2, 1799: d. Dec. 13, 1879, at Marshall,
        Mich.; m. Dr. Joseph Sibley. Had *Joseph*,[7] d. young;
        Harriet,[7] d. young; *Francis*,[7] who m. Louise Montgomery.
114. x. NATHANIEL,[6] b. July 21, 1803; m. first, Emma Rexford.

(47) ABIJAH[5] MANN

(*Abijah*,[4] *Nathaniel*,[3] *Richard*,[2] *Richard*[1]), the eldest son of Abijah
Man, Sr., by wife Sarah (Porter) Man, of Hebron, Conn., was born
in that town Dec. 21, 1761. It is said that at twenty-one or twenty-
two years of age, he located at Fairfield, Herkimer County, N. Y.,
and died at Batavia, N. Y., May 30, 1856 (was buried at Fairfield),
at the advanced age of nearly ninety-five years. He had a well-cul-
tivated farm of about two hundred acres at the time of his death.
He was one of the founders of the Fairfield Seminary, and one of
its first trustees. He was, no doubt, a man of considerable influence
in the community in which he lived. He married Levina Ford, who
was born Jan. 21, 1768, and by her had nine children, born at Fairfield, N. Y. It is said he married second, about 1825, Mary Wilsey.
Children :

     i. LEVINA,[6] b. Sept. 27, 1787; d. at Geneseo, Ill., Jan. 27,
        1882; m. Pliny Pomeroy, of Fairfield, N. Y., a hatter by
        trade, who d. in Leyden, N. Y., Aug. 21, 1856. They had:
        (1) *Ashbel S.*,[7] b. Aug. 27, 1810. (2) *Laura*,[7] b. July 24,
        1812; m. Daniel Knapp. (3) *Ralph M.*,[7] b. Jan. 8, 1815;
        m. Elmira Fleming; he is a retired merchant; resides in
        Boston. (4) *Mary S.*,[7] b. Nov. 18, 1816; m. James Smith.
        (5) *Sarah M.*,[7] b. Feb. 25, 1819; m. ――――. (6) *George*,[7]

b. Feb. 27, 1821; m. Nellie Blanchard; residence, Colona,
Ill. (7) *Almira*,[7] b. March 6, 1823; m. Steward Morton;
residence, Geneseo, Ill. (8) *Charles A.*,[7] b. June 20, 1825;
m. Sylvia West. (9) *Abijah M.*,[7] b. June 1, 1829; d.
March 20, 1831, at Leyden.

115. ii. JOEL,[6] b. Aug. 15, 1789; d. 1832; m. Betsey Cole.
iii. ELIZABETH,[6] b. Dec. 18, 1791; d. at Whitestown, N. Y.,
Dec. 31, 1876; m. Dr. Sylvester Miller, Aug. 10, 1809,
who d. at Lowville, N. Y., 1836. Their children were:
(1) *Hannibal*,[7] b. Sept. 10, 1810; m. Eliza Brownwer; no
children. (2) *Eliza F.*,[7] b. Dec. 5, 1812; m. Philip
Schuyler; they died, leaving a son, *Charles P.*,[8] who died
leaving a daughter, *Mary Van Rensselaer Schuyler*,[9] who is
now Mrs. L. Strade, of New York city. (3) *Levantia W.*,[7]
b. July 4, 1815; m. John Benedict, 1839, and had: *Miller*,[8] b. July 2, 1840, at Lowville, N. Y.; *J. Spencer*,[8] b.
1844, d. 1864 in Utica, New York, no children. (4)
Charles A.,[7] b. June 13, 1819; d. 1829. (5) *Mary L.*,[7] b.
January, 1825; m. Cornelius H. Wood, 1845, and resides at
Whitestown; children living, are: *Ela M.*,[8] *George L.*,[8]
Mary E.,[8] *Addison M.*,[8] *Spencer C.*,[8] *Annie K.*,[8] *James F.*[8]
(6) *Sarah F.*,[7] b. Aug. 26, 1828; d. Feb. 16, 1835. (7)
Addison C.,[7] b. Nov. 12, 1831; now a prominent lawyer
in Utica, of the firm of Miller & Fincke; he m. Cynthia
J. Brayton, April 29, 1863; has the following children:
Cynthia J.,[8] b. Feb. 24, 1866; *Charles A.*,[8] b. Dec. 29,
1867; *Howard C.*,[8] b. Dec. 18, 1872; *George Hervey*,[8]
b. Oct. 22, 1874; *Theodora*,[8] b. 1880; all reside with
their parents at Utica. (8) *Emma F.*,[7] b. Nov. 12, 1831
(twin sister to Addison C., Esq.); d. March 13, 1835.

116 iv. ABIJAH[6] (Hon.), b. Sept. 24, 1793; m. Mary Ann Bruce.
v. SARAH,[6] b. Feb. 27, 1795-7; unmarried; d. about 1870.
117. vi. AMASA,[6] b. Sept. 2, 1800; m. Alma Everett.
118. vii. CHARLES ADDISON[6] (Hon.), b. Jan. 16, 1803.
119. viii. WILLIAM H.,[6] b. Sept. 27, 1805.
ix. MARY ANN,[6] b. Aug. 19, 1812; d. Jan. 29, 1869; m. Madison
Merrill, Nov. 13, 1834; he was b. at Fairfield, N. Y.,
June 1, 1812, d. March 28, 1864. Children, born at Leyden, Lewis County, N. Y.: (1) *Martha B.*,[7] b. Feb. 8,
1837; m. 1855, Oscar L. Whetmore, civil engineer; d.
April 1, 1878, leaving one son, *Madison H.*,[8] b. Nov. 2,
1862, living with his mother at Boonville, N. Y. (2)
Abijah M.,[7] b. Jan. 2, 1839; m. Ellen R. Barrett (b. Jan.
23, 1844), of Talcottville, N. Y., Oct. 9, 1861, and have
four children: *Frederick Mann*,[8] b. July 30, 1862; *Walter
Booth*,[8] b. Aug. 29, 1869; *Augustus Divere*,[8] b. Sept. 11,
1872; *Louis Abijah*,[8] b. June 19, 1882. (3) *Helen E.*,[7]
b. July 15, 1844; m. Oct. 4, 1865, Roselle Jackson, a farmer in Boonville. (4) *Albert E.*,[7] b. Oct. 16, 1846; m.
Nov. 17, 1868, Sarah Bridgeman; he is a grocery and pro-

vision merchant in Boonville; had one son, *Herbert E.,*[8] b. Dec. 2, 1873. (5) *Charles F.,*[7] b. Sept. 23, 1849; m. March 5, 1872, Arvilla Jones, of Oswego; he is a carpenter, and resides at Thousand Island Park, Jefferson Co., N. Y.; had one daughter, *Ella M.,*[8] b. Nov. 15, 1877.

(48) AARON[5] MANN

(*Abijah,*[4] *Nathaniel,*[3] *Richard,*[2] *Richard*[1]), the second son of Abijah Man, Sr., was born in Hebron, Conn., Oct. 16, 1764. He married Chloe, daughter of Roger Clark, of Lebanon, Conn. About 1804, in company with his three brothers, Oliver, Daniel and Amasa, together with wife and four children, emigrated with an ox-team to Franklin, N. Y., and settled there, on a spot a little north of the present village. His wife died at Franklin, Sept. 7, 1805. Children:

    i. CLARVEY.[6]
    ii. ALTHA.[6]
    iii. AMASA,[6] d. February, 1826.
120.   iv. HORACE,[6] b. Jan 22, 1801; m. Sophronia Fitch.

(49) OLIVER[5] MANN

(*Abijah,*[4] *Nathaniel,*[3] *Richard,*[2] *Richard*[1]), the third son of Abijah Man, Sr., was born in Hebron, Conn., Nov. 14, 1768, and married first, Content Hills, of Mulberry, Conn. It is said he removed to Franklin, N. Y., in company with his brothers Aaron, Daniel, and Amasa, about 1804 (perhaps earlier); farmer. Children:

    i. AMASA PORTER,[6] b. Jan. 13, 1798; m. first, Sally Clark, 1823; m. second, Mary Kiniblor, of Franklin, N. Y., 1864. A physician and farmer in Meredith, N. Y., over forty years. Children: *Delos H.,*[7] *Onslow C.*[7]
    ii. PHILOXANIA,[6] b. 1799; d. about 1855.
    iii. ARISTOBULUS,[6] b. 1802; d. in infancy.
    iv. ARISTARCHUS,[6] b. 1802; d. 1871, Ill., widow living then and two children.
    v. LAURA,[6] b. 1804; m. Justin Judd, who died May, 1863.
    vi. ABIGAIL,[6] b. 1807; m. Joseph Judd, 1831 (brother of Justin). Three sons, one daughter.
    vii. OLIVER,[6] b. 1809; d. 1859; m. Jane, daughter of Samuel Kellogg, 1828, at Coventry, N. Y. He was a farmer "near Franklin, N. Y., and member of the Methodist church." Children: *Betsey,*[7] *Wallace,*[7] *Victory,*[7] *Washington,*[7] *Abijah,*[7] *Aristarchus,*[7] *Martha,*[7] *Emeline,*[7] *Nancy,*[7] *Josephine,*[7] *Carrie,*[7] *Frank,*[7] *Henry.*[7]
    viii. CONTENT,[6] b. 1811; d. April 1860; m. Osborne Knapp.

15

(50) DANIEL³ MANN

(*Abijah*,⁴ *Nathaniel*,³ *Richard*,² *Richard*¹), fourth son of Abijah
Man, Sr., of Hebron, Conn., was born in that town Jan. 18, 1771.
He married first, Molly, daughter of Roger Case, of Hebron, 1789.
He first settled at Franklin, N. Y. Sometime previous to 1840
he purchased a farm in Smyrna, N. Y., but soon after disposed of
this and purchased one in De Ruyter, N. Y., of Seth Shepard, in
1840. His wife died in De Ruyter, and he married second, Miss
Cone, of Lincklaen, N. Y. Children, by first wife:

   i. POLLY,⁶ b. Aug. 1795; m. Marvin Miller, 1819, who died
     1862, aged seventy. They had: (1) *Mary Ann.*⁷ (2)
     *Ezra.*⁷ (3) *Amasa.*⁷ (4) *Daniel.*⁷

121. ii. ERASTUS,⁶ b. Jan. 20, 1797; m. first, Diana Billings.

122. iii. HARVEY,⁶ b. Sept. 22, 1798; m. Marcia Collins.

   iv. PHEBE,⁶ b. Aug. 20, 1801; m. R. Sears, 1835, who lived in
     Columbus, N. Y.; four children, *Harland,*⁷ *Barney.*⁷

   v. DANIEL,⁶ Jr., b. May 20, 1803; m. first, Mary A. Jeffords,
     1829, who d. 1837; m. second, Miranda Sears, 1838.
     They had: (1) *Charles H.,*⁷ b. Jan. 19, 1830, resides at
     Concord, Mich.; farmer. (2) *Henry,*⁷ b. Nov. 27, 1831,
     Alleghany, Pa.; m. Eveline, daughter of Rev. Stephen
     Harrison, of Bloomingdale, Ill., 1857, and had *Mary
     Eva.*⁸ (Henry Mann was a farmer and organist in 1874,
     at Concord, Mich.) (3) *Mary Ann.*⁷ (4) *Sears.*⁷

   vi. HARRIET,⁶ b. Jan. 5, 1805; d. June 15, 1865; m. Timothy
     Sabin, 1828, of Oneonta, N. Y. He was in the butter
     and cheese trade at Oneonta, 1874. They had: (1) *Eg-
     bert R.*⁷ (2) *Algernon L.,*⁷ d. in civil war.

   vii. SALLY,⁶ b. March 31, 1806; d. about 1850; m. Joseph Bly,
     of De Ruyter, N. Y., had *James,*⁷ who was in civil war,
     and "confined one year in Salisbury prison." He was in
     Wood River, Kan., 1874.

   viii. AARON,⁶ b. June 20, 1808; d. Jan. 25, 1852, at Meredith, N.
     Y. He was a woollen manufacturer at Meredith. He m.
     Minerva, daughter of David Banks, of Mill Port, N. Y.

   ix. ALFRED,⁶ b. March 19, 1811; d. 1872; m. Annette, daugh-
     ter of Wm. Eaton, 1835, res. Leighton, Mich. They had:
     (1) *Harvey W.*⁷ d. civil war. (2) *Susan E.,*⁷ m. Mr.
     Barr, a Methodist minister. (3) *Mary F.*⁷ (4) *Philan-
     der,*⁷ Wayland, Mich. (5) *Hannah,*⁷ d. 1872.

   x. CYNTHIA,⁶ b. June 18, 1815; d. Feb. 24, 1859; m. Mr.
     Uebile.

   xi. JULIA,⁶ b. April 16, 1817; d. Dec. 10, 1871; m. Palmer
     Utter, 1836, at De Ruyter, N. Y., and had: (1) *Celestus.*⁷
     (2) *Adelbert,*⁷ in civil war, was a prisoner at Macon, Ga.,
     and "starved to death after a confinement of six months."

(3) *Williston,*[7] lost a limb in war. (4) *Harriet.*[7] (5)
Kendrick.[7]

xii. SUSAN,[6] b. Nov. 7, 1818; d. Dec. 1854; m. Asa P. Farns-
worth, of Aurora, Ill.

xiii. AUSTIN,[6] b. April 18, 1820; m. Mary E. Sexton, 1847, at
Smyrna, N. Y. He resides in Aurora, Ill., farmer and
merchant, deacon of Congregational church. Children:
(1) *Ella,*[7] m. and lives in Chicago. (2) *Libbie.*[7]

xiv. DEMIS,[6] b. Oct. 8, 1821; d. Dec. 17, 1870, at Aurora, Ill.,
unmarried.

(51) CHARLES[6] MANN

(*Nathaniel,*[5] *Josiah,*[4] *Thomas,*[3] *Thomas,*[2] *Richard*[1]), son of Nathaniel
of Scituate, Mass., by wife Abigail (Billings) Mann, was born there
Nov. 16, 1790. He married Mary D. Lathrop. Children, probably
born in Scituate:

i. REBECCA DAVIS,[7] b. Feb. 5, 1821; m. Samuel Thomas, Jr.,
who is in the Post Office department at Washington, D.
C.; has *George N. B.,*[8] a letter collector in Boston.

ii. ABIGAIL BILLINGS,[7] b. Oct. 11, 1825; m. Brooke Crane.

iii. MARY ANN HOWARD,[7] b. June 2, 1829; m. Thomas Rich-
ardson, res. Charlestown, Mass.

iv. LOUISA ADAMS,[7] b. March 26, 1833; d. June 23, 1855, unmarried.

v. ALMEDA CUSHMAN,[7] b. Aug. 15, 1836; m. William Wilds,
of Milton, Mass.

vi. CHARLES DEXTER,[7] b. Nov. 17, 1838; m. Lydia A. Gerrish
of Pembroke, Mass., resides at South Scituate, Mass.
Children: (1) *Charles E.,*[8] b. Nov. 14, 1863. (2) *George
H.,*[8] Sept. 25, 1865. (3) *William D.,*[8] Jan. 9, 1867; d.
1876. (4) *Samuel T.,*[8] Feb. 1, 1870. (5) *Lydia A.,*[8]
July 6, 1871. (6) *Barney D.,*[8] Sept. 17, 1874. (7)
Walter B.,[8] June 5, 1877. (8) *Mary A. A.,*[8] April 15,
1879. (9) *Sarah F.,*[8] Nov. 8, 1880.

vii. SARAH WALES,[7] b. March 2, 1841; m. first, Jeremiah R.
Hatch, of Quincy, Mass.; second, Charles Oldham. She
is now a widow, res. Quincy.

(52) PELEG[6] MANN

(*John,*[5] *Thomas,*[4] *Thomas,*[3] *Thomas,*[2] *Richard*[1]), the eldest son of
John Mann, Sr., of Scituate, Mass., by first wife, Patience (Rogers)
Mann, was born there Feb. 3, 1784. Early in life we find him a
resident at 73 Warren St., Boston, where for many years he was a

prominent builder and master mason; among the many buildings he erected was the Pine-Street church. He was married to Margaret Tufts, in Boston, March 12, 1809, by Caleb Blood, and died there, the record says, "with small pox, Aug. 17, 1840." Children, born in Boston, nearly all of whom were baptized in Old South church:

   i. WILLIAM TUFTS,[7] b. Dec. 8, 1810; d. unmarried in Boston, May 2, 1861. He lived some years in Puerto Cabello, South America. At one time was agent for the Middlesex Mills, at Lowell; subsequently went to Aspinwall, and California, as agent for the Pacific Mail Steamship Co. He corresponded with the late R. R. Hinman, of Hartford, Conn., on genealogical matters pertaining to this branch of the Manns.

   ii. PELEG ROGER,[7] b. April 11, 1813; d. unmarried in Boston, Nov. 2, 1838.

   iii. MARGARET,[7] b. Jan. 8, 1816; m. Rev. Thomas O. Rice, 1850, who settled first at West Killingly, Conn., was there eleven years; then pastor of the Circular church, Charleston, S. C., remaining until 1865. In 1867, became pastor of the Presbyterian church, Des Moines, Iowa. Returned to New England, preached at Plymouth, and lastly, since Nov. 1881, in Templeton, Mass.

   iv. HANNAH GREENLEAF,[7] b. Dec. 5, 1817; d. unmarried in Boston, April 29, 1833.

   v. ELIZABETH,[7] b. Nov. 1, 1819; m. John A. Whipple, formerly the well-known photographer of Boston. He is a resident of Cambridge, and publisher of religious tracts in Boston. Children: *Ella Melinda,*[8] m. 1874, George H. Lawrence; *Annie Adams,*[8] *Lucy,*[8] *John Adams,*[8] 1859, *William Newton,*[8] 1861.

   vi. SUSAN POOR,[7] b. June 12, 1823; d. in Boston, July 29, 1825.

   vii. DANIEL P.,[7] b. Jan. 12, 1826; m. Hattie Broad, of Brighton, Mass.; she d. Dec. 7, 1870. They had: (1) *Margaret Elizabeth,*[8] b. Nov. 7, 1852, who m. Eben Cook, 1878, and lives in Avoca, Iowa. (2) *George Harrington,*[8] died.

   viii. MARTHA STANWOOD,[7] b. Dec. 7, 1828; m. first, Geo. F. Harrington, 1850, of Hopkinton, who was drowned at St. Louis, in 1853; m. second, Joseph J. Whiting, 1862, who d. June, 1863; m. third, Hon. Samuel C. Pomeroy, United States senator from Kansas, in 1865, now residing at Washington, D. C.

(53) JOHN[6] MANN

(*John,*[5] *Thomas,*[4] *Thomas,*[3] *Thomas,*[2] *Richard*[1]) was born in Scituate, Mass., Nov. 1, 1785, and died in Boston, Aug. 16, 1848. He came to the town of Boston about 1803, and (it is said) learned the mason's trade of Mr. Harrington. For many years he was an owner of real estate on Charles Street, and resided there. He married Nov. 30, 1809, Kate Harrington, and had the following children, born in Boston:

i.   JOHN,[7] b. April 10, 1811; and died unmarried, Feb. 21, 1870. He was of the late firm of John Mann & Co., for many years the leading ribbon store of Boston.

ii. WILLIAM H.,[7] b. Nov. 7, 1813; unmarried. He is a retired ribbon merchant, residence Charles Street, Boston.

iii. CATHERINE,[7] b. 1817; d. April, 1818.

iv. CAROLINE E.,[7] b. March 9, 1820; m. July 5, 1842, Col. Lucius B. Marsh, of Boston, who for many years was head of the firm of Marsh, Talbot & Co. (wholesale woollen house), of Boston. He was colonel of the 47th Massachusetts regiment that participated in the late civil war. Col. Marsh having retired from active business, resides at Columbus Square, Boston. They have the following children: (1) *Lucius K.,*[8] b. May 28, 1843; m. Oct. 26, 1869, Charlotte E. Bates [and have *Lottie E.,*[9] b. Aug. 11, 1870], res. New York city. (2) *John G. L.,*[8] b. April 18, 1845; d. April 24, 1845. (3) *Catherine H.,*[8] b. Jan. 27, 1847; m. Jan. 7, 1868, George F. Kimball, of Boston [they have 1, *George Edward,*[9] b. March 7, 1869; 2, *Allen,*[9] b. May 20, 1872.] (4) *Elizabeth L.,*[8] b. Oct. 25, 1849, unmarried. (5) *William H. Mann,*[8] b. April 29, 1851; m. April 14, 1880, Mary Anna Harris, [issue: 1, *Anna Harris,*[9] b. in N. Y. city, Feb. 22, 1881; 2, *Caroline E. H.,*[9] b. in N. Y. city, July 3, 1882], res. New York city. (6) *Caroline B.,*[8] b. May 15, 1858; m. April 18, 1877, John F. Harris [had *Richard Brown,*[9] b. Feb. 23, 1878].

123. v.   JONATHAN H.,[7] b. June 3, 1825; m. Philena W. Dupee.

vi. SARAH A. T.,[7] b. July 5, 1827; d. in Boston, July 31, 1882; m. Sept. 21, 1853, James B. Macomber, of Boston. Issue: (1) *Caroline.*[8] (2) *Chandler.*[8] (3) *Sally.*[8] (4) *Harry W.*[8] (5) *Ethel.*[8]

vii. CHARLES H.,[7] b. Aug. 21, 1832; m. Dec. 4, 1856, Emily S., daughter of Rev. R. W. Cushman, D.D., a former pastor of Bowdoin Square Baptist church, Boston. Post Office address, Parker House, Boston. No children.

(54) DAVID[6] MANN

(*David,*[5] *Ebenezer,*[4] *Thomas,*[3] *Thomas,*[2] *Richard*[1]) was born in Pembroke, Mass., Nov. 29, 1782, and died there Oct. 11, 1858. He

was the eldest son of David Man, Sr., by wife Betsey (Bates) Mann.
He married in Pembroke, Jan. 24, 1805, Rebecca Oldham, born
Sept. 18, 1785, who died Jan. 7, 1855. David Mann, Jr., was by
trade a shipjoiner, a very skilful and industrious workman. He
took large contracts in Medford, and elsewhere, and employed many
men in his day. A resident of Pembroke. Children:

124.   i.   JOHN C.[7] (Capt.), b. April 6, 1806; m. Sylvia L. Hedge.
125.   ii. DAVID O.,[7] b. Dec. 13, 1808; m. Nancy Austin.
126.   iii. JONATHAN O.,[7] b. Dec. 13, 1808; m. Eliza A. Sears.
      iv. ALMIRA,[7] b. April 1, 1811; m. George Taber, Sept. 20,
         1835.
      v. ADELINE,[7] b. Feb. 13, 1813; m. John Oldham, Sept. 6,
         1843.
      vi. ELIZABETH,[7] b. Dec. 26, 1815; m. Robert Ramsdell, Sept.
         20, 1835.
      vii. MARY T.,[7] b. July 15, 1820; m. Seth Whitman, Jr., Sept.
         23, 1846.
      viii. LUCY P.,[7] b. Sept. 3, 1822; m. Horace J. Foster, Oct. 25,
         1846.

(55) EBENEZER[6] MANN

(*David,*[5] *Ebenezer,*[4] *Thomas,*[3] *Thomas,*[2] *Richard*[1]), son of David
Mann, Sr., of Pembroke, Mass., was born there Oct. 12, 1788, and
married July, 1812, Alma, born Nov. 20, 1793, daughter of Henry
and Lois (Stetson) Josselyn, of Pembroke. They removed to Leeds,
Maine, June 1, 1817, and settled upon a farm. He was living at
that place Feb. 3, 1884. His wife was a good penman at the advanced age of eighty-nine. She died Feb. 3, 1883. Children:

127.   i.   EBENEZER,[7] b. April 4, 1813; m. Lucetta Keen.
      ii. ISAIAH,[7] b. June 15, 1816; stone cutter; res. Leeds.
      iii. LOIS DELPHINA,[7] b. Feb. 1, 1830; d. 1831.
      iv. ALBERT HENRY,[7] b. Nov. 5, 1833; m. Polly Keene; lives
         on the old farm in Leeds; have *Isaiah Henry,*[8] b. May
         1, 1870.

(56) JOSIAH[6] MANN

(*David,*[5] *Ebenezer,*[4] *Thomas,*[3] *Thomas,*[2] *Richard*[1]), the youngest son
of David Mann, Sr., of Pembroke, Mass., was born in that town Oct.
16, 1801. He married first, Hannah Smith, of Hingham, Mass.;
second, Mary F. Curtis, of Charlestown, Mass. Mr. Mann is by

trade a ship chandler, and for many years owned a farm in the north part of Hanson, Mass. He resides in North Hanson, with his only son (by his second wife), who is in the Hanover tack factory.

    i. JOSIAH C.,[7] b. Nov. 13, 1847; m. Mary F. Gilbert. Resides at North Hanson, and has children: (1) *Minnie F.*,[8] b. May 11, 1870. (2) *Annie L.*,[8] b. March 3, 1873.

(57) JAMES BUFFINGTON[6] MANN

(*Ebenezer*,[5] *Ebenezer*,[4] *Thomas*,[3] *Thomas*,[2] *Richard*[1]), the youngest child of Ebenezer Mann, of Salem, Mass., by wife Sarah (Buffington) Mann, was born there June 14, 1809, and died Feb. 3, 1870. He married Susan F. Ruce (born June 8, 1812), April 7, 1844, she being a daughter of Mrs. Helen Ruce, who was a twin daughter of James Tytler, a Scotch historian, who died in Danvers, 1880, aged ninety-two. The widow survives, and resides in Salem. James B. Mann was a grocer in Salem, and was considered a man of strict integrity. He left a record worthy of emulation. It is said he had "quite an inventive genius," but labored under the infirmity of a severe lameness. Children, born in Salem:

    i. SARAH H.,[7] b. Feb. 13, 1845.
   ii. JULIA M.,[7] b. Nov. 17, 1846; teacher.
  iii. JAMES W.,[7] b. April 26, 1848; m. Eliza J. McNeil, of Salem, Aug. 1873. Children: (1) *Grace E.*,[8] b. in Chicago, Ill., Feb. 4, 1874. (2) *George P.*,[8] b. in Salem, Oct. 19, 1876. (3) *James Ernest*,[8] b. in Salem, July 10, 1879. (4) *Archibald McNeil*,[8] b. in Salem, Oct. 27, 1881.
   iv. SUSAN L.,[7] b. Dec. 8, 1850.

(58) JOSEPH[6] MANN

(*Joseph*,[5] *Joseph*,[4] *Joseph*,[3] *Thomas*,[2] *Richard*[1]), the eldest child of Joseph and Mary (Dyer) Mann, of Randolph, Mass., was born there Nov. 17, 1781. He married first, Eunice, daughter of Ebenezer Warren, who died 1828, and by her had eleven children; he married second, Azuba, sister of first wife, and had two children; he married third, Margaret Scarles. Mr. Mann resided in Randolph, and died there. Children:

128.   i. WARREN,[7] b. Jan. 21, 1806; m. Lois Niles.
129. ii. SIDNEY,[7] b. 1808; m. Hannah Sylvester.

iii. EUNICE,[7] b. 1810; m. Emery Delano, July 2, 1828; thirteen children; res. Randolph, Mass.

130. iv. JOSEPH,[7] b. April 1, 1812; m. Abigail E. Niles.

131. v. FRANCIS,[7] m. Sarah M. Spear.

132. vi. HENRY,[7] b. Feb. 28, 1816; m. first, Rhoda Faxon.

vii. HARRIET,[7] b. Nov. 22, 1818; m. Abraham Dyer, 1835; res. Quincy, Mass.; seven children.

viii. LOUISA,[7] b. Aug. 15, 1822; m. Francis Myers, 1838; had sixteen children.

133. ix. ANSEL,[7] b. Jan. 10, 1824; m. Jane Mann.

x. JANE,[7] b. Oct. 10, 1826; m. Adam Jones, May 8, 1842; res. Randolph, Mass.; six children.

xi. Infant,[7] d. young.

134. xii. ISAAC,[7] b. March 26, 1830; m. Louisa Goldthwait.

xiii. LUCINDA,[7] b. about 1835; m. Philips Myers, 1846; res. Canton, Mass.; nine children.

(59) JONATHAN[6] MANN

(*Joseph,*[5] *Joseph,*[4] *Joseph,*[3] *Thomas,*[2] *Richard*[1]), son of Joseph and Mary (Dyer) Mann, was born in Randolph, Mass., Sept. 4, 1786, and died there April 4, 1873. He married Polly Bradley (who was a daughter of his father's second wife), March 29, 1814; she died Nov. 29, 1873, aged eighty. Children:

i. DELAZON D.,[7] b. May 29, 1815; d. Jan. 26, 1883; m. May 18, 1852, Lucy Ann Nichols, of Middlebury, Vt. (He was a respected citizen and a member of the Stoughton Musical Society.—Randolph paper.) He resided in Randolph, Mass., and had: (1) *Lucy Eveline,*[8] b. Aug. 11, 1856.

ii. DELIGHT,[7] b. Aug. 31, 1818; m. Moses C. Ford, Nov. 7, 1839; res. Boston; seven children.

iii. JONATHAN,[7] b. March 11, 1821; m. Betsey Leeds; res. Milton; no children.

iv. JANE,[7] Aug. 26, 1823; m. Ansel Mann (cousin).

v. TAMZY,[7] b. Aug. 27, 1827; d. 1833.

vi. JACOB,[7] b. Oct. 25, 1829; m. Mrs. Nancy Green, and went to Topeka, Kan.; no children.

vii. MINOT T.,[7] b. Dec. 18, 1831; m. Sarah Handen; res. Black Hawk, Col.; three children.

viii. MOSES,[7] b. May 25, 1835; m. Mehitable R. Taylor, Jan. 1, 1862, who was killed by lightning June 16, 1882, aged forty-six; res. Randolph, Mass. They had: (1) *Alice M.,*[8] b. Dec. 30, 1862. (2) *G. Otis,*[8] b. April 28, 1867. (3) *Almira,*[8] b. April 10, 1871.

ix. IRA O.,[7] b. April 17, 1839; m. Eliza ——; res. Colorado; no children.

(60) SETH[6] MANN, Esq.

(*Seth,*[5] *Seth,*[4] *Joseph,*[3] *Thomas,*[2] *Richard*[1]) was born in what is
now Randolph, Mass., April 4, 1781, and at an early age removed
with all his father's family to
Braintree, Vt.   At about the
age of twenty-one years he re-
turned to Massachusetts, and thereafter resided permanently in his
native town.   A man of good judgment, energetic and enterprising.
He was early and all his lifetime engaged in widely extended business in team-work, transportation, as farmer, road contractor, merchant and manufacturer.   He was among the first to engage in the
manufacture of boots and shoes in Randolph (the boot and shoe
town), selling in Boston, later extending his trade through all the
cape towns and to all sections of the United States, his goods being
known as a standard article.   At his death he had a place of business
in Peoria, Ill., distributing there his manufactured goods in connection
with trade in general merchandise.   During the war of 1812 he was
much employed in providing transportation by land, as far north as
Bennington, Vt., and south as far as Richmond, Va., by officers of
the United States government, in supplying the army, and also in
transportation for the public in general, having at one time an office
in the then town of Boston.

He was much in public life, being for many years a justice of the
peace, for twelve years one of the selectmen of the town, and representative in the general court of the Commonwealth in the years
1823,–'24,–'26,–'27,–'28,–'29,–'31.   Director in the Randolph Bank
from its organization, and county commissioner of Norfolk County
from the year 1835 until his death, Oct. 23, 1843.

A Baptist in religious sentiment, he was liberal in his views, exemplary in character, ever anxious for the well-being of all, benev-
olent, and every object of charity found in him a cheerful giver.
To the poor he gave, and also assisted them by furnishing either the
means or the opportunity of aiding themselves, and more than once,
in times of greatest pressure, extended his business for their benefit.
Never of doubtful credit, or compelled to succumb to financial difficulties, he left a fair estate.   Many yet live to remember and speak
of his kindness, probity and usefulness as a citizen.

He married first, in 1806, his cousin Betsey Mann, daughter of Dea. Benjamin Mann, of Randolph; she was born Feb. 17, 1783, and died March 31, 1814. He married second, in 1816, Polly Mann, a sister of his first wife; she was born March 25, 1795, and died May 26, 1882. He had four children, viz.: two daughters by his first wife, and two sons by second.

   i. BETSEY,[7] b. July 31, 1807 (now living); m. in 1824, Alvan Kidder (b. in Braintree, Vt., Feb. 12, 1801), of Randolph. He was a manufacturer, and served the town several years as town clerk from 1835, also a representative to the General Court. He removed about 1846 to Peoria, Ill., where he died Nov. 19, 1871, leaving much property. Children: (1) *Alvan*,[8] b. Nov. 25, 1824; a farmer in Farmington, Ill.; m. Lucy Jane Ewatt, and has five children. (2) *Ann Maria*,[8] b. 1836; d. 1837, at Randolph. (3) *Ann*,[8] b. 1840; unmarried; residing at Peoria, Ill. (4) *George*,[8] b. Aug. 10, 1846; d. unmarried, Sept. 18, 1880.

   ii. EMILY,[7] b. Aug. 4, 1809; m. April 22, 1829, Charles Todd Woodman, who was born in Poultney, Vt., Dec. 31, 1807, and died in Boston, Dec. 15, 1879. For a time he resided in Randolph, and by occupation a tanner and currier. He was a representative to the general court from Randolph. He removed to Chelsea in 1842, subsequently to Boston, where for some years he carried on the leather trade, and served the city as an alderman. Children: (1) *Charles Eugene*,[8] b. May 27, 1832; d. in Boston, May 30, 1875. (2) *Ann*,[8] b. Nov. 30, 1835; died. (3) *Morton*,[8] b. Aug. 30, 1839; died. (4) *Emily*,[8] b. May 12, 1846; died. (5) *Frank*,[8] b. Oct. 27, 1850; resides in Boston; m. Florence Margaret Arnold, of Providence, and has: *Morton Arnold*,[9] b. April 22, 1877, and *Ethel F.*,[9] b. June, 1878.

135. iii. SETH,[7] 2nd (Esq.), b. Feb. 28, 1817; m. Eliza A. Cole.
136. iv. STILLMAN[7] (A. M.), b. June 27, 1819; m. Ella O. Tower.

(61) SAMUEL[6] MANN

(*Seth*,[5] *Seth*,[4] *Joseph*,[3] *Thomas*,[2] *Richard*[1]), the second son of Seth Mann, of Braintree, Vt., was born in what is now Randolph, Mass., July 16, 1783. He removed to Braintree, Vt., when young, with his father, and later in life purchased a farm in West Randolph, Vt., where he died Sept. 4, 1847. He married his cousin Rachel, daughter of Dea. Benjamin Mann, of Randolph, Mass., about 1806, who died Feb. 20, 1859. Children:

137. i. SAMUEL,[7] b. Aug. 12, 1807; m. Caroline Flint.
      ii. RACHEL,[7] b. Jan. 23, 1809; m. Luther Holman, March 23, 1837, who d. July 30, 1880, leaving three sons and two daughters; a son married and living in Cal., others in Vt.
      iii. CELINDA,[7] b. Sept. 1, 1814; m. (cousin) Samuel B. Mann.
      iv. LUCINDA,[7] b. Dec. 7, 1817.
      v. ALVIN KIDDER,[7] b. Aug. 8, 1820; m. Mary A. Holman, March 30, 1850. He is a farmer; no children.
      vi. MARY FLORETTA,[7] b. Sept. 1827; m. (cousin) C. B. Mann.

(62) MICAH[6] MANN

(*Seth,*[5] *Seth,*[4] *Joseph,*[3] *Thomas,*[2] *Richard*[1]), the third son of Seth Mann, of Braintree, Vt., was born at the "South Precinct" in Braintree, Mass. (now Randolph), June 21, 1785, and died in Vermont, Aug. 29, 1849. He removed early with his parents to Braintree, Vt., and later resided at Brookfield, Vt., subsequently Randolph, Vt. He married Sarah, daughter of Samuel and Elizabeth (Brackett) Bass, March 9, 1809, who was born March 7, 1787, and died Sept. 1872. Children:

      i. MICAH,[7] b. March 8, 1811; d. March 8, 1816.
      ii. LEVI,[7] b. Feb. 23, 1813; m. Mary Stephens, and for many years a manufacturer of boots and shoes at Randolph, Mass. He removed to Kappa, Ill. Children: (1) *James M.*[8] (2) *Horace.*[8] (3) *Mary A.*[8] (4) *Sarah.*[8]
138. iii. SAMUEL B.,[7] b. May 31, 1815; m. Celinda Mann.
139. iv. MICAH,[7] Jr., b. July 28, 1817; m. first, Minorra Ford.
      v. SARAH,[7] b. Nov. 2, 1819; d. Sept. 7, 1883; m. George Parrish, Feb. 3, 1841. Merchant at West Randolph, Vt.
      vi. GEORGE W.,[7] b. Sept. 30, 1821; d. Aug. 1883; m. Betsey Flint, July 16, 1847; a lumber dealer. No children.
      vii. JAMES M.,[7] b. July 27, 1824; d. June 11, 1833.
      viii. WILLIAM,[7] b. May 17, 1829; m. first, Cyntha Smith, June 15, 1857, who died 1862; m. second, Amanda E. Robinson, Jan. 10, 1864. He is a nurseryman. Children: (1) *Willie C.,*[8] b. Dec. 5, 1866; d. June 13, 1881. (2) and (3) twins, *Georgia E.,*[8] May 10, 1872; *Charles E.,*[8] who d. April 2, 1874.
140. ix. JOSEPH W.,[7] b. March 2, 1832; m. Ellen Whitcomb.

(63) LEVI[6] MANN

(*Seth,*[5] *Seth,*[4] *Joseph,*[3] *Thomas,*[2] *Richard*[1]), the fourth son of Seth Mann, of Braintree, Vt., was born at the "South Precinct," Braintree,

Mass. (now Randolph), May 21, 1789, and died March 18, 1829.
He married Jan. 16, 1817, his cousin Mary, daughter of Dea. Elisha
Mann, of Randolph, Mass., who survived her husband many
years, and married twice again; she died March 13, 1848. He was
a farmer in Randolph, Vt. Their children were:

141. i. LEVI,[7] b. June 14, 1819; m. Abby A. Spear.
      ii. ELISHA,[7] } (twins) b. 1821; d. in infancy.
      iii. STEPHEN,[7] }
      iv. Infant, d.
      v. MARY ABBY,[7] b. Dec. 4, 1827. She is a teacher in the
         American Asylum, at Hartford, Conn.

(64) JOEL[6] MANN

(*Seth,*[5] *Seth,*[4] *Joseph,*[3] *Thomas,*[2] *Richard*[1]), born May 28, 1791, at
"South Precinct," Braintree (now Randolph, Mass.), served in the
war of 1812, "hauled powder and flour from Albany to Burlington,
at night sleeping under his wagon." He married Oct. 14, 1815, his
cousin, Louisa Mann, at Randolph, Mass.; lived with his parents in
Braintree, Vt., about four years; in Randolph, Mass., two years;
then settled in Randolph, Vt.; had a farm of three hundred or more
acres, where he lived until April, 1852; farmed it extensively, built
a two-story brick house; from this time to May, 1862, resided on
another farm in town, and in the village, then removed to Gilmantown, Wis., built the second house in the place, and a large grist-
mill. He died there April 25, 1865. His widow, who survives,
lives there with her son Joel. Children: two first born in Braintree, Vt., the third in Randolph, Mass., all the others in Randolph, Vt.

      i. BENJAMIN,[7] b. Jan. 1817; d. aged about one year.
      ii. JOEL,[7] b. Dec. 18, 1818; unmarried; res. Gilmantown, Wis.
         He is a large landholder and a substantial farmer. He is
         a great reader withal, and has more than a local reputa-
         tion as being an "inventive genius."
      iii. LOUISA,[7] b. March 1, 1820; m. Harrison Amidown, farmer;
         res. Dover, Wis.
142. iv. MARSHALL,[7] b. Aug. 12, 1822; m. Sarah R. Ainsworth.
      v. ELVIRA PHILOEA,[7] b. Feb. 8, 1825; m. March 21, 1848, at
         Randolph, Vt., Isaac Parrish, who was born there Sept.
         5, 1817, a carpenter by trade, purchased a farm of 125
         acres in 1866 at Miller's Corners, N. Y., where they live.

Children, born in Vt.: (1) *Nathan*,[8] b. Sept. 19, 1850; m. Louvisa Hibbard, 1876, and live at Bloomfield, N. Y., farmer [and have children *Lyeta L.*,[9] b. Aug. 24, 1878; *Elmer L.*[9] and *Elma L.*,[9] twins, May 10, 1879; *Normand Garfield*,[9] March 13, 1881]. (2) *Rolla Clinton*,[8] June 28, 1855. (3) *Waldo George*,[8] April 26, 1857. (4) *Addie May*,[8] Nov. 16, 1859. (5) *Dora Louisa*,[8] Nov. 5, 1862.

vi. ROSANNA,[7] b. May 21, 1827; d. Feb. 8, 1883; m. March 21, 1848, Chauncy J. Leathers, of West Randolph, Vt., a drover, and have *Alice*,[8] who m. Allen Thayer, a farmer.

vii. HANNAH HOWARD,[7] b. Aug. 19 (?), 1829; m. June 29, 1854, Wm. Bass, Jr., of West Randolph, Vt. (owns the tavern buildings), farmer; no issue.

viii. DEBORAH DYER,[7] b. June 1, 1832; m. Seth M. Flint, of West Randolph, Vt., drover. Children: (1) *Minnie*,[8] b. Jan. 11, 1859; d. 1875. (2) *Mabel L.*,[8] b. June 2, 1865.

ix. CHARLES BENJAMIN,[7] b. July 26, 1834; m. Alice Densmore. A farmer, and has erected a brick mansion on the homestead. Children: *Lucien B.*,[8] b. Nov. 4, 1862; at school; res. West Randolph, Vt.

x. EMORY,[7] b. Nov. 28, 1837; d. Nov. 1842.

xi. ELLEN MARIA, b. June 14, 1839; m. Warren Kenyon, b. Sept. 24, 1837, a farmer in Gilmantown, Wis. Children: (1) *C. Sprague*,[8] b. Dec. 31, 1866. (2) *Minnie E.*,[8] Dec. 9, 1868. (3) *Elmer A.*,[8] Sept. 14, 1870. (4) *W. Burton*,[8] Jan. 18, 1872; d. Jan. 30, 1879. Mrs. Ellen M. Kenyon and her children reside with her mother and brother in Gilmantown, Wis. She has been a successful school teacher.

(65) STEPHEN[6] MANN

(*Seth*,[5] *Seth*,[4] *Joseph*,[3] *Thomas*,[2] *Richard*[1]), the sixth son of Seth Mann, of Braintree, Vt., was born in that town June 30, 1793, and died May 2, 1869. He married first, Eliphal, daughter of Henry and Eliphal (Burgess) Brackett [see Brackett Gen.], who were formerly of Boston. She was born April 2, 1795, and died at Randolph, Mass., Nov. 1, 1829. He married second, about 1836, Elizabeth Brackett (sister of first wife), born Jan. 26, 1804, who still survives.

Mr. Mann, in company with his brother Seth (about 1825), was engaged in manufacturing boots and shoes at Randolph, Mass. He left Massachusetts about 1830 and lived in Randolph and Braintree, Vt., up to about 1851, thence to Ferrisburg, Vt., spending much time with his son at Rutland. "He was engaged in various speculations, traded in wool, pork, butter and cheese. In the summer time bought and took to Brighton market, cattle and sheep." He was an active, efficient man of affairs, generally holding some official position in town or school district, and at one time a candidate of the whig party for state legislature. He had the following children—three by first wife, one by second, viz.:

143.   i.   WILLIAM BURGESS,[7] b. June 9, 1820; m. Orlinda A. Riford.
144.   ii.   CHARLES BRACKETT,[7] b. Oct. 20, 1822.
145.   iii.   HORATIO EUGENE,[7] Esq., b. Feb. 22, 1825; m. Mary Augusta Williams.
      iv.   STEPHEN ALLISON,[7] Esq., b. about Aug. 28, 1837; d. at Reno, Nevada, unmarried, Sept. 13, 1881. Hon. S. Allison Mann was a lawyer by profession, a graduate of the State and National Law School, at Poughkeepsie, N. Y. He early went to Salt Lake City, Utah. was very popular there, and filled many offices of trust. Under the appointment of President Lincoln or Grant, he was Secretary of Utah Territory, and for a long time Acting Governor.

(66) ELISHA[6] MANN

(*Seth,*[5] *Seth,*[4] *Joseph,*[3] *Thomas,*[2] *Richard*[1]) was born in Braintree, Vt., Oct. 4, 1795, and died there March 16, 1835. He married Ruth Smith, of Randolph, Mass., born May 13, 1801; died in Fond du Lac, Wis., July 17, 1882. Mr. Mann resided in Braintree, Vt., was a farmer and manufacturer of patent medicines. Children:

146.   i.   ELISHA,[7] b. Aug. 15, 1818; m. Mary Ann Partridge.
147.   ii.   SETH,[7] b. Feb. 4, 1820; m. first, Minoria A. Hutchinson.
      iii.   JUDSON,[7] b. Dec. 12, 1821; d. Aug. 25, 1827, by a fall upon a sharp stake.
148.   iv.   HOSEA,[7] b. Jan. 17, 1824; m. Mary Sophia Fitts.
149.   v.   STILLMAN,[7] b. Oct. 30, 1825.
      vi.   JUDSON,[7] b. Oct. 11, 1828; d. Feb. 22, 1829.
      vii.   JASON,[7] b. Oct. 11, 1828; unmarried; went to Kansas City, Mo.
      viii.   ELMIRA LUCINDA,[7] b. April 22, 1834; m. July 17, 1857, Lockhart R. Carswell (b. June 18, 1822), of Evanston, Ill. (were in Daytona, Florida, winter of 1883). They had: (1) *Mary Hattie,*[8] b. May 13, 1860; d. Oct. 23, 1864. (2) *William Mann,*[8] Aug. 23, 1862. (3) *Grace May,*[8] Sept. 3, 1871.

(67) BENJAMIN⁶ MANN

(*Benjamin,*⁵ *Seth,*⁴ *Joseph,*³ *Thomas,*² *Richard*¹), born at "South Precinct," Braintree (now Randolph), Mass., Dec. 3, 1776, and died there April 29, 1856. He married first, Polly Hunt, who died Aug. 31, 1852, aged seventy-two; he married second, Nov. 24, 1853, Eliza Taber (widow), who died Jan. 11, 1879, aged seventy-five. He was a farmer at the "West Corner." Children by first wife:

150.   i.   BENJAMIN O.,⁷ b. Oct. 6, 1802; m. Ruth Howard.
     ii. POLLY,⁷ b. March 6, 1809; d. April 25, 1876; m. Thomas B. Howard, Nov. 27, 1829, and had six children.

(68) JOSHUA⁶ MANN

(*Benjamin,*⁵ *Seth,*⁴ *Joseph,*³ *Thomas,*² *Richard*¹), born at the "South Precinct," Braintree, Mass. (now Randolph), Dec. 7, 1780, and died there Sept. 20, 1868. He married his cousin Sally, daughter of Micah White, Esq., Nov. 29, 1810, who died Dec. 3, 1876, aged ninety-two. He was a farmer at the "West Corner." Children:

    i.   SARAH,⁷ b. Nov. 7, 1811; d. Sept. 27, 1849; m. Daniel Sawin, April 6, 1831, who d. Jan. 5, 1849. Six children.
    ii. HANNAH,⁷ b. April 3, 1814; d. March 3, 1880; m. July 22, 1835, Dr. Salmon Morrill, a graduate of Dartmouth College, who was b. Aug. 15, 1812, in Sandwich, N. H.; d. Sept. 9, 1859. One son.
    iii. ELIZABETH,⁷ b. Nov. 21, 1817; d. July 16, 1865; m. April 6, 1839, Judson Smith; d. Feb. 3, 1843, aged twenty-nine. One son.
    iv. MARY JANE,⁷ b. July 20, 1821; m. Wales French, June 4, 1846. Have (1) *Sarah,*⁸ m. Geo. G. Spear. (2) *Mary W.*⁸ (3) *Lizzie,*⁸ m. E. O. Leach, of Randolph.
    v.   THOMAS B.,⁷ b. Aug. 29, 1825; m. Eliza Wilson, June 15, 1855. Was city surveyor of Providence, R. I., eight years. Have *Julia Ardelle,*⁸ b. March 6, 1863.
    vi. BENJAMIN J.,⁷ b. April 3, 1828; m. Clara A. Haskell, Oct. 23, 1861. They reside in Weymouth, Mass. Children: (1) *Susie Mabel,*⁸ b. Aug. 16, 1862; d. Nov. 24, 1865. (2) *George Henry,*⁸ June 22, 1864; d. Sept. 25, 1865. (3) *Bertram Haskell,*⁸ Nov. 15, 1866. (4) *Bessie Ada,*⁸ Nov. 15, 1870. (5) *Katie Isabel,*⁸ Jan. 29, 1874. (6) *Leo Russell,*⁸ Oct. 17, 1878.
    vii. HENRY M.,⁷ b. Dec. 16, 1831; m. Dec. 15, 1873, Nellie Fowler. They reside at Cambridge, Mass., and have children: (1) *Ada Frances,*⁸ b. Nov. 8, 1874. (2) *Murray Henry,*⁸ May 20, 1877.

(69) THOMAS JEWETT⁶ MANN

(*Ephraim*,⁵ *Seth*,⁴ *Joseph*,³ *Thomas*,² *Richard*¹) was born in Pownal or Bennington, Vt., in 1791, and died May 25, 1876, aged eighty-five years, two months, twenty days. He married Betsey Wideman, of Berne, N. Y., and resided for a time in Pownal and Bennington, Vt., subsequently in Berne, N. Y. He was a farmer and served in the 1812 war. Children:

    i. MALINDA,⁷ b. Aug. 3, 1815; d. 1849; m. April 21, 1836, John Cordwell, b. in Nottingham, England. He resides in Dalton, Ga. Children: (1) *Elizabeth*,⁸ b. May 13, 1837; m. Mr. Dyer; res. Dalton, Ga. (2) *Ephraim*,⁸ July 31, 1838; married; six children; res. Dalton, Ga. (3) *Sarah*,⁸ m. Henry Haggerty. (4) *Milicent*,⁸ m. Wm. Burney. (4) *Mary*,⁸ m. James Page.

151. ii. EPHRAIM JACOB,⁷ b. 1817; m. Sophia E. Engle.

152. iii. THOMAS,⁷ b. May 12, 1818; m. Catherine Weisgarver.

    iv. TRYPHOSA,⁷ b. Oct. 27, 1819; m. Aug. 8, 1840, George McBain, a builder and farmer, who d. 1873; res. Otsego, N. Y. Children: (1) *George*,⁸ b. April 23, 1841. (2) *Anna*,⁸ Sept. 8, 1842; m. H. Judson Traver, a dentist. (3) *Alexander*,⁸ Feb. 22, 1844; d. 1852. (4) *W. Henry*,⁸ Feb. 5, 1847; m. Ella J. Miller; 1872, builder, Paterson, N. J. (5) *Nancy H.*,⁸ Oct. 1, 1848; m. 1881, A. S. Guffin, Central Bridge, Scho. Co., N. Y. (6) *Malinda*,⁸ March 25, 1852; adopted, at the age of eighteen months, by her uncle Josiah Mann; m. Aug. 9. 1876, Matthias Bouck, and have three children. (7) *Monemia*,⁸ May 27, 1854; m. 1873, Charles A. Corbin, R. R. agt., Otsego, N. Y. (8) *Norman L.*,⁸ June 3, 1858; a telegraph operator, res. Wadena, Minn.

    v. ELIZABETH,⁷ m. John Mix; had among others *John Wesley*,⁸ b. June 20, 1847; res. Breakabeen, N. Y., farmer.

    vi. SOPHIA,⁷ b. July 26, 1824; m. Dec. 31, 1845, David P. Bergh, b. Dec. 23, 1824; d. 1865; res. Breakabeen, N. Y., farmer. Children: (1) *Oscar B.*,⁸ b. July 3, 1846; m. Sarah A. Smith, 1873. (2) *Sidney*,⁸ Aug. 27, 1850. (3) *Harriet E.*,⁸ Oct. 17, 1853; m. Charles Sholtis, 1876.

    vii. JOSIAH,⁷ b. Feb. 23, 1826; m. Dec. 31, 1850, Dinah Mattice, no children. Mr. Mann is a wealthy farmer at Fultonham, N. Y.

153. viii. ALMERIEN,⁷ b. Aug. 28, 1828; m. Hannah M. Chapman.

    ix. EUNICE,⁷ b. July 9, 1831; m. Aug. 2. 1847, Daniel Doncaster, b. Feb. 14, 1824, a machinist, res. Albany, N. Y. Children: (1) *Daniel Adolphus*,⁸ b. May 1, 1848; d. Jan. 27, 1850. (2) *Frances*,⁸ Oct. 1, 1849; d. Aug. 25, 1851. (3) *Daniel*,⁸ Feb. 10, 1851; m. 1872, Maggie O'Brien; res.

Albany, N. Y. (4) *William*,⁸ Oct. 3, 1852; m. Ada Van
Brocklin, 1874. (5) *Catharine Frances*,⁸ March 17, 1854;
m. Dr. Niles, dentist, at Ballston, N. Y. (6) *Nelson St.
John*,⁸ Dec. 6, 1857. (7) *Eunice A. I.*,⁸ Jan. 6, 1861; d.
Feb. 22, 1866. (8) *Lillie Jane*,⁸ April 27, 1866.

    x. ANDREW JACKSON,⁷ b. Sept. 30, 1832; m. Dec. 31, 1863,
        Harriet Pierce, res. North Blenheim, Scho. Co., N. Y.
        A keeper of bees; by trade a cooper.

154. xi. JOSEPH,⁷ b. July 22, 1833; m. Phebe Jane Pearson.

(70) JOSEPH P.⁶ MANN

(*Stephen*,⁵ *Seth*,⁴ *Joseph*,³ *Thomas*,² *Richard*¹), born 1796, (prob.)
in Claremont, N. H.; died April 14, 1864. He married Susan Jones,
who died Jan. 20, 1869, aged sixty-nine. Resided in Claremont, N.
H. Children:

      i. ESTHER,⁷ b. 1823; d. 1881.
155.   ii. LYMAN J.,⁷ b. Jan. 29, 1826; m. Maria E. Woods.
    iii. HARRIET E.,⁷ b. 1831; d. Dec. 16, 1849.
156.   iv. JOHN W.,⁷ b. 1832; m. Delia Clary.
     v. ELIJAH M.,⁷ b. Jan. 29, 1835; d. April 20, 1871; m. 1869,
        at Mt. Holly, Vt., Mrs. Charity Fuller, of that town; no
        children. He enlisted in 4th Vermont Vols. and served
        through the civil war.
157.   vi. AZRO J.,⁷ b. Aug. 20, 1836; m. Mrs. Clarissa E. W. Keyes.
    vii. AMY J.,⁷ b. 1839; d. April 16, 1840.
158. viii. CHARLES B.,⁷ b. Sept. 9, 1840; m. Mary Jane Young.
     ix. LUCIA P.,⁷ b. Dec. 27, 1841; d. April 1, 1859.
      x. GEORGE,⁷ b. June 5, 1844; m. Lucy H., daughter of Eben-
        ezer Tuttle, Esq., of Peru, Vt., who was born April 28,
        1846; first went to Minn., was there on a farm sixteen
        months, returned to Claremont, N. H., and located finally
        on a farm at Landgrove, Vt. No children.
     xi. ELIZABETH,⁷ and xii. MARIA,⁷ died.

(71) CHARLES HENRY⁶ MANN

(*Stephen*,⁵ *Seth*,⁴ *Joseph*,³ *Thomas*,² *Richard*¹), born April 28, 1806,
(prob.) in Claremont, N. H.; married Vespersia Howard, May 2,
1833. Had a farm, and lived in Claremont until burned out in
1858, when he sold the farm and located at Fairlee, Vt. Was representative from Fairlee to the General Court in 1866-67, and held
many other offices of trust, such as selectman, overseer of the poor,
district clerk, etc. Has been a member of the Methodist Episcopal

17

church fifty-three years. They reside in Bradford, Vt. The children were born in Claremont, N. H.

159.   i. CHARLES EDWIN,[7] b. Dec. 28, 1833.
     ii. MARTHA JANE,[7] b. Jan. 16, 1835; m. Sept. 16, 1857, Charles Curtis Doty. They res. Bradford, Vt.; had three children, two living, viz.: *Jennie Louise,*[8] and *Vernon Augustus.*[8]
    iii. STEPHEN HENRY,[7] b. June 6, 1836; res. Nashua, N. H., a carpenter by trade; m. Sept. 20, 1865, Belle A. B. Brewster. Children: (1) *Catherine Vespersia,*[8] b. June 16, 1866; d. Oct. 11, 1866. (2) *Eugene Brewster,*[8] June 12, 1869. (3) *Carrie Belle,*[8] July 15, 1872. (4) *Albert Henry,*[8] June 5, 1874; d. June 19, 1874. (5) *Karl Lee,*[8] Dec. 21, 1876; d. March 12, 1877. (6) *Harry Leon,*[8] Sept. 8, 1881.
    iv. JULIA ANNA,[7] b. June 19, 1839; m. Dec. 25, 1866, Willard H. Child, depot master at So. Newbury, Vt. Had four children, only one living, *Robert Alexander.*[8]

(72) IRA[6] MANN

(*Job,*[5] *Seth,*[4] *Joseph,*[3] *Thomas,*[2] *Richard*[1]), born July 23, 1811, in Braintree, Vt. Married first, Polly Morse, of Roxbury, Vt., who died April 12, 1851; married second, Mrs. Harriet K. (Spear) Thayer, Nov. 9, 1851. Mr. Mann is a substantial farmer at East Braintree, was selectman 1847-48, and a constable many years. He resides on the estate that formerly belonged to his father. (A bear and three cubs were killed in his woods in November, 1862. For account see Bass's His. of Braintree, p. 70.) Nine children, six by first wife, three by second:

   i. MARY JULIETTE,[7] b. Dec. 28, 1834; m. March 4, 1858, Francis Wright; res. Northfield, Vt.; two children.
   ii. IRA NATHAN,[7] b. May 2, or 21, 1838; d. May 5, 1841.
  iii. ALMA GEORGIANA,[7] b. July 13, 1841; d. Aug. 20, 1881; m. Irving Claflin, Dec. 15, 1860, who d. Sept. 1872; four children; res. Brookfield, Vt.
   iv. LUCY HELEN,[7] b. Sept. 10, 1845; m. Sept. 28, 1863, Ira O. Thayer; res. Roxbury, Vt.; three children.
   v. MINORA ADELIA,[7] b. Aug. 13, 1848; m. March 14, 1869, David B. Adams; res. Northfield, Vt.; one daughter.
   vi. Daughter,[7] died in infancy, April, 1851.
  vii. IRA,[7] b. Feb. 11, 1853; d. April 11, 1855.
 viii. ELLA VIRGINIA,[7] b. March 2, 1855; m. March 17, 1881, Wilmoth M. Terry [a student of the medical college in

Burlington, Vt.], and had at Bethel, Vt., (1) *Will Orman,*⁸ b. Jan. 27, 1882.

ix. FLORA MARION,⁷ b. Aug. 14, 1858; lives in Greenfield, N. Y., with her aunt.

(73) ELISHA⁶ MANN

(*Elisha,*⁵ *Seth,*⁴ *Joseph,*³ *Thomas,*² *Richard*¹), born in Randolph, Mass., March 31, 1803. He married first, Catharine Tucker; second, Naomi Mann. He resided at the "West Corner" in Randolph, a farmer. He had four children by first wife, two by second:

160.   i.   ELISHA,⁷ b. Dec. 17, 1829; m. first, Sarah Jane Howard.
      ii.   MINERVA,⁷ b. July 17, 1831; d. Feb. 4, 1847.
     iii.   NELSON,⁷ b. Jan. 23, 1834; m. June 9, 1864, Jennie, daughter of Nathaniel Howard, of R. Mr. Mann was a manufacturer (residing in Randolph, Mass.) for several years; a leader of the Randolph Brass Band many years, and leader of the choir at the First Baptist church about twenty years. Children: (1) *Howard Nelson,*⁸ b. 1865; d. 1870. (2) *Mary Peabody,*⁸ May 1, 1870.
     iv.   CATHERINE,⁷ b. March 5, 1836; d. Jan. ?
      v.   RACHEL LAVINIA,⁷ b. April 8, 1841; m. April 8, 1868, George M. French, of Randolph, and have: (1) *Herbert.*⁸ (2) *Charles.*⁸
     vi.   CHARLES HENRY,⁷ b. Nov. 4, 1842; m. June 11, 1867, Harriet Anna Phillips; res. Randolph. Children: (1) *Willie Orris,*⁸ b. Oct. 19, 1869. (2) *Florence Abby,*⁸ May 28, 1872. (3) *Elisha W.,*⁸ April 30, 1874. (4) *Ralph Henry,*⁸ Sept. 30, 1877. (5) *Bertha Anna,*⁸ March 12, 1881.

(74) ADONIRAM JUDSON⁶ MANN

(*Elisha,*⁵ *Seth,*⁴ *Joseph,*³ *Thomas,*² *Richard*¹), born March 28, 1805, in Randolph, Mass., and died there Jan. 28, 1882. He married, Feb. 8, 1827, Rosetta Howard, and resided at the "West Corner," in that town. He was admitted a member of the First Congregational church, in 1823, elected a deacon in 1855, resigned the office 1865. Children:

      i.   ADONIRAM JUDSON,⁷ Jr., b. Dec. 8, 1827; d. Dec. 6, 1851.
     ii.   ABIGAIL WHITCOMB,⁷ d. Aug. 12, 1866; m. Dec. 1846, Geo. Tabor, and had: (1) *George Elmer,*⁸ b. July, 1847; m. and res. at Campello, Mass. (2) *Warren White,*⁸ Oct. 12, 1850; m. and res. at Malden, Mass.
     iii.   ESTHER,⁷ b. April 15, 1835; d. April 12, 1836.

iv. ESTHER MARION,[7] b. Nov. 1, 1837; d. Nov. 26, 1881; m. first, Capt. Horace Niles, of the 35th Mass. regiment, was mortally wounded in the battle of Antietam, and died in a few days, aged thirty years, ten months. Mrs. Niles m. second, Jan. 30, 1867, John W. Bruce.

v. THOMAS HOWARD,[7] b. Sept. 20, 1839; m. May 12, 1866, Helen M. Wilbur; no children; res. Randolph.

vi. EMILY ROSSETTA,[7] b. Aug. 2, 1842; m. Nov. 16, 1862, Augustus J. Town, and had: (1) *Hattie Emma,*[8] b. June 30, 1863; m. Herbert Tabor. (2) *Alice Whitcomb,*[8] June 24, 1865. (3) *Arthur Mann,*[8] Feb. 26, 1867. (4) *Esther Maria*[8], Dec. 17, 1872.

vii. HARVEY NELSON,[7] b. Sept. 11, 1844; d. Sept. 27, 1846.

viii. HARVEY,[7] b. Sept. 28, 1847; m. May 26, 1870, Eliza Jane Arnold, of Canton, Mass., and have: (1) *Fred. Howard,*[8] b. Dec. 14, 1871. (2) *Esther,*[8] b. Jan. 20, 1883. Mr. Harvey Mann keeps a market in Dorchester District.

(75) REV. ASA[6] MANN

(*Elisha,*[5] *Seth,*[4] *Joseph,*[3] *Thomas,*[2] *Richard*[1]) was born April 9, 1816, in Randolph, Mass. He graduated from Amherst College, 1838, and Andover Theological Seminary, 1842; was settled in the ministry (first) in Hardwick, Mass., June 19, 1844; resigned Oct. 14, 1851; pastor at Exeter, N. H., 1851 to 1858; supplied at Wellfleet, Mass., 1862; Greenville, 1863; Springfield, Vt., 1864-5; Bath, N. H., 1866; pastor at Bath, 1867 to 1872; Raynham, 1873-4; Carlisle, 1875-6; supplied South Plymouth, 1878-9; and at Hardwick again, 1880 to 1881. Rev. Mr. Mann married April 16, 1848, Mary W. Bruce, of Springfield, Mass., who died Aug. 27, 1882, aged fifty-four. Mr. Mann's present residence and address is Braintree, Mass. Children:

i. ELLA LOUISE,[7] b. June 11, 1849.

ii. GRACE ELSIE,[7] b. Sept. 22, 1869.

(76) EPHRAIM[6] MANN

(*Elisha,*[5] *Seth,*[4] *Joseph,*[3] *Thomas,*[2] *Richard*[1]), a substantial farmer at Randolph, Mass., was born there April 18, 1820, and resides in that part of the town generally known as the "West Corner;" was selectman 1857-8; a member of the First Congregational choir since

1840, and its leader several years. He married Nov. 8, 1843, Mary Jane Leeds. Children:

    i. GEORGE WESTON,[7] b. March 17, 1845; d. March 6, 1846.
    ii. MARY LOUISA,[7] b. Nov. 11, 1851; m. Dec. 3, 1873, Dr. Augustus L. Chase, of Randolph, Mass., grad. of Eclectic Med. Institute, Cincinnati, Ohio. Children: (1) *Ella Louise,*[8] b. Oct. 4, 1874. (2) *Herbert Mann,*[9] March 7, 1877. (3) *Gilman Leeds,*[8] June 30, 1880.

(77) JOHN[6] MANN

(*John,*[5] *Seth,*[4] *Joseph,*[3] *Thomas,*[2] *Richard*[1]), born in Randolph, Mass., Jan. 11, 1805, and died at Randolph, Vt., June 29, 1874. He went to Randolph, Vt., and married April 4, 1841, Emily Howard, who died at Brookfield, Vt., March 9, 1863. They lived several years in East Braintree, Vt., where their children were born. For a time had a farm and lived in Brookfield, Vt. In 1864 sold the Brookfield estate, and ever after he and his son Laroy made their home with his son Gilman, at Randolph. He was a member of the Congregational church, and much respected. Children:

    i. JOHN GILMAN,[7] b. April 28, 1844; m. Oct. 27, 1868, Martha E. Granger. In 1863 Mr. Mann moved on to the farm in Randolph, the first one owned by his father in Vermont. In 1874 he engaged in the clothing business in West Randolph, still retaining the farm. They have one son, *John Laroy,*[8] b. Feb. 25, 1872.
    ii. CORNELIUS LAROY,[7] b. April 22, 1847; d. June 25, 1867.
    iii. EMMA MINORA,[7] b. May, 1855; d. June 8, 1859.

(78) ALVAN[6] MANN

(*John,*[5] *Seth,*[4] *Joseph,*[3] *Thomas,*[2] *Richard*[1]), born in Randolph, Mass., Dec. 6, 1806; married Emeline Mitchell, of Easton, Oct. 3, 1836. In early life he came into possession of nearly one-half of his father's estate at "West Corner," so called, a part of which he extensively cultivated, and marketed yearly large quantities of wood. This estate he sold some time since, to Deacon Royal Mann, his son, and retired from the more active pursuits, to enjoy the evening of life on the farm where he was born and always lived. Children:

161. i. AUGUSTINE ALVAN[7] (Dr.), b. Oct. 15, 1837.
      ii. LUTHERA NELSON,[7] b. July 22, 1839; d. Feb. 7, 1842.

    iii. ROYAL TILSON,[7] Esq., b. Feb. 10, 1843. He is a prominent citizen of Randolph, Mass., and unmarried. Was admitted a member of the First Congregational church in 1872; elected a deacon in 1878; served as selectman for the years 1880,–'81,–'82,–'83, is at present (1884) chairman of the board. He was appointed a justice of the peace in 1883. Is an extensive farmer, having about 150 acres of land which formerly belonged successively to his father grandfather, and great-grandfather.

162. iv. EDWIN MITCHELL,[7] b. March 23, 1849.

    v. LUTHERA HITCHCOCK,[7] b. July 3, 1851; unmarried, and living with her parents. It is through her efforts that much of the data concerning the Randolph family line is inserted in this volume.

(79) SETH[6] MANN

(*John*,[5] *Seth*,[4] *Joseph*,[3] *Thomas*,[2] *Richard*[1]), born April 1, 1810, in Randolph, Mass.; married Eliza Hunt, Nov. 27, 1834. He had about one half (112 acres) of his father's farm at "West Corner" in Randolph, and lived in the house which was built by his father. He died June 30, 1881. Children:

    i. JOHN ANDREW,[7] b. Nov. 1, 1835; m. 1860, Emily Jane Hayden; had two daughters, died young.

    ii. SARAH ANN,[7] b. March 7, 1839; m. 1856, Andrew Tracy. Children: (1) *M. Nellie*.[8] (2) *J. Louisa*.[8] (3) *Arthur*.[8] Res. Randolph, Mass.

    iii. MARY JANE,[7] b. Feb. 22, 1841; m. first, Frank Burpee; m. second, May 20, 1881, Kilburn Kendall; res. Worcester, Mass.

163. iv. SETH WESTON,[7] b. Dec. 20, 1847; m. Emma Fitts.

    v. ELIZA,[7] b. July 1, 1850; m. George Poole.

164. vi. MOSES FRANKLIN,[7] b. April 12, 1859, m. Julia Delano.

(80) DR. BENJAMIN[6] MANN

(*John*,[5] *Seth*,[4] *Joseph*,[3] *Thomas*,[2] *Richard*[1]). Benjamin Mann, A.M., M.D., for many years the well-known physician of Roxbury, Mass., was born in Randolph, Mass., March 31, 1814. He graduated at Amherst College, 1837, and "commenced professional studies under the direction of the well-known Dr. Ebenezer Alden of his native town, and Drs. Perry and Bowditch of Boston, attending also upon lectures and hospital practice at the Harvard Medical School, from which he received (1840) his degree in the usual course."

Soon after he commenced to practise in Foxboro' and remained there twelve years. He removed to Roxbury about 1852, and ever after practised in that city and Boston, where he enjoyed the confidence of the profession and the regard of a large circle of patients. At eighteen he became a member of the First Congregational church at Randolph, and maintained through life a high Christian character. He died in Brooklyn, N. Y., from hepatitis (on a homeward trip from Florida), April 21, 1874.

He married Jan. 25, 1842, Lydia E. Coffin Morse, daughter of John B. and Lydia Percy (Houston) Coffin, of Newburyport, Mass. [At the death of her parents, Morse was added to her name by her aunt with whom she was living.] Children:

165.   i. BENJAMIN HOUSTON[7] (Dr.), b. Nov. 6, 1842.
     ii. EMILY PERCY,[7] b. Sept. 12, 1844.
    iii. MARIETTA ROLLINS,[7] b. April 16, 1852.
    iv. HOWARD THORNTON,[7] b. June 26, 1863.

(81) DR. JONATHAN[6] MANN

(*John,*[5] *Seth,*[4] *Joseph,*[3] *Thomas,*[2] *Richard*[1]) was born in Randolph, Mass., March 16, 1816. At Amherst College from 1834 to 1836; grad. B. M. I., 1840; practised for a time in Kittery, Me.; went to Franklin, Mass., in 1843; to Valley Falls, R. I., in 1850; subsequently he practised in South Boston. Dr. Mann for a number of years has resided on Dartmouth Street, Boston.

He married first, Oct. 16, 1844, Marietta Rollins, born May 17, 1822, and died in Boston July 3, 1852 or '3. He married second, Jan. 16, 1854, Harriet Louise, daughter of Samuel and Harriet (Ham) Larrabee, of Bangor, Me. Children, three by first wife, five by second, viz.:

     i. JOHN ROLLINS,[7] b. July 8, 1845; d. Aug. 13, 1846.
    ii. SEWELL ROLLINS,[7] Esq., b. April 27, 1847; d. in Boston March 11, 1883.
   iii. JONATHAN EDWARDS,[7] b. 1848; d. aged four months.
   iv. SAMUEL LARRABEE,[7] b. Nov. 29, 1854; d. aged six months.
    v. FRANK EDWARDS,[7] b. 1856; d. aged ten months.
   vi. MARIETTA ROLLINS,[7] b. April 15, 1858; m. April 9, 1879, Fred W. Ayer, a lumber merchant in Bangor, Me. Children: (1) *Fred Rollins,*[8] b. Aug. 8, 1880. (2) *Nathan Chase,*[8] b. Feb. 22, 1881.
   vii. HARRIET LOUISE,[7] b. 1859; d. 1863.
  viii. ELLA FRANCES,[7] b. May 21, 1863.

(82) LEVI⁶ MANN

(*Levi,*⁵ *Benjamin,*⁴ *Benjamin,*³ *Thomas,*² *Richard*¹), born Jan. 6, 1782, in New York; died in No. Woburn, Mass., April 11, 1853. He married March 20, 1805, Margaret Ames, of Boston, who died at No. Woburn, Nov. 4, 1849, aged sixty-three years, ten months (grave-stone account at Hanover, Mass., where they were buried). Mr. Mann was a carpenter by trade, owned real estate in Boston, and resided there during the greater part of his life, his wife being a member of the Old South Church. Children:

i. LEVI,⁷ b. Dec. 15, 1805; d. March 7, 1851. He resided in Boston; m. Mary Ann Gilbert. [Boston rec. says Levi Mann m. Abigail Gilbert, Sept. 24, 1835.] She m. second, George W. Ellison, and d. Aug. 16, 1860. Children of Levi Mann, of Boston: (1) *Joseph,*⁸ b. April 6, 1838; m. 1866, Susan Glover, of Boston, and had 1, *Charles,*⁹ d. 1874; 2, *Laura M.,*⁹ d. 1869. (2) *Horace,*⁸ b. Dec. 9, 1839; d. May 29, 1873; m. April 7, 1869, Ruth J. Stetson, of Rockland, Mass., and have, 1, *Flora G.,*⁹ b. June 30, 1871-2. (3) *Laura A.,*⁸ b. Sept. 27, 1842; m. May 3, 1876, Charles F. Bryant. (4) *Charles,*⁸ b. Nov. 17, 1844; m. Ella E. Dove, Oct. 9, 1872. He is of the firm of Darrow, Mann & Co., State Street, Boston, and have, 1, *Susie Dove,*⁹ b. Jan. 13, 1874. (5) *Benjamin,*⁸ b. Nov. 1, 1846; m. Dec. 14, 1870, Georgiette Dodge. He is of the firm of Parker, Mann & Codman, Washington Street, Boston; res. Boston Highlands, and had, 1, *Georgiette Estella,*⁹ b. Sept. 21, 1874; d. April 12, 1880. (6) *George Washington,*⁸ b. Jan. 25, 1849; m. Feb. 25, 1880, Albenia Borden, and have, 1, *Nettie,*⁹ b. April 18, 1881. (7) *Levi,*⁸ b. Sept. 28, 1851; d. July, 1852.

ii. and iii. two daughters, died in infancy.

iv. REBECCA ANN,⁷ b. 1810; m. Harvey Hayden, 1832; res. Methuen, Mass.; no children.

v. SAMUEL,⁷ b. 1812; married and died in New Orleans. One child.

vi. MARGARET,⁷ April 2, 1814; d. May 18, 1842; m. first, Amos Boynton; second, Isaac Packard, and had: (1) *Ann Rebecca.*⁸ (2) *Lizzie.*⁹

vii. THOMAS D.,⁷ b. Aug. 1815; d. March 30, 1880; m. first, 1835, Lucy Damon, of Hanover, and had: (1) *Samuel,*⁸ b. 1842; d. in Danvers, 1864. (2) *Emily,*⁸ m. Nathaniel Davis, and has a son *Walter.*⁹ He m. second, Mrs. Mary E. Brown.

viii. HORACE D.,⁷ b. Dec. 5, 1817; d. June 3, 1876; carpenter by trade; m. first, Sept. 17, 1840, Caroline M. Wallace, who d. in Worcester, Feb. 1851; no children. He m. second, 1852, Caroline S. Deane, of Taunton, Mass., and had: (1) *Mary E.,*[6] b. Oct. 21, 1852. (2) *Horace,*[6] Sept. 12, 1855; d. March 3, 1882. (3) *Fanny D.,*[6] May 14, 1858. (4) *Ellsworth,*[6] March 11, 1861. (5) *George,*[6] Oct. 8, 1863; d. Sept. 6, 1864. (6) *John D.,*[6] May 21, 1872; res. No. Raynham, Mass.

ix. JOSEPH,[7] b. March 15, 1819; d. Aug. 19, 1866; carpenter by trade; m. in Boston, April 4, 1844, Mary Ann Hoyt. Children: (1) *Mary F.,*[8] b. Jan. 26, 1845; d. March 26, 1852. (2) *Sarah E.,*[8] Feb. 27, 1846; d. April 27, 1882; m. 1868, Joseph Dodds, of Champlain, N. Y. (3) *George H.,*[8] Nov. 27, 1847; d. Aug. 12, 1849. (4) *Susie M.,*[8] Sept. 12, 1850; d. Aug. 27, 1851. (5) *Charles J.,*[8] April 13, 1852. (6) *Mary Susie,*[8] Oct. 3, 1855; d. Nov. 6, 1877. (7) *John P.,*[8] Sept. 15, 1858. (8) *Benjamin Levi,*[8] Sept. 7, 1861; d. June 10, 1863. (9) *Edna F.,*[8] Oct. 4, 1865; d. June 7, 1866; res. Boston, Mass.

x. LAURA A.,[7] b. May 18, 1821; m. 1843, Rufus D. Larned, who lives in Minnesota; three children, *Frederick,*[8] *Levi,*[8] and *Mary,*[8] all married.

xi. ELIZABETH B.,[7] b. April 1, 1824; m. July 22, 1841, Noah Edgecomb; res. No. Woburn, Mass. They have had six children; only two lived to maturity, viz.: *George H.,*[8] b. Dec. 9, 1845; d. July 4, 1873; *Charles W.,*[8] Nov. 5, 1848; m. Netty E. Staggles, Aug. 15, 1871, and have three daughters.

xii. GEORGE W.,[7] b. Feb. 22, 1826; a carpenter by trade; m. first, Maria L. Bridges, of Boston, and had *Mary Ella,*[8] b. June 7, 1856; a teacher in a Boston public school. Mr. Mann m. second, Kate E. Chick, of Kittery, Me.; res. Boston, Mass.

xiii. HENRY,[7] b. Oct. 28, 1828; a shoemaker by trade; m. June 13, 1849, Isabella R. Stoddard, of Hanover, Mass. Children: (1) *Elizabeth R.,*[8] b. July 30, 1850. (2) *Isabella H.,*[8] Jan. 27, 1852. (3) *Charles H.,*[8] Dec. 16, 1855. (4) *Effie L.,*[8] Jan. 4, 1867; res. West Scituate, Mass.

xiv. EMILY,[7] d. aged thirteen months.

(83) JAIRUS[6] MANN

(*Levi,*[5] *Benjamin,*[4] *Benjamin,*[3] *Thomas,*[2] *Richard*[1]), born Oct. 7, 1787, in Hanover, Mass.; died at Charlestown, Mass., July 26, 1837. He married June 9, 1811, Desire, daughter of Enoch and Martha (Whiting) Whiting, of Hingham, who died in Charlestown, May 8, 1873, aged eighty-six. Mr. Mann had an estate on Austin

18

Street, in Charlestown, where he resided. Was a carpenter by trade. Children:

    i. ANN ELIZA,[7] b. Sept. 20, 1813; d. 1836.
166. ii. ALEXANDER,[7] b. July 30, 1817; m. first, Dorcas Rice.
    iii. MARY WHITING,[7] b. Aug. 4, 1819; d. Dec. 1837.
    iv. JAIRUS,[7] b. Aug. 17, 1822; d. 1822.

(84) JOHN[6] MANN

(*Levi,*[5] *Benjamin,*[4] *Benjamin,*[3] *Thomas,*[2] *Richard*[1]), born in Hanover, Mass., Jan. 25, 1795; died in what is now Rockland, Mass., March 16, 1876. He married Harriet, daughter of Ezekiel (Stetson) Turner, of Hanover (a granddaughter of Col. Amos Turner, of the Revolution). She was born in 1800, and died April 9, 1877. Mr. Mann was a school teacher, and by trade a shoe maker. Resided in East Abington, now Rockland, Mass. Children:

167. i. JOHN,[7] b. Dec. 28, 1819; m. first, Sarah V. Chandler.
    ii. JOSIAH,[7] b. March 13, 1822; m. Dec. 25, 1863, Charlotte Hammond, of Rockland, and had: (1) *Paul Grayson,*[8] b. and d. May 17, 1869. (2) *Gordon,*[8] April 3, 1871; res. Rockland, Mass.
    iii. ANDREW J.,[7] b. May 10, 1824; d. in Texas June 29, 1869; m. 1845, Abby O. Torrence, of Pembroke, and had an infant d. in Rockland Nov. 3, 1849.
168. iv. GUSTAVUS,[7] b. April 9, 1828; m. Elmira Vining.
    v. LUCY T.,[7] b. Aug. 4, 1829; m. first, Oct. 16, 1850, George Dunham, of Rockland, who d. Jan. 16, 1859; she m. second, Sept. 22, 1861, William Vining, of Rockland, a boot maker.
    vi. HARRIET N.,[7] b. Jan. 16, 1831; m. Aug. 25, 1844, Warren Lane, a boot and shoe maker, in Rockland, Mass.
    vii. LYDIA S.,[7] b. Feb. 9, 1832; d. Oct. 25, 1883; m. Oct. 14, 1850, Lorenzo D. Foster, of Rockland, Mass.; a boot and shoe maker.
    viii. SARAH,[7] b. May 18, 1834; m. May 14, 1866, Theodore B. Brooks, a shoemaker, of Rockland, Mass.
    ix. BETSEY,[7] b. Jan. 9, 1840; m. first, Feb. 16, 1862, Thomas Foster, of Rockland, who d. June 17, 1869; m. second, Anson Hicks, of Rockland, June 16, 1873.

(85) JOSEPH[6] MANN

(*Levi,*[5] *Benjamin,*[4] *Benjamin,*[3] *Thomas,*[2] *Richard*[1]), born in Hanover, Mass., Oct. 12, 1797; died in Austin Street, Charlestown,

Mass., where he resided, Dec. 2, 1835. He married Dec. 5, 1822, Eunice, born Dec. 12, 1799, daughter of Perez and Relief (Bowker) Jacobs, of Hanover, Mass. (she being a cousin to the mother of the late Hon. Charles Sumner). Mr. Mann was a ship carpenter by trade. The widow married second, Martin Stoddard and lived in Marshfield, Mass. Children of Joseph Mann, by wife Eunice, born in Charlestown, were:

169.
 i. JAIRUS,[7] b. Oct. 29, 1824; m. first, Emeline Runey.
 ii. CHARLOTTE B.,[7] b. May 12, 1827; d. Oct. 14, 1831.
 iii. EUNICE I.,[7] b. Feb. 16, 1829; m. William H. Smith, Nov. 29, 1848, and had: (1) *William Henry*,[8] b. May 23, 1851. (2) *Eunice A.*,[8] Sept. 22, 1853. (3) *Martha E.*,[8] June 22, 1858; residence Bunker Hill District, Boston.

(86) BENJAMIN[6] MANN, Esq.

(*Joshua*,[5] *Benjamin*,[4] *Benjamin*,[3] *Thomas*,[2] *Richard*[1]), born in Hanover, Mass., in 1788, and died there Dec. 11, 1861. According to Barry's Hist. Hanover, he married first, March 10, 1810, Lydia, daughter of Charles and Lucy (Dwelley) Josselyn. He married second, probably Lydia C. Waterman. He no doubt had a third wife. He was an influential citizen of the town, a trader and farmer, a justice of the peace for many years, and one of the original stockholders of Hanover Academy. He resided on Whiting Street. Had nine children by first wife, five by second:

 i. BENJAMIN L.,[7] b. April 19, 1812; d. New Orleans; m. Pamelia Whiting, of Scituate, Aug. 31, 1834.
 ii. ALBERT G.,[7] b. Aug. 22, 1813; d. 1817.
 iii. LYDIA J.,[7] b. Feb. 25, 1815; d. 1852; m. March 6, 1833, Jno. Pool, Jr.; had children: (1) *Jno. S.*,[8] b. Sept. 15, 1833. (2) *Lydia M.*,[8] May 18, 1836. (3) *Benjamin B.*,[8] Jan. 6, 1841. (4) *Margaret A.*,[8] July 11, 1849. (5) *Alonzo N.*,[8] Dec. 1851.
 iv. ELMIRA,[7] b. 1817; d. Nov. 1, 1817.
 v. CHARLES F.,[7] b. Sept. 5, 1818 (non compos.).
 vi. ELMIRA C.,[7] b. Jan. 11, 1820; m. Lysander B. Nash, of Weymouth, b. March 22, 1822, and had: (1) *Henrietta C.*,[8] b. April 15, 1846. (2) *Lysander W.*,[8] May 24, 1848.
 vii. HENRIETTA M.,[7] b. April 20, 1822; d. April 30, 1838.
 viii. NEWTON,[7] b. Feb. 20, 1825; d. Aug. 7, 1850.
 ix. LUCY A.,[7] b. Nov. 29, 1828; d. Jan. 24, 1855.
 x. MARCUS M.,[7] b. Nov. 22, 1840; m. Harriet Parks; res. Whiting Street, Hanover, Mass. Children: (1) *Mabel F.*,[8]

b. April 20, 1868. (2) *Jennie L.,*[8] July 11, 1875. (3) *Jacob F.,*[8] July 11, 1877. (4) Infant,[8] March 2, 1880.

xi. ALBERT G.,[7] b. July 17, 1843; d. July 28, 1865.

xii. Infant,[7] b. 1846; d. aged ten months.

xiii. EVERETT N.,[7] b. June 24, 1847; m. Henrietta Gardner, July 4, 1868; res. Webster Street, Hanover, Mass. Children: (1) *Abbie J.,*[8] b. Nov. 25, 1869. (2) *Edith E.,*[8] July 10, 1873. (3) *Preston G.,*[8] March 6, 1877. (4) *Minnie E.,*[8] April 7, 1879.

xiv. ABBY J.,[7] b. May 13, 1851; d. Aug. 29, 1869.

(87) MAJ. JOSHUA[6] MANN

(*Joshua,*[5] *Benjamin,*[4] *Benjamin,*[3] *Thomas,*[2] *Richard*[1]), born July 4, 1796, in Hanover, Mass., and died there Aug. 23, 1875. He married July 12, 1829, Bethia, born Jan. 27, 1808, daughter of Nathaniel Curtis, of Hanover, who died there Oct. 22, 1880. Barry's Hist. of Hanover says, "he was a farmer of respectable standing and lived on Centre Street." Children, born in Hanover:

i. JOSHUA W.,[7] b. March 19, 1830; d. in Mich.; m. Lydia Abbott, of Mich., and had: *Ellen,*[8] who is in Iowa.

ii. NANCY J.,[7] b. Oct. 1, 1832; m. first, M. T. Stetson, Oct. 6, 1850; second, —— Churchill.

iii. RODNEY,[7] b. March 9, 1835; m. Sept. 25, 1877, Sarah H. Hall, and had: (1) *Emerson Osborn.*[8] (2) *Otis R.,*[8] March 23, 1880. Mr. Mann is a crockery dealer; res. Hanson, Mass.

iv. MARY A.,[7] b. Nov. 10, 1838; unmarried; res. Hanover.

v. HORACE,[7] b. Nov. 12, 1842; unmarried.

vi. GEORGE W.,[7] b. March 12, 1845; m. Maria Rice, and have two children. Mr. Mann is a lawyer in Mich.; he grad. from Ann Arbor Coll., Mich.

(88) DAVID[6] MANN

(*Joshua,*[5] *Benjamin,*[4] *Benjamin,*[3] *Thomas,*[2] *Richard*[1]), of Hanover, Mass., was born there Sept. 7, 1798, and resides on Main Street. He married April 4, 1821, his cousin Betsey, daughter of Caleb and Betsey (Pratt) Mann. She died Jan. 29, 1873, aged seventy-three years, six months, twenty-eight days. Children:

i. DAVID J.,[7] b. 1822; d. at sea, 1846.

ii. GEORGE H.,[7] b. April 20, 1824; lives in Hanover.

iii. MARY J.,[7] b. Jan. 4, 1826; m. Wm. Church.

iv. JOSHUA,[7] b. Aug. 26, 1827; unmarried; res. in Hanover.

v. CALEB G.,[7] b. April 3, 1829; m. Amanda ———; res. in Hanover, and have: (1) *Caleb A.,*[8] b. Sept. 19, 185-, who m. Nov. 12, 1876, Abbie A. Hackett [they have *Lizzie J.,*[9] b. Dec. 8, 1877]. (2) *Hannah A.,*[8] Jan. 27, 1856; m. 1877, David D. Stoddard. (3) *Mary F. R.,*[8] Sept. 9, 1859; m. 1879, Elliot Bates. (4) *Charles H.,*[8] Oct. 29, 1860. (5) *James,*[8] July 26, 1862. (6) *Edward F.,*[8] Feb. 14, 1865. (7) *George H.,*[8] July 22, 1867. (8) *Eleanor E.,*[8] July 14, 1868. (9) *Abbie S.,*[8] Aug. 28, 1870.

vi. SOPHRONIA,[7] b. July 26, 1831; m. Jos. Hunt, of Rockland.

vii. PEREZ,[7] b. Jan. 1834; d. Aug. 20, 1835.

viii. RUSSELL C.,[7] b. July 30, 1836; unmarried; in San Francisco, Cal.

ix. ALBERT G.,[7] b. June 26, 1838; unmarried; res. Hanover.

x. HOWARD F.,[7] b. March 30, 1843; m. Cerena Measures, Aug. 8, 1875; res. Main Street, Hanover, Mass.; had (1) *Rena H.,*[8] b. Oct. 29, 1877.

(89) WILLIAM[6] MANN

(*Ensign,*[5] *Ensign,*[4] *Ensign,*[3] *Thomas,*[2] *Richard*[1]), born in Petersham, Mass., July 25, 1809. He was less than ten months old when his father died. After his mother married a second husband in 1815, he went to live with his uncle Samuel Mann, and remained in that family until he attained his majority. About this time, being somewhat of impaired health, by advice of physicians visited Lynn and took about a four weeks sail on the salt water. This trip having the desired effect, he returned and married Nov. 20, 1833, Abigail, born at Guildhall, Vt., Sept. 16, 1808, daughter of Benjamin* and Charity (Elliot) Cook (then of New Salem), of Athol, Mass. He lived at the easterly part of New Salem a year or two, where he had previously bought a farm of his father-in-law; from thence he removed to Barre and lived about a year. He then returned to Petersham, and carried on the John

---

* Benjamin[6] Cook, born at Wallingford, Conn., Jan. 24, 1764; died at Athol, about 1840; married Charity Elliot, born in Sutton, Mass., Aug. 1773, died at Petersham, aged ninety-seven. He was sixth in descent from Francis Cooke, of the Mayflower, in the following line: Benjamin,[6] John,[5] Israel,[4] Samuel,[3] Henry,[2] Francis.[1] See Hist. Wallingford, Conn.—ED.

Sanderson farm* a few years and finally purchased it. For many years subsequently he speculated in real estate and cattle, but the profits resulting therefrom largely vanished in supplying the many wants incident to a large family. He has owned about a dozen farms within a radius of five miles. About the year 1867, he purchased the Capt. Joel Brooks homestead estate in Petersham, of his son Horace Mann (who had previously bought it and cleared off the timber), where he has ever since resided. He is called a man of sound judgment, and enjoys the full confidence of his neighbors. A Jeffersonian in politics, and so are his sons, and firm believers in the sovereignty of the States. Of his children, the eldest was born in New Salem, the second in Barre, the others in Petersham. Children:

170.   i.   GEORGE SUMNER,[7] b. Nov. 25, 1834; m. Susan Alzea Stone.
171.   ii.   WILSON,[7] b. Jan. 28, 1837; m. Alice Putnam.
172.   iii.   HORACE,[7] b. Nov. 6, 1838; m. Martha E. Lamb.
173.   iv.   HORATIO,[7] b. Jan. 28, 1841; m. Abbie Louisa Payne.
       v.   MARY SANDERSON,[7] b. April 28, 1844; m. Nov. 3, 1869, Charles Kirke Wilder, a farmer in Petersham, who is much interested in agriculture. He was born in Petersham, Aug. 6, 1841. Children: (1) *George Kirke*,[8] b. Nov. 30, 1871. (2) *William Sumner*,[8] b. June 18, 1876. (3) *Charles Frederick*,[8] b. Dec. 22, 1878; d. Nov. 7, 1880.
      vi.   JANE LEVIRA,[7] b. Jan. 26, 1847; d. Dec. 27, 1864.
     vii.   LYDIA ANN,[7] b. July 6, 1849; unmarried; at home.

(90) LOT[6] MANN

(*Thomas*,[5] *Ensign*,[4] *Ensign*,[3] *Thomas*,[2] *Richard*[1]), born Oct. 24, 1818, in Petersham, Mass., resides at Athol, Mass. He married Jan. 11, 1862, Emily L., widow of Lot Dennis, of Petersham, and about that time purchased the well-known Seth Hapgood estate, at the Centre in Petersham, lived there a few years, and sold it to Hon. William B. Spooner, late deceased, of Boston, for a summer resi-

---

* This farm, formerly of more than 400 acres, is situated in the "Bennet Hill" district at the north part of Petersham. Sixty years ago it was extensively cultivated by John Sanderson, one of the wealthiest farmers in northern Worcester County. He was killed in his barn July 25, 1831, while in the act of taking a pair of unruly oxen off the cart-tongue. His only surviving son, Hon. John Sanderson, has been a resident of Bernardston, Mass., about fifty years.—ED.

dence. Mr. Mann by trade is a carpenter, and is said to possess a fair amount of property. One child, viz.:

i. THOMAS SIDNEY,[7] b. Oct. 18, 1864. He is unmarried, and of the grocery firm of Dennis & Mann, Orange, Mass.

(91) THOMAS MARSHALL[6] MANN

(*Thomas,*[5] *Ensign,*[4] *Ensign,*[3] *Thomas,*[2] *Richard*[1]) was born in Petersham, Mass., June 30, 1821, and died in Louisiana, Oct. 20, 1873. Mr. Mann probably had early instruction from his aged and learned grandfather, " Master Ensign Man" (as he was called), who lived in his father's family the last eighteen years of his life. This no doubt had an influence in shaping the future course of this young man. Be this as it may, we find him early an apt student among the many such at the locally well-known " Bennet Hill "* district school in Petersham. Later he taught this school, attended New Salem Academy, and was in Amherst College from 1846 to 1849, where he went to prepare himself to be a Universalist minister, but on account of ill health, after being there three years, went South to teach school, and finally settled at Vista Ridge, La., married M. E. Ferguson, about 1849, a wealthy planter's daughter (it is said), who died 1860. He settled on a plantation at that place and had many slaves before the war. His time was occupied mostly in teaching school and in " preaching the gospel." They had children born there as follows:

i. THOMAS WALTER,[7] b. Sept. 20, 1850; m. first, Sept. 27, 1871, Jennie C. Shage (divorced 1872); m. second, March 8, 1873, Gilley Yancy Davis, b. Sept. 22, 1855. He owns a farm and resides at Floyd, Carroll Co., La. Children by first wife: (1) *William Harris,*[8] b. Sept. 28, 1872. By second wife: (2) *Thomas Marshall,*[8] b. Dec. 28, 1873; d. June 26, 1880. (3) *James Lott,*[8] b. Sept. 17, 1880; d. Oct. 14, 1881.

---

* " Bennet Hill " school-house was of brick, situated at the north part of Petersham, on the old road and on the top of a hill so called, from a Mr. Bennet who lived there in the early history of the town. The road was discontinued about thirty-five years since, and the school-house taken down a few years later. In the remembrance of the author, the pupils of this school, for many years under the instruction of a superior teacher, Miss Eunice Sanderson (now Mrs. John Holman), were considered above the average in point of scholarship and literary attainment.—ED.

    ii. CHARLES ROBERT,[7] b. June 13, 1853; m. Dec. 28, 1876, Emma M. Franklin, b. July 14, 1852. He is a farmer; res. Hamburg, Ashley Co., Ark. Children: (1) *Mildred E.,*[8] b. Nov. 20, 1877; d. Oct. 17, 1880. (2) *James Ira,*[8] b. July 11, 1880. (3) *Alice Maria,*[8] b. May 11, 1883.

    iii. WILLIAM CLARK,[7] b. April 5, 1856; m. March 20, 1879, Nannie L. Sessons, b. March 1, 1859. He is a farmer; res. Oak Grove, Carroll Co., La. Children: (1) *Edith Evelyne,*[8] b. Feb. 26, 1882. (2) *William Marshall,*[8] b. June 16, 1883.

    iv. RICHARD BAXTER,[7] b. Oct. 22, 1859; m. May 4, 1879, Susie Ann Lawrence, b. July 23, 1856. He owns a farm at Oak Grove, Carroll Co., La. Children: (1) *Benjamin Lawrence,*[8] b. May 5, 1880. (2) *Richard Clark,*[8] b. Feb. 13, 1882. (3) *Earnest Linwood,*[8] b. Feb. 29, 1884.

(92) SAMUEL[6] MANN

(*Samuel,*[5] *Ensign,*[4] *Ensign,*[3] *Thomas,*[2] *Richard*[1]), the only surviving son of Samuel Mann, Sr., of Petersham, Mass., was born in that town October 21, 1832, and married his cousin Maria Antoinette Luce, July 3, 1854. He resides in the southerly part of Athol, within a few rods of Petersham town line and near his father's old homestead. The author of this work was a school-mate of his at the "Bennet Hill" district school. He was considered the intellectual genius of the neighborhood, and his services were not unfrequently in demand when difficult problems were perplexing to the student.

Sanford B. Cook, Esq., the present town clerk of Petersham, another school-mate and who has been associated with Mr. Mann in teaching, writes concerning him thus:

"Samuel Mann, Jr., is strongly developed physically, and in youth was quite an athlete. He has a mind of large calibre, and is almost constantly occupied in original thought. In childhood an apt scholar; in youth and mature years he delighted in the study of mathematics and the natural sciences, and became a proficient scholar therein. He was educated in the public schools of his own town, and in New Salem and Wilbraham Academies; has taught several terms in the public schools of Petersham, Athol, and Barre, with good success; was associate teacher in Farmer's Hall Academy at Goshen, N. Y., for about six months in 1866, where he did good work, having charge of the mathematical and scientific departments.

About 1856, he spent a season employed in the government survey on the frontier in the northwest, and here, from his superior mathematical ability, he was assigned the nice and critical work of 'meandering' the small lakes which abound in that country. In later years he has done much land surveying in the vicinity of his home. He has a great taste for drawing; though without special culture in this direction, he has nevertheless used his pencil to good advantage, having completed a large number of beautiful pictures, many of which are considered very valuable and would reflect credit upon the most accomplished artists. Since he was forty years old, his health has been considerably impaired, and in consequence he has only engaged in the lighter kind of work. He is a man of integrity, kind-hearted, and generous almost to a fault."

Children:

   i. CAROLINE ANTOINETTE,[7] b. April 11, 1858; d. Sept. 11, 1866.
   ii. HELEN A.,[7] b. May 13, 1860; m. Horace M. Stratton, March 28, 1878.
   iii. Sarah F.,[7] b. Dec. 20, 1865.
   iv. EUGENE S.,[7] b. Sept. 14, 1869.

(93) RODOLPHUS[6] MANN

(*Joel,[5] Joseph,[4] Nathaniel,[3] Richard,[2] Richard[1]*), born in Hebron, Conn., June 8, 1769, accompanied his father to Saratoga County, N. Y., and probably settled at Ballston or Milton in that county, where he died Oct. 22, 1828. He married first, Lydia Horton, born June 1, 1770, died April 14, 1812; married second, Phebe, born Oct. 10, 1779, widow of Thomas Sprague and daughter of Samuel Andrews; she died April 2, 1851. There were eight children by first wife, three by second, viz.:

   i. EZEKIEL,[7] b. Jan. 23, 1795; d. Dec. 1, 1865; m. ——; eldest daughter *Lydia,[8]* married Caleb Baxter.
   ii. LYDIA,[7] b. July 12, 1797; d. March 5, 1818.
   iii. JOEL,[7] b. July 16, 1799; d. Jan. 18, 1817.
   iv. RALPH R.,[7] b. March 19, 1802; d. May 20, 1803.
   v. RALPH R.,[7] b. Aug. 24, 1804; d. Dec. 23, 1882; married; res. Manlir, Mich. Children: *David R.,[8]* lives in Plainwell, Mich., and has two daughters.
   vi. MERCY,[7] b. Oct. 19, 1806; d. April 18, 1861; m. Samuel Rue; only child *Horton,[8]* resides at Ballston Centre, N. Y.
   vii. ALVAH,[7] b. Nov. 17, 1808; unmarried; d. in New York city. He built the Broadway Theatre.

19

viii. Horton,[7] b. March 29, 1812; d. 1865; m. in 1833, Elizabeth Curtiss, and had: (1) *Mary*,[8] b. and d. 1834. (2) *Mary E.*,[8] 1835; d. 1851. (3) *Mercy P.*,[8] 1843; d. 1872. The widow is living on her estate in Litchfield, Mich.

ix. Phebe,[7] b. Sept. 12, 1813; m William Miller, res. Litchfield, Mich.; they have (1) *Rodolphus*,[8] b. 1836. (2) *Elisha*,[8] 1838.

x. Joel,[7] b. Sept. 30, 1817; d. at Litchfield, Mich., March 25, 1856; m. Harriet Abele, 1839, and had: (1) *Rodolphus*.[8] (2) *Roger C.*[8] (3) *Phebe Ann.*[8] (4) *Harriet Emily*,[8] b. Nov. 11, 1846; m. Seymour D. Carroll, Oct. 3, 1867, and have: *Moses M.*,[9] b. April 7, 1875; *Harriet M.*,[9] Sept. 7, 1880; *Mercy C.*,[9] Aug. 19, 1882. (5) *Alvah R.*[8] (6) *William H.*[8] (7) *Joel A.*[8] (8) *Mary A.*[8] All except Harriet Emily are dead. The widow of Joel, Harriet (Abele) Mann, married second, Horace Jerome, who res. at Hillsdale City, Mich.

xi. John,[7] b. April 19, 1820; d. Aug. 7, 1822.

(94) JEREMIAH[5] MANN

(*Joel*,[5] *Joseph*,[4] *Nathaniel*,[3] *Richard*,[2] *Richard*[1]) was a substantial and well-to-do farmer in Milton Centre, Saratoga County, N. Y. He was born in Hebron, Conn., Nov. 14, 1771. About the year 1793 he accompanied his father, Joel Mann, to Saratoga County, N. Y., and settled in Milton Centre, where he died Jan. 3, 1839. He married first, Jan. 16, 1796, Lydia Norton, who was born Nov. 5, 1775. He married second, Rebecca Tallmadge, March 19, 1818, who died Feb. 16, 1852. The signature in this sketch was taken from his letter to "Much Respected Son" Francis Norton Mann, dated June 20, 1826. He had seven children—six by first wife, and Nathaniel (who resides on the homestead farm) by second wife:

i. Nathaniel,[7] b. July 16, 1798; killed Nov. 7, 1810, by a runaway horse.

174. ii. Jeremiah,[7] b. July 5, 1800; m. Clarissa Brockway.

175. iii. Francis Norton[7] (Hon.), b. June 19, 1802.

iv. George,[7] b. Nov. 8, 1804; d. Nov. 7, 1823.

v. William,[7] b. July 25, 1809; grad. from Union College. He died of consumption, May 25, 1839. Was unmarried, and a very promising young man.

vi. Mercy,[7] b. Oct. 28, 1813; d. Nov. 4, 1852; m. Dec. 23, 1840, Hon. Elias Plum (his second wife), a prominent citizen and ex-mayor of Troy, N. Y.; he died in April, 1883; by her had five children, viz.: (1) *Frank Mann,*[8] who died of consumption; he was in the cavalry service during the Rebellion, and badly wounded. (2) *Elias,*[8] Jr., now of New York. (3) *Sarah W.,*[8] now Mrs. E. G. Gilbert, of Troy. (4) *Lucetta,*[8] now Mrs. David Banks, of N. Y. (5) *Mercy Mann,*[8] living in Troy. Hon. Elias Plum had three children by first wife and one by third wife, who were no relation to the Manns.

176. vii. NATHANIEL,[7] b. Dec. 29, 1819; m. Sally Frances Slocum.

(95) SAMUEL[6] MANN

(*Joel,*[5] *Joseph,*[4] *Nathaniel,*[3] *Richard,*[2] *Richard*[1]), born in Hebron, Conn., June 18, 1776; died in Milton Centre or Ripley, N. Y., March 23, 1831 (?). It is said the widow of Samuel with her family of children, many of whom were then married, removed from Milton to Ripley, N. Y., before 1831. The widow soon after married a Mr. Van Sise, and died some years since in Ripley. It is also said that Samuel had about twelve children, probably born at Milton, some of whose names were: (1) *David,*[7] died in Westfield, N. Y., leaving a family. (2) *Samuel,*[7] lived in western New York, and left a family. (3) *Mary,*[7] married Wm. Freeman, of Lockport, N. Y. (4) *Margaret.*[7] (5) *Israel,*[7] went to Ohio. (6) *Horace.*[7] (7) *Nancy.*[7] (8) *Joel,*[7] went to Ohio. No doubt many of the descendants are living in Ohio and Michigan.

(96) DR. JOEL[6] MANN

(*Joel,*[5] *Joseph,*[4] *Nathaniel,*[3] *Richard,*[2] *Richard*[1]), born in Hebron, Conn., Sept. 16, 1784; accompanied his father to Milton, N. Y., about 1793, where he probably remained a few years and prepared himself to be a physician. He subsequently went to Cazenovia, N. Y., to practise; married Jan. 15, 1809, Sallie Merrick, and died there May 10, 1812, leaving only two children:

177.   i. DARWIN II.,[7] b. Dec. 15, 1809; m. Cordelia Newton.

      ii. JANE,[7] b. Feb. 21, 1812; m. April 12, 1833, Samuel C. Bliss (born March 1, 1808), of Cazenovia, N. Y., a farmer. They had seven children, the youngest, *Darwin II.,*[8] a physician in Kansas city, Mo.—(Bliss Genealogy.)

(96ª) ELIEL⁶ MANN

(*Zadock*,⁵ *Joseph*,⁴ *Nathaniel*,³ *Richard*,² *Richard*¹), born at Hebron, Conn., Sept. 3, 1781; died at Naugatuck, Conn., Nov. 7, 1864. He married first, Annis ——, who was born in 1784, and died Feb. 8, 1849. He married second, Lucy Judd, who was born 1786, and died Jan. 4, 1859. He had two sons by first wife. He was a millwright, and in early life was engaged in the lumber trade in eastern Ohio. A great portion of his life was spent in Naugatuck, where he died. Children:

    i. EMORY D.,⁷ b. in Hebron, Conn., May 8, 1805; d. Dec. 31, 1875. He m. Lucinda Atwater, of Naugatuck, Conn., April 28, 1828, who died April 26, 1873. He was a manufacturer and a skilful mechanic; res. Naugatuck. Children: (1) *Jane G.*,⁸ b. March 15, 1829; m. Nov. 28, 1847, Eli Nichols, who died March 22, 1875; he was a butcher; res. Waterbury, Conn. Children: 1, *Eli E.*,⁹ b. Jan. 14, 1851; m. Emma Potter; had one child. 2, *Eugene E.*,⁹ b. Feb. 14, 1852; d. Oct. 28, 1863. 3, *Lucinda E.*,⁹ b. Aug. 9, 1860; d. Sept. 28, 1861. 4, *Emmogene A.*,⁹ b. July 15, 1864. 5, *Eugene E.*,⁹ b. Jan. 6, 1865. 6, *Mabel A.*,⁹ b. Feb. 28, 1875. (2) *Fanny*,⁸ b. Dec. 4, 1831; m. June 3, 1851, Joseph N. Levenworth, a silver plater, now of New Haven, Conn. Children: 1, *Martha*,⁹ b. June 10, 1855; m. Elbert Sperry; had one child. 2, *Estella*,⁹ b. June 17, 1860; m. Frederic Farr. 3, *Hella*,⁹ b. June 17, 1860. 4, *Fred J.*,⁹ b. Sept. 8, 1875; d. 1879. (3) *Bela Atwater*,⁸ b. Sept. 4, 1835; m. Aug. 6, 1860, Prudence C. Spencer. He is a manufacturer of narrow cotton goods; res. Hamden, Conn. Has one son, 1, *Bela Hartley*,⁹ b. March 14, 1863. (4) *William Seymour*,⁸ b. July 11, 1838; m. Jan. 29, 1860, Mary E. Clark. He is a machinist; res. Hamden, Conn. One daughter, 1, *Fanny R.*,⁹ b. Nov. 14, 1860. (5) *Emily C.*,⁸ b. Sept. 9, 1840; m. Feb. 28, 1865, Capt. A. D. Hopkins, a farmer at Naugatuck. One daughter, 1, *Jane E.*,⁹ b. Oct. 4, 1870. (6) *Ella A.*,⁸ b. Sept. 7, 1845; m. Feb. 20, 1868, Dr. Frank B. Tuttle, a physician; res. Naugatuck. Children: 1, *Lerta Hunter*,⁹ b. Dec. 26, 1868; d. 1878. 2, *Frank J.*,⁹ b. Oct. 3, 1874. (7) *Annis R.*,⁸ b. Feb. 9, 1847; m. Nov. 21, 1870, Jacob T. Garrison, a dry goods merchant at Naugatuck. Children: 1, *Louisa L.*,⁹ b. July 2, 1871. 2, *Emily A.*,⁹ b. Oct. 27, 1875.

    ii. HIRAM ELIEL,⁷ b. in Connecticut, Nov. 14, 1813; m. May 18, 1837, Lucy Celesta Judd, who was born Sept. 23, 1816, and died Feb. 4, 1884. He is a farmer in Ashtabula

County, Ohio. Children: (1) *Harvey Eliel,*[8] b. Jan. 3, 1838; m. April 17, 1867, Elvira Cordelia Smith, who was born Aug. 9, 1850, died Dec. 27, 1877. Children: 1, *Lucy Margery,*[9] b. April 5, 1869. 2, *Laura Elvira.*[9] b. March 26, 1872. 3, *Henlen Cordelia,*[9] b. Oct. 28, 1877; d. June 10, 1878. (2) *Emery Burritt,*[8] b. June 17, 1842; d. April 20, 1855. (3) *Chauncey Hiram,*[8] b. June 4, 1845; address, Nyack, N. Y.

(97) WARNER[6] MANN

(*Zadock,*[5] *Joseph,*[4] *Nathaniel,*[3] *Richard,*[2] *Richard*[1]), the second son of Zadock Mann, was born (probably in Hebron, Conn.) Feb. 16, 1784, and died at Plymouth, Ohio, May 30, 1858, where he had resided for many years. He was a farmer and a highly respected citizen of that town. He married first, April 30, 1807, Amanda, daughter of Jude Blakeslee, of Plymouth, Conn., and by her had eleven children. He married second, J. A. Bragman, of E. Plymouth, O., and had four more children:

   i. SALLY AMANDA,[7] b. May 7, 1808; d. Jan. 21, 1810.
   ii. ESTHER,[7] b. Feb. 26, 1811; d. Oct. 10, 1847; m. Oct. 8, 1826, Stephen Buffum, and had: (1) *Rufus.*[8] (2) *Matthew.*[8] (3) *Joseph.*[8] (4) *Austin.*[8] (5) *George.*[8] (6) *Amanda.*[8] (7) *Olive.*[9] (8) *Silas.*[8]
178. iii. WILLIAM WARNER,[7] b. June 22, 1813; d. 1880.
   iv. LEVEA,[7] b. March 9, 1817; m. Bennett Seymour, Nov. 4, 1841, and have: *Emeline Eliza*[8] (a noted musician at Ashtabula, O.), who m. 1867, Francis E. Harmon; they have *Louise Gertrude,*[9] b. May 15, 1871.
179. v. BIELBY PORTENS,[7] b. May 18, 1819; m. Sarah Upson.
180. vi. BELA BLAKESLEE,[7] b. Jan. 15, 1822.
   vii. OLIVE,[7] b. Aug. 8, 1824; m. Dr. Chauncey Isbell, March 10, 1844; no children; res. Santa Paula, Cal.
   viii. AMANDA,[7] b. July 19, 1827; d. July 19, 1883; m. June 23, 1843, Isaac Mathews. Children: (1) *Cassius Mann,*[8] b. May 4, 1846. (2) *Minerva,*[8] April 8, 1848; m. Quincy A. Sloan, Oct. 16, 1871, and had *Frank Carleton,*[9] b. March 27, 1880; res. Iowa.
   ix. JOSEPH WARREN,[7] b. Sept. 3, 1829; d. July 8, 1853, in Cal., unmarried.
   x. JOHN HENRY,[7] b. May 7, 1831; res. Dakota; farmer; unmarried.
   xi. GEORGE SELDEN,[7] b. Nov. 5, 1833; d. Aug. 24, 1835.
   xii. GEORGE W.,[7] b. 1842; d. 1844.
   xiii. ANDREW W.,[7] b. Sept. 5, 1845; m. Martha Stevens; res. Burr Oak, Kan., and firm of Mann & Gilbert, merchants.

Children: (1) *Mattie M.,*[8] b. July 14, 1866; d. Feb. 23,
1870. (2) *Clara L.,*[8] June 22, 1868; d. Feb. 21, 1870.
(3) *Hattie M.,*[8] Feb. 19, 1870. (4) *Arthur Warner,*[8]
March 14, 1872. (5) *Edith,*[8] April 27, 1874. (6) *Mattie
Sarah,*[8] Dec. 4, 1882.

xiv.   MILES E.,[7] b. April 4, 1847; went to the war and never
heard from.

xv.   RUTH,[7] b. Dec. 31, 1849; m. Dec. 31, 1864, Solomon
Phillips, res. Akron, Ohio. Children: (1) *Eva,*[8] b. June
30, 1866. (2) *Levea,*[8] b. March 18, 1873.

(98) JOSEPH[6] MANN

(*Zadock,*[5] *Joseph,*[4] *Nathaniel,*[3] *Richard,*[2] *Richard*[1]) was born either
in Hebron, Conn., or Ashtabula, Ohio, April 12, 1792, and died Dec.
27, 1867. He married first, Alma ———; second, Mrs. Doyle,
July 3, 1865. He was a farmer and lived in Ashtabula County,
Ohio (probably the town of Plymouth). Children by first wife:

     i.   LAURA ADALINE,[7] b. Sept. 6, 1812; d. April 13, 1868; m.
Squire Jesse Smith, and had: (1) *Julia,*[8] b. June 8, 1834.
(2) *Joseph Willard,*[8] b. Aug. 11, 1839; d. in the war.
(3) *Laura C.,*[8] b. Jan. 31, 1842.

181.   ii.   MERRITT MARVIN,[7] b. June 29, 1814.

    iii.   BETSEY A.,[7] b. July 26, 1816; d. Feb. 26, 1876; m. Aug.
1, 1838, Edward Harper, b. Oct. 8, 1812, a carpenter and
farmer of East Plymouth, Ohio. Children: (1) *Helen E.,*[8]
b. Aug. 8, 1839; m. Joseph Graham. (2) *Charles E.,*[8]
Aug. 23, 1841; d. Nov. 4, 1856. (3) *Orpha J.,*[8] March
27, 1844; m. Wilber E. Mann, June 21, 1866. (4) *Lloyd
Mann,*[8] Aug. 31, 1846; m. Diadama Warren, 1871. (5)
Mary Louise,[8] Nov. 8, 1848; d. April 22, 1862. (6)
Lewis M.,[8] May 20, 1854; m. Elizabeth Waters, May 23,
1874. Edward Harper m. second, Mrs. Nancy Harrison,
Feb. 13, 1879.

    iv.   JULIA EMILY,[7] b. July 3, 1818; m. Nov. 1, 1838, William
R. Seymour, b. 1817; d. 1870; a stone mason. Children:
(1) *Randall Hart,*[8] b. Feb. 17, 1840; m. 1856, Sarah Edwards. He is a stone mason. (2) *Collins F.,*[8] July 19,
1841. (3) *Alma L.,*[8] Jan. 17, 1843; m. Philo W. Blakeslee, 1863. (4) *Merrick J.,*[8] Nov. 6, 1844; m. Harriet E.
Blakeslee; is a farmer. (5) *Marcus D.,*[8] Oct. 4, 1846.
(6) *Emily A.,*[8] Jan. 29, 1849; m. Chauncey Amidown.
(7) *Joseph Mann,*[8] May 17, 1851; d. Sept. 9, 1872. (8)
Harriet Ellen,[8] Feb. 17, 1854; a teacher. (9) *Levi L.,*[8]
Feb. 24, 1856; a teacher. (10) *William Homer,*[8] Oct. 16,
1858; m. Emma Pinney.

v. COLLINS ELIAL,[7] b. Oct. 4, 1820; m. Dec. 10, 1845, Minerva Wood, b. March 10, 1824, who d. April 29, 1880. Mr. Mann is a farmer at Geneva, Ohio. Children: (1) *Luroff C.*,[8] Oct. 28, 1846; soldier, d. April 25, 1865. (2) *Carlos A.*,[8] Sept. 11, 1849; m. Alice I. Cook, March 25, 1875, she b. Jan. 27, 1856. [Carlos A. Mann's res. is Portland, Oregon; a methodist, school-teacher, and farmer. Children: 1, *Lucy A.*,[9] b. Nov. 23, 1876; 2, *Olivia L.*,[9] July 28, 1878; 3, *Jeannie Alma*,[9] Jan. 13, 1881.] (3) *Elvira S.*,[8] Oct. 11, 1852; d. Nov. 24, 1869.

vi. ALMA AMANDA,[7] b. June 23, 1822; d. Jan. 8, 1865; m. Oct. 21, 1845, Frederick Smith, b. Oct. 22, 1818. Children: (1 and 2) *Albert*,[8] and *Adelbert*[8] (twins), b. Oct. 23, 1846 (Adelbert d. July 15, 1851). (3) *Maria A.*,[8] b. April 16, 1849. (4) *Eugene A.*,[8] March 24, 1856.

vii. ELECTA JANE,[7] b. May 12, 1824; d. March 28, 1883; m. first, Riley Castle, who d. Feb. 28, 1861. Children: (1) *Winfield*,[8] b. Nov. 3, 1848; m. Mary Ann Abbey; res. E. Plymouth, Ohio. (2) *Mary*,[8] Jan. 8, 1852; m. Shepard Fulkerson; res. Geneva, O. Electa J., m. second, Peter Thompson, and by him had *Marvin*,[8] b. Dec. 13, 1870.

viii. STEPHEN HENRY,[7] b. June 19, 1826; d. March 1, 1852; m. Sept. 1849, Amanda Saterlee, b. Feb. 26, 1821, and had: (1) *Clara Amanda*,[8] Aug. 31, 1850, who m. in 1870 Charles Cassady [and had 1, *Nellie E.*,[9] 1871; 2, *Clara A.*,[9] 1874; 3, *Charles*,[9] 1879]. (2) *Emily Suren*,[8] July 13, 1852; d. May 16, 1879; m. Wm. Mills, Nov. 12, 1875 [and had 1, *Merrill Henry*,[9] 1877, d. 1878; 2, *Eugenia Suren*,[9] 1879, d. 1879].

ix. CHARLES JOSEPH,[7] b. Oct. 25, 1828; d. Jan. 6, 1851.

x. AUSTIN WARNER,[7] b. Nov. 7, 1830; m. Sept. 27, 1855, Sarah E. Roscoe, who was b. Sept. 13, 1831. He is a farmer in Plymouth, Ohio, and has two children, viz.: (1) *Wilfred M.*,[8] b. March 19, 1858; a farmer. (2) *Frank E.*,[8] Dec. 10, 1869.

xi. HARRIET ELLEN,[7] b. Sept. 28, 1832; d. Aug. 2, 1856; m. Henry Richmond. No children.

xii. ORSON HIRAM,[7] b. Nov. 13, 1834; m. Mary Hoffman. He is a farmer at Plymouth, O., and has: (1) *Frances*,[8] who m. Wilber Warner; res. East Plymouth, Ohio. (2) *Edgar Orson*.[8]

xiii. ZADOCK,[7] b. Aug. 19, 1838; m. Elizabeth Hoffman. He is a farmer in Plymouth, Ohio, and has: (1) *Henry*.[8] (2) *Willie E.*[8] (3) *Mary*.[8]

(99) JAMES[6] MANN

(*James*,[5] *Joseph*,[4] *Nathaniel*,[3] *Richard*,[2] *Richard*[1]), born Aug. 10, 1792, in Ballston, N. Y.; died at his son Henry's home at Ballston

Spa, Sept. 23, 1873. He married Abigail Hedges, of Sag Harbor, L. I., who died at Ballston, May 30, 1882, aged eighty-four. His residence was at the old homestead in Ballston. One son, viz.:

    i. HENRY A.,[7] b. Jan. 23, 1823; m. Matilda Jones, Jan. 1, 1848. Henry A. Mann, Esq., is a resident of Ballston Spa, Saratoga County, N. Y. He was county treasurer for many years. They have had the following children: (1) *Henry A. Jr.*,[8] b. May 31, 1850; m. Frances A. Parcent, June 10, 1874, and have, 1, *Arthur J.*,[9] b. April 27, 1875; 2, *Harry Hedges*,[9] June 7, 1876. (2) *James R.*,[8] b. Dec. 25, 1851. (3) *William T.*,[8] b. Oct. 4, 1855. (4) *Edward J.*,[8] b. May 6, 1859; d. Oct. 6, 1874, at school, So. Williamstown. (5) *Ella M.*,[8] b. July 12, 1864.

(100) JOSEPH[6] MANN

(*James*,[5] *Joseph*,[4] *Nathaniel*,[3] *Richard*,[2] *Richard*[1]) was born in Ballston, N. Y., March 21, 1804, settled on a farm at Kendall, N. Y., and died there Sept. 1, 1881. He married first, in 1833, Delia Eveline Barrow, who died Aug. 28, 1865; second, Mrs. Harriet Sanford. Children by first wife:

    i. JAMES,[7] b. Oct. 3, 1834; unmarried; by trade an ornamental painter; res. Kendall, N. Y.

182. ii. WILLIAM BARROWS[7] (Dr.), b. June 15, 1838.

    iii. JOSEPH,[7] b. Jan. 5, 1840; m. in 1868, Laura Spicer; a farmer in Kendall, N. Y. Children: (1) *Charlotte*,[8] b. Dec. 15, 1869. (2) *Frederick*,[8] July 25, 1873. (3) *Ida*,[8] July 15, 1875. (4) *Mary*,[8] Dec. 8, 187?.

    iv. FRANCES TRYPHENA,[7] b. April 24, 1848; m. William N. Spicer. No children.

(101) JOHN[6] MANN

(*John*,[5] *John*,[4] *Nathaniel*,[3] *Richard*,[2] *Richard*[1]), the eldest of fifteen children, and the first child of American parentage born in the town, was born in Orford, N. H., May 21, 1766, and died there April 6, 1849. He married first, Feb. 25, 1788, Lydia, daughter of Deacon Timothy Dutton, of Hebron, Conn., who died Feb. 23, 1809. He married second, June, 1810, the widow of Jesse Smith, of Thetford, Vt., and daughter of Lemuel Hough, of Lebanon, N. H. He was a merchant and farmer at Orford, N. H., and occupied an important position in society; was major of a regiment; filled public offices, and was a member of the Congregational church. He had nine children by his first wife, all born at Orford, N. H., except the eldest son, who was born in Hebron, Conn. Children:

183.   i. JOHN DUTTON,[7] b. Feb. 15, 1789; m. Martha Phelps.

      ii. LYDIA,[7] b. Jan. 19, 1791; d. unmarried, Dec. 25, 1812.

184. iii. TIMOTHY,[7] b. Dec. 18, 1792; m. Eliza Louisa Poinier.

     iv. LUCY DUTTON,[7] b. March 24, 1795; m. Luther M. Harris, M.D., of Jamaica Plain, Boston. Children: *John*,[8] *William*,[8] *George*,[8] *Robert*,[8] *Lydia*,[8] and *Ellen*.[8] [For further account see Harris Gen., by Luther M. Harris, M.D.]

      v. SOPHIA,[7] b. May 4, 1797; d. Dec. 5, 1849; m. Jan. 26, 1817, George O. Strong [grad. Brown University 1814], whose residence was Boston, Mass., a boot and shoe merchant; had ten children, three died young. The surviving children were: *George*,[8] *Joanna*,[8] *Catherine*,[8] *Edwin*,[8] *Mary*,[8] *William*,[8] and *Lydia Ann*.[8]

185. vi. SILAS,[7] b. March 19, 1799; m. Rhoda Parker.

    vii. CLARISSA,[7] b. July 24, 1801; d. July 4, 1860;? m. Col. Squire Allen, Sept. 24, 1839, a merchant in Petersburgh, N. Y., d. Dec. 4, 1846.

186. viii. RUSSELL,[7] b. April 1, 1803; m. Mary Ann Hanchett.

     ix. ROYAL[7] (Rev.), b. Nov. 6, 1805; a grad. Dart. Coll.; Presbyterian clergyman; died at Marion, N. Y., in 1875. He m. first, Sarah P. Lee, in Rochester, N. Y., who d. Feb. 29, 1860, aged sixty-four. He m. second, Mary A. Raymond, daughter of Samuel Rich, of Penfield, N. Y., Jan. 21, 1861; she d. Sept. 30, 1865. He m. third, Laura Durfee, Oct. 16, 1866, at Marion, N. Y. He had one son, *Royal H.*,[8] a member of Mack's battery in the war, and died at Baton Rouge, La., aged twenty-one.

(102) SOLOMON[6] MANN[*]

(*John*,[5] *John*,[4] *Nathaniel*,[3] *Richard*,[2] *Richard*[1]) was born in Orford, N. H., Aug. 19, 1768, and died in Montpelier, Vt., Aug. 11, 1825. Farmer. He married Emily Parkhurst. Children:

      i. PHEBE,[7] m. Rev. George Hough, a missionary to Burmah; she was a woman of fine qualities of mind, and died aged seventy-one. They had a daughter who became the wife of Maj. Gen. Tremenheere, of the Bengal Engineers; and a son *George*,[8] Esq., assistant commissioner of the Rangoon district.

---

[*] The records of this family are meagre. See Rev. Joel Mann's pamphlet.

20

ii.   EMILY,[7] m. Henry Oakes, a merchant, who died at Fairlee, Vt., about 1815. The widow subsequently went to Little-ton, N. H., kept a public house and died there. Children: *Emily*,[8] m. Mr. Kent, a merchant in Lancaster, N. H. *Phebe*,[8] m. Mr. Stephenson, a lawyer. *Elizabeth*,[8] m. Rev. B. F. Fay. *Sarah*.[8] ~~*m.*~~   11.

iii.   SOLOMON,[7] m. Frances C. Kellam. He was a merchant and settled in Mich. Children: *Phebe*,[8] m. Mr. Hyatt, a mer-chant in Ann Arbor, Mich. *Frances Emily*,[8] m. Rev. Benj. F. Millard. *Hattie H.*,[8] died. *Solomon*,[8] a lawyer. *Gustavus*.[8] *Jennie Wells*,[8] m. David E. James, a lawyer. *Anna Green*,[8] m. Hon. George S. Becker, a member of Congress from Minn.

iv.   WILLIAM,[7] d. in Mich.; m. Ruth Hazeltine, and had: (1) *Henry*.[8] (2) *Jane*.[8] (3) *Mary Anne*,[8] who m. Waldron Hubbard Dame; d. Brooklyn, N. Y. (4) *Thomas*.[8] (5) *Elizabeth*.[8]

v.   ALMIRA,[7] m. Curtis Parks, a merchant, Concord, Vt.

vi.   GEORGE SPARROWHAWK,[7] b. (at Orford, N. H.) 1798; m. (at Bath, N. H.) June 30, 1819, Laura Mattocks. He re-sides in San Francisco, Cal. Of the children the three eldest were born at Fairlee, Vt., viz.: (1) *Laura Mat-tocks*,[8] b. March 9, 1820; m. (1836) Henry Baylis (Bay-lis Needles), of New York city. They had, 1, *Laura*,[9] b. June 22, 1837; 2, *Adalaide Louisa*,[9] June 16, 1845, who is married and has children in the tenth generation. (2) *George Mattocks*,[8] b. June 26, 1821; m. Aug. 17, 1846, Kate Cross Nash, of N. Y. city. For many years an im-porter of fancy goods in N. Y. city; res. Brooklyn, N. Y. Of their children *George H.*,[9] b. (New York) March 14, 1851 (fatally injured on the railroad in New Haven, and d. June 11, 1874). By profession a civil engineer; a man of unusual capacity and acquirements, and a good linguist. He m. (N. Y.) Oct. 31, 1872, Alphonsene T. Mousette, who had *George H.*,[10] b. (in Brooklyn, N. Y.) July 2, 1874 (this lad is with his maternal relatives in Paris, France, receiving an education). *Henrietta Kate*,[9] b. (Brooklyn) July 22, 1856; m. Jan. 4, 1879, Waldo I. Morse, a cloth com. merchant, N. Y. Children: 1, *Sidney F. Randolph*,[10] b. Jan. 29, 1880; 2, *Waldo I., Jr.*,[10] b. Feb. 12, 1883; res. Brooklyn, N. Y. (3) *Adaline*,[8] b. May 11, 1823; m. (N. Y.) May 11, 1845, Thomas H. Jenkins, who d. at Jamaica, L. I., 1870. Children: *Harry*[9] (died). *Adaline*.[9] *Samuel*.[9] *Charles*.[9] *Flora*.[9] Res. San Francisco, Cal. (4) *Ella*,[9] b. (in N. Y.) March 1, 1842; d. 1872; m. George Hawley, a merchant in San Francisco, Cal., and have, 1, *George M.*[9] 2, *Addie*.[9] (5) *William*,[8] b. (N. Y.) 1846; with parents at San Francisco, Cal. (6), (7), (8), (9), four children, died young.

vii.   HIRAM,[7] went West early.

viii. JOHN PARKHURST,[7] m. Hannah Bailey; a merchant, settled
in New York state, and had, *Marquis de Lafayette*.[8]

ix. HENRY,[7] injured by kick of a horse, d. at Brattleboro', Vt.

x. ALBERT,[7] a merchant in New Jersey, and has *Albert*,[8] a
Methodist minister.

xi. MARIA,[7] went South.

(103) JARED[6] MANN

(*John*,[5] *John*,[4] *Nathaniel*,[3] *Richard*,[2] *Richard*[1]) was born in Orford,
N. H., Nov. 6, 1770; died May 30, 1837, it is said, in Lowell, a
farmer. He m. Feb. 17, 1794, Mindwell, daughter of Samuel Hale,
M.D. He held some public offices in Orford, taught schools, and
was a useful citizen. Children:

187.
i. JARED,[7] b. Nov. 5, 1794; m. Hannah Mason.

ii. LUCRETIA,[7] b. April 11, 1796; d. Feb. 17, 1800.

iii. SUSANNA,[7] b. Jan. 5, 1798; d. July 14, 1870; m. March 14,
1825, Wm. Heard, of Wayland, Mass., a farmer, and had:
(1) *Samuel Hale Mann*,[8] b. March 23, 1826; m. Harriet
Sherman, of W., March 1, 1849; they have had five children. (2) *Wm. Andrew*,[8] Aug. 25, 1827; m. Emily Maria
Marston, of Sandwich, N. H., April 25, 1855; three sons.
(3) *Jared Mann*,[8] March 16, 1831; d. March 21, 1861;
m. Ellen Balch, of Prov. R. I., Oct. 19, 1858; Unitarian
clergyman; one child. (4) *Susan Elizabeth*,[8] July 16,
1835; d. Aug. 30, 1853.

iv. MARY HALE,[7] b. July 4, 1799; d. in Illinois; m. William
Darby, May 12, 1823, a farmer; have a son *Henry*[8]; res.
Illinois.

v. SAMUEL HALE,[7] b. May 25, 1801; d. Oct. 30, 1838. He
was a lawyer in Lowell, Mass., and m. Isabella Ross,
1829. Children: (1) *Isabella Ross*,[8] m. Mr. Parkyn, and
had, *Charles Cleghorn*.[9] (2) *Samuel H.*,[8] who resides in
Chicago, Ill.

vi. WILLIAM PRESCOTT,[7] b. Feb. 16, 1803; d. June 3, 1804.

vii. ELIZABETH,[7] b. March 3, 1805; d. March 18, 1805.

viii. WILLIAM PRESCOTT,[7] b. Nov. 4, 1806; d. May 5, 1807.

ix. ELIZABETH HALE,[7] b. Dec. 25, 1808; m. Sept. 13, 1832,
Abel Gleason, of Wayland, Mass., a farmer; no children.

(104) IRA[6] MANN

(*John*,[5] *John*,[4] *Nathaniel*,[3] *Richard*,[2] *Richard*[1]) was born in Orford,
N. H., Sept. 8, 1772; died in May, 1860, it is said, in Rome, Mich.
He married first, a Miss Bailey; married second, a Miss Scott.

He was a farmer and had seventeen children, the greater part of whom, it is said, settled West. Some of them were, *Ira*,[7] *Joseph*,[7] *Gilbert*,[7] *Abigail*,[7] *Anna*,[7] *Fanny*,[7] *Bailey*,[7] *Charles*,[7] and *Daniel*.[7]

(105) AARON[6] MANN

(*John*,[5] *John*,[4] *Nathaniel*,[3] *Richard*,[2] *Richard*[1]) was born in Orford, N. H., July 21, 1774, and died in Elgin, Ill., in 1851, having moved there with his family from Orford, in 1838. He married first, Sally Melvin; second, Sally Ingraham. Capt. Mann (as he was called) had sixteen children, eight by first wife, eight by second, viz.:

	i.	SALLY,[7] m. Reuben Roberts; res. Fisherville, N. H.
188.	ii.	AARON,[7] b. Feb. 28, 1799; m. Eliza Weld.
	iii.	HARRIET,[7] m. Francis Weld.
	iv.	PHILOXA,[7] b. 1803; d. Oct. 20, 1831, at Elbridge, N. Y.; m. Sept. 12, 1827, Peter Clark, a grad. from Union Coll. He was pres. of Washington College, Kent County, Md. Children: (1) *Philenus Mann*,[8] b. Sept. 23, 1831; d. Oct. 14, 1855, a gifted son.
	v.	ELIPHALET KIMBALL,[7] went to Elgin, Ill., about 1833; d. in Chicago, about 1880.
	vi.	ISAAC.[7] vii. CYRUS.[7] viii. Infant,[7] who was buried with its mother.

Children by second wife:

ix.	ADIN.[7]	xii.	BENNING.[7]	xv.	EUNICE.[7]
x.	WILLIAM.[7]	xiii.	MUNROE.[7]	xvi.	MARIA,[7] d. young.
xi.	LEONARD.[7]	xiv.	CHARLES.[7]		

(106) NATHANIEL[6] MANN

(*John*,[5] *John*,[4] *Nathaniel*,[3] *Richard*,[2] *Richard*[1]) was born in Orford, N. H., Dec. 29, 1779, and died May 13, 1860. He was an extensive farmer at Orford, and a useful citizen. He married Mary Mason, of Lyme, N. H., Nov. 27, 1804; she was born Nov. 26, 1785. Children:

189.	i.	JONATHAN MASON,[7] b. Jan. 27, 1806; m. Mary Kinsman.
	ii.	LEWIS,[7] b. March 2, 1810; died of consumption, Sept. 7, 1834; grad. Dartmouth College 1831.
	iii.	MARY,[7] b. Jan. 28, 1813; m. Oct. 10, 1833, Hon. Leonard Wilcox, who was a lawyer and judge in New Hampshire: he died at Orford, N. H., June 18, 1850, aged fifty. The widow survives, and lives in Orford. They have a son *Leonard*,[8] living in St. Louis, Mo.

iv. CARLOS,[7] b. Aug. 9, 1815; m. May 5, 1841, Eliza A. Willoughby, of Holderness, N. H., who d. Oct. 2, 1875. Children: (1) *Emma E.,*[8] b. Aug. 3, 1842; m. Charles M. Stratton, Oct. 30, 1870, of the firm of Stratton Brothers, at Greenfield, Mass. (2) *Julia A.,*[8] b. Nov. 11, 1845; m. July 19, 1870, Andrew A. C. Sears, of Plymouth, Mass., a carpenter. (3) *Zerah C.,*[8] b. March 21, 1850; m. March 30, 1875, M. Janie Hicks, at Orford; a farmer. (4) *Susan H.,*[8] b. Oct. 3, 1854. (5) *Bushrod W.,*[8] b. March 3, 1857; m. April 16, 1878, Cora Atwood, of Bedford, N. H.

v. HELEN,[7] b. Oct. 28, 1824; m. Charles A. Silver, a merchant, Brooklyn, N. Y. Children: (1) *Charles L.,*[8] b. 1849; d. 1882; m. Louise Jennings, of Brooklyn, April 16, 1875, who died May 6, 1883. (2) Dr. *Henry M.,*[8] a well known physician in the city of New York. (3) and (4) *Edward V.*[8] and *Lewis M.*[8] (twins), who are graduates of Yale College, and now studying medicine.

(107) Judge BENNING[6] MANN

(*John,*[5] *John,*[4] *Nathaniel,*[3] *Richard,*[2] *Richard*[1]) was born in Orford, N. H., Nov. 25, 1781. But little is known of his early life. With his two brothers, Cyrus and Joel, he preferred a professional course, and was educated at Dartmouth. He married his cousin, Phebe Mann (see p. 111), of Hebron, Conn., Dec. 25, 1806, and settled in Stafford, where he engaged in the practice of law. Here he remained some sixteen years, and here his children were born. It was during his residence here that he was Judge of Tolland County Court. About the winter of 1822, with his cousin Nathaniel Mann and Dr. Joseph Sibley, he engaged in some new business undertaking, and removed to Sidney, Delaware County, N. Y., where he remained three years. From this place he again removed to Hartford, Conn., where he passed the remainder of his life. Here he resumed the practice of his profession.

Without his solicitation and entirely unknown to himself, his friends procured his appointment as United States Marshal for Connecticut, under Polk, which office he filled to the satisfaction of all. He could have retained the position during the next term, but refused it. He also served with credit as Senator in the Legislature of the State. Afterward he was appointed Justice of the Police Court of Hartford, a position which he held for thirty years, when his term expired by law, he having reached the age of seventy. After that time he was Grand Juror and Clerk of the Police Court for nearly eleven years, which position he held at his death. He died Jan. 31, 1863, at his residence on Chapel Street, after an illness of one week. He was a man of strong common sense, and possessed a keen discernment of right and wrong, which led him to decide readily upon cases brought before him, and made him a terror to evil doers. Strict integrity and modesty were marked characteristics with him. He never sought any of the public honors held by him, but when they were thrust upon him he executed his trust with fidelity to all.

At the announcement of his death the officers of the police force and the newspaper reporters met in the court room, which had been draped in mourning, and after appropriate remarks by a number of gentlemen, resolutions of respect were offered and adopted. Resolutions of like tenor were passed by the Putnam Phalanx and the Masonic bodies of which he was a member. The funeral services were held in Christ Church, of which he was a member. The church and adjacent streets were filled with people, and a long procession followed the remains to the cemetery on North Main Street, where they were interred with Masonic honors.

The following lines were written by Mrs. L. H. Sigourney on his death:

"We miss him from our streets,
The good, brave man, who held old time at bay,
Taking from four score years their fill
Of vigorous health, and casting still
    Their frosts away.

We miss him in these days
When upright men are rare;
When the unvarnished purpose fails,
And gain o'er godliness prevails
    With haughty air.

Son of that honored State
Where granite boulders rise,
Amid the rocky cliffs that soar
Protective round New England's shore,
    Nearest the skies.

His virtues rooted deep,
Nor bowed to Fashion's train,
Nor truckled to the venal throng,
But frowned on violence and wrong
    With just disdain.

Unswerving was his course
To age from stainless youth:
So we with mournful reverence pay
The tribute of our praise this day,
    To sterling worth!
                    L. H. S."

Children :

i. MARTHA CORDELIA,[7] b. Sept. 21, 1810; d. at Grand Rapids,
Mich., June 1, 1863; m. Aug. 5, 1834, at Christ Church,
Hartford, Conn., Prof. Augustus Backus (son of Lieut.
Col. Electus Backus, of Greenville, N. Y.), who was born
May 9, 1802, and died Jan. 10, 1866; res. Troy, N. Y.
(until 1852), where the following children were born, viz.:

> (1) *Herbert Augustus*,[8] b. Sept. 6, 1835; m. April 8,
> 1869, Frances Gibbs Welton, of Grand Rapids;
> res. Detroit, Mich. He is connected with the
> house of Dean Godfrey & Co. Mr. Backus is
> interested in genealogy, and is expecting to pub-
> lish the history of the Backus Family in the near
> future. He has children: 1, *Augustus Welton*,[9]
> b. Jan. 4, 1870. 2, *Herbert Electus*,[9] b. May 31,
> 1872. 3, *Eleanor Frances*,[9] b. July 7, 1874; d.
> Oct. 17, 1876. 4, and 5 (twins), *Clarence Mann*,[9]
> b. Sept. 28, 1878, d. May 22, 1879, and *Francis
> Gibbs*,[9] b. Sept. 28, 1878.
>
> (2) *Isadore Cordelia*,[8] b. July 31, 1837; d. Dec. 6, 1840.
>
> (3) *Brady Electus*[8] (Rev., D.D.), b. March 24, 1839; m.
> Annie Taylor, of New York city, June 9, 1875.
> Dr. Backus was grad. from Trinity College, Hart-
> ford, Conn., and Gen. Theo. Seminary, New
> York city, and is Rector of Church of the Holy
> Apostles in New York city. Children: 1, *Cor-
> delia Mann*,[9] b. Feb. 14, 1878. 2, *Helen Amanda*,[9]
> b. May 6, 1881.
>
> (4) *Pauline Janette*,[8] b. April 18, 1841; m. Joseph
> Stringham, Jr., Sept. 14, 1869; res. East Sagi-
> naw, Mich. Child: 1, *Joseph*.[9]
>
> (5) *Arthur Mann*[8] (Rev.), b. Nov. 17, 1843; m. May
> 1, 1878, Elizabeth, daughter of Rev. Dr. Burton,
> of Cleveland, Ohio. Rev. Mr. Backus is at pres-
> ent Rector of St. Paul's Church, Dedham, Mass.
> Child: 1, *Jean*,[9] b. Aug. 14, 1881.
>
> (6) *Charlotte Cordelia*,[8] b. July 6, 1846; unmarried;
> res. Detroit, Mich.
>
> (7) *Albert Provost*,[8] b. Dec. 30, 1848; m. Aug. 13, 1874,
> Ada Farr, of Detroit, Mich.; res. Detroit; busi-
> ness, hardware. No children living.
>
> (8) *Clarence Lay*,[8] b. March 21, 1851; d. Nov. 23, 1851.

ii. BENNING E.,[7] died in Chicago, Ill., July 10, 1883, aged 72;
m. in 1834, Mary Ann Mygatt, in Hartford, Conn., and
had children: (1) *Julia*,[8] who m. —— Peck, a lawyer in
Chicago; res. Lyme, Conn. (2) *Edward B.*,[8] who is unmarried, and in New York city. (3) *Belle*.[8] (4) *Charles
Carrol*,[8] killed in the army. (5) *May*,[8] res. Chicago.

iii. EDWARD MANLIUS,[7] d. in Hartford, Conn.; m. first, Charlotte Pultz; m. second, Lucy Matthews. Children, by

first wife: (1) *Virginia,*⁸ b. June 27, 1841; m. Charles Long, of Chicago (now deceased), and had: 1, *Florence,*⁹ b. 1859; m. Dr. Horace Long, 1882, and lives in New York city; 2, *Charles,*⁹ b. 1862. (Mrs. Long now lives with her uncle, Edward Pultz, Jersey city). (2) *Ella,*⁸ b. 1846; m. William Kimball in 1865, who lives at West Bergen, N. J., and is a banker, of the firm of Ferris & Kimball, Exchange Place, N. Y.; child living, *William Adams,*⁹ Jr., b. Jan. 14, 1875. Child, by second wife: (3) *Stella,*⁸ m. Dr. Laban Hazeltine, April 20, 1876, of Jamestown, N. Y., and has *Mabel;*⁹ the widow (Lucy Matthews Mann) m. second, O. H. Hunter, and res. at Warren, Penn.

iv.   MARGARET PETERS,⁷ m. Samuel D. Hunter, a pioneer and leading citizen of Greeley, Colorado; he is a leading member of the Episcopal Church, and is engaged in well-known public enterprises. No children.

v.   CATHERINE VERNON,⁷ m. Sidney E. Strickland, of Chulahoma, Miss. No children.

vi.   CYRUS N.,⁷ d. Aug. 13, 1882, aged 59; m. Sept. 24, 1851, Angeline Slemmons, of Metamora, Ill. Children: (1) *Benning,*⁸ b. Nov. 22, 1853; d. Aug. 10, 1881. (2) *Harriet,*⁸ b. August, 1856; d. May 14, 1860. (3) *Charles,*⁸ b. May 7, 1863; d. March 12, 1884. (4) *Cyrus,*⁹ b. June 7, 1866.

(108) ASAPH⁶ MANN

(*John,*⁵ *John,*⁴ *Nathaniel,*³ *Richard,*² *Richard*¹), born in Orford, N. H., Sept. 30, 1783, and died Dec. 27, 1814. He married Mary Barber, daughter of his step-mother. He was a farmer in Orford, and inherited the homestead estate. Children:

i.   ASAPH,⁷ Jr., m. Ann Sawyer. He resides on the old homestead. Children: (1) *Abigail.*⁸ (2) *Francina.*⁸ (3) *John T.*⁸ (4) *Charles A.*⁸ (5) *Mary B.*⁸

ii.   THOMAS,⁷ m. Margaret Shaffer, of Savannah, Ga. He is a lawyer, practised a few years in Orford, then removed to Elizabeth, N. J. Child: (1) *William Little.*⁸

iii.   CATHERINE,⁷ d. young.

(109) REV. CYRUS⁶ MANN

(*John,*⁵ *John,*⁴ *Nathaniel,*³ *Richard,*² *Richard*¹) was born in Orford, N. H., April 3, 1785, and died at his son's in Stoughton, Mass., Feb. 9, 1859. He married Aug. 17, 1817, Nancy Sweetser, who was born Dec. 25, 1790, in Marlborough, N. H., and died at Fitzwilliam,

N. H., Aug. 9, 1871. He graduated from Dartmouth College in 1806, "having the Greek Oration." He was principal of Gilmanton Academy two years; teacher in Troy, N. Y., one year; tutor in Dartmouth College, five years; studied theology with Rev. Roswell Shurtliff; ordained and installed pastor of the Congregational church in Westminister, Mass., Feb. 22, 1815, where he faithfully labored twenty-six years over a large society. At his request was dismissed from this pastorate, and was stated preacher in Plymouth, Mass., three years, and lastly was acting pastor of the Congregational church at North Falmouth, Mass., four years. His publications were a "Treatise on Trigonometry," an "Epitome of the Evidences of Christianity," a "History of the Temperance Reformation," a "Memoir of Mrs. Myra W. Allen," and some sermons. Children, all born in Westminister:

190.
 i. CYRUS S.[7] (Dr.), b. April 12, 1820; m. Harriet P. Field.
 ii. ANN MARIA,[7] b. March 2, 1823; m. Rev. John F. Norton, A.M., Sept. 26, 1853 (second wife). Rev. Mr. Norton was the successful and beloved pastor of the Congregational church at Athol, Mass., for sixteen years; a man of genuine piety and scholarly attainments. He now resides at Natick, Mass. They have one son: *Lewis Mills*,[8] b. in Athol, Mass., Dec. 26, 1855; received the degree of Doctor of Philosophy, at "Gottingen University," Germany, in 1879, and is now (1883) Prof. of "Organic Chemistry" in the Mass. Institute of Technology, Boston; res. Auburndale, Mass. He was m. June 6, 1883, to Mary Alice, daughter of Rev. F. N. Peloubet, of Natick.
 iii. ADELIA PORTER,[7] b. Jan. 2, 1826; m. at Athol, Mass., Nov. 27, 1856, John Q. A. Johnson, of Charlestown, Mass., now (1883) at Washington, D. C. Children: (1) *John Norton*,[8] b. in Boston, May 31, 1859; grad. at Harvard University 1881, and received the degree of Doctor of Philosophy from the same university in 1883.

(110) REV. JOEL[6] MANN

(*John*,[5] *John*,[4] *Nathaniel*,[3] *Richard*,[2] *Richard*[1]) was born in Orford, N. H., Feb. 7, 1789, and died in New Haven, Conn., July 21, 1884. He graduated at Dartmouth College in 1810, valedictorian of his class. He taught Moor's Charity School in connection with the college, 1810–11. Studied theology with Rev. Dr. William Ellery Channing, of Boston, and with President John Wheelock, of Dartmouth College; was ordained colleague pastor with Rev. Dr. Henry Wright, Bristol, R. I., in 1815. In 1826 he left and became colleague pastor with Rev. Ebenezer Gay, of Suffield, Conn. He left in 1829, and in 1830 became pastor of the church in Greenwich, Conn. In 1837 he was installed pastor of the Free Presbyterian Church, New York City. In 1840 he became pastor of the Howard Street Church, Salem, Mass., where he remained until 1847. He preached in Kingston, R. I., from 1847 to 1857, and afterward at Hanover Four Corners, Mass. During the revivals of 1832 his preaching was in great demand, and attended with remarkable success. Some twenty years ago he gave up the active duties of the settled ministry, resided in Morrisania, N. Y., for a time, and then came to New Haven. During these latter years he has been a much esteemed and beloved member of a little circle of retired ministers, who have been accustomed to hold meetings for mutual pleasure and profit, among whom were professors Day, Olmstead and others. He has been an active member of the Third and Davenport churches, New Haven.

He has spent considerable time during the later years of his life upon his genealogy,* which he traced back hundreds of years through an old and honored English family. He had their coat of arms. He kept a copious diary. He took a decided and outspoken position against slavery. His sympathies in theology were with the old school. His decision of character and strength of purpose carried him through many exigencies and sicknesses to a good old age.

He has resided for many years with Mrs. C. E. Gorham, of New Haven. He was sick about a week with infirmities incident to extreme age rather than from any special disease, and died early on the morning of July 21, at the advanced age of ninety-five. The funeral was attended from the Davenport Church, July 23, and the remains were taken to Newport, R. I., for interment.—*The Congregationalist.*

He married May 10, 1816, Catherine, daughter of Samuel Vernon, president of Newport Bank, she died May 20, 1871. Children:

    i. SAMUEL VERNON,[7] b. Feb. 10, 1817; d. Oct. 10, 1836.

---

* Rev. Joel Mann published a twenty-four page pamphlet (heretofore alluded to on p. 109) about 1873, entitled "Genealogy of the Mann Family," in which his publications are mentioned.—ED.

191.   ii. EDWARD JOEL,[7] b. May 20, 1818; d. 1869.

      iii. MARY ELIZABETH,[7] d. in infancy.

      iv. ELIZABETH ELLEN,[7] d. in infancy.

      v. WILLIAM.[7]

      vi. CATHERINE VERNON,[7] b. Sept. 8, 1826; d. April 25, 1849; m. S. Stillman Field, of Boston, a merchant, and had: *Catherine V.*,[8] and *Frederick*,[8] both died.

192. vii. FREDERIC PORTER[7] (Dr.), m. Susan Martin.

(111) REUBEN[6] MANN

(*Andrew*,[5] *John*,[4] *Nathaniel*,[3] *Richard*,[2] *Richard*[1]) was born in Hebron, Conn., April 18, 1782; married there Maria Phelps, who was born in 1786, and died April 23, 1848. Mr. Mann went to Marshall, Mich., in the spring of 1836, and soon after purchased a farm near that place. From thence late in life he removed into the village of Marshall, and lived with his unmarried daughter Harriet Maria, where he died Jan. 24, 1868, aged eighty-six. Children, born in Hebron:

      i. HARRIET MARIA,[7]* b. May 11, 1813; d. unmarried at Marshall, Mich., Feb. 27, 1866.

      ii. HENRY REUBEN,[7] b. Sept. 30, 1815; d. at Marshall, unmarried, Oct. 6, 1842.

      iii. JULIETTE L.,[7] b. March 25, 1818; d. young in Hebron, Conn.

      iv. ANDREW PHELPS,[7] b. March 18, 1820; d. Jan. 12, 1848, at Marshall; m. (cousin) Anna Maria Mann; no children. The widow Anna Maria married second, in 1856, William D. Thomson, Esq., a banker of large wealth and influence, who resides in Jackson, Mich. They have two children. (See p. 165.)

---

* Harriet M. Mann, of Marshall, Mich., was a woman of superior character, and virtues and intellectual ability. A devout Christian, fond of home and literature, possessed of keen natural wit and a good memory, she was a charming companion and wise counsellor, was honored and beloved by all who knew her. She outlived her mother and brothers, and was never married; she devoted her later life to the care of her aged father, who survived her by a few years. Her death, which occurred in middle life, was deeply mourned by a large circle of friends and acquaintances, and by many who had experienced the benefits of her wise counsel and generosity of heart.

The following lines are from a number of other poems written by her, in which she seems to allude to her own life, and which show her to have been a woman of tender feeling and unusual literary ability.—Communicated by BRADY E. BACKUS, D.D., of New York city.

OUR FATHER'S HEARTH.

PILE on the wood—the winter blast
Bids household fires be bright;
Draw nigh the chairs—of seasons past
Shall be our talk to-night.

Were coldness in our hearts as rife
As snows that wrap the earth,
Soon, torpid love would warm to life
Beside our father's hearth.

(112) COL. ANDREW[6] MANN

(*Andrew,*[5] *John,*[4] *Nathaniel,*[3] *Richard,*[2] *Richard*[1]) was born in Hebron, Conn., Sept. 14, 1784, and married March 29, 1807, Nancy (or Anna) Phelps, of the same town, who was born Nov. 29, 1787. He removed to Unadilla, N. Y., about 1814, and followed the pursuit of farming. In 1834 he again removed, and this time to Marshall, Mich., where he erected a brick hotel and kept it for years. He was a man of enterprise and public spirit. It is said that "he built churches, school-houses, saw-mills and bridges." The first Episcopal church built at Marshall was erected by him and given to the society; the first printing-press in that town was purchased by him and a few others. He was a supporter of Andrew Jackson, was an active member of the militia in New York, and served as colonel in his district. His wife died at Athens, Mich., Sept. 9, 1850, and buried at Marshall. About this time, or a little later, he made his home at Madison, Wis., where his son had located. He died at Sun Prairie, Wis., Sept. 21, 1873, and was buried at Marshall, Mich. Children:

193.   i.   FRANCIS ANDREW,[7] b. March 16, 1808; m. Marian Mack.
194.   ii.   MANLIUS,[7] b. June 10, 1810; m. Pamelia Craig.
195.   iii.   JOEL PHELPS,[7] b. Nov. 19, 1814; m. Mary M. Crownover.

'Twas here we watched the ball's rebound,
  And shook the rattling dice;
Nor dreamed that pleasure e'er was found
  In fellowship with vice.
We thought, like Abyssinia's Prince,
  Within the wide world's girth,
All fair as it appeared—but since
  We've left our father's hearth,

Thou'st played another game than this,
  On the world's board; while I
Have risked the sum of happiness
  Upon a single die.
Unshrinking, we will bide the cast,
  For fullness, or for dearth;
So, our world centres to the last,
  Here by our father's hearth.

As brightly scintillates the flame,
  As in those hours of glee,
When grief, or care, was but a name,
  And words as thoughts were free:
But Time, the thief, can ne'er restore
  The effervescent mirth;
As once we met, we meet no more,
  Beside our father's hearth!

For some are gone. First the frail flower
  Drooped, gently, to the tomb;
Then the strong oak, in leafiest hour,
  Crushed, sudden, to its doom.
And thou and I, of all bereft
  Who owned a kindred birth,
Thou and I only, now are left
  Beside our father's hearth.

As waters close above the stone,
  And smooth their ruffled flow,
Till by no outward trace is shown
  The weight that rests below;
So we press back the tear that starts
  At mem'ry of their worth;
Though grief sits heavy at our hearts,
  And, by our father's hearth.

Earth's children we—and forth we must,
  To mingle in the strife
Begun in hope, to end in dust:
  For, brother, such is life!
Come heart-warm love, or cold pretence;
  Come misery, or mirth;
Our holiest thoughts will turn to whence
  They sprung—our father's hearth.

196. iv. JOHN EDWIN,[7] b. April 29, 1817; m. Emily Josephine
Bliven.

197. v. ANDREW LEWIS,[7] b. Aug. 5, 1819; m. first, Dolly M. Russell.

vi. GEORGE,[7] b. Sept. 16, 1822; d. May 12, 1841, at Marshall,
Mich.

vii. ANNA MARIA,[7] b. April 3, 1826, at Unadilla, N. Y.; m.
first, her cousin Andrew P. Mann, who died leaving no
children; she married second, 1856, William D. Thomp-
son, Esq., the enterprising and wealthy banker of Jackson,
Mich., where she now resides. Children: (1) *William
Mann,*[8] b. Feb. 24, 1858; m. Sept. 12, 1883, Kizzie
Adams Rogers, of Ann Arbor, Mich. (2) *Anna Louise,*[8]
b. June 26, 1861; m. Dec. 7, 1881, Clifford Wedworth
Clarke, of New York city, who died Jan. 25, 1884; they
have a son *Wedworth William,*[9] b. March 26, 1883. (3)
George Cooper,[8] b. Feb. 19, 1864; d. Sept. 15, 1865.
(See p. 163.)

viii. JULIETTE,[7] b. April 2, 1828; d. July 23, 1831, at Sidney
Plains, N. Y.

(113) JUDGE CYRUS[6] MANN

(*Andrew,*[5] *John,*[4] *Nathaniel,*[3] *Richard,*[2] *Richard*[1]) was born in Hebron, Conn., July 27, 1797. He fitted for Washington (now
Trinity) College with Rev. Dr. Bassett, of Hebron, but ill health
obliged him to relinquish his studies. He lived in the town of Hebron, and died there of asthma, Dec. 24, 1873. He married Elizabeth E., daughter of Artemas Worthington, Esq., of Colchester, Conn.
He was a merchant, farmer, and for many years a judge of probate.
He was a member of St. Peter's Protestant Episcopal Church in
Hebron, and a man universally respected in the community; in politics a democrat of the Jeffersonian type. Children:

i. MARGARET,[7] b. May 9, 1844; m. June 26, 1867, Charles E.
Jillson, a painter, and reside in Pawtucket, R. I. Children: (1) *Charles Herbert,*[8] b. at Hartford, Conn., Aug. 25,
1868. (2) *Eleanor Worthington,*[8] b. at Hebron, Conn.,
Sept. 14, 1871.

ii. CHARLOTTE M.,[7] b. Nov. 24, 1846; m. Charles L. Phelps,
May 11, 1870, and reside on the farm in Hebron, Conn.,
that has been in the Phelps family ever since the town
was settled. Children: (1) *Lewis Worthington,*[8] b. Oct.
20, 1880.

iii. C. EDWIN,[7] b. Dec. 20, 1848; d. Feb. 25, 1856.

iv. WILLIAM W.,[7] b. Jan. 30, 1851; unmarried; res. Littleton,
Colorado.

    v. ARTHUR,[7] b. July 8, 1854; d. May 12, 1863.
   vi. HERBERT,[7] b. Jan. 14, 1857; m. Aug. 21, 1883, Frances C.
        Mack, of Gilead, Conn. He is a partner in the firm of
        Burnell, Crisman & Co., wholesale and retail grain dealers,
        Denver, Col.

(114) NATHANIEL[6] MANN

(*Andrew,[5] John,[4] Nathaniel,[3] Richard,[2] Richard[1]*) was born in Hebron, Conn., July 21, 1803, and married first, March 29, 1826, Emma W., daughter of Judge Samuel R. Rexford, at Sidney Plains, N.
Y.; she died Dec. 23, 1845, in N. Y. city. He married second,
June 28, 1850, in N. Y. city, Eunice G., daughter of Rufus P. Green.
Mr. Mann has been successively a cabinet and shoe manufacturer.
Has resided at Rochester, N. Y., and No. Vineland, N. J. (now,
1884, Rochester). He has had ten children, three by first wife,
seven by second, viz.:

    i. SAMUEL REXFORD,[7] b. at Sidney Plains, Nov. 5, 1828; d.
        at Rochester, N. Y., May 5, 1873; m. Georgianna Teall,
        at Geneva, N. Y., and had: (1) *Samuel R.*[8] (2) *Ida Vic-*
        toria.[8] (3) *George Arthur.*[8] (4) *Fred.*[8] (5) *Wm. Sew-*
        ard.[8] The widow and family removed to Eau Claire,
        Wisconsin.
    ii. MILLY ANN,[7] m. George E. Lewis, in Chicago, Ill.
   iii. TOMPKINS,[7] b. Dec. 24, 1831; m. first, Mary B. Lestor, in
        Fredonia, N. Y.; had *Charles.*[8] His wife and son died;
        he then married second, ——— in N. Y. city, where they
        now (1883) reside. He is a professor of music, and organ-
        ist in a 5th Avenue church.
   iv. CHARLES N.,[7] b. at Elmira, N. Y., May 27, 1851; m. May,
        1875, in Rochester, N. Y., Ella Dates. He is by trade a
        carpenter, and "carries on farming" at North Vineland,
        N. J. Two children: (1) *Flora Ella.*[8] (2) *Charles Ber-*
        tram.[8]
    v. ALBERT A.,[7] b. at Elmira, April 12, 1854; m. Carrie Cooper,
        and have: (1) *Rena.*[8] (2) *Earl Addison.*[8] He is a me-
        chanic; res. Chicago, Ill.
   vi. EMMA JANE,[7] b. April 12, 1854, at Rochester, N. Y.
  vii. HANNAH SIBLEY,[7] b. at Elmira, Sept. 28, 1856; m. George
        W. Ashton, of N. Y. city, July 23, 1873. Four children:
        (1) *Edith Adell.*[8] (2) *Maud Eveline.*[9] (3) *May Belle,*[8]
        and an infant son. He is a mechanic; res. Rochester.
 viii. HARRIET M.,[7] b. at Port Crane, N. Y., Nov. 21, 1859; m.
        Dec. 25, 1876, Frank B. Cooper. Three children: (1)
        Frank Barnard.[8] (2) *Eva May.*[8] (3) *George Gebbie.*[8]
        Res. Chicago, Ill.

ix. RUFUS W.,[7] b. June 12, 1862; res. with parents (1884) in
     Rochester, N. Y.
 x. FLORENCE ADELL,[7] b. in N. Y. city, Aug. 22, 1865; res.
     at Rochester.

(115) JOEL[6] MANN

(*Abijah,[5] Abijah,[4] Nathaniel,[3] Richard,[2] Richard[1]*) was born in
Fairfield, N. Y., Aug. 15, 1789, and died March —, 1832, at ———.
He married Betsey Cole, who was born at Fairfield, May 29, 1789,.
and died at ———, April 9, 1866. Mr. Mann resided at Fairfield,
N. Y., Brockville, Canada, and perhaps other places.   Children:

  i. ELIZA L.,[7] b. (in Fairfield, N. Y.) Aug. 20, 1812; m. Peter
      E. Snell, of Manheim, N. Y. Children: (1) *Helen M.,*[8]
      m. and res. California; two children. (2) *Theodore,*[8] m.
      ———. (3) *Irving,*[8] m. ———; has children; one lives
      at Little Falls, N. Y. (4) *Orlando,*[8] m. ———.
 ii. HENRY W.,[7] b. (in Fairfield) Oct. 7, 1814; a farmer; res.
      Warsaw, N. Y.; m. Dec. 25, 1838, Mary A. Snyder, who
      was born in Frankfort, N. Y., March 6, 1817. They have:
      (1) *Theodore,*[8] b. Dec. 4, 1840, at Knoxville, Ill., who m.
      Rose Dibble, and resides at East Pike, N. Y., and have
      Emma.[9] (2) *Sanborn,*[8] b. Oct. 9, 1842; a tinsmith; res.
      Macon, Ill.; two children. (3) *Emma,*[8] b. April 21, 1844,
      at Middlebury, N. Y.; d. Oct. 1, 1874; m. Freedom Relya,
      of Warsaw. Children: 1, *Frank,*[9] b. Oct. 24, 1866; 2,
      Clarence,[9] b. Jan. 31, 1868. (4) *Mary,*[8] b. Jan. 28, 1846;
      d. Oct. 13, 1851. (5) *Ida P.,*[8] b. Nov. 9, 1849; d. Dec.
      31, 1850. (6) *Abijah F.,*[8] b. June 10, 1853, at Warsaw; a
      farmer at Warsaw; m. Oct. 10, 1881, Florence Gath. (7)
      Ada L.,[8] b. May 2, 1858; m. Dec. 10, 1879, Thomas J.
      Noblett; res. Attica, N. Y.; a grocer. Children: 1, *Roy*[9];
      2, *Grace.*[9]
iii. EUNICE ANN,[7] b. (in Brockville, Can.) Jan 27, 1818; m.
      George S. Campbell, who died April 26, 1863, at East
      Koy, N. Y. They have children: (1) *John Hoar,*[8] b. Oct.
      16, 1837, at Frankfort, N. Y.; m. first, March 6, 1866,
      Maria Walbridge, of Attica; m. second, May 16, 1882,
      Adelia V. Chamberlain, of Warsaw; no children. Mr.
      John Hoar Campbell is of the enterprising firm of Camp-
      bell Bros., manufacturers of Patent Socket Hand Rakes,
      etc. at East Koy. (2) *Timothy I.,*[8] b. July 3, 1842; m.
      Helen Miles; res. Wiscoy, N. Y. Child: 1, *Roy,*[8] b. Aug.
      15, 1879. (3) *Alma E.,*[8] b. Feb. 13, 1844; m. Nov. 30,
      1867, Charles E. Warne, a farmer; res. Pike, N. Y.; no
      children. (4) *George A.,*[8] b. June 8, 1851, at Attica; m.

Sept. 27, 1878, Angelia Ayers; res. East Koy, and is of the firm of Campbell Bros., as above.

iv.   JOEL,[7] b. (Brockville) Dec. 9, 1822; m. ———; res. Fairfax C. H., Va.; six children.

v.   CHARLES A.[7] (2nd), b. (Brockville) Oct. 20, 1825; d. June, 1870; m. first, Charlotte Burt, of Frankfort, N. Y., and had *Burt.*[8] He m. second, Betsey Fitch, of Bennington, N. Y., and had children. The widow and family reside at East Saginaw, Mich.

(116)   HON. ABIJAH[6] MANN

(*Abijah,*[5] *Abijah,*[4] *Nathaniel,*[3] *Richard,*[2] *Richard*[1]) was a politician and political leader in the State of New York. He was born in Fairfield, N. Y., Sept. 24, 1793, and died at Auburn, N. Y., where he had been spending some time, Sept. 6, 1868. He was early educated in the public schools of Herkimer County, aided by the instruction of an excellent mother, who being a woman of remarkable ability, bestowed great care upon his early training. He began life as a school teacher in Oneida County, but soon became a tradesman, and being a shrewd man of business, in time acquired considerable real estate property in the principal cities and villages in the State, at length purchasing an undeveloped coal mine in Lackawanna County, Penn. He early entered political life, was a Republican of the Tompkins school, and gloried in wearing the "bucktail." He soon became a man of mark; was elected Justice of the Peace, appointed Postmaster, and finally was chosen to the Assembly in 1828. He served three successive terms, obtaining a wide notoriety for his active hostility to the proposed Chenango Canal. "It cannot be of lasting benefit," he declared in a speech; "a man can as easily lift himself over the fence by the slack of his pantaloons." He remonstrated with Governor William L. Marcy for changing positions in regard to the enterprise, and was only silenced by the Governor's assurance that the Democratic party must support the Chenango Canal so that General Jackson might be re-elected President. Mr. Mann was elected to Congress in 1832, and re-elected in 1834.

Having been appointed on a committee to investigate the affairs of the United States Bank, he repaired to Philadelphia, but was denied access to the institution. He immediately procured laborers and set them to excavate their way under the building. This proceeding induced the officers to let Mr. Mann have his way; and he made a thorough investigation. Mr. Mann used to relate the story with great zest. "I had been desired by General Jackson," said he, "to come immediately to the President's house at any hour on my return to Washington. I arrived late in the night, and was refused admittance. 'My name is Mann,' said I, 'and the President wants to see me.' I was admitted; General Jackson had just risen from the bed, and walked up and down the room in an old woolen night-gown, which made him look like a ghost. 'Tell me,' he demanded, 'how stands the case?' I told him the names of members of both Houses of Congress who had received money from the bank; and he made comments as I told. Naming one most distinguished senator, I added, $70,000. 'That money is well spent,' cried General Jackson; 'he is an able man.' I named a southern Senator, adding $6,000. 'Too much, too much,' cried the old man; 'he is only a country village lawyer.' So I went through the whole catalogue, detailing one of the most extraordinary cases of official corruption then on record." The sequel of this investigation, the removal of the deposits, etc. are a part of the history of the times.

Mr. Mann left Congress at the expiration of General Jackson's term, and was elected that same autumn to the Assembly. Preston King was a member of the same House; and they were very uncomfortable members, and not over careful about the amount of trouble they gave the speaker, Mr. Luther Bradish. During one filibustering occasion, Mr. Bradish was tasked to the utmost. Mr. Mann would speak, and would not stop till three times called on by the speaker. "The gentleman from Herkimer is out of order," "The gentleman from Herkimer will take his seat," produced no effect. But he finally did sit down when Mr. Bradish shouted "Abijah Mann, Jr., take your seat." The courtly manners of Mr. Bradish were repulsive to the rough old political veteran. Several years afterwards Mr. Mann removed from Herkimer County, and opened an office in Jauncey Court, New York city, residing in Queen's County, and rep-

22

resenting that County in the Democratic convention, over which Governor Fenton presided. Preston King was nominated for Secretary of State, and Mr. Mann for Attorney General. The American party, however, carried the State. In 1857 Mr. Mann was nominated by the Republicans for the Senate from the second district, but was defeated by Samuel Sloan. This was his last appearance before the public. But he took a lively interest in political matters, generally acting with the Republicans, though retaining his early attachment for the distinctive financial views of the " Barnburners."—(Ext. from New York Times, in part.)

Mr. Mann married, Jan. 18, 1814, Mary Ann Bruce, who died Aug. 16, 1873, by whom he had several children, three of whom only lived to grow up, viz.:

i.   WILLIAM WALLACE,[7] who was a lawyer in New York city, and died in the spring of 1884. He m. first, Ann Palmer, and had several children, only one living, viz.: *Jane*,[8] who m. George Cothran, the author of the 7th edition of the Revised Statutes of New York.   He married second, ———, and had two more children, only one living, viz.: *William Barrett*.[8]

ii.   NANCY ANNA,[7] b. Nov. 6, 1822; d. Feb. 22, 1882; m. Sept. 13, 1843, Charles Fincke, of Little Falls, N. Y., a banker. They had five children, viz.:

    (1) *Charles Louis*,[8] b. June 16, 1844; m. Clara Hutchinson, Dec. 1, 1868.   He is a banker in New York city. Children: 1, *Anna Hutchinson*,[9] b. Dec. 20, 1870; 2, *Charles Louis*,[9] b. March 29, 1873; 3, *Clarence Mann*,[9] b. Oct. 12, 1874; 4, *Julia Hutchinson*,[9] b. June 20, 1880.

    (2) *Mary Rodman*,[8] b. Jan. 29, 1846; d. March 14, 1852.

    (3) *William Mann*,[8] b. July 30, 1848; d. April 15, 1879. He was a broker, and m. in 1872, Julia Clark.   Children: 1, *Benjamin Clark*[9]; 2, *William Mann*.[9]

    (4) *Frederick Getman*,[8] b. Jan. 28, 1850; m. Mary Ann De Shore Wood, June 23, 1875.   He is a prominent lawyer in Utica, N. Y., and member of the law firm of Miller & Fincke of that city. He has two children, viz.: 1, *Frances Amelia*,[9] b. June 12, 1876; 2, *Reginald*,[9] b. Nov. 26, 1878.

    (5) *Frances Amelia*,[8] b. Dec. 27, 1851; unmarried.

iii.   MARY,[7] m. Thomas H. Rodman, Esq., a prominent and influential gentleman of New York city, who was many years a law partner of his father-in-law, Abijah Mann, Jr. Mr. Rodman has had children, viz.: *Thomas Harvey*,[8] who is married; *Anna Fincke,*[6] died; *Frank,*[6] died; *Mary Washington,*[6] who married; *William Dudley,*[6] who is single; *Charles,*[6] died.

(117) AMASA[6] MANN

(*Abijah,*[5] *Abijah,*[4] *Nathaniel,*[3] *Richard,*[2] *Richard*[1]) was born Sept. 2, 1800, in Fairfield, N. Y. He learned the "wagon maker's trade" at Preston, Canada, and about the year 1822 settled at Frankfort, Herkimer County, N. Y., where in 1828 he married Alma Everett, and spent the remaining forty years of his life at that place, where he died July 23, 1868. Children:

 i. ABIJAH,[7] b. 1829: d. in infancy.
 ii. ABIGAIL,[7] b. Oct. 28, 1830; m. George R. Lewis, 1862; removed to Cedar Rapids, Iowa, in 1878, where he now resides. No children.
 iii. FRANKLIN,[7] b. Dec. 18, 1832. "He volunteered as a Federal soldier at Mt. Pleasant, Iowa, under Lincoln's first call for troops in 1861, and was killed at the battle of Wilson's Creek, 1861."
 iv. LAURA,[7] b. June 11, 1836; m. George Doolittle, of Utica, N. Y., July 23. 1857, b. Dec. 6, 1830. Have two children: (1) *Frank M.,*[8] b. Dec. 15, 1861. (2) *Clarence Everett,*[8] b. June 25, 1863. Mr. Doolittle res. in Washington, D. C.
198. v. AMASA,[7] b. July 28, 1839; m. Emily L. Devendorf.

(118) Hon. CHARLES ADDISON[6] MANN

(*Abijah,*[5] *Abijah,*[4] *Nathaniel,*[3] *Richard,*[2] *Richard*[1]) was born Jan. 16, 1803, in Fairfield, Herkimer County, N. Y. His father, Abijah Mann, removed from Hebron, Conn., among the *C. A. Mann* carliest settlers. He had married Lavina Ford, a woman of cultivation and strong character, by whom he had a large family of sons and daughters.

Abijah carried with him from his Connecticut home New-England ideas of education, thrift and industry, which he tried to impress upon his family and upon the community among which he lived. He was among the founders of the Fairfield Academy, an institution which equalled in its standard and in the character of its students nearly any institution of learning in the land at that time. The paternal farm was near the village; and Charles,

early showing a fondness for books and study, was allowed to cultivate his
tastes and to receive a thorough English and Classical education. While
attending school, as was then so frequently the custom, he helped out his
limited means by teaching during vacation, and after graduation he taught
in Lewis County for some time. At school he had as fellow students many
men who afterwards became famous, among them Judge Hiram Denio and
Rev. Dr. Barnes; with the former he maintained a life-long intimacy and
friendship.

In 1822, at the age of nineteen, he went to Utica, N. Y. He was accompanied by his brother, Abijah, Jr., who on introducing him, remarked,
that here was a boy "who knew nothing but Latin and Greek," adding,
however, that he was willing to work. He entered the law office of Lynch
and Varick, and struggled through three years of professional studies, under
all the discouragements of poverty. Although comparatively friendless on
coming to the city, his pleasant manners, studious habits, and general intelligence soon made him many friends, and these early friendships formed
with those who too were struggling for success against odds, remained firm
throughout life. In 1825 he was admitted to the bar, and was taken into
the firm, Mr. Lynch retiring. He entered at once on the active practice
of law, but never went very much into the courts. In 1830 Mr. Varick removed to New York, and Mr. Mann formed a partnership with the Hon.
David Wager, that lasted eight years, and on Mr. Wager retiring he
formed a partnership with John H. Edmunds, Esq., which lasted to the
time of his death.

The partnership with Mr. Varick had a very great influence on the course
of Mr. Mann's life. Mr. Varick was largely interested in real estate, and
on his removal to New York Mr. Mann purchased through him the remaining interests of the great Holland Land Company in the northern
towns of Oneida County. This property absorbed a large share of his time,
and led his attention to real estate and business, and away from his profession. Still, although he frequented the courts very little, he gradually
came to be considered the best real-estate lawyer in the County, and his
opinion on all legal matters was highly prized. This property was disposed of to settlers, many of them Welch, in plots and farms, and sold
largely on contract. The terms were always easy, and the creditor lenient
in pressing his claims, and "Squire Mann" was greatly respected and loved
by these simple folk with whom he was then brought into contact. This
land speculation was successful, and laid the basis of his fortune.

As the city grew, Mr. Mann's attention was directed to many new enterprises. Always public spirited and energetic, with a sound judgment, and
far-sightedness above the average, his aid was sought; his judgment fol-

lowed in very many of the new enterprises which so rapidly followed each other in a young and growing town. He was active among the projectors of the Utica & Schenectady Railroad, the beginning of our present magnificent system of railways. He was a leading spirit in the Oneida Bank after its disastrous robbery, and was successfully employed with Horatio Seymour, his life-long friend, in detecting and bringing to justice the robbers. He was president of the bank for a number of years before his death, and to his influence and labors must be attributed much of its present prosperity. He was one of the founders and for many years president of the Utica Steam Cotton Mills, and his theories as to the financial management of the institution which were adopted and have been followed, have had a great deal to do with its almost unprecedented success. In 1856, after a long term as director, he was unanimously elected President of the New York, Albany & Buffalo Telegraph Company. His election marked a new era in the company's history. His great executive ability here found scope for its display. The company was in a bad way, but by vigorous and decided action its wires were soon put in working order, its contracts fulfilled, and the value of the property greatly enhanced. In 1859 Mr. Mann's health compelled him to give up his position, but the work which he had done materially aided the permanent foundation for one of the greatest business enterprises of the day. Besides his business connections, Mr. Mann took an active interest in educational, charitable and religious enterprises.

He was one of the original managers of the State Lunatic Asylum, and for a long time chairman of the board. He devoted much time to this institution, and was particularly interested in perfecting its present admirable system of ventilation and heating. As a counsellor of the Utica Orphan Asylum he did good but humble service. The financial management of its affairs were largely in his hands,—his brother-in-law and wife having held the position in turn of treasurer from its foundation to the present time. He was one of the founders of the Utica Female Academy, as well as an active trustee of the Utica Free Academy before it was absorbed in the common school system. He also rendered excellent service as school commissioner for the five years previous to his death.

Mr. Mann's attention was early drawn to politics, but here he did not succeed so well. He was too honest and high-minded to stoop to the low methods of the politician, and the ideas which he advocated were not always the popular ones, though time has shown that they were right. His devotion to the public good, as well as his sound judgment and inflexible probity, early secured him a leading position in the community. He drafted the charter under which Utica was incorporated in 1832, and was elected a member of the Common Council at its first charter election, and re-elected for several succeeding terms. In 1840 he was elected to the Assembly by the Democratic party, and at once became a leader in that body. He had always given particular attention to financial questions, and the clearness and soundness of his views quickly attracted attention. He was from the first an advocate of the "pay as you go" policy, which he believed should be applied not only to individual affairs but to those of the State as well. In common with many of the leading minds of the day he realized the evils of the State debt system, and predicted the embarrassments which would ensue from its adoption. His speeches on State finances, and in defence of the policy of spending money no faster than it was earned, were widely published; and although the policy which he opposed was adopted, time has demonstrated fully the correctness of his views. In 1846, during the divisions of the Democrats, he was nominated to a seat in the Constitutional Convention. In 1848 he was an active member of the Free Soil party. He was nominated for Congress, but owing to party dissentions he failed of election. He returned to the Democratic party, but never hesitated to denounce the aggressions of the Slave Power, and to declare the necessity of opposition to them. In 1850 he was elected to the State Senate by the Democrats, and he at once assumed a leading position. On the impending passage of the unconstitutional "nine million bill" his sense of right and justice was so shocked that he advised the resignation of the Democratic Senators rather than to permit the consummation of the outrage. This act was not approved of by the electors, and a new Senate was elected which passed the bill; but the courts eventually affirmed its unconstitutionality, thus vindicating his judgment. Even those who condemned the resignation were forced to admire the unbending integrity and sacred regard for the constitutional prohibitions which impelled Mr. Mann as its leading adviser. This act really ended his political life. Business and local affairs engrossed his time, and after such an experience, he never had any heart again for politics. He therefore persistently refused all nominations, although his party friends had, on account of his well known financial skill, repeatedly urged him to accept of several subsequent nominations, particularly that of Comptroller. He was also tendered the office of Circuit Judge.

As has been already said, Mr. Mann's business success interfered with his success as a lawyer. Still, those who are competent to know speak of several cases which he argued with great ability and success. It was as a real estate lawyer that he was mostly known, and his opinion valued. A large share of his business was the management of trusts and estates for others, and few rendered more cheerfully and efficiently a greater amount of gratuitous services to women and those not capable or self-reliant enough to act in their own behalf, than he.

In his family life Mr. Mann was most happy. He married, Sept. 27, 1832, Miss Emma Bagg, whose father and grandfather had been prominent citizens of Utica from its earliest settlement. By her he had five children. As a husband and father Mr. Mann was fond and devoted. In his earlier life, before the cares and anxieties of business and public life absorbed him, he spent much of his time with his family, enjoying to the utmost their devotion and love. In the year 1851 he gave up his business and spent the year in European travel for the benefit of the health of his eldest daughter. This trip he greatly enjoyed, as his large reading and thorough knowledge of history, always a favorite study with him, enabled him to do to the utmost. His father's family were always objects of his most considerate care, and together with his brother, Abijah Mann, Jr., he extended continual and generous aid to his less successful and less fortunate brothers and sisters. During the last few years of his life, although suffering greatly from his disease,—an obscure form of brain disease,—he never complained, but was always hopeful and cheerful. His interest in the outside world never flagged, and one of the last acts of his life was to attend a meeting of the Board of his Cotton Mills. Returning from this, and while partaking of his dinner, he was seized with apoplexy, became instantly unconscious and never recovered.

An extended analysis of his character would be here uncalled for. Enough has been said to indicate his general excellence and worth, the depth and extent of his abilities. Still it may not be out of place to transcribe some of the kind words which have been said by his friends, those who knew him best.

In an editorial in the Utica Observer, Jan. 19, 1860, we find: "In him were combined, in harmonious proportions, so many of the most excellent traits of human nature, that any enumeration of his virtues would leave something still unsaid. He preserved in the highest positions the original simplicity of his habits, and was ever mindful of his early days, rejoicing in opportunities of assisting those who were similarly situated with himself and who seemed worthy of encouragement. His unswerving integrity, well balanced mind and excellent common sense pointed him out as the natural depositor of the most important trusts, while his great executive abilities enabled him to accomplish readily the vast amount of business which was thrust upon him. His moderation was wonderful; passion and excitement he never exhibited. He was governed throughout life by the firm conviction that permanent prosperity and happiness can follow only uprightness, and that retributive justice, though perhaps slowly, is surely following the dishonest and corrupt."

At the meeting of the Utica Bar, the Hon. Francis Kernan, long a friend and neighbor, remarked: "The citizens of Utica had special cause to lament the death of Mr. Mann. There were few to fill his place here. He possessed a clear, quick, comprehensive mind. He was unobtrusive in his habits, yet his usefulness was wide spread. In reference to every public movement his action and advice were always freely tendered, and were of the most beneficial kind. He was a conservative man, of far seeing sagacity, who had not only aided those enterprises useful to the community, but had stood as a bulwark against those often engaged in, which proved detrimental. In every deserving enterprise he was liberal, unselfish, wise and prudent." "As a legislator he was rather put forward into public stations by others; he did not desire it himself. Yet every one had confidence in his sagacity. No one had a suspicion that he was selfish. He possessed remarkable powers to present, either on paper or in oral debate, his views of public policy. As a lawyer he was well versed in the law, and could present his points clearly and aptly. He honored the profession to which he belonged."

Judge Ward Hunt remarked that, "professionally speaking, it was a great misfortune that he succeeded so well in business; otherwise he would have stood in the front rank as a lawyer."

The Hon. David Wager, his law partner, writes: "He was one of the gems of society, which astonish not so much by their brilliancy as by the justness and perfection of their workmanship. Like a well regulated timepiece, he was never out of order; and in relation to all his duties, public and social, he was true as the sun."

Though not a member of any church, he felt a high respect for religion, and was a faithful attendant at the Reformed Dutch Church, having been one of the original movers in its establishment in Utica. It is but just to add, that Mr. Mann's worth was fully appreciated by the citizens of Utica. The funeral was attended by most of the members of the Bar, Common Council, Mechanic Association, and other associations and companies. Nearly all the stores on Genesee Street were closed during the hours of the funeral, and the large attendance showed how closely Mr. Mann had linked himself not only with the fortunes but with the hearts and affections of his fellow citizens.

The Hon. Charles A. Mann married, Sept. 27, 1832, Emma Bagg, daughter of Moses Bagg and Sophia Darbyshire his wife; she was born Sept. 15, 1813. Children:

      i. SOPHIA,[7] b. Aug. 12, 1833; d. May 12, 1870; m. April 27, 1864, Alexander C. Coventry, of Utica, N. Y., who was b. May 8, 1832, and d. March 5, 1872. One child, *Emma*,[8] b. Oct. 12, 1865; d. Nov. 1, 1872.

199.   ii. CHARLES ADDISON[7] (Esq.), b. May 29, 1835.

200. iii. JAMES FORD[7] (Esq.), b. May 24, 1837.
201. iv. MATTHEW DARBYSHIRE[7] (Dr.), b. July 12, 1845.
    v. EMMA,[7] b. Sept. 17, 1847; m. April 27, 1870, Joseph R. Swan, Jr. Esq. (b. Sept. 10, 1842), a lawyer in Utica, N. Y.; he is a son of Judge Joseph R. Swan, of Columbus, O. Children: (1) *Sophia· W.,*[8] b. March 30, 1871. (2) *Andrews,*[8] b. Sept. 9, 1873; d. Dec. 5, 1873. (3) *Lois A.,*[8] b. May 21, 1875. (4) *Joseph R.*[8] (3d), b. Oct. 21, 1878.

(119) WILLIAM H.[6] MANN

(*Abijah,*[5] *Abijah,*[4] *Nathaniel,*[3] *Richard,*[2] *Richard*[1]) was born in Fairfield, N. Y., Sept. 27, 1805; married first or second, Eliza Sherrill, and had children: *Luman,*[7] *Levina,*[7] *Emily,*[7] *Henry,*[7] *Albert,*[7] *Mary,*[7] *Helen.*[7] Of this family, it is said, William H. (the father), Luman and Mary are now living, at or near Bloomington, Ill.

(120) HORACE[6] MANN

(*Aaron,*[5] *Abijah,*[4] *Nathaniel,*[3] *Richard,*[2] *Richard*[1]) was born in Hebron, Conn., Jan. 22, 1801. His father removed from Hebron with his family of children about 1804, to Franklin, N. Y., and the subject of this sketch (Horace) is the only surviving child of the above family, and resides in the village of Franklin. He married Feb. 26, 1825, in Franklin, Sophronia, daughter of Col. Silas Fitch, of Franklin, both (1883) living. Children:

    i. GEORGE W.,[7] m. Asenath Phelps, and have: (1) *Leslie,*[8] a farmer. (2) *Carrie.*[8]
    ii. SUSAN MARIA,[7] m. Rufus Wood, a farmer. They have: (1) *Irving*[8] (a physician), res. Woodbine, Iowa. (2) *Carrie.*[8]
    iii. SILAS,[7] m. Elmira Nichols, of Sardinia, N. Y.; res. Arcade, N. Y. He is a merchant.
    iv. ALMIRON,[7] m. Orline Potter, a farmer; have one daughter, *Flora.*[8]

(121) ERASTUS[6] MANN

(*Daniel,*[5] *Abijah,*[4] *Nathaniel,*[3] *Richard,*[2] *Richard*[1]) was born Jan. 20, 1797, probably in Hebron, Conn., and died April 19, 1871, at New Woodstock, N. Y. He married first, Diana, daughter of Joseph Billings, Nov. 16, 1820, at Smyrna, N. Y.; she died Sept. 20,

23

1829. He married second, Abby Billings (a sister of first wife); she died July 6, 1873. Mr. Mann was a farmer and resided at Franklin, N. Y., from a boy up to about 1829, then removed to Georgetown, N. Y., where he lived twenty-nine years. In 1858 he removed to New Woodstock, N. Y. He was a deacon of the Baptist church in New Woodstock, and in his will bequeathed $500 to the American Baptist Home Missionary Society. Children, three by each wife, viz.:

    i.   WILLISTON,[7] b. April 14, 1822; d. March 29, 1830.

    ii. CARLTON E.,[7] b. Sept. 24, 1824; m. March 8, 1849, Emily Northrop, of Smyrna, N. Y., and resides in Hamilton, N. Y.; one son, *Hervey W.*,[8] b. 1850, who resides at West Eaton, N. Y.; school-teacher; no children.

    iii. HARRIET D.,[7] b. Nov. 3, 1827; m. Alfred Parmley; had one son; all dead.

    iv. CLINTON D.,[7] b. Sept. 7, 1835; d. Feb. 16, 1874, buried in New Woodstock; m. Hannah, daughter of Hannah Gipson.

    v.   DELINA A.,[7] b. Dec. 20, 1839; d. Jan. 9, 1869.

    vi. JOSEPH B.,[7]* b. June 8, 1849; m. July 31, 1872, Delana, daughter of Thomas Eastman, and granddaughter of Timothy Eastman, of Boscawen, N. H. In 1874 Mr. Mann was taking a course of study in the Rochester Theological Seminary, N. Y. He died at his home in New Woodstock, N. Y., in June, 1877. The widow married second, Mr. Barrett, and resides at New Woodstock.

(122) HARVEY[5] MANN

(*Daniel*,[5] *Abijah*,[4] *Nathaniel*,[3] *Richard*,[2] *Richard*[1]) was born (probably in Hebron, Conn.) Sept. 22, 1798, and died at Franklin, N. Y., where he always lived, March 8, 1883. He married May 4, 1825, Marcia, daughter of Joseph Collins. Mr. Mann was a farmer and deacon of the Presbyterian church. They have one son, who is a resident of Franklin, N. Y., viz.:

    i.   GILBERT,[7] b. March 25, 1830, in Franklin, N. Y.; m. first, Jan. 15, 1854, Elmira, daughter of Daniel Carr; she d.

---

* Mr. Joseph B. Mann was the author of a little book printed in 1874 in Rochester, N. Y., entitled "Chronological Record of the English Manns," a work quite readable and credible in dealing with some of the New York branches; but in adopting the ideas of the late R. R. Hinman, of Hartford, Conn., and dealing with other branches of the family, he was in error and considerably mixed.—ED.

March 23, 1855, aged twenty-eight. He m. second, in
1857, Phebe J., daughter of John White, of Unadilla, N.
Y.; res. Franklin, N. Y. Children: (1) *Arthur D.*,[8] b.
1855; m. Dec. 1877, Amelia Merchant, of Worcester,
N. Y.; res. Kansas City, Mo. (they had, *Elmira*,[9] b. Dec.
4, 1879, d. April 3, 1881; and *Herman*,[9] July, 1882).
(2) *Mary E.*,[8] b. 1858; d. 1865. (3) *Minnie A.*,[8] b. Aug.
1859. (4) *William T.*,[8] b. July, 1861. (5) *Helen G.*,[8] b.
Feb. 1863.

(123) JONATHAN H.[7] MANN

(*John*,[6] *John*,[5] *Thomas*,[4] *Thomas*,[3] *Thomas*,[2] *Richard*[1]) was born in
Boston, Mass., June 3, 1825. He married Philena W. Dupee, Nov.
12, 1848, and resides on Brookline Street, Boston. For many
years he has been a deputy collector in the United States Internal
Revenue Department. Children, born in Boston:

    i.   SARAH S.,[8] b. Sept. 15, 1849; m. Hugh Macdonald.
    ii. JOHN,[8] b. Sept. 12, 1851; unmarried.
    iii. WILLIAM H.,[8] b. April 3, 1859; unmarried.
    iv. JONATHAN H.,[8] b. Aug. 15, 1862; unmarried.

(124) CAPT. JOHN C.[7] MANN

(*David*,[6] *David*,[5] *Ebenezer*,[4] *Thomas*,[3] *Thomas*,[2] *Richard*[1]) was born
in Pembroke, Mass., April 6, 1806. For many years he was a fore-
man in Alger's foundry in South Boston; was captain of the Pulaski
Guards, at one time; and it is said, "was fond of gunning and fishing." He was married March 1, 1827, in Boston, by Rev. Wm.
Jenks, D.D., to Sylvia L. Hedge, who was born Nov. 25, 1806, and
died June 23, 1875. He died April 23, 1867. Children:

    i.   MARIA H.,[8] b. Feb. 26, 1828; m. Sept. 1, 1847, James R.
         Josselyn, of Pembroke; he d. 1882. Children: (1) *Ella
         F.*,[9] who m. E. M. Jones, of Pembroke. (2) *Gilman S.*,[9]
         of Boston. (3) *James E.*,[9] of Pembroke.
    ii. PRISCILLA J.,[8] b. April 9, 1830; m. April 29, 1849, Francis
         Collamore, M.D., of Pembroke, Mass. Dr. Collamore is
         a well-known physician practising in Pembroke and ad-
         joining towns. They have: (1) *Francis*,[9] Jr., b. Oct. 23,
         1855. (2) *Florina Mann*,[9] b. June 28, 1862.
    iii. CHARLES E.,[8] b. April, 1832; d. Aug. 1833.
    iv. CLARA H.,[8] b. April 6, 1834; m. Sept. 12, 1858, Josiah
         Dean Bonney, of Pembroke, and have *Charles Dean*.[9]

v.   JOHN H.,⁸ b. Sept. 1836; d. Aug. 1842.
vi. FREDERIC C.,⁸ b. Jan. 22, 1839; m. Nov. 23, 1864, Millie
     L. Hill, and lives in East Bridgewater, Mass.   Children:
     (1) *Charles Frederic*,⁹ b. April 12, 1869.   (2) *Mary Isa-
     belle*,⁹ March 12, 1876.   (3) *Grace L.*,⁹ April 19, 1882.
vii. LOUISA F.,⁸ b. Aug. 1, 1841; m. Jan. 29, 1865, Henry B.
     White; res. Boston.   Children: (1) *Harry H.*⁹ (2) *Fred.*⁹
viii. FLORENCE E.,⁸ b. July 28, 1843; d. Nov. 26, 1860.
ix. EDWIN F.,⁸ b. Sept. 1845; d. Nov. 19, 1860.
x.   JULIA A.,⁸ b. Aug. 7, 1848; m. William P. Bates; res. Bos-
     ton; one son, *Willie.*⁹

(125)   DAVID O.⁷ MANN

(*David*,⁶ *David*,⁵ *Ebenezer*,⁴ *Thomas*,³ *Thomas*,² *Richard*¹) (a twin
brother to Jonathan O.), was born in Pembroke, Mass., Dec. 13,
1808; resided there and died Jan. 1, 1874.   He married May 14,
1844, Nancy Austin.   He was an iron moulder by trade, and called
a skilful workman.   Children:

i.   DAVID AUSTIN,⁸ b. Feb. 20, 1845; m. Emily B. Ramsdell;
     res. Pembroke, Mass.; a poultry dealer.
ii. ALFRED W.,⁸ b. Aug. 12, 1850; unmarried; res. Pembroke,
     Mass.; a house painter.

(126) JONATHAN O.⁷ MANN

(*David*,⁶ *David*,⁵ *Ebenezer*,⁴ *Thomas*,³ *Thomas*,² *Richard*¹), a twin
brother of David O. Mann, was born in Pembroke, Mass., Dec. 13,
1808, and married Nov. 4, 1834, Eliza A. Sears, of E. Dennis, Mass.
He is by trade an iron moulder, and for many years resided in
Boston, where most of his children were born, but now follows farming with his son George H., at Pembroke.   Children:

i.   CHARLES H.,⁸ b. March 4, 1836; d. at sea July 20, 1854.
ii. ELLEN ELIZA,⁸ b. Aug. 24, 1837; m. Oct. 30, 1858, Gor-
     ham B. Howard; res. Brockton, Mass.
iii. GEORGE HARRISON,⁸ b. Jan. 22, 1839; m. in Fall River,
     Nov. 28, 1871, Ellen, daughter of John Bury.   Mr. Mann
     served in the war of the rebellion three years; for a time
     resided in Fall River.   He now owns a farm in Pem-
     broke, Mass., and resides there.   They have *Edith Sears*,⁹
     b. Jan. 12, 1873.
iv. MARY EMMA,⁸ b. Sept. 24, 1842; m. Nov. 13, 1870, Eben
     G. Rhodes; res. Brockton, Mass.

(127) EBENEZER⁷ MANN, Jr.

(*Ebenezer,⁶ David,⁵ Ebenezer,⁴ Thomas,³ Thomas,² Richard¹*) was born in Pembroke, Mass., April 4, 1813. His father moved from Pembroke, to Leeds, Maine, when he was about four years old. Ebenezer, Jr., married in 1833, Lucetta Keen, of Greene, Maine, and for a time lived in Wales, Maine. He is a farmer, and has been a resident of Auburn, Me., for many years. Children:

 i. EUDORA R.,⁸ b. Jan. 9, 1839; m. 1865, Horace F. Waterhouse, a brick mason, who d. in 1883. The widow resides with her parents.
 ii. ELISHA K.,⁸ b. March 1, 1841; m. first, —— Savage, and had: (1) *Ulysses.*⁹ (2) *Elisha.*⁹ He then got a divorce, went to Fall River, Mass., and married again. He served in the late war three years.
 iii. ANN M.,⁸ b. Jan. 1, 1843; m. 1863, A. B. Caswell, a machinist in Auburn, Me. No children.
 iv. EBENEZER M.,⁸ b. April 9, 1845; m. in 1869, Sarah Dearborn, of Monmouth, Me. He is a farmer at Monmouth. Children: (1) *Susan,*⁹ b. 1870. (2) *Ida,*⁹ about 1872.
 v. JACOB J.,⁸ b. July 15, 1847; m. 1881, Emma Ayers, and has *Myrta.*⁹ Mr. Mann, by trade a carpenter, is in the employ of the Maine Central R. R. Co.; res. Greene, Maine.
 vi. LOIS L.,⁸ b. Oct. 2, 1849; d. March 7, 1850.
 vii. MARY A.,⁸ b. April 19, 1854; d. 1879-80.
 viii. LUCY K.,⁸ b. May 18, 1857; d. March 8, 1858.

(128) WARREN⁷ MANN

(*Joseph,⁶ Joseph,⁵ Joseph,⁴ Joseph,³ Thomas,² Richard¹*) was born in Randolph, Mass., Jan. 21, 1806, and is a farmer, residing in that town. He married Oct. 28, 1827, Lois Niles, who died Oct. 17, 1881, aged seventy-three years, ten months, nine days. Children:

 i. LUTHER W.,⁸ b. Sept. 20, 1828; m. Feb. 5, 1854, Rhoda Waite, and has: (1) *Hubert W.,*⁹ b. April 12, 1855. (2) *Fred. H.,*⁹ Dec. 20, 1856. Res. Randolph, Mass.
 ii. LUCY A.,⁸ b. Oct. 12, 1831; d. June 26, 1882.

(129) SIDNEY⁷ MANN

(*Joseph,⁶ Joseph,⁵ Joseph,⁴ Joseph,³ Thomas,² Richard¹*) was born in Randolph, Mass., in 1808, and died Aug. 30, 1868. He married Hannah Sylvester. Children:

i.   ELIZABETH,[8] m. Aug. 19, 1862, Jonathan S. Niles; res.
     Randolph, Mass.; one son.
ii. GEORGE W.,[8] b. 1838; m. May 14, 1858, Sally A. Hollis.
     He was a member of Co. C. in Col. Barnes's regiment, and
     was killed May 8, 1864, at Laurel Hill, Va. They had:
     (1) *Jane*,[9] d. 1859. (2) *George E.*,[9] b. Aug. 23, 1861;
     m. Aug. 6, 1879, Alice A. Goldthwait, and resides in
     Stoughton, Mass.
iii. JOHN E.,[8] b. May 18, 1840; m. Mrs. Sally A. (Hollis) Mann,
     Aug. 3, 1865; resides in Stoughton, Mass. Children: (1)
     Emily A.,[9] b. Feb. 17, 186-. (2) *James E.*,[9] b. Oct. 29,
     1877.
iv. SIDNEY AUGUSTUS,[8] b. about 1841; was a member of Co. H,
     in Col. Barnes's 18th Mass. Reg., and died in a hospital in
     Virginia, June 4, 1863.

(130)   JOSEPH[7] MANN

(*Joseph*,[6] *Joseph*,[5] *Joseph*,[4] *Joseph*,[3] *Thomas*,[2] *Richard*[1]), a farmer in
Randolph, Mass., was born there April 1, 1812. He married Abi-
gail E. Niles, Jan. 26, 1837, who died March 9, 1876, aged fifty-
nine years, seven months, two days. Children:

i.   LUCIUS H.,[8] b. Feb. 28, 1838; m. May 2, 1861, Elizabeth
      A. Withington. Children: (1) *Lester W.*,[9] b. April 8, 186-.
      (2) *Ernest W.*,[9] Aug. 10, 1864. Res. Randolph, Mass.
ii.   WALTER A.,[8] b. Feb. 4, 1840; m. Jan. 4, 1863, Sarah L.
      Withington. Children: (1) *Edith L.*,[9] b. Dec. 16, 1866.
iii. LAURA A.,[8] b. Sept. 28, 1842; m. Nov. 22, 1866, Frederick
      A. May; res. Canton, Mass.
iv.   ABBY L.,[8] b. Feb. 2, 1845; m. John W. Dunnells, Oct. 21,
      1865; d. Oct. 31, 1865.
v.   JULIUS W.,[8] b. Nov. 17, 1847; d. Feb. 14, 1874; m. Jan. 1,
      1870, Irene Drake, of Stoughton, Mass. Children: (1)
      Julius E.,[9] b. Nov. 14, 1871. (2) *Jason E.*,[9] Aug. 16,
      1873.
vi.   MARIANNA,[8] b. Nov. 22, 1850; m. April 15, 1868, Edward
      Walker; res. Stoughton, Mass.
vii. HORACE W.,[8] Sept. 4, 1853; m. June 20, 1878, Lizzie Bird,
      of Stoughton, Mass., and have *Linna*,[9] b. July 8, 1880.
viii. EMMA F.,[8] b. Oct. 22, 1856.
ix.   ALTON H.,[8] b. Nov. 26, 1857.
x.   ALMIRA N.,[8] b. July 20, 1859; d. Nov. 25, 1865.

(134)   FRANCIS[7] MANN

(*Joseph*,[6] *Joseph*,[5] *Joseph*,[4] *Joseph*,[3] *Thomas*,[2] *Richard*[1]) was born in
Randolph, Mass., about 1814. He married Nov. 6, 1836, Sarah M.
Spear, and resides in Sherborn, Mass. Children:

i. FRANCIS EDWARD,[8] d. aged eight years.
ii. MARIA ELLEN,[8] m. Warner Gilson; res. Vineland, N. J.; two children.
iii. ROSALINE,[8] m. Leonard Jones; res. Ashland, Mass.; three children.
iv. THERESA CREANIER,[8] m. Edwin Ward; res. Ashland, Mass. No children.
v. JESSE ALBERTUS,[8] unmarried; res. Ashland, Mass.

(132) HENRY[7] MANN

(*Joseph,*[6] *Joseph,*[5] *Joseph,*[4] *Joseph,*[3] *Thomas,*[2] *Richard*[1]) was born in Randolph, Mass., Feb. 28, 1817, and married first, June 13, 1852, Rhoda Frances Faxon, born in Braintree, Mass., Feb. 17, 1825, died Oct. 1, 1874. He married second, June 1, 1876, Sarah Louisa Dickerman. He resides in Braintree; was representative to the General Court in 1870. Children by first wife:

i. CHARLES HENRY,[8] b. March 28, 1853; m. March 28, 1876, Susan Elizabeth Hollis, who d. Feb. 3, 1877; and has *Lizzie Hollis,*[9] b. Jan. 23, 1877; res. Braintree, Mass.; a butcher.
ii. FRANK HERBERT,[8] b. July 3, 1857; d. March 4, 1860.
iii. NELLIE FRANCES,[8] b. Dec. 13, 1860; d. Sept. 22, 1861.

(133) ANSEL[7] MANN

(*Joseph,*[6] *Joseph,*[5] *Joseph,*[4] *Joseph,*[3] *Thomas,*[2] *Richard*[1]), born in Randolph, Mass., Jan. 10, 1824; m. (his cousin) Jane, daughter of Jonathan and Sally (Bradley) Mann, February, 1846. They reside in Randolph. Children:

i. ANSEL A.,[8] b. Dec. 10, 1850; unmarried; lives in Boston.
ii. MARY J.,[8] b. Oct. 16, 1856.
iii. IDA F.,[8] b. Oct. 8, 1860; d. young.
iv. VIRGINIA C.,[8] b. Aug. 10, 1862; d. young.

(134) ISAAC[7] MANN

(*Joseph,*[6] *Joseph,*[5] *Joseph,*[4] *Joseph,*[3] *Thomas,*[2] *Richard*[1]), born in Randolph, Mass., March 26, 1830; married Dec. 25, 1848, Louisa Goldthwait. He is a farmer, residing in Canton, Mass. Children:

i. M. LOUISA,[9] b. June 8, 1851; m. Oct. 31, 1868, James M. Holbrook, who resides in Holbrook, Mass.; three children.

ii. ISAAC H.,[8] b. Jan. 20, 1853; d. Feb. 22, 1881; m. Dec. 24, 1878, Lucy Myers; res. Canton, Mass. No children.

iii. RUFUS E.,[8] b. April 28, 1856; m. Feb. 28, 1876, Susie L. Guild; res. Stoughton. Mass. Children: (1) *Lulu*,[9] b. April 18, 1877. (2) *Mabel E.*,[9] Oct. 23, 1879. (3) *R. Henry*,[9] Nov. 1880; d. Sept. 10, 1881.

iv. MARY A.,[8] b. June 15, 1858; m. Aug. 15, 1877, Elbridge Jones; two children; res. Randolph, Mass.

v.   SILAS,[8] b. Sept. 2, 1861.

vi. ELISHA A.,[8] b. Oct. 4, 1864.

vii. WALTER,[8] b. Sept. 17, 1867.

viii. LILLA,[8] b. Feb. 12, 1872.

(135) SETH[7] MANN, 2ND, ESQ.

(*Seth*,[6] *Seth*,[5] *Seth*,[4] *Joseph*,[3] *Thomas*,[2] *Richard*[1]), the eldest son of Seth Mann, Esq., by second wife Polly (Mann) Mann, was born in Randolph, Mass., Feb. 28, 1817. Graduated from Brown University, 1839, and received the degree of A. M. in 1842. After leaving college he aided his father in his business until his decease in 1847, and subsequently with his younger brother assumed for a time the manufacturing and mercantile branches until a sale. He has always resided in Randolph at the old family homestead, and has principally been engaged in public business; a justice of the peace since 1855, selectman and assessor twelve years, whenever other duties allowed, between the years 1855 and 1877. A member of the school committee four years; United States assessor or collector of internal revenue from 1862 to 1875; county commissioner 1856 to 1859; representative to the legislature 1861, 1876, 1877. During all these years he has been and is now engaged as fire insurance agent, as conveyancer in probate courts, assisting and advising others, also acting himself as administrator, executor, trustee, guardian, etc. He is the owner of considerable real estate in Randolph and Boston. It is a fact worthy of record that all his business, official and personal, has been conducted with honor and integrity, and he has enjoyed fully the public confidence.

He married at Braintree, Oct. 9, 1839, Eliza A., daughter of William and Lois Cole, who was born at Middleboro', Mass., May 13, 1819. They have had seven children, five of whom, two daughters and three sons (including twins), died in infancy. The others are:

> ADELAIDE ELIZABETH,[8] b. Nov. 30, 1846; is unmarried.
> LOIS T.,[8] b. Feb. 23, 1849; d. Sept. 17, 1850.

(136) SAMUEL STILLMAN[7] MANN, A.M.

(*Seth,*[6] *Seth,*[5] *Seth,*[4] *Joseph,*[3] *Thomas,*[2] *Richard*[1]), of San Francisco, Cal., was born in Randolph, Mass., June 27, 1819, and was graduated from Brown University in 1841. From 1841 to 1849 he was engaged variously at Randolph, in business, representative to the General Court, and school committee. In February, 1849, amid the excitement caused by the gold discoveries in California, he went thither via Cape Horn, in a sailing vessel owned and provisioned by the passengers. After remaining in California a few years, he passed on to Umpqua City, Oregon, and again to Marshfield in the same state. Here he became interested in coal lands. These were developed by a co-partnership, requiring buildings, railroad, cars, and vessels. During his residence in Marshfield he was for several years judge of the probate court of Coos County.

In 1863, he visited his native town, remaining a year, returning in 1864 with a wife, Miss Ella O. Tower, whom he married June 16, 1864, being the daughter of Isaac and Minora Tower, of Randolph. He remained at Marshfield till the fall of 1883, when he sold his interest in the coal mine and its appendages for a considerable sum, and removed to San Francisco, retiring from all business, intent only on the education of his two sons, "as a recompense for what his father had done for him." Children:

> i. CHARLES STILLMAN,[8] b. March 20, 1864.
> ii. FREDERIC AUGUSTUS,[8] b. Sept. 20, 1866.

24

(137) SAMUEL⁷ MANN

(*Samuel,⁶ Seth,⁵ Seth,⁴ Joseph,³ Thomas,² Richard¹*) was born Aug. 12, 1807 (probably in W. Randolph, Vt.). He married first, May 1, 1832, Caroline Flint, who died Dec. 25, 1847. He married second, June 7, 1848, Mrs. Esther Kinney; she died Nov. 23, 1859, and he married third, in 1861, Mrs. Eliza L. Harback, who died June 9, 1869; he then married fourth, July 20, 1870, Malissa F. Stickel. He is a farmer in W. Randolph, Vt. Two children by first wife; one by second, viz.:

    i. MARTIN F.,⁸ b. June 28, 1839; d. Sept. 1, 1869; m. first, April 3, 1864, Helen M. Flint, who d. March 25, 1867. He m. second, 1869, Clara P. Clark. One son by first wife, viz.: (1) *Horace,⁹* b. March 25, 1867.

    ii. ALBINA,⁸ b. April 1, 1840; d. Dec. 13, 1845.

    iii. WALLACE S.,⁸ b. May 4, 1850; m. Oct. 22, 1874, Ida Boyce. Children: (1) *Georgia E.,⁹* b. April 23, 1877. (2) *Winiford,⁹* Feb. 5, 1880. (3) *Orrin W.,⁹* Aug. 22, 1881.

(138) SAMUEL B.⁷ MANN

(*Micah,⁶ Seth,⁵ Seth,⁴ Joseph,³ Thomas,² Richard¹*) was born in Vermont, May 31, 1815. He married Oct. 6, 1842, his cousin Celinda Mann, and lives in West Randolph, Vt. He was a merchant in that town and a director in Orange County Bank some fifteen years. Children:

    i. LEISTER G.,⁸ b. July 2, 1843; d. June 26, 1864.

    ii. MARION C.,⁸ b. Dec. 12, 1846.

    iii. ELLA C.,⁸ b. Nov. 12, 1848; d. July 7, 1852.

    iv. ADA E.,⁸ b. March 19, 1851; d. July 15, 1852.

    v. SAMUEL F.,⁸ b. Dec. 4, 1852; m. Luie M. Raymond, July 26, 1876. He is a farmer in West Randolph, Vt.

(139) MICAH⁷ MANN

(*Micah,⁶ Seth,⁵ Seth,⁴ Joseph,³ Thomas,² Richard¹*) was born in Vermont, July 28, 1817. Mr. Mann is an old inhabitant of the town of West Randolph, Vt., where he now resides. He married first, Minora Ford, Feb. 2, 1841, who died April 14, 1851; he married second, Dec. 8, 1852, Alethea Gaines. Mr. Mann was in the mercantile business at West Randolph, about seventeen years; at present he is a nurseryman. Children, one by each wife, viz.:

    i. SARAH M.,[8] b. Sept. 5, 1845; m. H. E. Sharp, Jan. 27 1864; a carpenter; res. West Randolph, Vt.
    ii. CLARENCE M.,[8] b. July 26, 1860; clerk in store at West Randolph, Vt.

(140) JOSEPH W.[7] MANN

(*Micah,*[6] *Seth,*[5] *Seth,*[4] *Joseph,*[3] *Thomas,*[2] *Richard*[1]) was born (probably in W. Randolph, Vt.) March 2, 1832, and married Ellen Whitcomb. He is a merchant at West Randolph, Vt. Children:

    i. NELLIE E.,[8] b. Dec. 6, 1868.
    ii. HATTIE W.,[8] b. Feb. 7, 1871.

(141) LEVI[7] MANN

(*Levi,*[6] *Seth,*[5] *Seth,*[4] *Joseph,*[3] *Thomas,*[2] *Richard*[1]) was born in Randolph, Vt., June 14, 1819, and married Oct. 23, 1839, Abby A. Spear, who was born in Randolph, Mass., July 23, 1819. Mr. Mann lived a few years in Randolph, Mass., where all of his children were born. For many years he has lived in California. His present residence is 520 Clapp Street, San Francisco. Children:

202.   i. AZRO LEVI.[8] b. Sept. 2, 1840; m. Sarah Jane Shuey.
203.   ii. CHARLES HERBERT,[8] b. June 23, 1845; m. Mary Effie Shed.
    iii. iv. v. Three children, died under two years.
    vi. SETH,[8] b. June 29, 1861; unmarried; a lawyer, and teacher of an evening mission school in San Francisco, Cal.

(142) MARSHALL[7] MANN

(*Joel,*[6] *Seth,*[5] *Seth,*[4] *Joseph,*[3] *Thomas,*[2] *Richard*[1]), a farmer, was born in Randolph, Vt., Aug. 12, 1822, and married in 1849, Sarah R. Ainsworth, of Northfield, Vt., where he resided three or four years, then settled on his father's old homestead in Randolph, which he owned and lived upon until recently. He now resides in the village of West Randolph, Vt. Children:

    i. O. EUGENE,[8] b. April 22, 1850; m. Nov. 1, 1876, Orra Peeva, or Peavy, a farmer, who reside on a part of the old homestead in Randolph, Vt. Children: (1) *Rupert Gerald,*[9] b. Nov. 9, 1877.

ii. H. CLAYTON,[8] b. Sept. 16, 1851; m. Dec. 10, 1881, Ruth Frances Thayer; a farmer, and lives in the brick house on the old homestead in Randolph, Vt.

iii. HATTIE E.,[8] b. Nov. 16, 1859; with her parents.

(143) WILLIAM BURGESS' MANN

(*Stephen,*[6] *Seth,*[5] *Seth,*[4] *Joseph,*[3] *Thomas,*[2] *Richard*[1]) was born in Randolph, Vt., June 9, 1820, resided first in Randolph and Rutland, Vt. He married Orlinda A. Riford, Feb. 28, 1843, who was born July 1, 1822, in Braintree, Vt. He went to California in 1852, and was last heard from at Carson City, Nevada. Orlinda A. (Riford) Mann married second, Feb. 22, 1866, Alex. Russequie, and had *Elbert Alex. Riford*, born Sept. 2, 1867. Children of William Burgess Mann are:

i. CHARLES EUGENE,[8] b. Sept. 8, 1844; m. 1872, Elizabeth A. Husted, of Burlington, Iowa; res. Mason City, Iowa; no children.

ii. RACHEL ELEPHAL,[8] b. Dec. 13, 1849; m. Oct. 14, 1873, Egbert Clayton Tuttle, of the firm of Tuttle & Co., Rutland, Vt., booksellers, stationers and official printers for the state of Vermont. Children: (1) *William Stearns,*[9] b. July 20, 1874. (2) *Charles Egbert,*[9] May 28, 1878. (3) *Berenice Rachel,*[9] March 24, 1880; res, Rutland, Vt.

(144) CHARLES BRACKETT' MANN

(*Stephen,*[6] *Seth,*[5] *Seth,*[4] *Joseph,*[3] *Thomas,*[2] *Richard*[1]) was born (in Randolph, Mass. or Vt.) Oct. 20, 1822, and died at Rutland (probably Vt.), Aug. 13, 1869. He married his cousin Mary Florette Mann, Dec. 2, 1847. The widow married second, Sept. 28, 1871, A. B. Bruneau, who resides in Fall River, Mass.; no children by this marriage. Children of Charles Brackett Mann, are:

i. MARY IDA,[8] b. March 4, 1849; res. Fall River, Mass.
ii. AMA VIOLA,[8] b. Dec. 24, 1850; d. June 26, 1852.
iii. CHARLES ORIC,[8] b. March 14, 1852; d. March 28, 1853.
iv. CHARLES ORIC,[8] b. Feb. 10, 1854; m. June 3, 1881, Jeanie Barr Weir; res. Worcester, Mass.
v. CARLTON IRVING,[8] b. Dec. 21, 1855; d. Jan. 30, 1870.
vi. FREDDIE BRACKETT,[8] b. Jan. 17, 1860; d. Aug. 20, 1860.
vii. STEPHEN ELMER,[8] b. May 11, 1861; in college (Brown University).

(145) HORATIO EUGENE[7] MANN, Esq.

(*Stephen,*[9] *Seth,*[6] *Seth,*[4] *Joseph,*[3] *Thomas,*[2] *Richard*[1]), by profession a lawyer, was born Feb. 22, 1825, in Vermont, and was the third son of Stephen and Elephal (Brackett) Mann of that state.

Mr. Mann entered the University of Vermont in 1849, but on account of poor health he left and subsequently studied law at the State and National Law School, then at Ballston Spa, N. Y. He first commenced the practice of law in Charleston, Ill. He went to Minnesota in the Spring of 1857, and after that territory was admitted as a state he was a member of the first legislature, taking his seat as representative of Hennipin County, December, 1859. In October, 1862, he received from Hon. Samuel F. Miller, associate justice of the United States Supreme Court, the appointment of clerk of the United States Circuit Court, which office he held, residing at St. Paul, Minn., up to his resignation which occurred in 1883. Judge Nelson, in his remarks accepting Mr. Mann's resignation, bore warm testimony to the ability he had displayed in the discharge of the duties of the office with which he had been so long connected, and the great regret he felt that their very pleasant official and social relations were to be thus severed. Judge Nelson was followed by Judge E. C. Palmer and ex-Gov. C. K. Davis, of St. Paul, and Hon. Eugene M. Wilson, of Minneapolis, each speaker highly complimenting Mr. Mann, and manifesting the regret that his resignation had caused them, a regret that would be fully shared by every member of the bar, not only of St. Paul and Minneapolis, but of the state and sister states practising before the court. Mr. Mann, whose wife's health has been benefited by a more congenial climate, anticipates removing to some point near the coast and further south.

Mr. Mann married, Sept. 6, 1854, Mary Augusta, daughter of the late Hon. Charles Kilborn Williams,* who for many years was Chief Justice of the Supreme Court of Vermont, and governor of that state 1850–51. Children, born in Minnesota, as follows:

---

* Charles Kilborn Williams, LL.D., b. Jan. 24, 1782, was a great-grandson of Rev. John Williams, of Deerfield, who was captured by the Indians.—See "Memorial Biographies of N. E. Hist. Gen. Society," vol. ii. pp. 17 to 34.

    i. LAURA WILLIAMS,[5] b. Feb. 23, 1858; m. Sept. 6, 1883, in
        St. Paul, Minn., to Robert Bond Whitacre, Esq.; res.
        St. Paul.

    ii. EUGENE LANGDON,[9] b. May 20, 1861; was graduated from
        Hobart College, N. Y., in 1883. At the graduation serv-
        ices, June 28, Mr. Mann delivered a well written oration
        on " The Spoils System."

    iii. CHARLES KILBORN WILLIAMS,[9] b. March 16, 1871; d.
        April 24, 1871.

(146) ELISHA[7] MANN

(*Elisha,[6] Seth,[5] Seth,[4] Joseph,[3] Thomas,[2] Richard[1]*), born in Brain-
tree, Vt., Aug. 15, 1818, and died there Jan. 9, 1854. He married
May 5, 1840, Mary Ann, daughter of Samuel Partridge, of Braintree,
Vt. By trade a carpenter; was a farmer at the time of his death.
The widow survives and is living with her son's family in Chicago,
Ill. Children:

        i. JUDSON E.,[8] b. June 22, 1841; d. aged ten weeks.
        ii. Infant, b. May 22, 1842, died.
204. iii. HORACE EDWIN[8] (Dr.), b. April 23, 1844.
205. iv. FRANK EUGENE,[8] b. March 17, 1846.

(147) SETH[7] MANN

(*Elisha,[6] Seth,[5] Seth,[4] Joseph,[3] Thomas,[2] Richard[1]*), a wholesale and
retail dealer in lumber, at Freeport, Ill., was born in Braintree, Vt.,
Feb. 4, 1820. He married first, Minoria Antoinette, daughter of
Rufus Hutchinson; she was born in Braintree, Vt., Sept. 16, 1826,
and died April 10, 1848. He married second, Oct. 18, 1849,
Minora Adelia, daughter of Isaac Tower, of Randolph, Mass.; she
was born Feb. 19, 1831. Children:

        i. CLIFTON SETH,[8] b. March 9, 1853; d. March 10, 1853.
        ii. IDA ADELIA,[8] b. April 2, 1855; m. Oct. 7, 1874, Charles
            D. Knowlton, of Freeport, Ill., who was b. Jan. 27, 1848.
            He resides at Freeport, Ill. Children: (1) *Edith,[9]* b. Sept.
            25, 1877. (2) *Charles D.,[9]* Nov. 25, 1878.
        iii. MORTON TOWER,[8] b. June 4, 1864; d. June 9, 1865.

(148) HOSEA[7] MANN

(*Elisha,[6] Seth,[5] Seth,[4] Joseph,[3] Thomas,[2] Richard[1]*), of Sioux City,
Iowa, was born in Braintree, Vt., Jan. 17, 1824. The first twenty-

four years of his life were spent on the homestead farm in Vermont. In May, 1848, in company with his brother Stillman went to Fond du Lac, Wis. He writes, "I left my brother to teach school in Milwaukee County, and I came up into the pine woods some seventy miles up Wolf river, and went into the log and lumber business, when there were twenty Indians to one white man, and have followed the trade about ever since."

He has lived in Portage City and New London, Wis.; now resides at Sioux City, Iowa. He married Aug. 30, 1859, Mary Sophia Fitts, of New Lisbon, Wis. Children:

    i. FLORA BELL,⁸ b. at Portage City, Oct. 3, 1861; m. Oct. 16, 1879, Lyman A. Page, a book-keeper in Sioux City, Iowa, and have: (1) *Edith*,⁹ b. Sept. 5, 1882.
    ii. LUELLA RUTH,⁸ b. June 1, 1863; d. Sept. 8, 1864.
    iii. HERBERT CARLTON,⁸ b. New London, June 5, 1865.
    iv. DELLA MAUD,⁸ b. New London, Jan. 13, 1867.
    v. CHARLES WINSLOW,⁸ b. Fond du Lac, April 3, 1873.
    vi. EDNA,⁸ b. Sioux City, May 8, 1881.

(149) STILLMAN⁷ MANN

(*Elisha*,⁶ *Seth*,⁵ *Seth*,⁴ *Joseph*,³ *Thomas*,² *Richard*¹) was born in Braintree, Vt., Oct. 30, 1825, went to Wisconsin in 1848 with his brother Hosea, and taught school there in Milwaukee County. He now resides at Russell, Kansas, and is keeping a hotel. He married first, Sarah Sophia Hubbard, of Pittsford, Sept. 20, 1855, who died Oct. 4, 1865. They had a son and daughter by this marriage (both dead). He married second, A. Louise Dunham, and had children:

    i. RAY ERNEST,⁸ b. March 23, 1870.
    ii. JAY DUNHAM,⁸ b. July 1, 1872; d. March 1, 1878.
    iii. GILBERT HAMLIN,⁸ b. Aug. 22, 1874.

(150) BENJAMIN O.⁷ MANN

(*Benjamin*,⁶ *Benjamin*,⁵ *Seth*,⁴ *Joseph*,³ *Thomas*,² *Richard*¹), born in Randolph, Mass., Oct. 6, 1802; died Feb. 8, 1870. He married Ruth, daughter of Dea. Abiel Howard, of Braintree, Vt., May 16, 1833. He was a farmer at "West Corner," Randolph. Children:

206.   i. HORACE P.,⁸ b. June 7, 1834; m. Annie M. Belcher.

ii. LAURA A.,[8] b. Feb. 28, 1837; m. Henry Tileston, Dec. 11,
     1860. Children: (1) *Frank H.*,[9] b. 1861; m. Cora L.
     Ross, Nov. 28, 1882. (2) *Harry*,[9] b. 1870. (3) *Leroy*,[9]
     d. young.

iii. MARY E.,[8] b. Dec. 27, 1840; m. Wm. F. Reynolds, Jan. 1,
     1859. Children: (1) *Herbert F.*,[9] b. 1862; m. Alice F.
     Buck, Dec. 25, 1883. (2) *Weldon*,[9] 1865. (3) *Henry*,[9]
     1867. (4) *Orren*,[9] 1870. (5) *Howard*,[9] 1873. (6)
     Wallace,[9] 1878.

(151) EPHRAIM JACOB[7] MANN

(*Thomas Jewett*,[6] *Ephraim*,[5] *Seth*,[4] *Joseph*,[3] *Thomas*,[2] *Richard*[1]), who
resides at Schoharie, N. Y., is a miller and machinist. He was born
in Bennington, Vt., in 1817. He married Sophia E. Engle, in 1844.
A correspondent writes, "Ephraim Jacob Mann has lost heavily at
times by fire, but is now prospering. He was nearly killed in the
summer of 1881 by being caught by a large moving belt." Children:

i. IDA,[8] b. 1846; m. in 1864, Charles B. Stevens, a miller, and
    has: (1) *Charles Willis*,[9] b. 1865; d. 1866. (2) *Francis E.*,[9] 1867. (3) *Louisa V.*,[9] 1870. (4) *Samuel Byron*,[9] 1872.

ii. EDWARD V.,[8] b. 1854; m. 1881, Missouria Rickard, and have
    (1) *Porter J.*,[9] b. 1881.

(152) THOMAS[7] MANN

(*Thomas Jewett*,[6] *Ephraim*,[5] *Seth*,[4] *Joseph*,[3] *Thomas*,[2] *Richard*[1]) was
born May 12, 1818 (probably in Bennington, Vt.), and resides in
Fultonham, Schoharie County, N. Y. He served in the Rebellion
and was wounded in the hand. He married in 1843, Catherine
Weisgarver. Children:

i.   ELIZABETH,[8] b. June 5, 1844; m. William Teller, a cooper;
     res. Fultonham, N. Y., and have, (1) *Eva*.[9]

ii. JOHN WHEELER[8] (Dr.), b. Sept. 11, 1847; d. Feb. 14,
     1884; m. June 20, 1848, Isabella Clark. Dr. Mann was
     a physician in Albany, N. Y., and had, (1) *Bertha*,[9] b.
     Nov. 19, 1874.

iii. EUNICE,[8] b. Sept. 11, 1849; d. July 31, 1877; m. Charles
     Gardinier, of Albany, N. Y. No children.

iv. MARY,[9] b. June 5, 1850; d. Feb. 12, 1883.

v.   ALICE,[8] b. Feb. 14, 1853; d. Sept. 4, 1877; m. Rodman G.
     Day, of Albany, N. Y.

vi. ELLA,[8] b. Nov. 3, 1851; m. ———, and has *Sheridan Mann*,[9] b. Dec. 28, 1875.

vii. ANNA,[8] b. June 5, 1857; m. Merritt Rosekrans. Children: (1) *Florence*.[9] (2) *Alice*.[9]

viii. DAVID P.,[8] b. May 7, 1860.

ix. FRANK,[8] b. March 9, 1867.

(153) ALMERIEN[7] MANN

(*Thomas Jewett*,[6] *Ephraim*,[5] *Seth*,[4] *Joseph*,[3] *Thomas*,[2] *Richard*[1]) is a farmer living near West Fulton, Schoharie Co., N. Y. He was born Aug. 28, 1828, probably in Berne, N. Y. On the death of his mother was "bound out" to Mr. Gideon Hills, of Breakabeen, N. Y., with whom he lived till he attained his majority. He married Aug. 18, 1849, Hannah M. Chapman, and had thirteen children:

i. MARY ALICE,[8] b. Oct. 6, 1850; m. Nov. 29, 1871, Andrew Phaneuff, who resides in West Fulton, N. Y., a mechanic by trade, and have, *Algenora*.[9]

ii. JACOB HENRY,[8] b. Aug. 9, 1852; res. West Fulton, Schoharie Co., N. Y., living with his father. Jacob H. Mann, Esq., was graduated from the Albany Normal School in 1874, and has been teaching since that time. He is school commissioner of the second Com. Dist. of Schoharie Co. The author of this work is under great obligations to him for many records obtained and sent pertaining to this family.

iii. THERON W.,[8] b. Aug. 11, 1854; a telegraph operator; res. Clitherall, Minn.

iv. CHARLES,[8] b. Nov. 2, 1856; m. Nov. 27, 1879, Bertha Terpenning, and had, *Edna*,[9] d. April, 1882.

v. ROSELTHA,[8] b. Dec. 3, 1858; m. Feb. 2, 1877, Jesse Keyser. Children: (1) *Grace*.[9] (2) *Blanche*.[9]

vi. WELLINGTON,[8] b. Dec. 14, 1860.

vii. LILLIE,[8] b. Nov. 18, 1862.

viii. GEORGE ERWIN,[8] b. Nov. 29, 1864.

ix. JULIA E.,[9] b. Dec. 13, 1866.

x. HOMER N.,[8] b. Dec. 11, 1868; d. Dec. 20, 1868.

xi. HARRIET,[8] b. Dec. 6, 1871.

xii. JOSIAH,[8] b. March 30, 1874.

xiii. MANLY BURR,[8] b. April 1, 1878.

(154) JOSEPH[7] MANN

(*Thomas Jewett*,[6] *Ephraim*,[5] *Seth*,[4] *Joseph*,[3] *Thomas*,[2] *Richard*[1]), a farmer in Hillsboro', Washington Co., Oregon, was born in Berne,

25

N. Y., July 22, 1833, and went West in 1853. He married April 1, 1861, Phebe Jane Pearson. Children:

   i. ELIZABETH U.,[8] b. Oct. 3, 1862.
   ii. FREEMAN GRANT,[8] b. Feb. 23, 1864.
   iii. JOSEPH GIDEON.[8] Dec. 16, 1866.
   iv. LULU JANE,[8] b. Oct. 3, 1868.
   v. THOMAS WELCOMLY,[8] b. Feb. 11, 1879.
   vi. ABBIE GRACE,[8] b. Jan. 18, 1881.

(155) LYMAN J.[7] MANN

(*Joseph P.,*[6] *Stephen,*[5] *Seth,*[4] *Joseph,*[3] *Thomas,*[2] *Richard*[1]), born June 29, 1826, in Claremont, N. H. He married March 28, 1855, Maria E. Woods, at Henniker, N. H., and emigrated to Minnesota, arriving there April 27, 1855, "squatted on 160 acres of government land, built a log house, and lived a pioneer life for twelve years." Within four miles of his farm now (1882) is the pleasant town of Claremont, with railroad facilities, etc. He writes, "we are now in a very pleasant and prosperous farming community." Five children, all born in Claremont, Minn.:

   i. RANSOM J.,[8] b. Oct. 13, 1857. He teaches school winters.
   ii. HATTIE E.,[8] b. April 21, 1860; grad. State Normal School, at Winona, Wis., May 5, 1880; teacher.
   iii. WILLIE P.,[8] b. April 13, 1864. At Rochester Seminary.
   iv. CHARLES O.,[8] b. Oct. 14, 1865. At home.
   v. FRANK,[8] b. June 4, 1867. At home.

(156) JOHN W.[7] MANN

(*Joseph P.,*[6] *Stephen,*[5] *Seth,*[4] *Joseph,*[3] *Thomas,*[2] *Richard*[1]) was born 1832, in Claremont, N. H. He went to Illinois in November, 1855, and to Minnesota in June, 1856. He married July, 1858, Mrs. Delia Clary, of N. Y. He enlisted in Company E, 3d Minnesota Infantry, Oct. 1861; discharged the following July on account of illness at Murfreesboro'. In September, 1864, he enlisted in the 2d Minnesota Battery, and served through the war. He is a farmer and has held several town and school district offices; resides at Fort Ripley, Minn. Children:

   i. HORACE H.,[8] July 7, 1861.
   ii. LUCIA R.,[8] b. Feb. 5, 1865.
      Three children died in infancy.

(157) AZRO J.[7] MANN

(*Joseph P.,*[6] *Stephen,*[5] *Seth,*[4] *Joseph,*[3] *Thomas,*[2] *Richard*[1]), who resides at Claremont, N. H., was born there Aug. 20, 1836. He enlisted in the 7th New Hampshire Regiment, Co. H, Nov. 12, 1861, was wounded July 18, 1863, between twelve and one at night, while on fatigue duty at the siege of Charleston, S. C., and was discharged on account of wound, July 31, 1864. He married Mrs. Clarissa E. W. (Cook) Keyes, Jan. 8, 1872. Children:

    i. JOSEPH P.,[8] b. March 18, 1873.
    ii. CHARLES W.,[8] b. May 4, 1877; d. Sept. 6, 1880.

(158) CHARLES B.[7] MANN

(*Joseph P.,*[6] *Stephen,*[5] *Seth,*[4] *Joseph,*[3] *Thomas,*[2] *Richard*[1]) was born in Claremont, N. H., Sept. 9, 1840. He enlisted in Co. G, 9th New Hampshire Volunteers, July 24, 1862; was wounded near Cold Harbor, Va., May 31, 1864, and discharged July 4, 1865. He married Aug. 22, 1877, Mary Jane, daughter of Eli Young, who was born April 14, 1855. He resides in Claremont, N. H. Children:

    i. LUCIA P.,[8] b. Nov. 25, 1878.
    ii. CLYDE E.,[8] b. April 14, 1880.
    iii. MAUD B.,[8] b. Dec. 11, 1881.

(159) CHARLES EDWIN[7] MANN

(*Charles Henry,*[6] *Stephen,*[5] *Seth,*[4] *Joseph,*[3] *Thomas,*[2] *Richard*[1]) was born in Claremont, N. H., Dec. 28, 1833. He married April 3, 1861, Maria Ann Gordon. He is a farmer, and resides in Bradford, Vt. Children:

    i. CHARLES JAMES,[8] b. June 18, 1862.
    ii. ALICE MARTHA,[8] b. April 13, 1863.
    iii. ROSAMOND VESPERSIA,[8] b. Dec. 9, 1867.
    iv. ARTHUR EDWIN,[8] b. Oct. 10, 1871.
    v. WALTER GORDON,[8] b. Jan. 26, 1873.
    vi. STEPHEN HENRY,[8] b. June 14, 1875.
    vii. HOWARD ALBERT,[8] b. Sept. 25, 1879.

(160) ELISHA⁷ MANN

(*Elisha,⁶ Elisha,⁵ Seth,⁴ Joseph,³ Thomas,² Richard¹*) was born in Randolph, Mass., Dec. 17, 1829. He married first, July 7, 1852, Sarah Jane Howard, who died April 17, 1870. He married second, Dec. 7, 1871, Justena, daughter of Hiram Alden. Mr. Mann has been an extensive manufacturer of boots and shoes; factory at Randolph, then at Boston, where he was burnt out; subsequently had a wholesale boot and shoe house on Summer Street, Boston, under the firm name of Mann & Brackett, having their factories at Stoneham, Lynn and Abington, Mass. He retired from business three or four years since; resides at Randolph. Children, all by first wife except the youngest:

    i. EMMA JANE,⁸ b. Nov. 10, 1854; m. Nov. 10, 1872, Carroll Alden Thayer, who is the Receiving Teller of the Elliot National Bank, Boston, and resides at Randolph, Mass. Two sons.

    ii. ARTHUR ELISHA,⁸ b. Aug. 28, 1856. Of the wholesale boot and shoe firm of Mann & Sanborn (1883), Lincoln Street, Boston.

    iii. MARY ELLEN,⁸ b. Jan. 29, 1860; m. June 19, 1879, Horatio B. Alden, Jr.; res. Dorchester District, Boston. One daughter.

    iv. JENNIE,⁸ b. June 1, 1862; d. Nov. 29, 1862.

    v. MAUD JUSTENA,⁸ b. May 29, 1875.

(161) DR. AUGUSTINE ALVAN⁷ MANN

(*Alvan,⁶ John,⁵ Seth,⁴ Joseph,³ Thomas,² Richard¹*) was born in Randolph, Mass., Oct. 15, 1837. He received the degree of M.D. from the Jefferson Medical College, Philadelphia, in March, 1860, settled in Valley Falls, R. I., the same year. He entered the United States service as assistant surgeon of the 1st Rhode Island cavalry. He was taken prisoner June 18, 1863, and remained in Libby Prison, Richmond, Va., until Nov. 26, 1863. He left the service but few months before the close of the war, and settled in Central Falls, R. I., where he now resides, enjoying a large and lucrative practice. He married June 6, 1865, Sarah T. Bucklin, of Valley Falls, R. I. Children :

i. ARTHUR BUCKLIN,[8] b. June 19, 1866.
ii. CHESTER AUGUSTINE,[8] b. March 7, 1870; d. Aug. 21, 1871.
iii. ERNEST,[8] b. Dec. 12, 1871; d. Nov. 1873.
iv. RUTH MITCHELL,[8] b. July 7, 1873.
v. EDITH,[8] b. June 22, 1875.
vi. EVERETT AUGUSTINE,[8] b. April 3, 1877.
vii. BERTIE,[8] b. Nov. 23, 1879; d. Aug. 4, 1880.

(162) EDWIN MITCHELL[7] MANN

(*Alvan,*[6] *John,*[5] *Seth,*[4] *Joseph,*[3] *Thomas,*[2] *Richard*[1]) was born in Randolph, Mass., March 23, 1849. He is a farmer and wood dealer, resides in Randolph. He and his brother, Deacon Royal Mann, enlarged the cemetery in 1876. This burial lot was first laid out by Lieut. Seth Man, in June, 1792, on land that he bought of Simeon Haywood for the sum of two pounds, being situated at the "West Corner," so called. Having enlarged and beautified the grounds, they now call it "Oakland Cemetery." He married Jan. 19, 1881, Jennie Hall Taber. Children :

i. WALDO EDWIN,[8] b. Nov. 22, 1881.
ii. CLARA TABER,[8] b. Dec. 29, 1883.

(163) SETH WESTON[7] MANN

(*Seth,*[6] *John,*[5] *Seth,*[4] *Joseph,*[3] *Thomas,*[2] *Richard*[1]) was born in Randolph, Mass., Dec. 20, 1847, and married Emma Fitts in 1869. Mr. Mann is a farmer. Children :

i. WESTON LEONE,[8] b. Aug. 27, 1870.
ii. GEORGE EMERSON,[8] b. April 29, 1873.
iii. HENRY JEFFERSON,[8] b. Sept. 27, 1875.
iv. MABEL BESSIE,[8] b. Feb. 20, 1879.

(164) MOSES FRANKLIN[7] MANN

(*Seth,*[6] *John,*[5] *Seth,*[4] *Joseph,*[3] *Thomas,*[2] *Richard*[1]), the youngest son of Seth and Eliza (Hunt) Mann, of Randolph, Mass., was born there April 12, 1859. He married, 1877, Julia Delano. He is a farmer. Children :

i. FRANK ERNEST,[8] b. July 24, 1878.
ii. WALTER C.,[8] b. Feb. 19, 1880.
iii. JULIA ETTA,[8] b. July 21, 1882.

(165) Dr. BENJAMIN HOUSTON⁷ MANN

(*Benjamin,*⁶ *John,*⁵ *Seth,*⁴ *Joseph,*³ *Thomas,*² *Richard*¹), formerly of the Highland District, Boston, was born at Foxboro', Mass., Nov. 6, 1842, and died in Boston, Oct. 26, 1881. Benj. H. Mann, M.D., was the eldest son of the lamented Benjamin Mann, M.D., of Roxbury. Young Dr. Mann, as he was familiarly called, was educated in the public schools of Roxbury, finishing with a course in the Latin school, subsequently about a year at Union College, N. Y., which he left to go to the war. He was the hospital steward of the 24th Massachusetts regiment, and served throughout the rebellion. On his return he entered Harvard Medical College, from which he was graduated in 1868, and at once began to practise at Boston Highlands. He developed rare skill, especially in surgical cases, and his practice grew rapidly, till his failing health obliged him in a measure to relinquish it. It is said, " the number of his benevolences to the poor were legion." He married Feb. 22, 1871, Martha E., daughter of Charles M. Foss, of Boston. Children:

     i.   BENJAMIN PERCY,⁸ b. Nov. 9, 1871.
     ii.   CHARLES FOSS,⁸ b. April 23, 1873; d. April 4, 1877.
     iii.   HOUSTON,⁸ b. Dec. 31, 1875.
     iv.   ARTHUR MEAD,⁸ b. Feb. 5, 1879.

(166) ALEXANDER⁷ MANN

(*Jairus,*⁶ *Levi,*⁵ *Benjamin,*⁴ *Benjamin,*³ *Thomas,*² *Richard*¹) was born in Charlestown, Mass., July 30, 1817, where he always lived, having a summer residence at Hull. He was educated in the common schools, and at the early age of seventeen commenced to learn the currier's trade with Benj. Myrick. In 1837 he went into partnership with a Mr. Hartshorn. The first year they lost all their capital, when Mr. Mann assumed the business, which was successfully continued by him until 1877, when he retired with a handsome property. He was honest and upright in all his dealings, and enjoyed the confidence of the community. During the last part of his life he was afflicted with a heart trouble, which terminated his life Sept. 23, 1882. He left a will bequeathing his large estate to his second wife. He married first, in 1838, Dorcas Rice, of Bedford,

Mass., who died Feb. 28, 1860. He married second, Sept. 3, 1860, Sarah Roberts, of Lyman, Maine. Children, born in Charlestown, all but the two youngest by first wife, viz.:

    i.   MARCUS H.,[8] b. Dec. 21, 1840; d. June 2, 1884; m. Adeline Abbott, of Charlestown, Mass. Children: (1) *Edwin Alexander.*[9] (2) *Adeline.*[9] Residence, Bunker Hill District, Boston.

    ii. MARY E.,[8] b. July 13, 1842; m. M. H. Gilman, of Charlestown; had *Arthur B.,*[9] b. Oct. 23, 1865, d. Feb. 20, 1870.

    iii. ROBERT O.,[8] b. June 1, 1844; d. March, 1867.

    iv. ENOCH W.,[8] b. Sept. 16, 1846.

    v. HARRIET,[8] b. Aug. 1848; d. Jan. 18, 1849.

    vi. FRANKLIN,[8] b. Jan. 25, 1850.

    vii. MARTHA W.,[8] b. Aug. 17, 1853; d. July 21, 1854.

    viii. MARTHA ROBERTS,[8] b. June 26, 1861.

    ix. HORACE,[8] b. Jan. 14, 1863; d. Aug. 5, 1864.

(167) JOHN[7] MANN

(*John,*[6] *Levi,*[5] *Benjamin,*[4] *Benjamin,*[3] *Thomas,*[2] *Richard*[1]), of Rockland, Mass., by trade a shoemaker, was born Dec. 28, 1819, and died April 22, 1878. He married first, Aug. 25, 1844, Sarah V. Chandler, of Rockland, who died Oct. 21, 1861. He married second, Oct. 14, 1862, Sophia Willis, of Rockland. He had eleven children, four by the first wife, seven by the second, viz.:

    i.   JOHN,[8] b. March 22, 1849; m. March 22, 1866, Hannah L. Cook, of Rockland, Mass. He is a shoe manufacturer in Rockland. Children: (1) *Bertha Estella,*[9] b. Dec. 20, 1867; d. April 10, 1868. (2) *Forest Clinton,*[9] b. Sept. 24, 1869. (3) *Idella Wayland,*[9] b. Sept. 29, 1873. (4) *Sarah Vincent,*[9] b. Aug. 3, 1876.

    ii. SARAH EUDORA,[8] b. Aug. 24, 1850; m. Aug. 4, 1867, Charles Lawrence Stevens, of Rockland, Mass., a shoe dealer.

    iii. JOSEPH P.,[8] b. March 17, 1853; d. Dec. 11, 1860.

    iv. LILLIAN AUGUSTA,[8] b. Sept. 15, 1855; m. Aug. 3, 1872, Wm. H. Wheeler, of Rockland, a shoemaker.

    v. HATTIE MAY,[8] b. March 31, 1863; d. May 22, 1869.

    vi. ELAMINA,[8] b. July 28, 1864; d. Aug. 8, 1866.

    vii. CHARLES NELSON,[8] b. April 30, 1866.

    viii. MARY JOSEPHINE,[8] b. Jan. 26, 1868; d. May 28, 1869.

    ix. JOSEPH HENRY,[8] b. Jan. 12, 1871; d. Dec. 16, 1877.

    x. LOUIS GRAYSON,[8] b. April 14, 1873.

    xi. LESTER RAYMOND,[8] b. Nov. 3, 1874.

(168)　GUSTAVUS' MANN

(*John,⁶ Levi,⁵ Benjamin,⁴ Benjamin,³ Thomas,² Richard¹*), by trade
a carpenter, residing at Rockland, Mass., was born April 9, 1828,
in East Abington (now Rockland), Mass. He married in October,
1849, Elmira Vining, of Rockland. Children:

    i. GUSTAVUS N.,⁸ b. July 9, 1850; m. Feb. 14, 1873, Rosalie
        Shores, of Weymouth, Mass., a shoemaker; resides in
        Rockland. Children: (1) *Nelson E.,⁹* b. Aug. 23, 1873.
        (2) *Percy E.,⁹* b. April 7, 1875.
    ii. HORACE E.,⁸ b. Aug. 11, 1852; a carpenter; res. Arizona.

(169)　JAIRUS' MANN

(*Joseph,⁶ Levi,⁵ Benjamin,⁴ Benjamin,³ Thomas,² Richard¹*) was born
in Charlestown, Mass., Oct. 29, 1824, and for many years has been
a resident of the city of Somerville in the same state. He is the city
messenger. He married first, Emeline Runey, of Somerville, who
was born Oct. 25, 1823, and died July 5, 1861. He married second,
Aug. 3, 1863, Martha A. Spofford, of Portland, Me., who was born
March 1, 1842. He has had three children by first wife and two by
second, viz.:

    i. MARY EMMA,⁸ b. Aug. 21, 1848; d. Jan. 6, 1866.
    ii. FANNY JOSEPHENE,⁸ b. Jan. 20, 1850; died.
    iii. ALFRED EUGENE,⁸ b. Nov. 17, 1851; m. Emily Gulletty, of
        Somerville, Mass.
    iv. HORACE CROSBY,⁸ b. Sept. 16, 1864; died.
    v. HARRIET ASENATH,⁸ b. May 6, 1866.

(170)　GEORGE SUMNER' MANN

(*William,⁶ Ensign,⁵ Ensign,⁴ Ensign,³ Thomas,² Richard¹*), a resident of Boston since 1858, and the author of this Memorial, was born
in New Salem, Mass., Nov. 25, 1834. His father removing early to
Petersham, his native town, the subject of this sketch lived at home,
worked on the farm and attended the "Bennet Hill" district school
until 1852. In the autumn of that year was in Bernardston at
Goodale Academy. In 1853 engaged as clerk in the old Theodore
Jones store in Athol, remained in that town about four years and

George S. Mann

subequently a few months in the post office at Erving; came to Boston as clerk in 1858. He with others formed a partnership soon after, and embarked in the dry goods trade on Tremont Row, later having also branch stores on Hanover and Tremont streets, under the successive firm names of Mann & Co.; Barker, Mann & Co., and George S. Mann & Co. Closed up business in 1878. Mr. Mann for the last fifteen or twenty years has also been interested in real estate, conveyancing, care of trusts, etc., and has been a justice of the peace since 1873; also is a member of the New-England Historic Genealogical Society. He married, March 26, 1865, Susan Alzea, born in Topsfield, Mass., Feb. 23, 1834, daughter of Dr. Jeremiah and Esther (Wildes) Stone,[*] late of Provincetown, Mass. Children:

    i. CARRIE WILDES,[8] b. Feb. 28, 1868.
    ii. GERTRUDE WHITNEY,[8] b. Nov. 21, 1871.

(171) WILSON[7] MANN

(*William,*[6] *Ensign,*[5] *Ensign,*[4] *Ensign,*[3] *Thomas,*[2] *Richard*[1]), a retired dry goods merchant residing in Orange, Mass., was born in Barre, Mass., Jan. 28, 1837. He married Sept. 12, 1864, Alice, b. Aug. 25, 1846, daughter of John and Mary S. (Merriam) Putnam, of Orange. Mr. Mann has been in the mercantile business in Athol, Greenfield and Boston; in the latter place was a member of the firm of Mann & Co., in 1865, and a few years later one of the firm of Barker, Mann & Co. Mr. Mann for the past six or seven years has resided in Orange, where he is interested in real estate and timber. He has identified himself in the welfare of the town where he resides, and is a director in the Orange National Bank. One child, born in Orange:

    i. MAY ALICE,[8] b. Feb. 15, 1872.

(172) HORACE[7] MANN

(*William,*[6] *Ensign,*[5] *Ensign,*[4] *Ensign,*[3] *Thomas,*[2] *Richard*[1]) was born in Petersham, Mass., Nov. 6, 1838, and married April 6, 1866,

---

* Jeremiah[8] Stone, M.D. (Shubael,[7] Eliphalet,[6] Hezekiah,[5] Nathaniel,[4] John,[3] Gregory,[2] Rev. Timothy[1]), born in Marlborough, N. H., Nov. 2, 1798; d. April 23, 1875; m. Esther, daughter of Moses and Esther (Dwinell) Wildes, of Topsfield, Mass.— See Hist. of Marlborough, N. H., by Charles A. Bemis, for Stone Genealogy.—ED.

Martha E., born Oct. 30, 1842, daughter of James Lamb, of Athol, Mass. Mr. Mann was educated in the common school at "Bennet Hill," Athol High School, and New Salem Academy. After teaching a few terms in Athol and vicinity, he engaged in the furniture business in Athol, and speculated in real estate and timber. In the fall of 1881, he removed with his family to Jacksonville, Fla., then in 1882 to Asheville, N. C., where he has erected a house and still resides. Like his honored parents, he is conscientious in all his dealings and has strong religious convictions. Children, born in Athol:

    i.   JAMES LAMB,[8] b. Aug. 14, 1870.
    ii. WILLIAM,[8] b. June 14, 1875; d. Aug. 14, 1875.
    iii. MABEL ABBIE,[8] b. July 31, 1876.

(173) HORATIO[7] MANN

(*William,[6] Ensign,[5] Ensign,[4] Ensign,[3] Thomas,[2] Richard[1]*), who is a farmer by occupation, was born in Petersham, Mass., Jan. 28, 1841; married March 1, 1871, Abbie Louisa, born Oct. 14, 1849, daughter of John F. and Mary (Brewer) Payne, of Montague, Mass. Mr. Mann has lived in his native town, where he has owned real estate, also in Barre and Montague, where he has had the management of farms. For the last ten or eleven years he has lived in Boston and superintended the well-known Weld Farm in West Roxbury District. Children, the oldest born in Petersham, the youngest in Boston:

    i. JENNIE DELL,[8] b. April 17, 1872.
    ii. LOUISE ALICE,[8] b. July 21, 1877.

(174) JEREMIAH[7] MANN

(*Jeremiah,[6] Joel,[5] Joseph,[4] Nathaniel,[3] Richard,[2] Richard[1]*), who was a farmer in Ripley, N. Y., was born at Milton, Saratoga County, N. Y., July 5, 1800. He settled at Ripley in 1824, and married Oct. 5, 1825, Clarissa Brockway, of Ripley, who was born May 23, 1803, at Geneva, N. Y., and went to Ripley in June, 1814. She is (Aug. 8, 1883) living. He died Sept. 11, 1868. Children:

    i. AUGUSTA,[8] b. Nov. 25, 1826; m. Sept. 2, 1844, William Hunt, of Ripley, N. Y., a farmer. He died Dec. 1, 1869, leaving no children. Mrs. Hunt resides at Ripley, N. Y.

Francis N. Mann

ii. CAROLINE,[8] b. Aug. 22, 1828; d. March 12, 1875; m. April
     21, 1852, William Bell, Jr., of Erie City, Penn.; a mer-
     chant. Children: (1) *Augusta M.*,[9] b. Dec. 28, 1854; m.
     Oct. 26, 1881, Wilbur F. Smallwood, a banker, res. Erie
     City. [They have one son, *John Bell*,[10] b. Sept. 19,
     1882.] (2) *Caroline M.*,[9] b. April 9, 1866. (3) *William
     Jeremiah*,[9] b. Nov. 20, 1873.
iii. LYDIA,[8] b. Dec. 13, 1833; m. Dec. 6, 1870, Lucius G. Ham-
     ilton, a farmer, of Ripley, N. Y. He d. March 16, 1874.
     One son, born Jan. 23, 1874.

(175) Hon. FRANCIS NORTON[7] MANN

(*Jeremiah*,[6] *Joel*,[5] *Joseph*,[4] *Nathaniel*,[3] *Richard*,[2] *Richard*[1]), one of
the oldest and most prominent citizens of the city of Troy, N. Y.,
died there at 1.30 o'clock Sunday morning, Feb. 8, 1880, in the
seventy-eighth year of his age.

The following obituary is taken from the Troy Daily Times of
Feb. 9, 1880:

Judge Mann was born in the town of Milton, Saratoga County, on
June 19, 1802. His parents were Jeremiah Mann, who was a son
of Joel Mann, a pioneer settler of Milton, and Lydia Norton, who
was a daughter of Francis Norton, of Hebron, Tolland County,
Conn. The subject of this sketch early evinced a disclination to
follow the business of farming, in which his father was engaged. As
a boy he displayed a singular fondness for books and study. The
more he gratified himself in this direction the more ambitious he became to acquire a liberal education, but was obliged to content himself with the meagre facilities afforded by the common school, until
having reached his eighteenth year, he resolved to leave his home and
seek a residence in some place in which better opportunities for educational advancement were to be found. He went forth to win
success in the race for wealth and distinction. On foot and alone
he proceeded to the house of a Presbyterian clergyman, the Rev.
Joseph Sweetman, in the town of Charlton, about sixteen miles from
Milton. The result of the interview between the youth and the
minister was that the former became a member of the latter's family
for a period of two years, during which he performed such service as
was required of him in return for his maintenance. He next entered
the Lansingburgh Academy, where he remained one year, and on

June 24, 1823, was admitted into the junior class of Union College, whence he was graduated on July 24, 1825. On the 4th day of the following October he began the study of the law in the office of Ashley Sampson and John Dickson, of Rochester, and throughout his stay there he supported himself by performing the ordinary duties of a clerk. Leaving Rochester, he continued his studies in the office of Daniel Cady, at Johnstown. A short time afterward he became a student in the office of Samuel G. Huntington, of Troy, where he remained until his admission to the bar as Attorney and Counsellor of the Supreme Court in August, 1828. Then he opened an office in this city, and here practised his profession for more than half a century, although the last twenty years of his life were chiefly devoted to the care of his large and increasing estate. As a lawyer he declined to engage in any cause devoid of merit, and he was more than ordinarily successful in the courts. He was elected a Supervisor of the second ward in 1835, and again in 1857, and as an Alderman he represented the same ward from 1844 to 1847. From 1840 to 1845 he was one of the judges of the Court of Common Pleas of Rensselaer County. He was chosen Mayor of Troy in March, 1847, and was thrice reëlected to the office by increasing majorities. At all times during his manhood Judge Mann manifested a profound interest in religious matters. He early became a communicant of the Protestant Episcopal church: was one of the founders of St. John's Church in Troy in 1830, and ever afterward continued to be a member of its vestry, occupying the position of senior warden at the time of his death. On October 25, 1848, Judge Mann was married to Mary J. Hooker, daughter of Marquise de Lafayette Hooker, of Poultney, Vt., a lineal descendant of the Rev. Thomas Hooker, founder of the city of Hartford, Conn. The fruits of this union were two sons and one daughter, all of whom survive their parents, Mrs. Mann having died July 28, 1875. About a year ago Judge Mann sustained a fractured limb by a fall upon the sidewalk, and since that time had been confined to his house. More recently he suffered a stroke of paralysis, from the effects of which he died.

Careful economy, strict attention to the performance of whatever duties, public or private, were imposed upon him, the possession of shrewd business qualities and sound judgment, enabled the deceased to amass a large competency. His property consists principally of real estate situated in this city, West Troy, Cohoes and vicinity. Judge Mann's honesty and integrity were above questioning. His obligations were always promptly met, and he rigidly exacted the same promptness from those with whom he had business dealings. The management of his large estate kept his time fully occupied, and he found little opportunity to indulge in the pursuit of enjoyment, but he was far from being unsocial, and, especially during the last few years of his life, took delight in talking of the scenes and incidents of the past. He was very closely identified with the growth and prosperity of Troy, and his wisdom and judgment were of great value in the administration of municipal affairs. He had the honor of being the chief executive officer of the city when Gen. Wool returned in triumph from the Mexican war, and presided over the public meeting of welcome held in the front of the court house, upon which occasion the mayor, in behalf of the citizens of Troy, presented the general with a magnificent sword.

Judge Mann was always a liberal contributor and earnest supporter of St. John's Church. He was for many years one of the most prominent members of the parish, and evinced a lively interest in its welfare up to the time of his death. He took a great interest in the Troy Orphan Asylum, and was a Trustee and a member of the Finance Committee, also President of the Board of Directors of the Troy Academy. He was one of the founders of the Young Men's Association, and was the member from the second ward of the committee appointed to obtain signatures to the constitution of that organization. At the time of his death he was a director of the Mutual National Bank.

Children :

207. i. FRANCIS NORTON[8] (Col.), b. Aug. 2, 1849.
     ii. ELIAS PLUM,[8] b. March 12, 1852; unmarried. He graduated from the Rensselaer Polytechnic Institute, in the class of 1872. He has been Alderman (2d ward) of Troy two terms, and is at present a Fire Commissioner of the city. His business is the care of real estate, belonging to his father's estate and that of others who are non-residents.
    iii. EMILY M.,[8] b. July 22, 1854; m. April 28, 1880, Hamilton Fish, Jr. (a son of the Hon. Hamilton Fish), who is a lawyer in New York city. They have one daughter, *Jeannette Mary*,[9] b. April 7, 1883.

(176) NATHANIEL[1] MANN

(*Jeremiah,*[6] *Joel,*[5] *Joseph,*[4] *Nathaniel,*[3] *Richard,*[2] *Richard*[1]), the youngest of a family of seven children and only child of Jeremiah Mann by a second wife, is a substantial citizen and farmer, occupying the old homestead at Milton Centre (Ballston), Saratoga Co., N. Y. He was born in that town Dec. 29, 1819, and married Feb. 24, 1841, Sally Frances Slocum, who was born Feb. 23, 1819, and died Feb. 24, 1867. He and his only son Jeremiah carry on the farm that was purchased by his grandfather Joel Mann about the year 1693. P. O. address, Ballston, N. Y. Children:

	i.	ANNA,[8] b. Feb. 17, 1842.
	ii.	MERCY P.,[8] b. Dec. 23, 1843; m. Aug. 7, 1883, John Hudson Peck, Esq., a lawyer in Troy, N. Y.
	iii.	ELIZA P.,[8] b. Oct. 11, 1845.
208.	iv.	JEREMIAH,[8] b. Oct. 24, 1847; m. Ella Riggs.
	v.	MARY WILLARD,[8] b. Sept. 10, 1854; d. Dec. 2, 1866.

(177) DARWIN H.[7] MANN

(*Joel,*[6] *Joel,*[5] *Joseph,*[4] *Nathaniel,*[3] *Richard,*[2] *Richard*[1]), by occupation a farmer, was born in Cazenovia, N. Y., Dec. 15, 1809, and died in that town, Dec. 28, 1844. He married Jan. 8, 1835, Cordelia Newton, who survived her husband and died at Cazenovia, Aug. 1, 1883. Children, born in Cazenovia:

209.	i.	NEWTON M.[8] (Rev.), b. Jan. 16, 1836.
	ii.	SARAH,[8] b. Oct. 11, 1839; m. Daniel S. Maycumber, Nov. 22, 1865, who d. about 1867, and had *Daniel,*[9] who d. aged 20 months; res. Cazenovia, N. Y.
210.	iii.	EUGENE H.,[8] b. Nov. 11, 1841; m. Jane Allen Fradd.
	iv.	MARCIA J.,[8] b. Dec. 27, 1842; unmarried.
	v.	HELEN E.,[8] b. July 23, 1844; unmarried.

(178) WILLIAM WARNER[7] MANN

(*Warner,*[6] *Zadock,*[5] *Joseph,*[4] *Nathaniel,*[3] *Richard,*[2] *Richard*[1]), who was a merchant in Ashtabula, Ohio, was born (probably at Plymouth, Ohio) June 22, 1813, and died there May 24, 1880. He was the first post carrier in that part of the state. He first commenced in the store of Wm. W. Reed, in Ashtabula, subsequently he settled upon a piece of wild land, cleared it up summers and taught school winters. He was the first postmaster of Plymouth, Ohio, which office he held for twelve years. For a time he was in the mercantile business with Mr. Bennett Seymour. In 1859, removed to Ashtabula, and built a part of a block on Centre Street. From 1866, to April, 1873, the firm was Mann & Noyes; after that Mr. Mann carried on the business alone, until his health failed in 1879–80, at which time he sold out to Mr. H. J. Noyes. He has filled many offices of honor and trust, and was an exemplary member of the Episcopal Church for over forty-five years.—Ext. Ash. paper.

He married, October, 1833, Rebecca ———. Children:

    i. DOTHA REBECCA,[8] b. Aug. 21, 1835; d. Oct. 30, 1861; m. R. Radford, Dec. 24, 1860; had *Freddie*,[9] who died.

    ii. LEVEA HARRIET,[8] b. June 25, 1837; m. June 21, 1867, H. J. Noyes, and had: (1) *William Horatio*,[9] b. March 6, 1871. (2) *Edward Mann*,[9] Aug. 13, 1873. (3) *Harrie Castle*,[9] March 3, 1876. (4) *Rebecca Harriet*,[9] July 24, 1878.

    iii. JULIA AMANDA,[8] b. Sept. 14, 1839; m. Oct. 21, 1860, J. W. Morgan. Children: (1) *Allen Hiram*,[9] b. Nov. 24, 1861; m. Hattie Avery, 1881. (2) *Julia Ellen*,[9] Dec. 28, 1863. (3) *Harriet May*,[9] Jan. 8, 1867. (4) *Gertrude Minerva*,[9] April 11, 1869. (5) *Alice*,[9] May 12, 1871; d. May 28, 1871. (6) *Ruth Rebecca*,[9] April 25, 1872. (7) *Matthew Mann*,[9] July 4, 1874; d. June 30, 1877. (8) *Mary Catherine*,[9] Jan. 12, 1877. (9) *John Josiah*,[9] Aug. 31, 1879.

    iv. SARAH MINERVA,[8] b. Oct. 18, 1841; m. Sept. 9, 1874, C. H. Noyes. No children.

(179) BIELBY PORTEUS' MANN

(*Warner*,[6] *Zadock*,[5] *Joseph*,[4] *Nathaniel*,[3] *Richard*,[2] *Richard*[1]), a highly respected citizen of Plymouth, Ohio, was born in that town May 18, 1819. He has always resided within two miles of the place of his birth; by trade a blacksmith, but for many years has been an extensive farmer and dairyman. He has been township clerk and held other town offices; a member of the Episcopal church. He married May 19, 1842, Sarah Upson, of Plymouth, Conn. The children were all born in Plymouth, Ohio:

211.   i. WILBER ELIAS,[8] b. March 29, 1844; m. Orpha J. Harper.

ii. ELLEN SINA,[8] b. Oct. 17, 1845; m. first, Oct. 10, 1865, John
J. Pancost.   Children: (1) *Elmer J.,*[9] b. Nov. 5, 1866; d.
Feb. 3, 1869.   (2) *Minnie Elma,*[9] b. Oct. 29, 1868.   (3)
Bertha Emma,[9] b. Aug. 1, 1870.   (4) *Frank Layton,*[9] b.
March 31, 1872. [Obtained a divorce.] Mar. second,
June 7, 1876, John W. Lockwood, and had *Alice Carey,*[9] b.
March 22, 1877.   Many thanks are due Mrs. Lockwood
for collecting material and furnishing the author with most
of the data regarding the Ohio families.

iii. ESTHER JANE,[8] b. Jan. 20, 1848; m. Feb. 23, 1865, J. L.
Flint.   Children: (1) *William Arthur,*[9] b. Jan. 14, 1866.
(2) *Lucy Ann,*[9] b. Nov. 7, 1867.   (3) *Charles Jay,*[9] b.
Nov. 4, 1869.   (4) *George Porteus,*[9] Nov. 11, 1872.   (5)
Mary Estella,[9] b. March 13, 1877.   (6) *Sarah Irene,*[9] Jan.
27, 1881.   (7) *John Bielby,*[9] Feb. 20, 1883.

iv. EMMA MIRANDA,[8] b. April 20, 1850; m. March 13, 1869,
George W. Topper.   Children: (1) *Fred Porteus,*[9] b.
Nov. 24, 1870.   (2) *Clara Ellen,*[9] April 12, 1872; d.
July 6, 1875.   (3) *Lucy Ella,*[9] Sept. 2, 1875.   (4) *John
Carleton,*[9] Feb. 10, 1877.   (5) *George Raymond,*[9] May 13,
1879.

212.   v. WATSON EDWIN,[8] b. March 22, 1852; m. Millie A. Wood.
213.   vi. WARREN EDWARD,[8] b. March 22, 1852; m. Ada L. Jones.

vii. MIRA IRENE,[8] b. April 11, 1859; unmarried; has a good
musical talent, is an organist.

viii. OLIVE AMANDA,[8] b. Oct. 22, 1864; m. Aug. 26, 1883, Stew-
art D. Terrill, a farmer.   No children.

(180) BELA BLAKESLEE[7] MANN

(*Warner,*[6] *Zadock,*[5] *Joseph,*[4] *Nathaniel,*[3] *Richard,*[2] *Richard*[1]) was
born at Plymouth, Ohio, Jan. 15, 1822.   He was a farmer, and died
in Iowa, Sept. 16, 1856.   He married Mary Ann Seymour, March
20, 1845.   Children:

i. LEVERETT WARREN,[8] b. Oct. 9, 1851; m. —— Leverett.
He is a telegraph operator, and resides at Ocala, Florida.
Three children.

ii. JOHN HENRY,[8] b. Oct. 4, 1853; m. Nov. 9, 1881, Madora
Tyler.   He is a machinist by trade; res. Ashtabula, Ohio.
He has *Leverett Bela,*[9] b. July 24, 1882; a son, b. Aug. 4, 1884.

(181) MERRITT MARVIN[7] MANN

(*Joseph,*[6] *Zadock,*[5] *Joseph,*[4] *Nathaniel,*[3] *Richard,*[2] *Richard*[1]) was
born (probably in Plymouth, Ohio) June 29, 1814, and died July

18, 1855. He married first, Minerva Matthews, who died July 24, 1841. He married second, Feb. 6, 1844, Almira Taft, who was born May 1, 1819. He was a farmer and had seven children, three by first wife, four by second, viz.:

- i. MARVIN HENRY,[8] b. Sept. 1835; d. New Orleans, May 28, 1862, aged twenty-seven years.
- ii. JOHN FRIEND,[8] b. Nov. 29, 1839; m. Nov. 28, 1861, Mary Ann Newberry, who was b. July 8, 1838; res. McGregor, Iowa; a drayman. Children: (1) *Minerva Isbell,*[9] b. June 5, 1866. (2) *Martin Newberry,*[9] b. Feb. 13, 1868. (3) *Georgia Anna,*[9] Oct. 5, 1870. (4) *William Warner,*[9] June 26, 1877.
- iii. MERRITT EDWARD,[8] b. July 22, 1841; d. April 26, 1882.
- iv. OLIVER PERRY,[8] b. Dec. 23, 1844; m. Aug. 1, 1868, Nancy Jane Hawkins; a laborer; res. Plymouth, Ohio. Children: (1) *Artie Alonzo,*[9] b. Aug. 28, 1869. (2) *Frank Lorenzo,*[9] May 22, 1871. (3) *Flora Almira,*[9] Dec. 8, 1873. (4) *Charles Thomas,*[9] Sept. 26, 1876. (5) *Earl Taylor,*[9] March 14, 1878.
- v. GEORGIA A.,[8] b. Feb. 13, 1849; m. May 4, 1870, Charles A. Stanley, b. May 3, 1849. Children: (1) *Jessie M.,*[9] b. May 9, 1872. (2) *Florence G.,*[9] Sept. 30, 1874. (3) *Maria C.,*[9] Aug. 15, 1876. (4) *Charles F.,*[9] Nov. 15, 1878. (5) *Birdie,*[9] Oct. 9, 1880. P. O. address, Chippewa Falls, Wis.
- vi. CHARLES F.,[8] b. Dec. 6, 1853; d. June 24, 1872.
- vii. MERRITT ALTON,[8] b. Jan. 4, 1855; m. June 5, 1877, Florence E. Brumagin, who was b. March 23, 1859. He is an industrious farmer in Geneva, Ohio. Children: (1) *Alton H.,*[9] b. May 14, 1879. (2) *Mary A.,*[9] July 8, 1880. (3) *Ina E.,*[9] Nov. 10, 1882.

(182) DR. WILLIAM BARROW[7] MANN

(*Joseph,*[6] *James,*[5] *Joseph,*[4] *Nathaniel,*[3] *Richard,*[2] *Richard*[1]), an eminent and well-known physician residing at Brockport, N. Y., was born in Kendall, N. Y., June 15, 1838. Dr. Mann was commissioned Assistant Surgeon U. S. Navy, Sept. 17, 1861. Resigned in May, 1865. He married Nov. 7, 1865, Sophronia E. Clark, and has the following children:

- i. HORACE,[8] b. Oct. 13, 1866.
- ii. WILLIAM B.,[8] Jr., b. Aug. 1, 1869; d. 1874.
- iii. SOPHRONIA E.,[8] b. Oct. 11, 1873.
- iv. JAMES,[8] b. June 27, 1878.
- v. CHARLES THEODORE,[8] b. Sept. 19, 1880.

27

(183) JOHN DUTTON[7] MANN

(*John,[6] John,[5] John,[4] Nathaniel,[3] Richard,[2] Richard[1]*), who was a merchant, was born in Hebron, Conn., Feb. 15, 1789, and married, at his father's house in Orford, N. H., Jan. 19, 1809, Martha Phelps (probably daughter of Dr. Phelps, of Chester, Mass.). He resided first at Orford, N. H., subsequently at Troy, N. Y. He died at Ashfield, Mass., Feb. 20, 1878, and his only son deposited his remains in Oakland Cemetery, Troy, by the side of his wife who died there May 28, 1863. Child:

214.　　i.　John Henry,[8] b. March 10, 1810; m. Martha Dean.

(184) TIMOTHY[7] MANN

(*John,[6] John,[5] John,[4] Nathaniel,[3] Richard,[2] Richard[1]*), who was a hardware merchant, in Troy, N. Y., was born Dec. 18, 1792, in Orford, N. H. He married Nov. 25, 1828, Eliza Louisa, daughter of John Poinier, Esq., of Newark, N. J.; she died Nov. 17, 1839, aged thirty-four. He died at the home of his son in Brooklyn, N. Y., Feb. 23, 1872, and was buried in Oakland Cemetery, Troy.   Children :

　　i　John Poinier,[8] b. at Troy, Sept. 25, 1829; m. Elizabeth Laidlair, Brooklyn, N. Y. Three children. P. O. address, New York city.
　　ii.　Elizabeth Johnson,[8] b. July 23, 1831; m. first, May 9, 1850, Henry H. Sweetland, who died June 19, 1852; she married second, May 17, 1855, Walter J. Seymour, since separated; she married third, James Cumming, and resides in Yonkers, N. Y. No children.
　　iii.　Amelia Ashley,[8] b. Sept. 16, 1833; d. March 25, 1834.
　　iv.　Charles Ogden,[8] b. at Troy, May 22, 1835; m. May 26, 1859, Eliza Jeanette Dodge, New York city. P. O. address, 11 Wall Street, N. York.

(185) SILAS[7] MANN

(*John[6], John,[5] John,[4] Nathaniel,[3] Richard,[2] Richard[1]*) was born March 19, 1799, at Orford, N. H., and married Feb. 23, 1823, Rhoda, daughter of Elisha Parker, Esq., of Bradford, Vt. He settled in Jordan, N. Y., and for many years he and his son Silas E.

Mann were hardware merchants there, under the firm name of S. Mann & Son. He and wife both living (1884). He was an "elder in the Presbyterian church," in 1874. [J. B. M.]   Children:

    i.   LYDIA JANE,⁶ b. Thetford, Vt., Dec. 28, 1823; m. Samuel K. Bennett, April 30, 1850; res. Port Byron, N. Y. Children: (1) *Martha A.*,⁹ b. March 19, 1851; d. March 30, 1873; m. Loren S. Colby. (2) *Ella J.*,⁹ b. Sept. 11, 1853. (3) *Lewis M.*,⁹ b. July 13, 1856. (4) *Charles A.*,⁹ b. June 25, 1859; m. Emma Lovejoy. (5) *Fannie M.*,⁹ b. May 1, 1862.

215. ii. SILAS ELBRIDGE,⁶ b. March 3, 1826.

    iii. FRANCES ERMINA,⁶ b. in Troy, N. Y., Nov. 3, 1827; m. March 19, 1848, Lyman E. Phelps, who died Aug. 22, 1849, leaving a daughter, *Jennie E.*,⁹ b. Jan. 17, 1849, d. Oct. 8, 1873.

    iv. MARTHA PHELPS,⁶ b. in Starkey, N. Y., April 29, 1836; she resides with parents.

(186) RUSSELL⁶ MANN

(*John,*⁶ *John,*⁵ *John,*⁴ *Nathaniel,*³ *Richard,*² *Richard*¹) was born in Orford, N. H., April 1, 1803, and died at his home, 152 Second Street, Troy, N. Y., Jan. 7, 1867. He was a stove and hardware merchant in Troy for many years. He married Dec. 1, 1829, Mary Ann, daughter of Dr. Elijah Hanchett [whose wife was Mercy Mann, see p. 107], at Milton, Saratoga Co., N. Y.; she was born Oct. 26, 1804, in Salisbury, N. Y.   Children:

    i. MERCY,⁶ b. in Troy, N. Y., Aug. 29, 1830; d. in New York city, Feb. 13, 1837.

    ii. MARY,⁶ b. in Troy, Aug. 29, 1830; unmarried; res. Troy.

    iii. GEORGE RUSSELL,⁶ b. in Troy, March 1, 1833; m. in New York Jan. 10, 1858, Mary Frances Davis. He was acting assistant surgeon on board the steam sloop-of-war "Pocahontas," and died on board at Sabine Pass, Texas, Aug. 20, 1864. His widow is a practising physician in N. Y. They had: (1) *Mary Ella,*⁹ b. Sept. 12, 1859. (2) *Julia Frances,*⁹ died.

    iv. JULIA FRANCES,⁶ b. Troy, May 25, 1836; d. Oct. 8, 1849.

    v. WILLIAM AUGUSTUS,⁶ b. in New York city, Oct. 1, 1839; m. Sept. 7, 1868, at Raleigh, N. C., Frances Lee Smith. Children: (1) *Euphemia Mary,*⁹ b. Jan. 22, 1873. (2) *Gertrude Lee,*⁹ b. June 26, 1876. Res. Dakota, "Liston Indian Agency."

(187) JARED⁷ MANN

(*Jared,⁶ John,⁵ John,⁴ Nathaniel,³ Richard,² Richard¹*) was born Nov. 5, 1794. He was a farmer by occupation. He married June 29, 1826, Hannah Mason, of Lyme, N. H., who was born May 27, 1794. He died April 14, 1831. Children:

i. ISABELLA,⁸ b. May 2, 1827; m. May 29, 1848, Henry Wight, now resides in Wayland, Mass.
ii. CATHERINE,⁸ b. July 5, 1829; m. Sept. 27, 1848, Joseph Stevens Abbot, the celebrated coach manufacturer of Concord, N. H., and have: *Edward A.,*⁹ who resides in Boston; *Mary,*⁹ who m. Oct. 31, 1883, Gerald Wyman, of Boston; perhaps others.
iii. MARY COOLIDGE,⁸ b. May 7, 1831; m. Samuel M. Wixcox, Esq.; res. Washington, D. C.

(188) AARON⁷ MANN

(*Aaron,⁶ John,⁵ John,⁴ Nathaniel,³ Richard,² Richard¹*), who was a farmer and lime manufacturer, and lived in the easterly part of Orford, N. H., was born in that town Feb. 28, 1799, and died March 10, 1854. He married Eliza Weld, who was born April 25, 1800, and died Aug. 9, 1876. Children:

i. CAROLINE,⁸ b. Jan. 17, 1825; m. first, Oliver Chase, of Paxton, Mass.; second (1883), Calvin Proctor, of Claremont, N. H.; has *Henry M. Chase,*⁹ of Worcester.
ii. ALBERT G.,⁸ b. July 19, 1827; m. first, Julia Maria Sanborn, of Orford, N. H.; m. second, Dec. 13, 1864, Harriet A. Bigelow, of Worcester, Mass. No children. Mr. Mann is a granite merchant, in Worcester.
iii. HENRY A.,⁸ b. Sept. 1, 1832; d. Jan. 9, 1835.
iv. LOUISA,⁸ b. Oct. 8, 1836; d. Feb. 9, 1859; m. Jan. 14, 1857, John E. Spaulding, of Worcester. No children.

(189) JONATHAN MASON⁷ MANN

(*Nathaniel,⁶ John,⁵ John,⁴ Nathaniel,³ Richard,² Richard¹*), for many years a well-known and much respected citizen of Greenfield, Mass., was born probably in Orford, N. H., Jan. 27, 1806. He married Feb. 21, 1832, Mary Kinsman, at Thetford, Vt., who died May 22, 1868. He died at Greenfield, Sept. 16, 1883. He was court house messenger twenty-one years, and one of the oldest Free Masons in that part of the state. Children :

    i.   LUCY HARRIS,[8] b. May 30, 1838; res. Greenfield, Mass.
    ii.   HELEN LYDIA,[8] b. March 30, 1840; res. Greenfield, Mass.

(190) CYRUS S.[7] MANN, M.D.

(*Cyrus,*[6] *John,*[5] *John,*[4] *Nathaniel,*[3] *Richard,*[2] *Richard*[1]), a physician residing in Brooklyn, N. Y., was born in Westminister, Mass., April 12, 1820, he being the eldest child and only son of Rev. Cyrus Mann, deceased. Dr. Mann was some time at Amherst College, and graduated from Harvard Medical School, 1843. He went from Newton, Mass., as Assistant Surgeon of the 31st Massachusetts Volunteers, to Louisiana, in the civil war. He married, June 28, 1849, Harriet P., daughter of Justin Field, of Boston. Children :

    i.   EDWARD CYRUS[8] (M.D.), b. in Braintree, Mass., April 21, 1850; m. Nov. 10, 1870, Barbara, daughter of J. W. Busteed, of New York city. Dr. Edward C. Mann has an office in New York city, and is the author of works entitled " Inebriety and the Opium Habit," and " Manual of Psychological Medicine."
    ii.   WILLIAM JUSTIN,[8] Esq., b. Aug. 16, 1853; a lawyer in New York city; res. Brooklyn, N. Y.
    iii.   HENRY F.,[8] died, aged two years.

(191) EDWARD JOEL[7] MANN

(*Joel,*[6] *John,*[5] *John,*[4] *Nathaniel,*[3] *Richard,*[2] *Richard*[1]), the second son of Rev. Joel Mann, was born May 20, 1818, and died March 26, 1869. " He was for many years a commission and exporting merchant in New York, and was connected with the house of Messrs. Bell & Grant, in London. Afterwards had a commercial connection with an important firm in Liverpool." (Ext. Rev. Joel Mann's pamphlet.) He married June 3, 1839, Abby Ophelia, daughter of Col. Edward Martin. She was born Nov. 7, 1816. Residence, Flushing, N. Y. Children :

    i.   CHRISTOPHER V.,[8] b. March 26, 1840; d. Feb. 3, 1842.
    ii.   SARAH R.,[8] b. Nov. 3, 1840(?); d. Jan. 26, 1861.
    iii.   SAMUEL VERNON,[8] b. June 23, 1843; m. Harriet Onderdonk (granddaughter of the late Bishop Onderdonk, of N. Y.),

who d. March 23, 1881. Children: (1) *Edith Vernon,*[9] b. March 2, 1871. (2) *Alice,*[9] b. May 11, 1872; d. in infancy. (3) *Vernon,*[9] May 2, 1873. P. O. address, 58 Wall Street, N. York.

    iv. MARTHA LITTLEFIELD,[8] b. April 16, 1845; m. June 1, 1869, L. M. Franklin.

    v. MARY,[8] b. Aug. 20, 1847; d. Sept. 2, 1848.

    vi. MARY L.,[8] b. Dec. 19, 1848.

    vii. ROBERT O.,[8] b. July 7, 1849; d. July 13, 1850.

    viii. EDWARD MARTIN,[8] b. July 3, 1852.

[The above names, births, etc., are mostly taken from Martin Genealogy. —ED.]

(192) DR. FREDERIC PORTER[7] MANN

(*Joel,*[6] *John,*[5] *John,*[4] *Nathaniel,*[3] *Richard,*[2] *Richard*[1]), the youngest child of Rev. Joel Mann, was born about 1828, and married Susan E. Martin, who was born April 13, 1827. Dr. Mann resided many years in Brooklyn, N. Y., but it is said some two or three years since the family removed to California, thence to Chicago, where they are now living. Children:

    i. FREDERIC P.,[8] b. Dec. 25, 1851.

    ii. Daughter, born and died June 20, 1853.

    iii. Son, born Aug. 17, 1854; d. Sept. 22, 1854.

    iv. CLARENCE M.,[8] b. Feb. 3, 1856.

    v. HARWOOD P.,[8] b. Oct. 22, 1857.

    vi. LILA A.,[8] b. March 20, 1860.

    vii. HERBERT F.,[8] b. Sept. 16, 1863.

(193) FRANCIS ANDREW[7] MANN

(*Andrew,*[6] *Andrew,*[5] *John,*[4] *Nathaniel,*[3] *Richard,*[2] *Richard*[1]) was born in Hebron, Conn., March 16, 1808, and died in Marshall, Mich., Jan. 8, 1851. He was a farmer, and resided in Athens, Mich. He married in Chenango, N. Y., December, 1835, Marian Mack. Of the children, the eldest was born in Chenango, all the others in Athens, Mich., viz.:

    i. CHARLES HENRY,[8] b. Dec. 30, 1836; m. at Athens, Mich., Oct. 12, 1870, Rebecca S. Briggs; a farmer. They have, *Frank Sibley,*[9] b. at Sherwood, Mich., Feb. 20, 1874. Residence now, Union City, Mich.

    ii. CALVIN ANDREW,[8] b. Jan. 11, 1839; m. at Middleton, Wis.,

Nov. 25, 1871, Emily Adelia Gammons; a farmer; no children; res. Sherwood, Mich.

iii.   GEORGE LEWIS,[8] b. Aug. 14, 1841; d. at Athens, Mich., March 10, 1861.

iv.   HARRIET PARMELIA,[8] b. June 10, 1844; d. at Athens, April 28, 1845.

v.   JULIA ANN,[8] b. July 6, 1846; m. at Athens, Oct. 11, 1871, Walter B. Webb. They have, *Nettie Emma*,[9] b. at Jackson, Mich., March 1, 1876. Mr. Webb is of the firm of C. E. Webb & Brother, Wholesale Druggists and Sole Proprietors of Webb's Family Medicines, of Jackson, Mich.

vi.   HANNAH MARIA,[8] b. Sept. 22, 1849; d. at Athens, Nov. 30, 1876.

(194) MANLIUS[7] MANN

(*Andrew*,[6] *Andrew*,[5] *John*,[4] *Nathaniel*,[3] *Richard*,[2] *Richard*[1]), a merchant in Marshall, Mich., was born in Hebron, Conn., June 10, 1810. He married Oct. 4, 1836, at Bainbridge, N. Y., Pamelia Craig, and located the same year in Marshall, where he has resided ever since. He is a well-known and highly respected citizen of that city. They have had six children, three boys and three girls, all of whom except the two following daughters died young:

i.   JOSEPHINE,[8] b. Oct. 4, 1840; m. Jan. 14, 1863, William Page Van Vechten, of Auburn, N. Y., where she now resides. No children.

ii.   CATHERINE FITCH,[8] b. Feb. 3, 1844; m. Oct. 10, 1867, George Perritt, of Troy, N. Y., now a merchant in Marshall, Mich. Children: twin boys, born Jan. 28, 1869, and named after their grandparents, *Manlius M.*,[9] and *George R.*[9]

(195) JOEL PHELPS[7] MANN

(*Andrew*,[6] *Andrew*,[5] *John*,[4] *Nathaniel*,[3] *Richard*,[2] *Richard*[1]), a substantial farmer in Longmont, Colorado, was born in Unadilla, N. Y., Nov. 19, 1814. He married Mary M. Crownover, June 2, 1840. She was born at Mifflin, Penn., March 2, 1821. He first resided in

Athens, Mich., where two children were born. From thence he removed to Madison, Wis., where the rest of the children were born. He removed to Colorado in 1860. Besides being a farmer, Mr. Mann has been in the mercantile, lumbering and livery business. He writes, "taking all things combined, Colorado is one of the best states in the Union." Children:

    i. ESTHER ELIZABETH,[8] b. Sept. 6, 1842; m. Maj. William F. Wilder; res. Denver, Colorado; has a family.

    ii. ALMIRA,[8] b. Oct. 27, 1844; died.

    iii. JOEL SIBLEY,[8] b. March 7, 1847; died.

    iv. JAMES ANDREW,[8] b. March 12, 1848; died.

    v. FRANK I.,[8] b. July 4, 1850; stock raiser; P. O. Littleton, Colorado.

    vi. FANNY FLORENCE,[8] b. March 3, 1853; died.

    vii. HARRY,[8] b. Sept. 20, 1858; res. Longmont, Col.

(196) JOHN EDWIN[7] MANN

(Andrew,[6] Andrew,[5] John,[4] Nathaniel,[3] Richard,[2] Richard[1]) was born in Unadilla, N. Y., April 29, 1817, and married July 5, 1842, Emily Josephine Bliven, of Fall River, Mass., and resided a few years at Marshall, Mich. He then removed to Madison, Wisconsin. He now resides at Sun Prairie, Wis. He is a hotel keeper, and agent of Geo. T. Smith's Middlings Purifier Co. Children:

    i. FRANCES JULIETTE,[8] b. at Marshall, Mich., March 3, 1844; d. 1879; m. A. M. Seymour. They have one daughter, born in 1870.

    ii. JOSEPH ANDREW,[8] b. at Marshall, Mich., June 28, 1846; d. 1873.

    iii. HARRIET MARIA,[8] b. 1849; m. George E. Knapp, of Dupont, N. Y.

    iv. LOUIS,[8] b. at Madison, Wis., Feb. 26, 1853; m. 1881, Nellie Ransom; res. Jackson, Mich.; furniture dealer. They have one daughter.

    v. LOUISE,[8] b. at Madison, Feb. 26, 1853; m. Charles H. Chittenden, of Petersburgh, Mich.

    vi. JOSEPHINE BLIVEN,[8] b. April 18, 1855; now at St. Paul, Minn.

    vii. WILLIAM THOMPSON,[8] b. Jan. 19, 1857; m. March 24, 1881, Sarah Haner, of Bristol, Wis. P. O. Madison, Wis.

    viii. FRED. B.,[8] b. Dec. 31, 1858; res. Jackson, Mich.

    ix. GEORGE ALLEN,[8] b. Aug. 12, 1862; res. Sun Prairie.

    x. CHARLES EDWIN,[8] b. Nov. 1864; res. Sun Prairie.

    xi. CATHERINE ALMIRA,[8] b. July 16, 1867; res. Sun Prairie.

(197) ANDREW LEWIS⁷ MANN

(*Andrew,⁶ Andrew,⁵ John,⁴ Nathaniel,³ Richard,² Richard¹*), a farmer, and a resident of Madison, Wis. He was born at Unadilla, N. Y., Aug. 5, 1819. He married first, Sept. 8, 1851, Dolly M. Russell. She died at Madison, Wis., Sept. 17, 1852. He married second, June 18, 1856, Isabella J. Knapp, of Colchester, N. Y., and moved to Fitchburg, Wis. She died Sept. 21, 1880.   Children:

    i. RUSSELL DEFOREST,⁸ b. May 21, 1852; d. Aug. 30, 1852.
    ii. JUNIUS KNAPP,⁸ b. at Fitchburg, Wis., May 12, 1857.
    iii. ANNA GRACE,⁸ b. at Fitchburg, Wis., March 30, 1865.

(198) AMASA⁷ MANN

(*Amasa,⁶ Abijah,⁵ Abijah,⁴ Nathaniel,³ Richard,² Richard¹*), a dry-goods merchant, of the firm of Devendorf & Mann, Cedar Rapids, Iowa. He was born in Frankfort, N. Y., July 28, 1839. He married in 1867, Emily L. Devendorf, of Frankfort, and removed the same year to Cedar Rapids, Iowa, where he now resides. Children:

    i. FRANKLIN,⁸ b. July 24, 1868.
    ii. ALMA,⁹ b. Feb. 2, 1870.
    iii. MARGARET,⁸ b. April 9, 1873.
    iv. EVERETT,⁸ b. 1876; d. 1879.
    v. CHARLES,⁸ b. 1882; d. 1882.

(199) CHARLES ADDISON⁷ MANN, Esq.

(*Charles A.,⁶ Abijah,⁵ Abijah,⁴ Nathaniel,³ Richard,² Richard¹*), eldest son of the Hon. Charles A. Mann, is a retired lawyer residing at Cazenovia, N. Y. He was born in Utica, N. Y., May 24, 1835. He was at Williston Seminary, Easthampton, Mass., in 1852, and graduated from Yale College in 1856. He married first, June 15, 1864, Alice Couselt Paterson, of New Jersey [a granddaughter of Charles King, President of Columbia College], who died Aug. 10, 1869. They had children by this marriage, but none surviving. He married second, July 2, 1874, Mary Elizabeth Lee, of Washington, D. C., a daughter of William Barlow Lee, of the War Department, who was formerly of Boston. Mr. Mann has also lived in Utica,

28

N. Y., New York city, and St. Paul, Minn., where he is largely interested in real estate.   Children, by second wife :

    i. CHARLES ADDISON,[8] Jr., b. May 4, 1875.
    ii. MARION,[8] died.
    iii. MARY LEE,[8] b. Aug. 22, 1882.

(200)   JAMES FORD[7] MANN, Esq.

(*Charles A.,*[6] *Abijah,*[5] *Abijah,*[4] *Nathaniel,*[3] *Richard,*[2] *Richard*[1]), the second son of Hon. Charles A. Mann, of Utica, N. Y., is a prominent lawyer residing in that city.   He was born in Utica, May 24, 1837, and was graduated from Yale College in 1859.   He married May 16, 1861, Emma L. Obertenffer, of Philadelphia, who was born March 13, 1837, and died March 9, 1875.   Children, born in Utica :

    i. JULIA D.,[8] b. May 11, 1862.
    ii. JOHN H.,[8] b. May 11, 1863.   He was graduated from Yale College (Scientific Department), 1883; in law office at Utica.   The author is indebted to him for letters containing valuable data.
    iii. SOPHIA,[8] b. Feb. 18, 1866.
    iv. ALBERTINE O.,[8] b. April 25, 1867; d. Nov. 16, 1873.
    v. FREDERIC J.,[8] b. Oct. 13, 1870.
    vi. CLARENCE C.,[8] b. Feb. 18, 1875.
    vii. HERMAN O.,[8] b. Feb. 18, 1875; d. Aug. 23, 1875.

(201)   DR. MATTHEW DARBYSHIRE[7] MANN

(*Charles A.,*[6] *Abijah,*[5] *Abijah,*[4] *Nathaniel,*[3] *Richard,*[2] *Richard*[1]), the youngest son of the late Hon. Charles A. Mann, was born in the city of Utica, N. Y., July 12, 1845, and was graduated from Yale College in 1867.   He is a physician residing in Buffalo, N. Y., where he occupies a high position.   He is Professor of Obstetrics and Gynæcology in the Buffalo Medical College.   He married Nov. 11, 1869, Elizabeth, daughter of Daniel Pope, of Philadelphia, Penn., who was born Oct. 19, 1844.   Children :

    i. HELEN,[8] b. Sept. 12, 1870.
    ii. ETHEL,[8] b. Jan. 19, 1873.
    iii. EDWARD COX,[8] b. Sept. 5, 1874.
    iv. EMMA,[8] died.
    v. ARTHUR SITGREAVES,[8] b. Aug. 18, 1878.
    vi. PAUL FORD,[8] b. July 12, 1881.
    vii. MATTHEW D.,[8] Jr., b. April 11, 188–.

(202) AZRO LEVI⁵ MANN

(*Levi,⁷ Levi,⁶ Seth,⁵ Seth,⁴ Joseph,³ Thomas,² Richard¹*), who is a professor of Greek and Latin, residing in San Francisco, Cal., was born in Randolph, Mass., Sept. 2, 1840, and married Sept. 18, 1868, Sarah Jane Shuey, who was born Sept. 25, 1849, in Illinois, and graduated there at the State Normal School. Her father, Robert Martin Shuey, born Aug. 24, 1820 (a farmer), moved from Illinois to California in 1859, "across the plains."

The following is extracted from "The Pacific School Journal," regarding him.

Mr. Mann was educated in the public schools of Massachusetts, until he entered Middlebury College, Vermont, from which institution he graduated with distinction in 1860. During his career in college he taught three winters in New England, and "boarded around."

On leaving college in 1860, he came to California and began his career in this State as a teacher of a country school in Sutter county. He subsequently taught a country school in Yuba county. He taught in the town of Colusa one term, and was afterwards vice-principal of the Grammar School in Marysville for about three years. During his residence in Marysville, Mr. Mann read law in the office of Belcher & Belcher, and was about to apply for admission to the Bar, when he was attacked with a malarial disease and forced to seek a more salubrious climate. He next taught one term as principal of the East Oakland Grammar School. In 1866 he came to San Francisco, and was appointed to a position in the Boys' Latin School. When this school was consolidated with the Boys' High School Mr. Mann was placed at the head of the classical department, a position which he held up to the time of his election as City Superintendent in 1877.

His sterling character, correct habits and manly bearing have secured for him the admiration and hearty support of the parents of the pupils he has taught. In fact Mr. Mann was one of the most popular teachers in the Department, both with his pupils and with their parents.

Mr. Mann has filled the office of City and County Superintendent in this city since December, 1877, and has made, in our opinion, the most capable, efficient and conscientious Superintendent that we have ever had in San Francisco. He is a clear, an able and an original thinker, a good speaker and a ready and forcible writer. A few weeks after his election he delivered an address before the Dashaway Association of this city, which deservedly attracted public attention at the time.

In that address Mr. Mann ably and forcibly pointed out the evils of the existing administration of school affairs, and fearlessly advocated most important and salutary reforms.

Mr. Mann was president of the State Teachers' Association for 1877–78, and delivered an able and thoughtful address on the "American Idea of Common Schools," before that body at its annual meeting at Sacramento. This address was published in the "School and Home Journal," and is considered by our leading educators as one of the ablest educational addresses ever delivered in this State. During the past two years he has delivered many able and practical addresses before the students of the State University and several educational associations in various parts of the State. These addresses have placed him in the foremost rank of leading American educators, and have been republished in nearly all the leading educational journals of the United States. One of these addresses on "Ungraded Schools," delivered at Los Angeles last year, secured for Mr. Mann a high place in the esteem of all friends of public schools in the southern portion of the State. Mr. Mann's report of the public schools of San Francisco for the year 1878, is one of the most able, complete and valuable reports ever published in this city, and has been highly complimented by the leading journals at the East. Mr. Mann's private life is above reproach, and in his public acts he has ever adhered to right, honor and duty.

Children :

    i.   ROBERT LEVI,⁹ b. Feb. 20, 1870.
   ii. MARY ABBY,⁹ b. Nov. 20, 1872.
  iii. HORACE,⁹ b. April 20, 1884.

(203)   CHARLES HERBERT⁸ MANN

(*Levi,*⁷ *Levi,*⁶ *Seth,*⁵ *Seth,*⁴ *Joseph,*³ *Thomas,*² *Richard*¹), who holds a prominent position in the well-known business house of C. C. Hastings & Co., San Francisco, Cal., was born in Randolph, Mass., June 23, 1841, where his father lived for a number of years. Mr. Mann, like his brother, has won an honorable distinction in the city where he resides, though in another department of life. He married, May 4, 1864, Mary Effie Shed, who was born Oct. 9, 1842. Children :

    i. LIZZIE HERBERT,⁹ b. Jan. 24, 1865.
   ii. MARY ELLEN,⁹ b. April 4, 1866.

(204) Dr. HORACE EDWIN[8] MANN

(*Elisha,*[7] *Elisha,*[6] *Seth,*[5] *Seth,*[4] *Joseph,*[3] *Thomas,*[2] *Richard*[1]), a well-known practising physician at Marinette, Wis., was born in Braintree, Vt., April 23, 1844. At the age of eleven he in company with his mother and brother removed to Fond du Lac, Wis. At eighteen he enlisted in the 32d Regiment Wisconsin Volunteers, serving in various campaigns with that regiment. In February, 1865, he was promoted to Adjutant of the 1st Mississippi Mounted Rifles. After the war he returned to Fond du Lac, and was assistant postmaster for six years and studied medicine. He graduated from Long Island College Hospital in 1874, and located in Marinette the same year. He is a member of the Wisconsin State Medical Society, and American Medical Association. He was appointed in 1882 County Superintendent of Schools. His early advantages were limited, but by energy of purpose and unrelenting toil he has been eminently successful. He married July 8, 1867, Flora A. Tracy. Children :

    i. FRED. EUGENE,[9] b. March 14, 1869.
    ii. GUY TRACY,[9] b. Feb. 23, 1870; d. July 10, 1870.
    iii. IDA FLORA,[9] b. Dec. 16, 1873; d. March 22, 1879.
    iv. WILLIAM HENRY,[9] b. May 3, 1876.

(205) FRANK EUGENE[8] MANN

(*Elisha,*[7] *Elisha,*[6] *Seth,*[5] *Seth,*[4] *Joseph,*[3] *Thomas,*[2] *Richard*[1]) was born in Braintree, Vt., March 17, 1846. About 1855 his mother and family removed from Vermont and settled in Fond du Lac, Wis., where the subject of this sketch learned the printing trade. By his industry and skill he won his way to the head of the mechanical department of one of the largest printing houses in Chicago, Ill., where he died July 9, 1882, leaving a large family (his mother living with them). He married Sept. 2, 1869, Sarah Ella Livinggood. Res. Chicago. Children :

    i. NELLIE MARIA,[9] b. June 6, 1870.
    ii. EDWIN ORLANDO,[9] b. Nov. 18, 1871.
    iii. HATTIE ELMIRA,[9] b. Aug. 12, 1873.
    iv. EUGENE LIVINGGOOD,[9] b. June 13, 1877.
    v. FRANK SIBLEY,[9] b. July 15, 1879.
    vi. HORACE,[9] b. March 8, 1882.

(206) HORACE P.[8] MANN

(*Benjamin,*[7] *Benjamin,*[6] *Benjamin,*[5] *Seth,*[4] *Joseph,*[3] *Thomas,*[2] *Richard*[1]) was born in Randolph, Mass., June 7, 1834, and married Nov. 12, 1861, Annie M. Belcher. He owns a farm, and delivers coal for R. W. Turner & Co., Randolph. Children:

 i. HORACE BURTON,[9] b. July 5, 1863.
 ii. JENNIE MARIA,[9] b. Nov. 5, 1864.
 iii. MARY EVA,[9] b. Sept. 30, 1867.
 iv. NELLIE GERTRUDE,[9] b. Feb. 19, 1872.
 v. ARTHUR LYMAN,[9] b. Jan. 29, 1874.

(207) COL. FRANCIS NORTON[8] MANN*

(*Francis Norton,*[7] *Jeremiah,*[6] *Joel,*[5] *Joseph,*[4] *Nathaniel,*[3] *Richard,*[2] *Richard*[1]), who is a lawyer by profession and a prominent citizen of Troy, N. Y., is the eldest son of the late Hon. Francis N. Mann, of that city. He was born there Aug. 2, 1849, and graduated from Yale College in the class of 1870. Mr. Mann represented the City of Troy in the New York legislature in 1879, and was aid de camp, with rank of colonel, on the staff of Governor Cornell, of New York State, for the years 1880–2. He married Jan. 19, 1878, Jessie Melville, daughter of Thaddeus W. Patchin, of Troy. Children:

 i. MARY JEANNETTE,[9] b. Feb. 27, 1879.
 ii. JESSIE MELVILLE,[9] b. Aug. 7, 1880.
 iii. EMILY HOOKER,[9] b. March 28, 1882.

(208) JEREMIAH[8] MANN

(*Nathaniel,*[7] *Jeremiah,*[6] *Joel,*[5] *Joseph,*[4] *Nathaniel,*[3] *Richard,*[2] *Richard*[1]), an only son and farmer occupying the old ancestral homestead at Milton Centre (Ballston), N. Y., was born there Oct. 24, 1847. He married June 5, 1877, Ella Riggs. They have a son Nathaniel. Five generations of Manns have lived successively on this same farm. Child:

 i. NATHANIEL,[9] b. March 28, 1878.

---

* The author acknowledges his indebtedness to Colonel Mann for the interest he has manifested in this work, and for favors received.

(209) Rev. NEWTON M.⁸ MANN

(*Darwin H.,*[7] *Joel,*[6] *Joel,*[5] *Joseph,*[4] *Nathaniel,*[3] *Richard,*[2] *Richard*[1]), a Unitarian clergyman residing in Rochester, N. Y., was born in Cazenovia, N. Y., Jan. 16, 1836. He probably married Eliza J. Smith, Aug. 8, 1857, at Bristol, Wisconsin. Mr. Mann taught school from 1856 to 1860, and was principal of the High School at Alton, Ill., for the year 1861. He then engaged in the ministry. He organized and built a church in Kenosha, Wis., and went from that place to Troy, N. Y., and thence to Rochester, where he now resides. Children :

  i. DARWIN HORACE,[9] b. June 19, 1858; m. Sept. 30, 1880, Ruth Siddons. He is in the U. S. Postal Service; res. Rochester, N. Y. They have a son in the tenth generation, viz.: *Herbert Siddons,*[10] b. Aug. 27, 1881.
 ii. ADELAIDE,[9] b. March 22, 1860; m. Aug. 30, 1882, C. E. Bowen.
iii. CHARLES,[9] b. Aug. 29, 1861.
 iv. HERBERT SPENCER,[9] b. May 23, 1867.

(210) EUGENE H.⁸ MANN

(*Darwin H.,*[7] *Joel,*[6] *Joel,*[5] *Joseph,*[4] *Nathaniel,*[3] *Richard,*[2] *Richard*[1]) was born in Cazenovia, N. Y., Nov. 11, 1841. He married Dec. 31, 1867, Jane Allen Fradd, and resides in Rochester, N. Y., where he is employed by a horse-railroad company. Children :

  i. DARWIN RICHARD,[9] b. Feb. 20, 1869.
 ii. EDNA NORA,[9] b. Nov. 4, 1870.
iii. MARCIA JANE,[9] b. Aug. 7, 1872.

(211) WILBER ELIAS⁸ MANN

(*Bielby Porteus,*[7] *Warner,*[6] *Zadock,*[5] *Joseph,*[4] *Nathaniel,*[3] *Richard,*[2] *Richard*[1]), the present postmaster of East Plymouth, Ohio, was born in Plymouth, Ohio, March 29, 1844. He has been a farmer and is a natural mechanic; has held town offices. At present runs a grocery store in connection with the post office. He married June 21, 1866, Orpha J. Harper. Children :

  i. BERTHA MAY,[9] b. Oct. 21, 1867.
 ii. ALTA LOUISE,[9] b. June 8, 1870.
iii. IDA EUGENIA,[9] b. July 17, 1875.
 iv. MARY EDNA,[9] b. March 18, 1883.

(212) WATSON EDWIN⁸ MANN

(*Bielby Porteus,*[7] *Warner,*[6] *Zadock,*[5] *Joseph,*[4] *Nathaniel,*[3] *Richard,*[2] *Richard*[1]), who has a twin brother, was born March 22, 1852, in Plymouth, Ohio. He married Sept. 6, 1875, Millie A. Wood; resides in Ashtabula, Ohio, "where he has a nice home;" is a member of the Episcopal church, and in the employ of Wm. Seymour, a miller in Ashtabula. Children:

    i. Son,[9] b. and d. Sept. 18, 1878.
    ii. JULIA MAY,[9] b. Jan. 15, 1880.

(213) WARREN EDWARD⁸ MANN

(*Bielby Porteus,*[7] *Warner,*[6] *Zadock,*[5] *Joseph,*[4] *Nathaniel,*[3] *Richard,*[2] *Richard*[1]) was born at Plymouth, Ohio, March 22, 1852, and married Aug. 22, 1874, Ada L. Jones. He lives in Ashtabula, Ohio, where he has a good house near his twin brother, and is employed in the plow handle works of W. A. Ellis & Co. Mr. Mann is a Methodist. Children:

    i. SARAH BLANCHE,[9] b. Aug. 30, 1875.
    ii. MARGARET AMANDA,[9] b. Nov. 10, 1879.

(214) JOHN HENRY⁸ MANN

(*John Dutton,*[7] *John,*[6] *John,*[5] *John,*[4] *Nathaniel,*[3] *Richard,*[2] *Richard*[1]) was born in Orford, N. H., March 10, 1810. He lived in Orford until about 1836, at which time he located at Woodstock, Vt., where for three years he was employed in a woolen factory, then carried on the tin ware and stove business about fifteen years. Being in delicate health, and by advice of his physician "to work in the open air," he removed in April, 1866, on to a farm in Ashfield, Mass., where he still resides. Mr. Mann, who is a fine penman, has furnished the author with valuable family data. He married March 14, 1841, at Woodstock, Vt., Martha Dean, and had the following children, born in Woodstock:

    i. MARTHA MARIA,[9] b. March 25, 1842; m. April 25, 1861, at Woodstock, Vt., George E. Dimick, a carriage maker. They separated in 1875, and she resides with her parents in Ashfield, Mass.

   ii.   JOHN HENRY,[9] Jr., b. March 11, 1844; m. Nov. 24, 1870, at Ashfield, Gracia Almeda Franklin. By trade a carpenter; resided at Orange, Mass., a few years, now on a farm in Ashfield, Mass. Children: (1) *Charles Henry*,[10] b. at Orange, Oct. 22, 1873. (2) *Lewis Edward*,[10] b. at Orange, Feb. 18, 1879; d. at Orange, Nov. 17, 1880.

   iii. MARY ELIZABETH,[9] b. Aug. 25, 1846; d. July 26, 1848.

   iv. CHARLES WESLEY,[9] b. March 25, 1850; a farmer in Ashfield.

   v. EDWIN ALONZO,[9] b. July 3, 1853; m. Dec. 25, 1879, in New York city, Cecelia I. Armstrong, of N. York.

   vi. WALLACE ALBERT,[9] b. July 12, 1855; m. at Northampton, Mass., May 6, 1880, Delia M. Searle. A farmer in Northampton.

   vii. MARY LOUISA,[9] b. Dec. 26, 1857; m. April 22, 1880, at Conway, Mass., Francis M. Payne, a farmer in Conway. Children: (1) *Ernest Clinton*,[10] b. Aug. 1, 1881. (2) *Eva May*,[10] b. April 10, 1883.

   viii. HORACE WILLIAM,[9] b. May 29, 1862; a farmer in Ashfield.

(215) SILAS ELBRIDGE[8] MANN

(*Silas*,[7] *John*,[6] *John*,[5] *John*,[4] *Nathaniel*,[3] *Richard*,[2] *Richard*[1]), of the firm of S. E. Mann & Son, dealers in hardware, stoves, agricultural implements, etc., in Jordan, N. Y., was born in Thetford, Vt., March 3, 1826. He first commenced business in Jordan with his father in 1852, under the firm name of S. Mann & Son. He married first, May 28, 1848, Almira D. Woolsey, who was born Aug. 10, 1825, at Summer Hill, N. Y., and died in Jordan, Feb. 23, 1857. He married second, April 13, 1858, Nancy M. Hicks, who was born in Homer, N. Y., Jan. 7, 1836. Children, two by first wife, four by second:

   i. ROSA,[9] b. in Jordan, March 27, 1851; m. June 19, 1878, F. DeWitt Wright; res. Syracuse, N. Y.

   ii. IVAH,[9] b. in Syracuse, March 21, 1855; res. Syracuse, N. Y.

   iii. CLARA,[9] b. in Jordan, Nov. 2, 1859.

   iv. EUGENE E.,[9] b. in Jordan, April 6, 1861.

   v. MARY,[9] b. in Jordan, May 8, 1862.

   vi. JESSIE,[9] b. in Jordan, Jan. 7, 1864.

29

ERRATA.

Page 22, 4th line from bottom, *for* George Henry *read* George Hervey.
24, 21st line from top, *for* George Henry *read* George Hervey.
24, 16th line from bottom, *for* July 13, 1881, *read* June 13, 1881.
38, 14th line from bottom, *for* Joel Negus *read* Joseph Negus.
92, 9th line from bottom, *for* Mary Dyer *read* Eunice Warren.
106, 18th line from top, *for* Lott *read* Lot.
110, 20th line from bottom, *for* Barker *read* Barber.
122, 9th line from bottom, *for* Stillman *read* Samuel Stillman.
149, 17th line from bottom, *for* Portens *read* Porteus.
152, 16th line from bottom, *for* Barrows *read* Barrow.
163, 21st line from bottom, *for* Thomson *read* Thompson.
176, last line, *for* May 29 *read* May 24.
187, 15th line from bottom, *for* 1845 *read* 1841.
212, 13th line from top, *for* Wixcox *read* Wilcox.

NOTE.—Persons discovering other errors will please communicate the same to the author, who has interleaved a copy of this work for the purpose of noting corrections and additions.

INDEX I.

MAN AND MANN.

* The first sixteen pages (English Records) not indexed.

INDEX II.

NAMES OTHER THAN MANN.*

Those who are known to have died under 10 years of age are omitted in this Index.

* The first sixteen pages (English Records) not indexed.

32